The Well of the Silent Harp

1791-1796

These are the years of fulfilment for Robert Burns. The passions of his youth are almost spent. The sensual desire that burned so fiercely is beginning to dim; only the abiding love for Jean remains.

But there is a shadow over the family. Despite the recognition of his genius, Burns has never been so poor. His health is failing, and mingled with back-breaking work and his financial worries is the young man's knowledge that death is not far away.

Immortal Memory

The Story of Robert Burns

JAMES BARKE

The Well of the
Silent Harp

A Novel of the Life and Loves
of Robert Burns

Collins
FONTANA BOOKS

First published by Wm. Collins 1954
First issued in Fontana Books 1975

Copyright

Made and printed in Great Britain by
William Collins Sons & Co Ltd Glasgow

TO THE MEMORY OF
JEAN ARMOUR BURNS
whose serene star grows brighter
with the years

'*Something in ilka part o' thee
To praise, to love, I find.*'

NOTE

Burns's last years in Dumfries (1791-1796) were, like most years of his life, years of ill-rewarded drudgery shot through with pain and shadowed in tragedy. But, for all that, they were years of fulfilment and intellectual and spiritual vigour.

The nature of Burns's activity as an Exciseman has, fortunately, been removed from the field of speculation, prejudice and ignorant gossip. Excise records prove that he was, with the possible exception of his Supervisor, the most hard-working *and hard worked* officer in the Division. His Excise responsibilities were onerous: he discharged them in the most exemplary manner. That (in addition) he succeeded in discharging his unpaid labours to Johnson's *Scots Musical Museum* and Thomson's *Select Scotish Airs* is ample proof (for those who need proof) that his creative genius was never higher nor more productive.

Above all, in Dumfries he came to final terms with man in relation to human society: his philosophy ripened to full maturity. He knew all there was to know: saw everything there was to see. Deep in his soul, for him, the Ancient of Days had grown ancient indeed.

He died in his bed in the 38th year of his life: had he not so died, society would have found it necessary to crucify him.

It is for the reader to judge whether this early death of Burns was or was not a tragedy; and, if a tragedy, to what extent.

In one sense the Dumfries years were barren: they were barren of notable characters. There were no flaming loves— apart from the brief interlude of Anna Park; and she belonged to the Ellisland-Dumfries days. The evidence that Jean Lorimer had turned whore before she left Dumfries is not as satisfactory as I could wish. Certainly before his end Burns turned away from her; and her Edinburgh days do not belong to these pages. But I should hate to think I had wronged her memory even by an odd year.

It remains to notice two controversial incidents. The first concerns the allegation that Burns sent four carronades to the French. There is some evidence that he purchased four carronades from the brig *Rosamond*: there is no evidence that he despatched them to the French.

They each weighed some six hundredweights. The cost of their transportation alone was far beyond Burns's means. Moreover, twenty-four hundredweights of ordnance cannot be smuggled around in the pockets of a tailed-coat. His enemies would have known of their movement; Dundas would have known; the Excise would have known—and he would, as a consequence, have shared " Muir and Palmer's fate."

Historians are of the opinion that the essential evidence of their despatch to the French may reside somewhere in the *Journal* of John Lewars. But Lewars's *Journal* has not been seen since Sir Walter Scott is alleged to have passed it through his hands.

Until the reappearance of Lewars's *Journal* and the proving of his evidence, the carronades incident must be left to lie on the table.

The second event concerns the place where the Burns-Riddell quarrel originated. Much violent controversy has raged over this relatively-unimportant incident. But the protagonists have plumped either for Friars Carse or Woodley Park. One steady glance at the facts proves, however, that the incident occurred at neither house but at the " hospitable mansion " of a lady who remains to this day unidentified. Should the "Letter from Hell " ever turn up, the name of the addressee may establish her identity: if not, she is likely to remain unknown. Meanwhile Woodley Park and Friars Carse are eliminated from the controversy.

My portrait of Robert Burns is unashamedly romantic and idealistic; but it is more solidly related to historical fact than any other portrait. This is not to say that it is the best portrait. Time has settled the hash of innumerable portraitists of Robert Burns; and it would be foolish of me to look for partiality where none has ever been granted. All I claim is that I have done the best I can for my generation. It is a pioneer effort at clearing the field of much nonsense and a rank and wicked crop of calumny.

The last word has not been written about Burns—nor will it ever be. The last word will remain with Burns even as the last word on Beethoven remains with Beethoven and on Rembrandt with Rembrandt. Of such, ordinary mortals (however gifted) are only vouchsafed a glimpse or two of their essential immortality.

Acknowledgments due to those who have helped me on this last lap are many.

My debt to Professor J. DeLancey Ferguson grows with the years. As my Court of Appeal he has always delivered judgment with admirable humanity, incomparable knowledge and uncanny insight.

Mr Thomas McCrorie, curator of the Burns House in Dumfries, has been a happy source of much knowledge and fortunate lore. With Tam as guide, many a useful and always pleasant day (and night!) has been spent exploring the neuks and crannies of Dumfries. Would that those connected with Burns in official capacity had a tithe of Tam's love for the Bard, for his haunts and for his work and worth. To care for the house in which Burns died is no light responsibility. Mr McCrorie discharges that responsibility in a manner worthy of the Bard's memory. I am proud to acknowledge my indebtedness to him.

Mr John S. Clarke made me free of his unique library and supplied me with many rare documents concerning the trial of Thomas Muir and his associates of the days when reason-in-revolt was thundering across the closing years of the eighteenth century. Mr Clarke's long service in the task of explaining and interpreting Burns to every kind of audience is known to all Scots—and many thousands of his fellow-Englishmen. I salute him.

Many others have helped me in various ways. Mr A. M. Donaldson of Vancouver passed on to me an important discovery without reservation, exemplifying the true spirit of research workers everywhere. Mr. James Urquhart of Dumfries had only to learn that I was dubious of the whereabouts of the Jerusalem Tavern than he dug up the facts for me. But to true Burns lovers everywhere, no task is too mean or too arduous if only the result will add another stone, however small, to the cairn of his Immortal Memory.

There is a fairly sound convention that an author should not pay tribute to his publishers in a book bearing their imprint. But there are times when a convention needs to be broken. In issuing these volumes, the House of Collins has been rather more than publishers. It has sustained, encouraged, advised—and shown a remarkable degree of patience. Directors, editors and representatives have been helpful in a manner that owes nothing to the demarcations of commerce. To Mr W. A. R. Collins and Mr F. T. Smith I lie under a specially heavy debt of gratitude. It is a debt I am happy to acknowledge.

It is a rather shadowy Burns that is revealed to the research worker or to the writer confined to his study. Burns can only be fully understood in relation to his effect on contemporary life and letters. Deprived of the living contact with innumerable lovers of Burns (who have shared with me the flesh and blood of his world and the quickening of his spirit) this series of novels could not have been envisaged, far less written.

But I end as I began. In the *Note* to *The Wind that Shakes the Barley* I wrote: " This is a novel; and since a novel is devised for entertainment it should be read for pleasure: or not at all." If, as a by-product, a number of readers are induced to read the works of Burns, this will be a " consummation devoutly to be wished."

J.B.,
Daljarrock, Ayrshire,
5th March, 1953.

CONTENTS

Part One

THE HAWK THAT SWOOPS ON HIGH

Part Two

THE ROCK AND THE WEE PICKLE TOW

Part Three

THE POOR MAN'S DEAREST FRIEND

CHARACTERS

in their order of appearance
(Fictional characters are printed in *Italics*)

ROBERT BURNS.
JEAN ARMOUR BURNS.
NELLIE FORSYTH, barmaid, The King's Arms, Dumfries.
ALEXANDER FINDLATER, Supervisor of Excise, Dumfries.
MRS LOVE, landlady, Cowgate, Edinburgh.
JENNY CLOW, maid-servant, Edinburgh.
MRS AGNES MacLEHOSE, Edinburgh.
ANNA PARK, Leith.
WILLIAM NICOL, teacher, Edinburgh.
ADAM ARMOUR, mason, Machlin.
FANNY BURNES, wife to Adam Armour.
AGNES (NANCY) BURNS, sister of Robert.
MARIA WOODLEY, wife to Walter Riddell.
WALTER RIDDELL, brother of Robert Riddell.
HENRY CLINT, The King's Arms, Dumfries.
ROBERT RIDDELL, squire, Friars Carse.
JOHN MacMURDO, Chamberlain, Drumlanrig.
JOHN SYME, Collector of Stamps, Dumfries.
JOHN MITCHELL, Collector of Excise, Dumfries.
GEORGE HAUGH, blacksmith, Dumfries.
JEAN LORIMER, Kemys Hall.
EDMUND BURKE, politician, London.
CHARLES JAMES FOX, politician, London.
JOHN LEWARS, Excise officer, Dumfries.
WILLIAM SMELLIE, printer, Edinburgh.
STEPHEN CLARKE, musician, Edinburgh.
LOUISE FONTENELLE, actress, Dumfries.
HUGH BELL,
THOMAS MUIR,
WILLIAM SKIRVING,⎫ Members of The Society of the
LORD DAER, ⎬ Friends of the People, Edinburgh.
ROBERT FOWLER,
COLONEL DALRYMPLE,⎭
FRANCES ANNA DUNLOP, Dunlop House, Ayrshire.
WILLIAM CORBET, Collector-General of Excise, Edinburgh.

JESSIE LEWARS, Millbrae Vennel, Dumfries.
ELIZABETH HYSLOP, the Globe Tavern, Dumfries.
DR PITT SMITH, citizen of New York, U.S.A.
LORD BRAXFIELD, Lord Justice Clerk, Edinburgh.
WALTER AULD, saddler, Dumfries.
MRS ECKS, " Hospitable Mansion," Dumfries.
JOSEPH GERRALD, reformer, Edinburgh.
DAVID NEWALL, lawyer, Dumfries.
WILLIAM HYSLOP, the Globe Tavern, Dumfries.
ROBERT BURNS, first son of Robert.
FRANCIS WALLACE, second son of Robert
A. S. De PEYSTER, colonel, Mavis Grove, Dumfries.
JOHN ANDREWS, merchant, Dumfries.
WILLIAM MAXWELL, physician, Dumfries.
GRACE AIKEN, daughter of Robert Aiken, lawyer, Ayr.
HOST AND HOSTESS, Inn of Ruthwell, Solway.
WILLIAM NICOL BURNS, third son of Robert.
THOMAS BOYD, architect, Dumfries.
GILBERT BURNS, brother of Robert, Mossgiel.
JOHN RANKINE, farmer of Adamhill.

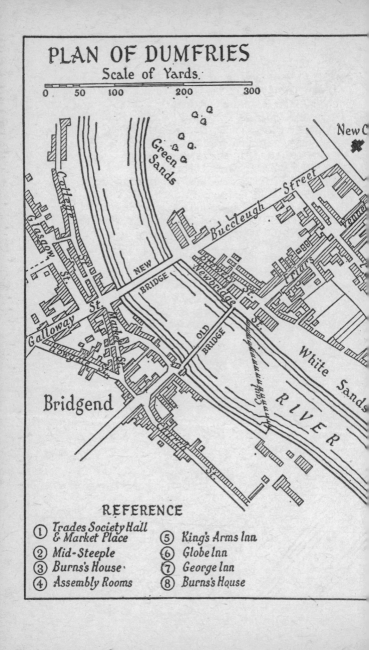

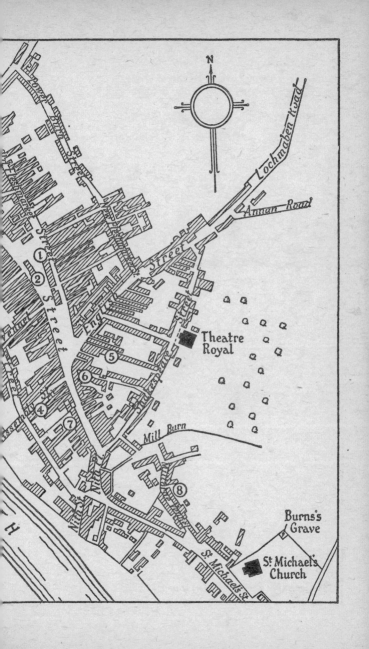

Here's freedom to them that would read,
  Here's freedom to them that would write!
There's nane ever feared that the truth should be heard
  But they whom the truth would indite!

Part One

THE HAWK THAT SWOOPS
ON HIGH

THE DRUMMING OF THE NITH

As the river Nith flowed to the sea it met a ridge of ground at Dumfries, swung right and then left in a great broad sweep, drummed proudly over the caul below the bridge and then settled quietly into the comfortable channel that led to the firth of the Solway.

The town was built tightly on and about the ridge. Its vennels were narrow, its innumerable closes narrower. Humanity had cluttered together closely on the ridge, for it was dry and drainage could escape from it down into the river. As the river was subject to floods, the houses stood well back from it. In normal conditions, a broad stretch of 'sands' lay between the town and the river, providing an excellent venue for fairs and sales of live-stock.

Built substantially of red sand-stone, Dumfries was a bonnie town and reasonably well appointed. It was much favoured by the gentry and had a uniquely residential air about it. It was annually patronised by the Noblemen and Gentlemen of the Caledonian Hunt – to say nothing of their ladies and retinues of servants, flunkeys and hangers-on.

A bonnie town indeed and in many ways a brave one. The 'trades' flourished and the merchants were prosperous. The port thrived, and there was exporting and importing. . . .

On the brow of the High Street stood the Mid-Steeple of the Council-House and in front of it the market-place of Queensberry Square. This was the town centre, the hub of the Dumfriesshire and Galloway universe.

It was a long time now since the first clutter of houses had appeared on the ridge above the Nith. The days of Devorgilla and Baliol and the building of Sweetheart Abbey might be romantic days; but there had been little romance about when the villainous Bruce murdered the Red Comyn before the altar in Greyfriars; nor had the Dumfries cobbles paved any welcome to Prince Charlie and his Highlanders. . . But Dumfries had survived and matured and sometimes it had dovered and dozed for an odd generation. . .

Robert Burns had found it dovering away pleasantly enough. There was a new bridge a-building, the new theatre and, here and there, a new house was going up. But it was not a town he warmed to. True, he had been made a Freeman in the year of his Edinburgh triumph and he had a few friends in and about the burgh. Yet it was not a town he would have settled in from choice.

The High Street ran with rough parallelism to the Nith and just below it, and between it and the river, Irish Street bisected the narrow vennels. The principal vennel through which most of the traffic went north and south across the bridge was the Friars; a shorter vennel lay to the south: the Stinking Vennel. A nasty open sewer ran down the middle of the causeway, emptying into the Nith as rainfall and drainage permitted.

But in the matter of stinks, the Stinking Vennel was by no means unique. The town stank. Everywhere drainage was at a minimum and great boglands surrounded the town.

Machlin had its stinks too; but in a more personal, identifiable sense. Dumfries stank as Edinburgh stank – vastly, persistently and impersonally.

Coming from the freshness of the Ellisland farm acres, Mrs Burns was more conscious of the indefinable stench than her husband was. Not that the Bard was insensitive to the offence to his nostrils.

'You'll get used to it, Jean.'

'Aye . . . I suppose folk can get used to onything . . . in time.'

'In time. . . Damnit, lass: had there been ony other road out of Ellisland I wad hae taken it. But you ken there was nae other road. I ken it's hell to be living in the Stinking Vennel up a narrow stair wi' a table-cloth o' a back-court and no' a green blade onywhaur. . . I ken —'

'Noo then, Rab: I'm no' complainin' —'

'That's your fault, Jean: you dinna complain enough.'

Jean changed her foot on the rocker of the cradle.

'There's nae use in complaining.'

'What about the pair o' us taking a bit walk? It's dry. There's a blink o' sun. Let Fanny see to the bairns. . . Come on: get your plaidein.'

They turned right on the causeway at the close-mouth and a dozen steps took them to the White Sands. Several women had taken advantage of the sun to do some washing in the river: each was busy with her tub. The river, though swollen, was in no angry mood.

'I'll no' hae far to go for my washing.'

'Aye. . . You'll miss Fanny and Nancy – I'll miss them mysel'.'

'I'll miss them. But we canna help it, Rab. There's nothing here for your sister: she kens that. And noo that Adam wants to marry Fanny — '

'Oh, we canna stand in their way.'

'And you agree we should give Fanny her wedding gown?'

'Yes: the best we can afford. She's turned into a fine woman: she'll make a grand wife to your brother.'

'Weel . . . I think he'll mak' her a guid husband.'

'I've nae fear for them – things couldna hae turned out better.'

From time to time the Bard interrupted the talk of family matters to point out something to Jean. He spoke of the beauty of the old bridge with its arches and the significance of the new bridge a-building a little up-river. But Jean merely nodded at the mass of scaffolding and excavations. At the moment Jean cared nothing for bridge-building or architecture or even the lay-out of the town. She took everything in with a casual sweep of her eye and accepted. Well Jean knew there was nothing for her but acceptance. Comment was a mere waste of breath.

They went up the Friars Vennel and here Jean was more interested in the shops and the appearance of the people.

'A body need want for nocht about Dumfries. . . There's a wheen drinking howffs.'

'Aye: it's a drucken town, lass.'

'Whaur's the Globe?'

'I'll show you when we come to it. This tak's us up onto the market – though, gin we were in a hurry, Irish Street here wad bring us out at our house. . .'

'Are there mony Irish in Dumfries?'

'Aye . . . there's an odd Irishman. They drive cattle across from Donaghadee – drive frae Portpatrick and Portlogan. . . Mind you, Jean, there's waur towns nor Dumfries. This is a grand place for a market, is it no? And when they finish the new brig the traffic'll gang doon the new Buccleuch Street and that'll tak' the weight off the vennel. It'll be a great improvement. . . This is the centre o' the town. That red building in the middle o' the street is called the Mid-Steeple. Quite an imposing tower with a guid knock set into it. . .'

'How long d'ye think you'll be in Edinburry?'

'Ten or twelve days at the outside.'

'Nancy says she'll wait till you get back.'

'I see. . .'

'But she wants hame for the New Year.'

'And Fanny?'

'Adam was thinking they could a' gae back thegither – if Gilbert could spare a conveyance — ? '

'Aye: that micht be the best way. . . And what d'you think o' the place?'

'Oh, the place is richt enough. I see the folk gi'ing us some queer looks.'

'That's the King's Arms Hotel facing us there. . . The Globe's down a bit and up a narrow close: will we ca' in and pay our respects to the Hyslops . . . ? '

But Jean didn't feel like visiting yet. There was too much to plan and to discuss – and so much to assimilate. She was in her twenty-sixth year and her constitution was as magnificent as ever. She was in her full-blossomed bloom. She had been his when the glory of her womanhood was at its freshest. . . They'd had their trials and tribulations. . . But now it seemed settled that her husband would live by the Excise; that farming was finished and over. . . She was neither glad nor sorry. She had her husband and her children. Her first-born, Robbie, was coming six; Frank was coming three; William and Anna Park's Betty were still at her generous breasts. . . Her twins she called them. She could have done with the companionship of Nancy and Fanny. But she would manage; she would only have the children and her husband to look after and she had all the strength and goodwill and good-nature this called for.

And yet somehow there was uncertainty. She felt that the three small rooms in the Stinking Vennel constituted a temporary, makeshift abode. And Rab was uncertain: he was desperately hoping that he would get promotion in the Excise and that promotion would take him out of Dumfries. . . Well, sufficient unto the day . . .

'The bairns'll be needing a feed, Rab – but on you go! Tell Bess Hyslop she can come doon ony time and that I'm looking forward to seeing her. . . You'll no' be late?'

The November dusk was gathering quickly. Already it was lying heavy in the narrow vennels and in the narrow closes. Here and there candles and tapers were being lit. Beyond Criffell hill the sky was red and menacing. The Nith drummed dully and monotonously over the caul.

22

The Bard, having seen Jean to the close-mouth, retraced his steps towards the Globe. But he didn't visit the Globe. He had several problems to think out by himself; and at the Globe he was not so much a customer as a valued friend. . .

He wanted half-an-hour by himself. He passed the Globe close and entered the King's Arms, went down the long narrow lobby and looked into a side-room. It was empty. He returned to the tap room where Nellie Forsyth was serving beer from a barrel and borrowed a lighted candle.

'Fetch ben a drop, Nellie, when you're ready. I've a wee bit writing to do.'

'Certainly, Mr Burns: I'll be ben on the instant.'

The Bard took out the letter he had received from Mrs Agnes MacLehose. He read it again; but the message it contained was already burned in his memory.

Mrs MacLehose informed him – in acid lines – that Jenny Clow was sick unto death and in the direst of poverty.

Poor Jenny! Poor silly independent stubborn proud bitch! So Jenny was going to die on him – and the son she had borne him? Of course Mrs MacLehose was justified in writing as she had. Mrs Mac could always justify herself – in her own eyes. And she'd flitted from General's Entry in the Potterrow to Lamont's Land in the Canongate! Just so . . . and she was for Jamaica and her brute of a husband.

Aye: it was a damned chancy world. Folk changed and in the end, despite all protests, did no more (or could do no more) than things would do with them.

Nancy was going to rejoin her husband in the Indies. Maybe had he gone to the Indies with Mary Campbell he would have met Nancy MacLehose in very different circumstances. Aye: Kingston would have been very different from Edinburgh in the year of the golden dream of '87.

But Jenny Clow? Jenny's problem was more immediate. He would write Nancy and ask her to go immediately to Jenny's assistance and he would repay Nancy the moment he arrived in Auld Reckie and had laid his bag in with MacKay at the White Hart Inn in the Grassmarket. He had put up at MacKay's when he had first visited Edinburgh in '86 – he would put up with MacKay again.

He took his quill, uncorked his ink-horn and wrote to Nancy. . .

Dear sweet-curved luscious amorous pious Nancy! They had loved that second winter in Auld Reekie; loved hotly, feverishly, tempestuously – and damned-near unnaturally. But they had loved and quarrelled. The quarrel didn't matter now. He had escaped, almost at the last moment, from her clutches. But he had escaped. Now he could in safety remember the loving, the caressing, the kissing, the love-making. . . What if he hadn't dismounted at the Grassmarket? What if he'd put dearest Nancy in the family-way? Aye: she'd been a lucky lass, damned lucky . . .

And what would the Reverend John Kemp and cousin William Craig have done had she become pregnant?

It would be glorious to see Nancy again. . . To share a bottle of wine with her and, after a long hour of gossip, to go to bed with her in the candle-light as they'd so often done in the Potterrow. . .

And, by God! they'd go to bed! Now that she was leaving Scotland forever, he'd see to that. Oh . . . he'd be careful, as always. Nancy would not arrive at Jamaica with his child, embryonic, in her fruitful womb. But she'd remember him. Yes: she'd remember him.

Nellie came through with the third drink as he finished his letter to Mrs MacLehose. . .

He could see her sitting in her chair – and the children through the wall. Prim and proper in her terrible poverty, pious in her religion and genteel in her respectability – semi-Anglified in her smattering culture – and hot as hell in the loving lust of her rich blood; biting her lips and groaning in her amorous frenzies. . .

Mrs Agnes MacLehose; Miss Nancy Craig; and the same age as himself – coming into her thirty-third year. Damn! just the prime of life . . . just the sweating-prime. He'd thought he'd been in his prime at twenty-six! Hell: he'd been but a laddie then.

This would be his last fling for a while. He would visit Jenny Clow and see what could be done for her. If Jenny had only been sensible he would have had her son – and his son – in the Stinking Vennel by now along with Betty Park. . . But Jenny had been independent. Proud . . . adamant . . . scornful! He recalled the last time he'd seen her. In Haddington in the George Inn. Jenny pale and scornful. And now, if Nancy was to be trusted, lying at death's door. God! life was a pell-mell of trial and adversity. . . If one could only see what lay ahead, round the corner, to the end of the week after next! But no: things happened and fate added up the consequences and then, out of the blue, presented the bill and demanded immediate payment, regardless of how money-matters stood at the time. . .

Yet Jenny had been worth the outcome. Jenny had been bright and keen and willing at a time he had sorely-needed her. And she'd known the consequences before they had loved. Maybe he should have been as considerate of her as he had been of her mistress, Nancy. But then he hadn't loved Jenny as he had loved Nancy. He'd been as hot for Jenny as Jenny had been for him. Neither of them had heeded the consequences. Their love-making had been desperate and urgent and without thought of consequences. Consequences! What had Jenny or he cared for consequences? Up yonder in Willie Cruickshank's attic room . . . and his dislocated knee not the most of his physical pain. . . No, no: Jenny had asked for no preferment and wouldn't have understood such nature-circumventing niceties. Jenny had wanted love, violent and vigorous – and nothing barred. She'd gotten it. There were no regrets. Only: she was dying – and there was the problem, immediate and heart-searing, of their son. . .

What would Jean think of him if she only knew the truth? But then Jean had never made the mistake of thinking that she could wholly possess him – or any husband. Jean knew that nature didn't make men that way. At least not vital, full-blooded, vigorous men.

God knows no man could wholly satisfy the amorous needs of any one normal woman. But God knew just as truly that no one woman could wholly satisfy one man. Aye: Jean knew this truth. His experience with Anna Park had more than proved that. There was little that Jean didn't know – instinctively, intuitively. . .

And while he was ruminating about Jean and Nancy and Jenny the door opened and Alexander Findlater, the new Supervisor of the Dumfries Excise, put his head in at the door, hesitated and then came boldly in.

Alexander Findlater had been promoted to a supervisorship and transferred from Edinburgh. He was just getting into his stride in Dumfries.

Findlater was a strong personality. Probably there was no more efficient Supervisor in Scotland. He came of the stock of Presbyterian clergymen; but he was no Calvinist and he liked the Bard.

'Weel, Robert . . . settling into Dumfries?'

'As weel as ever I'll settle, Sandy.'

'What are ye drinking? Tuts: you can aey man another drap. I'll tell ye what I want to speak to you about. It's all right for you to go to Edinburgh – permission has come through – only a matter of form. But form's something we've got to attend to in the Service. I've a message I'd like you to do for me in Edinburgh . . .'

Off duty they were friendly and intimate. On duty, Findlater was like his immediate superior, Collector John Mitchell – he was very much the Excise official and he let everybody know that, including the Bard.

'. . . and I wanted to warn you about Lorimer at Kemsy Hall. The man's little short o' a smuggler, Robert. D'ye realise that?'

'No . . . I don't. Maybe he's no' just what he should be, and you ken how things are wi' his wife — '

'I ken you're friendly wi' them, Robert. There's nae harm in that. But folks' tongues wag and Lorimer's going to give us a bit o' trouble afore long. He's crafty, Robert. I just want to warn you – and it's nae mair than a friendly warning – if you hae ony official business wi' Lorimer take good care he doesna put you in the wrong. He could mislead you, trip you, gin you werena just exactly on your toes. You understand?'

'I understand well enough. But I hope you don't think I'd let my friendship with the Lorimers stand between me and my duty?'

'No . . . no' exactly. But you might be off your guard just sufficiently. He's gotten a bonnie daughter – Jean . . .'

'Does Jean need to come into this?'

'No . . . no . . . Just she's a beauty, Robert – and I've nae doubt but you'll hae made a sang on her.'

'Maybe more than one!'

'Just so! Oh, I dinna fau't you for that.'

'You don't think that Jean and me — '

'No, no: that would never cross my mind. And even if it did it still wouldn'a worry me. I'm as fond o' a lass as ever you could be.'

'Are you?'

Findlater didn't reply. Maybe he wasn't. But he felt he had already committed himself. He was a strong personality with a strong sharp face and a strong sharp way of speaking. He was ambitious. He aimed to be a Collector with the minimum of service. He'd been married some ten years and had four of a family. His wife, Susan Forester, was well-enough connected. His background alone would make for promotion. But Findlater liked good company and he liked a dram. And he was only in his thirty-eighth year . . .

'See John Syme lately?'

'No. . . Old Maxwell o' the Stamp Office is still hanging on. You ken Syme's waiting to fill his shoes — '

'Dead men's shoes often tak' a while to wear out. Syme'll fill the job. He's gotten a lang head — '

'And a good one – and a heart o' the finest.'

'A good man Syme. Drink up, Robert.'

'I'm in nae mood for heavy drinking, Sandy. And I couldna fight against – far less drink level wi' – your constitution.'

'How's your health thae days?'

'I'm fine. But I aey need a day to recover from hard drinking.'

'It doesna worry Syme.'

'Syme's a port drinker. Maybe the gout'll catch up on him.'

'What d'ye think o' your colleagues in the Service?'

'Unofficially – strictly?'

'You ken me. You like Lewars?'

'Do you?'

'He'll mak' a grand officer. Though dinna tell him I said so. Penn?'

'Penn's all right. I look upon John Lewars as a friend, Sandy. There're no others in that category.'

'I see . . . I think you're wise, Robert.'

'How d'you get on wi' the Collector?'

'I've nothing but admiration and respect for Mr Mitchell.'

'Mitchell's a solid-enough man . . . Weel, once you're properly settled in, you'll bring Mrs Burns round to meet Mrs Findlater?'

'I'll be honoured. The twins are still at the breast – I think Mrs Findlater will understand. . . And my sister and my niece that were helping us at Ellisland will be gone afore the New Year — '

'But there's nae need for ony formalities – a friendly visit, Robert – just a friendly visit. My wife's an utter stranger in Dumfries and, to tell the truth, she's no' hellish enamoured o' the Dumfries folk.'

'They take a wee bit kennin'.'

'That's one o' the drawbacks o' the Service, Robert. You get settled into a district and then you're transferred. I kent some fine folks about Cupar-Angus. Different folk frae the south here.'

Suddenly Findlater took his leave.

'I was expecting a friend, Robert. I'll maybe look in at the George.'

A good friend Findlater: a man he felt he could lean on as a friend and an officer who would act squarely with him on official duties. But there was no softness of any kind about him – no all-embracing warmth as there was about Syme.

The Bard had still some writing to do. He had friends to contact in Edinburgh, friends that neither Mrs MacLehose nor Jenny Clow nor Anna Park knew anything about. He would have a busy time indeed during his stay there.

He'd also to see James Johnson and Stephen Clarke and drive them on with the fourth volume of songs. And he'd promised to see Cleghorn and Robert Ainslie and Alexander Cunningham and Willie Nicol and Peter Hill. No . . . there wouldn't be an idle moment for him in Edinburgh.

Before he left the King's Arms he re-read the passage in Mrs MacLehose's letter that cut him. Jenny Clow was dying. 'In circumstances so distressing, to whom can she so naturally look for aid as the father of her child, the man for whose sake she suffered many a sad and anxious night, shut from the world, with no other companions than guilt and solitude?' That was Nancy gilding the emotional lily. But then followed the cut! 'You have now an opportunity to evince you indeed possess these fine feelings you have delineated, so as to claim the just admiration of your country.'

Aye: that held and hurt. It was half truth. But Nancy didn't scruple to use it for all it was worth. That was the kind of loving bitch Nancy MacLehose could be. But then, in woman, the voluptuary and the virago were inextricably mixed.

Just as suddenly as Findlater had left, he felt lonely and empty. He needed companionship. He didn't want to go home: not yet.

He put his papers away and rose up hurriedly. Outside there was a drizzle of rain and the broad street was empty.

He turned into the warmth and friendliness of the Globe. Bess Hyslop would have a message for him to take to her niece Anna Park at Leith. There would be a song maybe. . .

THE GLIMMERING BLINK

It rained in the Grassmarket; but the busiest place in Edinburgh was rarely ever empty. He'd been cramped in the fly and he stamped his chilled feet on the wet causeway.

There was a note waiting for him giving Jenny Clow's address and direction in the Cowgate.

He took a good meal, fortified himself with a good drink and set off up the Cowgate.

It was an old wife who admitted him into her ill-smelling, ill-lighted kitchen.

'You're Mr Burns? I'm glad you've come, sir. The lass is in sair need o' a shilling or twa — '

'How is she?'

'You'll no' be fashed wi' her lang. She's wasting awa' fast.'

'Let me see her!'

'Through the door there and along the passage. You'll need the can'le.'

Jenny struggled into a sitting position. The effort brought on a fit of coughing. The Bard turned away his head.

The bed-clothes were worn and dirty. Her shawl was ragged and dirty. Her arms were pathetically thin.

'Well, Jenny — ?'

Her eyes were sunk but burning. She still gasped for breath.

'So . . . you came! That was kind o' ye.'

'The boy?'

'I buried him afore I cam' here. God saw to that.'

'When?'

'Weeks ago. He . . . didna suffer . . . just faded awa'. I'll be wi' him afore lang. . . I'm glad to see you . . . Robert. It was kind o' ye to send the money wi' Mrs Mac.'

'Was she here?'

'Aye . . .'

'Have you no' seen a doctor?'

'Mrs Mac wanted me . . . but I'm past seeing a doctor. Will you no' sit doon?'

'Is there onything you want?'

'Aye . . . if I could be buried decently aside my wee son.'

'You'll be buried decently. God, Jenny, couldn't you hae written me long afore this?'

'I was too prood . . . I was aey too prood. I'm no' too prood noo. . . As lang as wee Robbie lived I didna want to dee.'

'And you'll no dee. I'll get you a doctor.'

'Aye, I ken you wad. But . . . no . . . I dinna want to see ony doctor. I'd give up hope o' ever meeting wi' you again. Mrs Mac was affa upset and said ill things aboot you. But . . . I wouldna let her . . .'

'Could you take a drink o' gin – or brandy?'

'A taste o' brandy and water – aye.'

'Who's your landlady?'

'Mrs Love. She drinks a lot; but she's no' bad-hearted.'

'Could I trust her to go for some brandy?'

She nodded and the Bard called her in.

'Here, wife! Gae doon and fetch a bottle o' brandy and if you touch a drap I'll break your neck. And fetch a gill o' gin – and if it's a gill when you come back you can drink it. And nae taiglin'!'

He gave her the money and, muttering protestations and blessings at the same time, she shuffled away.

The Bard knew that Jenny was dying. He had watched his brother John die. . . And Jenny had changed: she was humble in death. Her sufferings must have been fearful.

'You're weel yourself – and a' yours, Robert?'

'Yes, Jenny —'

'I'm no' a bonnie sicht. . . I wasn't aey this way. . . Try and mind me as I used to be.'

She fumbled at the neck of her shawl and fingered a thin piece of blackened ribbon.

'I had to spend a guinea to bury him: ye dinna blame me? I said I wouldna . . .'

The Bard turned away. He felt as if his guts were being squeezed in a vice. If only the old hag would come with the brandy. He hadn't looked forward to this meeting with Jenny. He hadn't realised it would be so painful. But Jenny was right. She was far past the aid of any doctor. It was only a matter of time: a few hours at least . . . a few days at most.

And yet he was glad he had come – if he could give her some tithe of comfort at the end.

Mrs Love came with the drink and was persuaded to bring some water. A cracked mug sat on the chair beside the bed.

He held the bottles against the light: they had not been tampered with.

'Here, wife: you've earned your gin. Jenny: how strong can ye tak' it?'

'The same o' water.'

'There, then! Sip it – or it'll maybe start your cough. But if you can get it down —'

It was a slow and painful business for her to get the first few mouthfuls over. But the effect of the drink was almost instantaneous. A flush crept into her cheeks and her eyes burned even brighter – if that were possible. Her breathing quickened, but seemed easier.

'Ah . . . that's better . . . that's easier. I've nae pain. Only my cough and my breathing . . . and when the blood comes. . . I'm affa weak after the blood comes.'

'You've nae relations . . . kith or kin?'

'Naebody that would want me or I would want to hae wi' me. Auld Mistress Love kent my mither. . . Mrs Mac's gaun to join her man in Jamaica.'

'Mrs Mac can go to hell, Jenny. Drink up your brandy: it'll gar you sleep.'

'I'll hae lang enough to sleep. Dinna be, angry wi' Mrs Mac: you ken you were fond o' her and she's still fond o' you.'

'Did she say that?'

'A woman kens anither woman. She's silly to go to Jamaica – d'ye no' think so?'

'Mrs Mac's an auld sang noo, Jenny.'

'No' that auld. She's a richt bonnie woman still.'

Jenny could now drink more freely. The Bard was secretly glad to see her doing so. He felt he couldn't go away as long as her eyes held him. Her voice was very low and husky: sometimes he lost a phrase.

She was becoming drunk. Once she giggled pathetically and once she cried, the big tears pouring relentlessly down her flushed pinched face. She half wiped her face with the back of a hand that was so emaciated it looked like a claw.

'D'ye mind, Robert, when I first came wi' yon message – in Saint James's Square. . . Oh, I'm glad you came . . . to . . . see me. I was bitter when I saw you at Haddington. . . I said bitter words. . . But . . . you forgive me, Robert? Maybe I should say Mr Burns. . . I wad hae asked ye . . . to kiss me . . . but . . . you micht . . . get . . . the smit. . .'

'Cuddle doon, Jenny, and try and sleep.'

'Aye . . . cuddle doon. . . I'm no' cauld noo . . .'

She half-slid, half-crawled down into the bed. He happed the thin bed-clothes about her. He brushed her brow with his lips.

'Guid-nicht . . . Robert. . . Guid. . .'

She sighed and her eyes closed. Her lips were parted and her breathing was in soft gasps.

He backed slowly towards the door. She was asleep.

In the kitchen he said to Mrs Love:

'Listen, wife: be guid to her. I've left the brandy wi' her: see that you dinna touch it. She hasna lang to go. It wad be better for her if she went in the nicht. Noo listen: I'll go out now and fix on – the final arrangements. There'll be a man up here in the morning. D'ye understand?'

But Mrs Love could only nod. This man was something of a terror to her – a man of authority not to be disobeyed in any particular. She kept nodding.

He threw a guinea on the table.

'I'll pay for everything – and you for your trouble.'

'God bless you, sir: I'll be as guid to her as if she were my ain. I've done that a' the time.'

'Guid-nicht to you then.'

Out in the dank Cowgate he was suddenly overwhelmed with loneliness, remorse, pity and a strange unpredictable terror. The wind knifed down the grey-black cleft of the Cowgate. The whipped rain stung. Folks moved by instinct for visibility was wretched. Once in the same Cowgate he had courted Peggy Cameron. . .

He found himself plodding up Libberton's Wynd making for John Dowie's tavern. His need for drink was overwhelming – after that . . . company, distraction . . . anything to make him forget the pitiful physical wreck of Jenny Clow – a wreck in which the soul still glimmered and wavered.

SENSIBILITY HOW CHARMING

Mrs MacLehose returned his embrace almost too ardently. Her legs weakened, her midriff tautened. She broke away hastily.

'I got your note. Mary Peacock has taken the children out for a walk. . . Oh, Robert . . . it's been so long.'

'Well, Nancy: you ken whose fault that was – but for Godsake, no recriminations!'

'And no kissing . . . I just canna thole it, Robert. I meant to be cold – and cross – wi' you.'

'I meant to be a bit off-hand mysel', Nancy. You havena been over-kind to me. . .'

'I'd no cause to be. You're looking well. Come and sit down.'

'You're looking as magnificent as ever, Nancy.'

'No flattery, please!'

'You were always magnificent, Nancy – even in your anger. And I couldna flatter you: that's beyond my powers —'

'Robert! You mustna talk like that. My dear: I canna thole it – as I've told you. You ken how much the silly, weak woman I am.'

'Neither silly nor weak —'

'Have you seen Jenny Clow?'

'Yes. . . By God! I saw Jenny Clow. . . . I saw her kisted this morning!'

'Robert! No, no! Surely not —'

'Jenny died last night. I'd a long talk with her before she died. . . No: I didn't see her die. But I knew she was dying. Oh, maybe I hastened her death – by a few hours. If so, God help me: I did my best. . . Nancy, you could have told me before . . . you did.'

'I didn't know. . . And Robert! how could you: not with Jenny! She was my maid when it happened —'

'Yes: I know. But you made the mistake of sending her instead of coming yourself.'

'You mean to Saint James's Square —'

'Yes: to Saint James's Square. When – I did what I did to Jenny Clow maybe I was thinking of you, Nancy. Certainly I was thinking of you —'

'No, no, no . . .'

'Why not? Anyway, Nancy, I saw Jenny before she died. She was a brave lass.'

'She's being buried —'

'As to burial: I've arranged all that. No: I won't be there, Nancy. That's too trivial a business for me to attend to –

besides, I couldn't bear the hypocrisy of it and my emotions micht get the better o' me.'

'But I thought you had made your peace. . . I mean you canna treat death as trivial —'

'Trivial? No, no, Nancy: there's nothing trivial about death. Dinna worry, lass: once you've sat at the bed-side o' death – but I forgot: you lost a son. . . Well, I lost a son. . .'

'But how could you, loving me, resort to Jenny: and my own servant! How could you, Robert?'

'It was simple enough. . .'

'No: don't tell me. I who loved you as no woman has ever loved a man. . . I who would have gladly gone through life with you – and beyond life to all eternity. Oh, that I should sin my immortal soul! Robert: you know that I would have done anything for you —'

'Nancy, Nancy! Why must you torture yourself? I was in love with you: I was never in love wi' Jenny Clow. . . Dinna interrupt me. I was in love with *you*. You were in love wi' me.'

'You know I forbid that word.'

'The word, Nancy my dear, always the word – but never the deed.'

'Dinna say that —'

'Aye, I'll say that and a lot more —'

'No —'

'Nancy: you maun face it. Face the truth —'

'I don't want to hear anything —'

'Right! You dinna want to hear the truth. So why should I try to tell you?'

'But I want to know the truth —'

'No: only the truth that – well, the truth that doesn't offend you. Now I'm tired, Nancy. Have you a drink in the house?'

'Robert! This isn't my house: I've no house. I've sold my furniture – what was left of it: I'm leaving Scotland for good —'

'You're going to rejoin your husband in Jamaica —?'

'And – why shouldn't I? You married your Jean!'

'Well . . . well . . . I couldn't have married you, could I?'

'I'd have gone away with you —'

'To where?'

'I'd have made you a good wife —'

'Not wife, Nancy – mistress!'

'I never thocht you'd use that expression to me. You've become unkind, unthinking —'

'I'm merely telling the truth. Come, Nancy: there's no point now in trying to deceive each other in a net o' words and evasions. Love's one thing: marriage is another. I do love you and always will – no matter what happens. But if we were married we'd hate each other at the end o' the week —'

'That's insulting —'

'What does insulting matter? You think you would like me for a husband, Nancy. But you've no idea what I'd be like as a husband.'

'I suppose your Jean kens?'

'That she does – and loves me the more for it.'

'So you're happily married?'

'As happy as a married man can be and a damn-sight happier than most.'

'And what, pray, do you think I would lack as a wife?'

'The ability to leave a man alone when he needs to be alone and not to interfere with his friends when he must hae friends. But I don't know, Nancy. All I'm certain of is that either as the wife of a farmer or a common gauger you'd be a failure —'

'Oh, yes: I grant you all that willingly. But you can't deny that I could be a wife to a poet!'

'No. . . But then you canna judge a poet by his best verses. And when your poet has had a hard day searching auld wives' barrels and comes home tired and wet and has to sit in at the board-end with a wheel sheets o' Excise accounts to fill up. . . No, Nancy: you were made to be a poet's *mistress*. You should have lived in simple elegance, in a grand but unpretentious house – had fine clothes, fine carpets, fine china, fine pictures and a fine library of finely-bound volumes – and fine wine – and waited for your poet-lover.'

'When it suited him to call?'

'Well, you wouldn't want to see him when it didna suit him: that would ruin everything.'

'Oh, you can be cruel, Robert.'

'No, my dear: I'm no' cruel and I could never be cruel to you. But now that we're parting – and unfortunately it looks like forever – let's face and acknowledge the truth in each other. The lies we told each other were lovers' lies, poetic lies

– but lies, however pleasant. But the truth need be no less pleasant – and it's certainly more invigorating. I always knew the truth about you, Nancy.'

'And do you think I didn't know the truth about you?'

'And was the truth so terrible?'

'I – I did think you were different from all other men.'

'And am I not different?'

'I thought you were supremely the man who would be faithful to the woman he loved. But you married your Jean – and you had Jenny Clow. And how many others? And all the time I believed in your most sacred vows.'

'Did you? Honestly, Nancy?'

'Well . . . I wanted most desperately to believe you.'

'That's better. But I married my Jean – and you're going to rejoin your husband!'

'Robert! If only you know how afraid I am of meeting my husband. But what can I do? I've my boys to think about. I owe them something more than the terrible poverty I've endured all these years. You know how ashamed I was of my mean rooms in General's Entry. Now my boys will have a father and have their education and their future provided for and I – I was at the end of my tether, Robert. You were lost to me. I could have endured so much more with you at my side — But no: that would have been sinful. You dinna ken how fervently I've prayed to be forgiven the terrible sins we've committed.'

'Praying does you good, Nancy. A good prayer purges you like writing a good song purges me.'

'I've never convinced you about the necessity for constant prayer, Robert. I've failed even in trying to bring you to a proper relationship with the Almighty. I fear you're a heathen at heart, Robert.'

'No, I'm no heathen, Nancy. But maybe a man has a different approach to the Deity than a woman – especially a woman of fine poetic sensibility.'

'Canna you see you're in danger of blaspheming away your immortal soul?'

'Fine I do, Nancy. But I'll listen to the Reverend John Kemp at the proper time and place; and I'm not going to sit here and have you sermonising. Can you fill me another drink? And fill one for yourself. . .'

Nancy had got her rooms in Lamont's Land from a friend who had to go out to the country on a long visit to a sick relative. They were only slightly better than her own rooms had been in the Potterrow. Yet somehow, for all their digniness, the old rooms and the poor furniture had had something of Nancy's personality stamped on them. Here it was obvious that Nancy was in lodgings.

The meeting ended as the Bard knew it would end. Nancy was in his arms, passionate, protesting, weeping and succumbing in turn.

'On the sixth of the month I've a friend coming to stay with me, Robert. But come to-night and every night till then. Come after the drums – I'll be waiting for you.'

'I can stay all night?'

'Till the morning, my love. Oh, that you could stay forever! Now run: Mary's due back with the children.'

NO PARTING KISS

In a Leith tavern, in a private room, with a touch of frost and a bright sun outside and a warm fire within, the Bard sat with Anna Park and shared with her a pint of wine.

The bloom had died on Anna. The bright flame of her loving had sunk to a glimmer. She was still a fine woman. Men still stared at her and stared with lust in their eyes; but there was no response in Anna. For the time being at any rate, her experience with the Bard had burned her out.

'Maybe we shouldna hae met again, Robert?'

'Of course we should. I'm mair nor glad to see you again. But you're worrying about something?'

'No. . . I'm no' worrying. No' now. I'm thinking about getting married.'

'That's grand news: the best thing you can do.'

'The *only* thing I can do. But I dinna think I'll ever love a man again.'

'Nonsense, my dear! Of course you'll love again. You're fond o' this fellow you're thinking o' marrying?'

'Fond? Well . . . he's decent enough. Been a sodger: wants to settle doon. Kens I've had a bairn: says it'll mak' nae difference.'

'Were you wise to tell him about the bairn?'

'I couldn'a deceive him and he would hae found out onyway. He didna speir ony questions. I said it was to a married

37

man – and had died. That's near enough the truth for me. But she's a' richt, isn't she?'

'Aye, she's perfect, Anna – and she's my lassie . . . and aey will be. The wife couldna be fonder o' her.'

Anna looked into her glass of wine, lifted it slowly and took a slow meditative drink. The sun caught her hair and it flamed.

'It was kind o' you to bring the money, Robert. Are you sure you can spare it: I mean. . .'

'Not a word, my dear. I only wish I could make it more. I wish I saw you happier.'

Anna forced a smile. Even her eyes brightened.

'I'm happy enough.'

Her hand shot out impulsively and grasped his as it rested palm-downwards on the table.

'I'm glad you came, Robert. Glad and sorry too.'

'Why the sorrow?'

'We dinna love ony mair. We canna love ony mair. It's a terrible gnawing want deep inside. Make's me feel terribly empty – and lonely. You see there's no' another man like you. Ony other man's an insult after you — '

'Ony other woman's an insult after you, Anna.'

'Dinna tell lies, Robert. You'll aey hae women and women will aey be glad to hae you. It's different wi' me. No: I'll never richt get ower it – never! We were too happy when we were loving. Oh, yon nichts in the Globe . . .! I did mean a lot to you then, Robert, didn't I?'

'God, Anna: dinna talk like that. There never were nights like you and never can be again. All right, lass: I'll hae women to the end o' my days, I suppose. But my sang for you will always be true and for me the gowden locks o' Anna will never turn grey. If we can never recapture our love, at least nothing can prevent us taking the memory o' it to the grave.'

Anna took her hand away. But she looked at him with deep, almost melancholic gratitude.

'Will I ever see you again?'

'Why not? Do we no' mean something to each other that's precious beyond the naming? It's true we canna love again – because we couldna love as intensely again. . . Anna, there were times when I was completely transformed in my loving – times that didna properly belong to this earth. Let's be grateful that we ever loved sae intensely. . . So why shouldna we meet again and pledge the memory in a glass o' wine?'

'You're a great man – and a guid man. There's no' a spot o' badness or evil in you. It does me good just to be wi' you and hear you speak. The world's a different place when you talk. I don't think I ever told you that. And there's something about your eyes that mak's me feel – oh, I just canna describe the feeling it gives me – but it's a guid feeling. Even yet, Robert, I think I wad dae onything you asked me and never question the richts or wrangs o' it; for wi' you somehow there's nae wrangs. I canna put words thegither the way you can; but aey tellt you I was nae gowk – I've ideas about things; and I think.'

She lifted her glass and drained it.

'Och, maybe I'm just a silly bitch too, Robert. I'll need to leave you. I'm late already. They'll smell drink aff me and I never drink noo – but I enjoyed that.'

They were both on their feet. She shook her head and, retreating, held out her hand.

'Dinna kiss me, Robert – I couldna stand it. Ta-ta: and God bless you.'

He released her hand and she turned and was out of the room on the turn of her heel.

The Bard sat down, lifted his glass and watched the light break and shimmer in the blood-red wine.

In many ways, Anna Park was the most terrific woman he had ever known. But strangely – even more than Jenny Clow fresh in the grave – did she belong to the past; that, as far as he was concerned, she had no future. And Anna knew this in a way that was at once shattering and reassuring.

Vaguely but deeply relieved, the Bard took off his drink slowly.

THE WARNING

He saw most of his old Edinburgh friends. He even looked in at the Crochallan Club and introduced them to some bawdy songs he had collected since his last visit. Willie Smellie and Willie Dunbar were as friendly and as bawdy as ever. He spent half a day out at Corstorphine with Robert Cleghorn of Saughton Mills and revelled in the lusty farmer's sterling good-fellowship. Cleghorn was disappointed that Ellisland had turned out a bad bargain, but was reassured to learn that The Excise would give the Bard more leisure for his pen. He promised that, at the first opportunity, he would pay him a visit at Dumfries.

So did Alexander Cunningham, who asked many questions about their mutual friend John Syme. Cunningham was a genuine fellow and a real friend. His admiration for the character of the Bard was boundless. There was an almost staid quality about him that the Bard liked. There was no need to exert himself in his company. He could enjoy an hour with him quietly but with deep satisfaction. And Cunningham was deeply stirred by the events in France. Cunningham, too, believed that the world had begun anew.

With Willie Nicol it was impossible to relax – unless when Willie was half-way towards a drunken oblivion. And Willie was drinking heavier than ever, now that his wife had come into money and he had purchased the estate of Laggan Park over the hills from Ellisland.

'I dinna suppose you'll ever be oot about Laggan Park?'

'Seldom, Willie. But sometimes I hae to relieve a fellow-officer. Any time I'm that way I'll look your tenant up and report progress.'

'That'll dae me, Robin. I want to ken if there's ony limestone. . . Sae you think you'll dae weel in the Excise Service?'

'I'm on the list for promotion to a Supervisorship. At worst it'll only be a matter o' waiting.'

'There's something bluidy unnatural about you being in the service o' this government o' graft and corruption and incompetency.'

'I'm no' thirled to the politics o' the government: I'm there to exact the law.'

'By God and that's funnier! *You* exacting the law! Getting some puir auld ale-wife fined for some paltry offence!'

'There's no occasion for me to have the law on ony puir auld ale-wife. I've used my office to save mony such a wife – and maist officers dae likewise. It's the big folk we're after.'

'But to hell, Robin: it's a' wrang for you to be on the side o' that law. We pay enough for our drink as it is, do we no'? I suppose I could hae been arrested for brewing you a peck o' maut at Moffat?'

'Technically, yes: you could.'

'God damnit, that I should hae lived to see the day when the greatest poet the world has ever seen sat and talked about the technicality o' arresting a scholar for brewing a bit drink for himself and his friends! It's monstrous, Robin – it's no' natural. Damnit, you canna get away frae the fact that it's degrading work for a poet – ony poet.'

'And you knocking Latin into the heads o' the gentry's bastards?'

'So you admit your degradation, do you? Dinna tell me you glory in it. Scotland's played you a dirty trick, Robin. I mean Scotland's gentry. Whaur's your Duke o' Atholl and your Duchess o' Gordon noo? Whaur's your Gentlemen o' the Caledonian Hunt to whom you dedicated your Edinburgh volume? They spend mair on a hunt ball than wad keep you in comfort for a decade. No; but they'll let you stamp leather and gauge barrels for a pound a week – a common gauger. Even at that they could hae started you at the level o' a Supervisorship – without ony bother. You would hae mastered the job in a week. But they'll put you through the mill and fob you aff by placing your name on the promotion list. No: I dinna blame you, Robin. Of course you've got to live. But you should be able to find something else – and something that would give you independence. You think you're independent. But wait, my bonnie boy – just wait till you stick out your neck ower far. This is no' France, you ken. And the French king's no' finished yet. Louis has plenty o' friends in Europe – and plenty nearer hame —'

'But hell, Willie – you're for the French! Since when did you become a Royalist?'

'I'd cut the heads aff every king and throw them to the mob to mak' kick-ba's – and they'd be shouting for a new king the morn! You've got to get rid o' the damned rotten trash o' aristocracy. Taking spite out on a bit king because he wears a crown's a silly business.'

'But the French have no parliament like ours.'

'Weel, they've gotten this Legislative Assembly! They've got their Three Estates. You'll see where a parliament'll get them. Look at Dundas wi' damn-near every Scottish member in his pocket. Naebody kens that better than you. . .'

'We can press for reform. We're pressing for it already. And in a perfectly legal and constitutional manner.'

'That's what I'm warning you against. You, an Exciseman. Dinna spout your constitutionalism in my lug. If you go

41

against the politics o' Henry Dundas you'll no' reign lang in the Excise. Damnit, Robin, your job's to write poetry and sangs. You can sing o' Liberty and Fraternity and Equality – if you were Robert Burns, Poet, and dependent on nae man. But let you, as common gauger, cock your snout at the Powers on High and they'll smash your face in – and damn quick. You're ower damn trusting – that's what aey told you. If a duke tak's you by the hand then he must be a good fellow. If some lousy clergyman thinks weel o' your Holy Fair then he maun be a fine independent fellow worthy o' your friendship. And because Graham o' Fintry's gotten you placed on the promotion list you think he's a damn fine fellow too. Aye: they're a' damn fine fellows until you want something aff them that would mean them dipping their hands into their weel-lined pouches. When Fintry gave you the privilege o' riding ower some dizzen muirland parishes, summer and winter, what was he giving you – and what was it taking out o' his pocket? When Glencairn – but Glencairn's a sair point wi' you. . .'

'No: say what you like about Glencairn. I ken what Glencairn did for me and nothing you can say can change my mind about that. Say what you like about Fintry. But I ken damn-well it cost Fintry nothing to make me an Exciseman – except the trust he had in me that I'd make a good Exciseman. But if it cost him nothing to push my interest –obviously it would hae cost him less no' to hae pushed it. No, no, Willie: fine I ken the truth o' what you're saying – by and large. But if I canna be allowed the privilege o' taking a man on his individual merits, then I want nae privileges whatsoever and I micht as well be a labouring ox. You see nae difference in Henry Erskine frae Lord Braxfield. To me, there's a' the difference in the world. Braxfield's only a bluidy beast dressed in the wig and gown o' the judiciary. Dean-o'-the-Faculty Erskine's a man who lends human worth and human integrity to his office. Braxfield does whatever dirty work Dundas commands. Erskine stands up against him whenever he gets the opportunity.'

'Listen, Robin: the moment Harry Erskine proves a danger – a real danger – to Dundas then Dundas'll hae him removed and thrown out o' his office like a drunk flunkey — '

'Aye . . . and maybe Dundas'll get flung out o' his office — '

'And wha is there to throw Dundas out? That's the

42

poet in you again. Mind you: I'd tak' a richt willing part in the hanging, drawing and quartering o' Dundas the morn. I ken fine there's a restless, reforming spirit abroad the now and I ken there're certain influential Whigs ahint a lot o' the agitation – and guid luck to them. But still, they're a' far ower canny for Willie Nicol, and I dinna trust them. When Dundas cracks doon on them they'll find scapegoats to tak' the brunt o' the blows. It's you I'm feared o', Robin. You'd mak' a grand scapegoat – and you ken how fond o' you Dundas is. You see you're sae bluidy impulsive *and* trusting. They'll get you to write some bluidy blinding rant for them – and then you'll be a mair marked man that you are — '

'Hell, Willie! What wad you hae me dae?'

'Man, it's just that I'm feared for you – feared that you get into a lot o' bother ower nothing that really matters. Oh, I ken that Freedom and Liberty are great ideals and great sources o' poetic inspiration. But once the poet has to fight with the harp in one hand and the sword in the other . . . Weel: it's a noble spectacle – for the onlooker! And I'd rather see you as the onlooker than the one that's looked onto – understand? I want you to be the onlooker – the poet looking on and recording. And for every Heroic Ode you could compose, you could dash aff twa-three blazing satires. Your Tree o' Liberty's hardly a bush yet: you could get mair shelter under a docken-leaf. . . I ken you canna see things this way. That's why I keep hammering at you. . . Oh, you'll gang your ain gate as you've aey done. I don't suppose you can help that. But for Godsake go canny! Watch your step! We're living in damned kittle times and I fear the powers that be. Some folk think you're a big strong fellow fearing neither God nor devil – and maybe whiles you see yoursel' in that role. But I ken you better, Robin. You're easy hurt, and you'd be easy broken. And if they savaged you, by God! I think I'd go out and choke them wi' my bare hands — Noo drink up! for I canna trust mysel' on this theme.

'And noo, tell me how you got on wi' your lass wi' the bastard boy? You should hae sent the bitch to hell lang ago. What did it cost you this time? I told you lang ago you'd be better saired i' the hure-shop. But no: you're too damned fussy for an honest hure. . . '

But the Bard said nothing. He noted with regret that Willie Nicol was showing the wear and tear of his constant drinking. The whites of his eyes were muddy brown and blotched with ruptured blood-vessels. . . Yet there was about Nicol a downrightness and a forthrightness that could not disguise the warmth of his friendship. And there was something touching about Nicol, the atheist and republican, advising him caution. . .

AE FOND KISS

He remained sober and left Willie Nicol dead drunk. This was to be his last night with Clarinda.

They sat for a long time in front of the fire sharing a bottle of wine and talking in calmness and friendship of their own particular problems. Their love had ripened into a deep, if limited, friendship. They had no secrets that mattered from each other; and by some subtle arrangement neither of them mentioned Robert Ainslie. Indeed, during a brief meeting with Ainslie, Mrs MacLehose's name had not been mentioned. He took it that Nancy didn't intend that Ainslie should know of their meeting.

An observer, eavesdropping on them might have taken them for husband and wife whose love had mellowed with the years and who were about to separate for a journey. The Bard's top-boots stood by the fireside and Nancy's stays draped the back of a chair along with her linen drawers and scarlet stockings. . . Her ample bosom was almost bare. The Bard's breeches were undone at the knees.

They were completely relaxed and at their ease. The wine sat on a small delicate table.

At last the wine began to mellow in Nancy's veins. Her body was warm: she felt deliciously drowsy.

'And to think this is the last night we'll ever have together, Robert. . . The last on this earth. . .'

'It's a queer world, Nancy. We never know what Fate has in store for us. We *may* meet again.'

He said this to reassure her. But he felt like her that this was indeed the end. And he was sorry. There was a something about Nancy that was infinitely soothing and comforting. When she forgot about her religion and her sensibility and her poetry, Nancy was a very natural, homely, affectionate woman. But it was only at night-time, by the light of the fire or taper, that she was wholly so – just as it was only in bed that her amorousness became frenzied and transcendent.

And yet he knew now, with more certainty than ever, that she could never have been more than a holiday wife, or the occasional mistress.

So he sat there with her in the glow of the firelight, relaxed, enjoying the taste of the wine, talking softly and easily about their common friends and common problems. He was in no hurry to go to bed – there was no clamorous urgency about that relationship now. Ultimately in bed, slowly, with the mood dictating its own rhythm, that it would come. But there was no need to anticipate. Every woman had her own rhythm and sometimes, if not indeed most times, it was better to let that rhythm develop within itself. And why not, since he could always dictate and dominate the climax?

'And I've not to write?'

'Please dinna write – at least until I can get some word to you through Mary Peacock. A letter might well place my whole future in jeopardy.'

'Fine I ken. . . But I'll be desperate to hear how you progress.'

'I'll write Mary regularly – but Mary won't be able to say anything about you in reply. At least not at first. . . I'll need to be doubly cautious, Robert. But I suppose MacLehose must have changed. . .'

'But you're no' too sure about that?'

'I must keep my assurance – till I find out: I must have something to sustain me. Everybody agrees that I can do no other than join him.'

'Including Mr Kemp?'

'You never liked Mr Kemp – yet I canna think why.'

'Aye, fine you ken, Nancy – but that's an old story and there's nae point in raking it up noo. . .'

Nancy was quite prepared to let the question of Kemp drop: she didn't want anything to disturb this last meeting.

'It was kind of you to bring the wine, Robert – and so characteristic of you to remember what I like.'

'It would be difficult to forget — '

'If only I'd met you the first winter you cam' to Town — '

'Aye: that would hae been a different story. And if I hadna smashed my knee —'

'Does it ever trouble you now?'

'Whiles. Once my horse fell on it. After a long ride it bothers me – and sometimes when I've had a chill.'

'You should rub it with hot oil. . . And yet it was your injured knee that really brought us together. . . Tell me, Robert – why can't men be faithful to the women they love, even their wives?'

'Some men are, Nancy. Because they're made that way —'

'I've never heard of any. I understand most men go to the bawdy houses – surely that canna be true?'

'It's a matter of taste, I suppose. I hae good friends that go regularly. I dinna count it a virtue, Nancy; but I've never been able to bring myself to frequent them.'

'Somehow I couldna think of you. . . Maybe that's why it had to be puir Jenny?'

'Weel . . . it didna *have* to be Jenny. It just *was* Jenny.'

'It could have been anybody?'

'No . . . no' just anybody. But you canna foresee such things. It just happens and that's all. It so happens that Jenny was the least consequential of a' the women I've ever known in that sense.'

'How many hae there been?'

'It so happens, Nancy, that I'm a poet and no' a counting-house clerk?'

'As many as that?'

'Now, damn you, dinna jump to conclusions! You seem to ken mair o' the ways o' men than you should!'

'That's unfair, Robert. All women ken – and all women talk.'

'About themselves?'

'Now that's silly – coming from you. Women aey talk in the third person – except perhaps to one real friend. Mary Peacock kens – well, nearly everything.'

But this knowledge was not new to the Bard. Nancy hadn't been shocked about Jenny's morality – only shocked at his seeming neglect of her. It was amazing how she kept her religion in a shut-off compartment in her mind. She had many shut-off compartments in her mind.

There were no hysterics, no scenes, no heroics at their parting. There were tears, yes. Nancy wept: she was genuinely

46

broken-hearted at the parting. The Bard was deeply touched too. There had grown up between them a love that was unique and precious – a love that no outsider could have understood.

It was a love that ended – or began – on a high note of emotional intensity. They were in each other's arms and in a moment they were separated – across the years and forever.

As the Bard laboured his way back to the Grassmarket in the mirk and gloom and shivering dampness of that Edinburgh December, he felt intensely the pain of parting from what was one of the great loves of his life. Already Nancy belonged to the past – the irretrievable irrecoverable past. God knows: Nancy had been real enough. But already she was becoming transformed into the intense symbol of the parting of love: of the separation of lovers. . .

Had he never met Nancy; had they never fallen in love so blindly, so cumulatively, then, of course, there would have been no sorrow, no heart-break. . .

But the heart-break was there: the longing; the terrible feeling of loneliness; the agonising inevitability of never meeting again. . . And all against the heartless background of Edinburgh's unutterable December gloom. . .

THE MEASURED TIME

Immediately he got back to Dumfries the Bard took his brother-in-law, Adam Armour, into the Coach and Horse tavern at the corner of the White Sands and the Stinking Vennel for a farewell pint of ale.

Adam enjoyed the Armours' robust health. He was broad and stocky and had a round ruddy honest face. As a boy he had worshipped Robert Burns. As a man he had come to admire him almost to the point of idolatry.

'Had you a good time in Embro, Robert?'

'Weel . . . I dinna ken about a good time. My time was gey crowded what wi' the folk I'd to see. And there were some trying moments. Adam: I'm no' the man to listen to guid advice; but I can seldom resist giving it.'

'I'd aey listen to your advice.'

'You're getting a guid wife in my cousin Fanny.'

'It's me kens that.'

'I ken you'll be guid to her just as she'll be guid to you. But the strange thing is that even the best o' wives – and I hae the finest God put breath in – aye: even the best o' wives pall. They mother your bairns and they work awa' – and sometimes they get trachled and lose their looks. Aye; and sometimes they get irritable. Oh, and sometimes you're awa' frae hame and you fa' in wi' a bonnie lass and you're tempted. . . I havena been a' I should hae been in this respect. When I was a bachelor I gloried in the lassies. I socht them high and socht them low – and sometimes they socht me. But once you're married, Adam, you've got to resist that at all costs."

'I dinna think I'll hae ony bother: Fanny'll dae me.'

'Aye: that's what you think now and that's what you should think. But you've got to be on your guard. You'll be awa' on jobs here and there and you'll get lonesome a wee; and maybe you'll coup back twa-three pints if the yill's guid. And then maybe there's a lass handy. It doesna seem a great sin – and then the next thing you ken maybe is that she's knocked-up wi' a wean. . . Noo I ken you, Adam: you're a lusty young beggar goupin' fu' o' the best red Armour blood. And by God! I'm the last man to moralise. But – be cautioned, Adam! It's a mistake. It's a hell o' a thing when your sins come staring you in the face.'

'But you're different, Robert: you're a poet.'

'And what difference does that make?'

'Weel . . . a poet's different frae ordinary men. Maybe a poet needs plenty o' lassies. I think Jean understands – in fact I ken she does. So does Fanny. I'm no' sure about your sister Nancy . . .'

'Oho! So you've discussed a' this, have you?'

'Weel . . . I wouldna say we discussed it . . . it was kind o' mentioned . . . back and forward.'

'Listen, Adam: I want nae damned sophistry. I'm telling you, straight and plain, that when you bairn lassies bye your wife you're committing a grave offence against your wife, your bairns, your marriage and yourself. And you pay for it – unless you've gotten a conscience like saddle-leather. And I'm warning you that you'll be tempted and I'm warning you to fight the temptation – like the devil. I'm no' giving a damn about the morality o' the business. I'm just telling you it hurts – and hurts a' round. And whether it hurts a poet mair or less is beside the point.'

'Right – I'll mind your warning and I'll dae my best. You

ken I sowed a wheen wild oats afore I met in wi' Fanny. But no' since then.'

'That's the lad. By God! I think a lot o' Fanny. I'd be a proud father if I'd a dochter like her. And I like you, you randy beggar! But by the Holy, Adam, if I ever heard that you ill-treated Fanny, I'd come up to Machlin and lib you wi' a kail-gullie.'

Adam grinned broadly. But he felt that the Bard's threat was no idle one. He'd little doubt but that he'd do just what he said. Adam Armour respected him the more for it.

'And d'ye think you'll settle doon into Dumfries?'

'There's damn-all else for it, Adam. Damn-all else, boy. No: I canna say I'm looking forward to things; and yet I ken I could be worse off. There's a lot to be said for the town in the winter months. It's cosy enough and you're no' layerin' in glaur to your boot-taps – you can aey keep your feet dry in the town. But in the spring – and on the lang summer nichts. . . But needs must, Adam, my boy. I've a wife and a cleckin' o' weans and I've got to provide for them.'

'I think you'll dae weel enough.'

'It'll no' be for want o' application if I dinna. There's no' a lazy inch in me though I say it mysel'. Only I get that damned melancholy at times – richt doon in the depths . . . a black bluidy bog o' depression. I aey had thae black fits, ye ken; but nothing to what I get noo. And then I want drink and company; and then I discover neither drink nor company's ony bluidy guid to me. That's the real hell o' my disease, Adam – when man and woman delighteth not and neither wife nor weans. Without Jean I'd be the most useless miserable soul alive when I'm in the depths. Jean understands — '

'I aey got on weel wi' our Jean. She was guid to me.'

'You're the only one in the family that realises Jean's real worth. There's no' another woman like her. She's unique, precious beyond rubies. I could hae searched the length and breadth o' Scotland and never found her equal.'

'Fanny says the same.'

'Weel she may! And yet there's the mystery, Adam. I've a wife like Jean – and still I got skiting over the dyke.'

'Ach, there's nae harm in your skiting, Robert. And you worry ower much aboot it. Come on: you'll hae this pint o' yill wi' me. Fanny says she doesna richt ken how to thank

49

you and Jean for the wedding gown. God, Robert, she was actually greetin' to me aboot it – she's that touched.'

'She's entitled to the best. It's a damned pity Jean and me canna be at the weddin'.'

'Aye . . . and it's a pity aboot Daddy Auld.'

'What about Daddy Auld?'

'Did naebody tell you? He died at the beginning o' the week – Tuesday, I think it was — '

'Daddy Auld dead! Dear, dear. . . Damned, I'm real hurt to hear that, Adam. Mind you: Daddy Auld was a big man, narrow Calvinist though he was. Aye: a big man, Adam; and, at bottom, a kindly, far-seeing minister. I had my quarrels wi' him and I'd to thole mony a rebuke – and I was never a guid tholer in that direction. . . But I admired him for a' that. He did his best for Jean and me according to his lights. . . Half the clergy nowadays are but bags o' theological wind and water compared wi' the like o' Daddy. The last time I saw him was at Gilbert's weddin': he was gey frail then. . . Come on: drink up. I'll need to hae a word wi' Jean about this. . .'

That night there was something of a farewell party in the Stinking Vennel.

The Bard was in his best humour and he tried to make everybody happy. He well knew the underlying sorrow of the occasion.

Jean was sorry she was losing the companionship of Fanny and Nancy. Nancy was sorry she was going back to the dull monotony of Mossgiel and the uncertainty of how she would get along with Gilbert's wife. Fanny – though she was radiantly happy at the prospect of her marriage to Adam and setting up in a house of her own – was sorry for the immediacy of the parting from Jean and Robert, to whom she had developed a filial affection deeper than she had known towards her own parents. Adam felt the parting least, because he was not so emotionally involved. Yet Jean was his favourite sister, and Robert was the greatest man who had ever lived.

Fanny was coming twenty. When she first joined Jean and Robert at the Isle she was sixteen and thin and elfin and undernourished. She had blossomed in the four years of hard work and good homely faring. Her hair was auburn, her eyes brown, her bone-work strong but finely grained: her complexion healthy but dusky. Her breasts were small but well-defined; her hips plump and round. She had all the makings of a good and fecund mother.

Fascinated, Fanny seldom took her eyes from the Bard. She had watched him in many moods. But in his rare jocular, almost boisterous, moods, he was irresistible. He sat for a while with Robbie on his knee and made Jean sing – almost against her will.

And now Fanny had to take her glass of toddy along with the others, for her uncle was proposing a toast specially in her honour. But she protested.

'I've never drunk toddy afore, Uncle Robert!'

'I ken fine you havena. D'you think I wad ask you, unless it was a byornar special occasion? Would you rather hae port wine?'

'Dinna start her on port, Rab.'

'Aye: you're better wi' the toddy – it's weel watered doon and can dae you nae harm.'

'A' richt! I'll tak' a wee drap.'

'You'll find as you go through life that, on special occasions when either your health or the event demands it, a drap o' toddy's the best drink o' a'. We used to have it at hame on the New Year's morning wi' a drap o' sugar in it – and we thocht it grand. Brandy and port and claret were never heard o' in cot-houses in the auld days.'

'You'd dae weel to mind that, Robin.'

'Ah, there you are, Nancy! Aey to the fore wi' guid advice! But I'm coming to your toast too, my lass. Noo, there's to be nae lang faces and nae regrets. The morn's nicht ye'll a' be back in Machlin and meeting wi' auld friends again; and it's Jean and me will ken the vacant chairs round the fireside. But Lord! Machlin's no' at the end o' the earth. There'll aey be some o' us making the journey up or doon. . .'

But somehow, though everybody tried to put a face on things, the sadness was here – the sadness of parting. . .

There came a point when the Bard had had enough of leave-taking.

'I'm feeling like a breath o' fresh air afore I turn in. It'll be an early start in the morning.'

He turned down onto the Sands. There was a moon and it sent slanting shivers across the swollen Nith. The drumming of the caul was incessant. The Sands were deserted, though many windows were still lit and there was a merry laugh about the tavern.

He turned his back on the caul and strolled, with the moon in his face, towards the Dock Park.

He had been working feverishly on three songs commemorating his parting with Nancy. He began to rehearse them – a final rehearsal. He hummed them over. The tunes were good: *Cornwallis's Lament* to go with Sensibility how charming, thou, my friend, can'st truly tell! But distress with horrors arming thou alas! hast known too well!

A better tune was *Through the Lang Muir*. The words here fitted the long sweep of the melody: Ance mair I hail thee, thou gloomy December! Ance mair I hail thee wi' sorrow and care! Sad was the parting thou makes me remember: parting wi' Nancy, O' ne'er to meet mair!

And then, and perhaps best of all, *Ae Fond Kiss to Rory Dall's Port*: Ae fond kiss, and then we sever! Ae farewell, and then forever! . . . I'll ne'er blame my partial fancy – naething could resist my Nancy! But to see her was to love her, love but her, and love forever. Had we never loved sae kindly, had we never loved sae blindly, never met – or never parted – we had ne'er been broken-hearted. . . Ae fond kiss, and then we sever! Ae farewell, alas, forever! Deep in heart-wrung tears I'll pledge thee, warring sighs and groans I'll wage thee. . .

Yes: that was a song worthy of his parting wi' Nancy. It had brought the tear to his eye.

God! and they *were* parted. There she was in Edinburgh waiting on the *Roselle* that he might have once boarded himself – and here he was by the banks of the Nith putting the finishing touches to the farewell songs.

He'd had a surfeit of farewells – and all women. Jenny Clow, Anna Park, Nancy – and now Fanny and his sister. . . But the poet in him was touched only at the parting with Nancy.

In bed, Jean said to him:

'There's nae guid in takin' things sae sair to heart, Robin. It's no' like a death in the family.'

'True enough, Jean. What does it really matter who goes or who stays as lang as we hae each other?'

'Just! As lang as we hae each other. . .'

MARIA WOODLEY RIDDELL

It was late on a January afternoon that a coach drew up at the Stamp Office in the Stinking Vennel, and a moment later that the coachman announced the presence of Maria Riddell. The Bard was finishing some Excise returns and the announcement set him in something of a flutter. He told the coachman to show his mistress up and set about to tidy the table.

'It's Captain Walter Riddell's wife, Jean.'

'And what will she be wanting here?'

'I've nae idea, Jean – but we'll hae to receive her.'

Mrs Riddell was in a gay mood. She was small made. But she was enveloped in a warm travelling cloak trimmed with fur. A light brisk step brought her into the kitchen.

'Ah! the Bard at home! How are you?'

She held out a small hand.

'My usual self, Madam. Jean, this is Mistress Riddell. . .'

Jean and Maria shook hands. Jean indicated a chair. Maria's eyes were darting into every corner of the room.

'No: thank you, Mistress Burns, I can't stay. I've been looking for your celebrated husband for over a week. So I just had to risk bearding the lion in his . . . den. I wonder if I could spirit him away for an hour. We're at the King's Arms. My husband has some business — '

She turned to the Bard and smiled her sweet cynical smile.

'I want an introduction to an Edinburgh publisher: I've decided to venture my Voyage to the Leewards.'

'Certainly, Madam. If you can allow me half-an-hour to finish my Excise work I can be with you.'

'Oh, thank you. . . Good-bye, Mistress Burns – I do so hope you'll forgive my intrusion. . .'

Jean said nothing. Mrs Riddell was as foreign to her as would have been the Bey of Algiers's harem favourite.

But when the door had closed, she turned to Robin.

'God help you, gin you've got to listen to that. What age will she be?'

'Nae mair than nineteen or twenty.'

'Fu' o' her ain importance onyway. Did you meet her at the Carse?'

'Aye: I thocht I told you about her. She's no' long married

to Walter Riddell – Glenriddell's younger brother. His wife died out about the Indies and she left him a big sugar plantation. Then he met Maria Woodley – her father was Governor o' the Leeward Isles oot there. She got married – she'll no' be much more than a year married. She'd a dochter no' that long ago. . . She's written a book on her voyages . . . she writes poetry. Oh, a clever-enough woman – but young. She'll learn.'

The Bard talked rapidly and somehow hoped Jean wouldn't ask too many questions.

'I've aey told you, Rab: if that's your dirt o' gentry you're welcome to them! English too!'

'I wouldna describe a sister-in-law o' Glenriddell's as dirt, Jean.'

'Och weel . . . dinna worry me aboot them. And the less they come aboot the hoose the better.'

But the Bard, hurrying through with his Excise work thought it better to say nothing.

Maria Riddell was no beauty. She had dark brown hair and light brown eyes and thin bandy legs. She had no breasts worth mentioning, though what she had were cunningly corseted and pushed up and forward: as they were low-placed she could afford to show a large exposure of bosom (the skin well dusted with a mother-o'-pearl powder). Her mouth was a large animated gash, accentuated by a pointed chin and an uptilted nose.

No: coldly analysed, Maria was no beauty. But what she lacked in beauty she made up for in vitality. The Bard was quick to acknowledge that she was one of the most vivacious, intelligent and attractive women he had ever met.

Round a fire in the King's Arms, they enjoyed a tête-à-tête.

'And you will introduce me to someone in Edinburgh – I can pay to have my Voyage printed. What about Mr Smellie – I find his Natural History quite fantastically en lightening.'

'Smellie? Smellie's a genius, Madam, and, like his kind, apt to be difficult.'

'But if you gave me an introduction – I could talk to him?'

'Just so – but maybe Smellie would do the talking. He can be direct to the point of rudeness – and he stands on no ceremony.'

'What nonsense! Any man can be handled. A little judicious flattery — '

'No . . . nobody – and certainly no woman – could flatter Smellie.'

'Then I insist on the introduction – I must meet so wild and so learned a boar – or should I say bear?'

'A good bit of both, Madam – I assure you — '

'Then I'll bring you back either a tusk or a claw to prove my prowess as a huntress. . . Would you order me a glass of wine, kind sir?'

'Walter – Captain Riddell – has purchased Godielea. Just four miles out of town – know it? I think it's delightful. Of course Captain Riddell will have to lay out a lot on improving – Oh yes; and it's to be re-named Woodley Park – in my honour, of course. You must come out and visit us just as soon as we are settled in. I promise you it won't be at all stodgy like the Carse.'

'Glenriddell is one of my firm friends and I am one of his staunchest admirers. Many a happy and entertaining evening I've spent at the Carse. I hope to spend many yet.'

'Ah, yes . . . but I promise you happier nights at Woodley Park. I'm going to have all the gay, intelligent young people at my parties – and all the wittiest men. My men must be witty and gallant and remarkable. And you, my friend – there will be a special welcome for Scotland's Poet – the Caledonian Bard. You will be my special social protégé. What fun we'll have! What discussions! And if we have an odd aristocrat then we'll bait him! Liberty, Fraternity, Equality! Vive la France!'

'You are determinedly for the French, Madam!'

'Certainly. Of course, of course! Away with the dull heavy-witted aristocrats! We welcome Freedom! I must make some red caps so that we can wear them at dinner. Can't you see what nights we'll have! How we'll stir up the county and make a name for ourselves?'

'Your very presence, Madam, has already stirred up the county. I can see how an invitation to Woodley Park will be eagerly sought after. But I can't see county folk and the best families taking to the Red Cap of Liberty . . .'

'Pouiff! What do I care for your best families? I'm a Woodley in my own right and I'm married into the Riddell family! It will all be such fun – and I'll play over some of

55

your wonderful songs – and sing them. But I must insist that you teach me the best Scotch – I insist . . .'

It amazed the Bard that a woman so young could talk so maturely and with such superb assurance. And how had she managed, in so short a time, to acquire such a width of culture? True, her tongue rattled on at a fearful rate; but she put so much animation of tone and gesture into her talk that the listener was held – and often despite himself.

Finally, Captain Walter Riddell came to claim his wife. Whereas Glenriddell was red and massive and huge-fisted and stentorian, Walter was pale, slim, delicately-handed and cursed with a peculiar tenor sneering tone of voice. He was haughty with all whom he considered his social inferiors.

'Well, Burns: my wife entertaining you?'

'That, I think, is her privilege, Captain.'

'Don't let her abuse it.'

'Walter! Mr Burns must join our parties?'

'Yes, do, Burns – we shall be glad to have you to Woodley Park. I can always assure you of an excellent cellar! The coach is waiting, Maria. 'Night, Burns.'

Walter Riddell gave his wife his arm.

Maria bestowed one of her best smiles on the Bard.

'And you will remember my introduction to Mr Smellie. . ."

Henry Clint, the proprietor of the King's Arms, came across to him – having seen the Riddells to their coach.

'Hoo are ye to-night, Mr Burns? A handsome couple – the Captain and his wife. By God, sir, she can talk. I hear they've paid a bonnie price for Goldielea. Ah weel, Mr Burns – the toon can aey dae wi' spenders . . .'

'Aye: I suppose wit and youth and intelligence canna be computed in the ledger nor counted in the cash-box. Will you join me in a drink, Harry?'

'No, no, Mr Burns: you'll join me in one. By the by: Mr Syme and some other gentlemen are in the smoke-room. He was asking for you.'

'In that case — '

'You'll hae a drink wi' me just the same. I'm just going to join the company for a few moments.'

Clint was the right man for the King's Arms. He had the

ight touch of obsequy and deferment to the gentry; and he
had an easier familiar touch for his regulars. He saw to it
that no low company entered his door. He always knew just
when to stand a drink and when not to. A stout little man,
he took care to dress the part and wash himself regularly.

The Bard was delighted to find that the company consisted
of Glenriddell, John MacMurdo the Drumlanrig chamberlain
and John Syme of Barncailzie.

Glenriddell bellowed his welcome.

'Ah! the Bard himself! Welcome, Robert. You're well?
Good, good. . . Draw in your chair. I wanted to see you
about your schoolmaster Clarke at Moffat.'

The Bard greeted MacMurdo and Syme warmly just as
soon as Glenriddell gave him an opening.

'Captain Walter just left me this moment. His good-lady
wants an introduction to Smellie, the printer.'

'Yes: I saw Walter. . . What the devil does Maria want
with Smellie?'

'She's thinking of publishing her Voyages —'

'Voyages, bah! Yes: Mr Clint?'

'I was just waiting to see what the company would like –
on the house, sir – of course – on the house.'

'Oh—that's good of you, Mr Clint.'

'What about a nice bottle o' port, sir?'

'Port? What d'you say, gentlemen?'

They all agreed to the port.

'Now, Robert, you're not long back from Edinburgh, I
understand? How's our old friend Johnson coming on with
your fourth volume? We must keep at them. Stephen Clarke's
the laziest hound I've ever met. Gifted, of course. . . No: of
course we can't do without him – and he kens that.'

'When's he coming down to Drumlanrig?'

'I spoke to him, John. He seems to be tied up in every
direction. But he assured me he was keeping the young ladies
in mind.'

'Any fresh intelligence frae Edinburgh about France?'
John Syme was as avid as any of them for news of France.

'No: things seem to be hanging fire the now. But the
best intelligences are predicting that Brunswick micht put a
lowe to things. Mrs Walter Riddell seems to be a most
enthusiastic votary —'

Glenriddell snorted.

'My sister-in-law, Robert, is too damned enthusiastic in hearing her tongue wag three score to the dizzen.'

'Come, Glenriddell: she's barely nineteen!'

'Nineteen or ninety: it mak's nae difference to me. I detest women who talk down their menfolk. Don't you agree gentlemen?'

But the others knew better than take sides in a family dispute. Not that the Bard was going to be silenced in this fashion.

'No: she's young and impulsive – and she's got brains.'

'Brains! What the devil does a woman want with brains? But yes: I suppose she is young, and being abroad so much. . . I must say I find a little of Maria's conversation goes a damned long way. . . But I must get back to the Carse to-night, Gentlemen; and I want to hear your Edinburgh news Robert.'

John MacMurdo left with Glenriddell and Syme ordered another bottle of port.

'You can see that Robert Riddell doesna like Maria – and damned! I canna just blame him.'

'What? I'd have expected better from you, John. I tell you Maria Riddell is an outstanding woman – she's got every gift.'

'Except the gift o' silence, Robert. You maun admit that's important?'

'In a wife, yes – not necessarily in a friend.'

'Oh, you're friends, are you?'

'What the hell do you think we are – lovers?'

'I can picture you in love wi' a hundred women; but canna picture you in love wi' Maria Riddell.'

'Uhuh – and just why?'

'God! she's nae beauty!'

'Maybe – but she grows on you.'

'I wadna want Maria Riddell to grow on me.'

'I'll tell you the trouble wi' the whole bluidy lot o' you as far as Maria's concerned. You're a' jealous o' her. That was a' the trouble at Friars Carse – that's what set old Mrs Riddell and young Mrs Riddell against her. Glenriddell had to follow suit. Glenriddell's mother has a hell o' a temper. I mind one nicht she turned on Captain Grose — '

'Dinna tell me, Robert. I ken about her temper – aye, long ago.'

'Well – and you ken that Glenriddell's wife is a kindly body and a bit hauden-doon between Glenriddell and his mother. Then wow! along comes Maria and fingers her nose at convention, at age, at decorum. And that's what Maria's been doing ever since.'

'No' just the maist elegant behaviour for a young lady of quality!'

'Ah! but she's elegant – even her rudest gesture has style aboot it!'

'But young ladies dinna make rude gestures.'

'Of course they don't: that's just the point. That's where Maria has them beaten to a shocked silence – and the men-folks too. . . I wonder what Grose would have thought of her?'

'Ah, Captain Grose! He was a character!'

'One o' the finest men I've ever met. Grose was supreme! Glorious! Fantastic!'

'Would you place Grose at the supreme head of the men you've known, Robin?'

'Yes – and no. Yes for certain unique qualities that Grose had. No for certain qualities I have known to a greater degree in other men. In my native Ayrshire there was perhaps a candidate for supremacy: John Rankine – a farmer – cele-brated in my Rough, Rude, Ready-Witted Rankine. And oddly enough, now that I come to think of it, he had many of Grose's characteristics. . . There's Willie Nicol, my best Edinburgh friend next to Cunningham. Nicol's the best Latin scholar in Europe – which means the world: I remember sitting in the company of some of the finest Latinists in Edinburgh and he translated my verses into Latin, clean extempore, in a manner that amazed and astounded all present. Yet on the surface you'd think maybe that Nicol was the most savage-tongued, savage-mannered brute in creation. Nicol can strip the pretence from a subject or an attitude quicker and more surely than any other man I've ever known. . . There was my worthy parent. . . . There was a man too of quite extraordinary character – and I can view him without the partiality of the filial relationship. . . My late parish priest, the Reverend William Auld of Machlin – Daddy Auld of familiar context – was another such. . . Such are or were giants in their own particular line. No: I havena met wi' ony giants in Dumfries. Oh yes: many worthy, excellent fel-lows. But giants . . . no. Glenriddell narrowly escapes. A

59

touch o' something and Glenriddell could have been out standing. I think principally that he lacks a sense of real humour. Patrick Miller has greatness in him too. . .'

'You've nae cause to think weel o' Miller. . .'

'No: that I havena. But that doesna mean I'm blind to his qualities. That would be damned stupid o' me, would it no' . . .? But you canna place men within absolute limits. You can do no more than recognise greatness and smallness and herd the ruck o' mankind in between. Wi' women it's ever more difficult – for we're a' apt to partiality where the sex are concerned. But to come back to Maria Riddell! That girl's gotten real greatness in her. If she matures and develops she'll be one of the outstanding females of this generation. Of course, she may never ripen into the maturity of her promise. For one thing, she's married to the wrong man –'

'But how can you tell that?'

'Ah, you can sense it the moment the pair o' them are thegither. There's something fundamentally rotten about Walter Riddell. There's nae depth to him. He's as shallow as a girdle and as proud as Lucifer; and nae mair brains in him than you'd find in an addled egg. He's only a gentleman by the cut o' his coat, the size o' his purse and the length o' his pedigree.'

'You can be devastating in your criticisms, Robert. And how did your Goddess o' Sapience come to marry him?'

'That's where sex enters. When Maria met wi' him she was a couple o' years younger than she is now. Walter can cut a figure to a young lass in the first throes o' passion. When a man's kissing you and exploring the wonders o' your body and the blood's drumming in your ears like the Nith ower the caul, you dinna stop to ask if the man has brains or character or onything but the physical processes o' his love-making. . . If men looked only for beauty in their wives and wives looked only for character in their husbands, then there would be damned little giving and taking in matrimony – holy or otherwise.'

'Aye: you've gotten a' the answers, Robin. And it a' sounds the simple truth the way you lay it off. I'll admit, mind you, that Maria Riddell's a quite exceptional lady – quite exceptional.'

'Weel: we can dae noe mair than leave it at that. But it beats me to forecast what Willie Smellie will think o' her.'

'D'you think she'll meet her match?'

'Honestly, John. . . It's on the cards that Willie Smellie'll tak' one look at her and tell her to go and — '

'Never!'

'It wouldna cost Willie Smellie a lift o' his bushy eyebrows. . . Smellie's like Willie Nicol in that respect: no respecter o' persons – far less personages. And our Maria still thinks she's something o' a personage.'

'Weel, Robin: unless I'm far wrong in my calculations, I think we'll see some fun aboot Dumfries wi' Maria and Walter.'

'Agreed! So let's hae a bumper to Maria afore we go. . .'

THE SWORD AND THE BOOK

When he was meeting with the big folks, the people of rank and fashion, it was usually in the King's Arms or the George tavern that ran into Irish Street: or the adjacent Assembly Rooms. With intimate friends to whom rank and fashion mattered nothing, his favourite howff was still the Globe tavern.

And many a merry night he had. But he never allowed anything to interfere with his Excise work. He spent the greater part of most evenings with Jean and the bairns round the fire-side or sitting alone in the tiny room – more of a closet – writing songs or letters; or making a copy of a bawdy ballad or a political piece extolling France. . .

By the end of February he had won his promotion in the Excise. He was now in the Port Division and his salary was raised from fifty pounds a year to seventy pounds. There was no saying just what his perquisites might be; but Findlater assured him they would be no less than twenty pounds. With a bit of luck, he might be said to be earning a hundred pounds a year.

The news so gratified the pair of them that Jean promptly conceived.

But though his Excise work in the Port Division promised to be a matter of busy routine, on the last day of the month he found himself at Annan waterfoot, with a cutlass in his hand, leading a boarding-party in an attack on a smuggling brig that put up a fight against capture.

It was an exciting and highly-dangerous adventure. But

the Bard enjoyed it. He had proved that a poet need be no physical coward. Jean was quite distressed when she heard all about it.

'You never said a word to me aboot having to wade oot to smugglers wi' dragoons and what-not; and them firing on you and you wi' a sword. . .'

'Aye . . . and I was in the mood to hae used it to purpose gin they hadna fled.'

'You that wouldna hurt a mouse wad cut a man's heid aff?'

'Wad you expect me to stand like a gowk and let them blaw the head aff me? Mind you: I wadna like to think that I had cut aff a fellow creature's head. But war's war; and when you're attacked you've got to defend yourself. But dinna you worry yoursel' – I micht never need to be out on the same errand again.'

'I would hope no'. Was John Lewars there?'

'Aye, John Lewars was there. We were a' there that were ony worth. You can speir Lewars the next nicht he's up.'

John Lewars was a young man in his early twenties. He lived in the Millbrae Vennel and his father had been a Supervisor in the Service.

Both Jean and Robert liked him and he was often at the house. He was clever, well-mannered and was devoted to the Bard in an honest and downright way. He seldom drank and when he did he avoided spirits. But he was partial to a bottle of good porter and Jean always saw to it that there was a bottle in the house. Jean hoped that he might make a match of it with Jean Lorimer. But though the two of them got on well enough, it didn't seem that John was in any hurry to get married or to involve himself with women. He was a keen reader, a keen student of history and an enthusiast for the turn of events in France.

Young Robbie was also becoming an avid reader – or rather an avid listener. He had an amazing memory and could retain great stretches of poetry. Often enough if John Lewars arrived and the Bard was out he would take the lad in his poetry and patiently explain to him the meaning of any new words. It warmed Jean's heart to see him at this – and it warmed young Robbie's heart too. He liked John Lewars and he liked to strive the harder to please him.

Robbie was a fine-natured boy with a fine, almost delicate, temper. He had become the apple of his father's eye. And nothing pleased him better than to take the lad not only in poetry and reading but in writing and arithmetic and even a little Latin – though here Lewars could score over the Bard.

Jean would sometimes say:

'You used to never hae a good word for education, Rab?'

'Aye; but there's learning and there's education and there's knowledge. It would be a damned shame to let the bairns grow up without the ability to read and write – and to read the best writers and to write like the best authors. I hae nae notion o' filling their heads wi' a lot o' damned philosophic nonsense or theological clishmachlavers. But the tools o' honest learning, Jean! I maun see that they get the best tools I can provide. That was the basis o' my own father's method. You saw the kind o' letters William could write us. I want the bairns to grow up honest men and bonnie lassies. But I want them all to have the ability to understand whatever they may read and the ability to tak' pen to paper and put down their thochts in a plain but not inelegant fashion. Your college pass-men can do nae mair; and damned few o' them can do as much. I'm no' expecting ony o' them to turn out geniuses and poets and great men. There's nae reason why they shouldna, of course. But if the boys turn out manly, guid-mannered, well-read and well-spoken like John Lewars, for example, I'll be happy enough.'

GOD AND DEVIL

Everybody that came about the house remarked on the harmony that reigned there between husband and wife; and between parents and children. It was always a happy house to come into. No one could ever recall an angry word spoken in it. Above all, never a lewd word or a lewd hint!

Findlater once talked to his superior, Collector Mitchell, about this aspect of their celebrated subordinate.

'The Bard's an amazing man, John. I was wi' him the other night in the Globe wi' John MacMurdo and John Syme – and that beggar Lorimer o' Kemys Ha'. We got fu' a bit and then someone got the Bard on to his bawdy songs. The like o' you I never imagined possible. By the Lord, but yon's no' canny! And he'd dozens o' examples. Syme told me later that he felt his hair rising on his scalp. And then, damn it, he made it sound so natural. . . In the end there was nae offence in it. And then what d'you think? I had to call in on him the following nicht. He's sitting there reading the Bible to his eldest laddie. He asked me to wait till he'd finished the chapter. And honestly, John: I've never heard the Bible read like yon. No: I'm no' trying to paint a picture. You'd hae thocht he was a saint. And he meant it. To tell the honest truth, I had to ask him no' to stop and the bairn backed me up and he read to us for half-an-hour. A strucken half-hour and me in a hurry. The Bible mind you! Me – that comes aff generations o' ministers. How d'you explain it, John?'

'I've lang given up trying to understand Robert Burns. His ways are like the Almighty's – beyond explanation. He's a genius: he's gotten a gift frae on high – and a touch o' something frae below. I'll be frank wi' you. I'd rather no' hae him under me.'

'I ken what you're for saying, John. . .'

'Yes: I'd rather no' hae him under me. I'm aey uncomfortable in my official relations wi' him. I hate like hell to hae to check him. And yet, what are we to dae? It wad be a mistake to treat him ony other way. We're in a Service wi' rules and regulations; and, above all, discipline maun be maintained. In my day I've worked under a drunk Supervisor and an ill-beast o' a Supervisor; and once under a Collector that I wadna just ca' honest. But I took my medicine as I went along. Baith as Supervisor and Collector, I've tried to do my duty honestly and to be fair to the men under me. Besides, it wouldna be fair to the other men to show Burns favouritism.'

'Exactly my own position, John. You couldna hae put the point fairer. Mind you: I can see the Bard being a Collector lang afore me. He's got influence – and guid luck to him. It behoves us a' to hae as mony friends at court as we can. But in day-to-day duty we canna make ony distinctions between one efficient officer and another.'

'And off-duty at least we can show – in whatever way may occur to us – that we appreciate both the man and the poet. But, if you ask me, there's baith God and the Devil in him.'

'Maybe there is that in all of us — ?'

'Nae doubt; but no' to the same excess; no' to the same strength o' neat spirit.'

GEORGE HAUGH

Immediately above the Bard in the vennel lived an honest blacksmith, George Haugh, and his equally-honest wife Aggie. Sometimes the Bard went up and had an hour with George and sometimes Aggie came down and spent an hour with Jean.

But if George Haugh was an honest blacksmith, his politics certainly reeked of the smiddy: for George was a rebel. He was the leader of many such in the town of Dumfries. George was a canny rebel. He thought much and said little. Nobody who was considered anybody in Dumfries gave a second thought to honest Geordie Haugh, the smith. He would not have had it otherwise.

'You see, Rab,' said George, one night, 'this is how I view things.' He puffed slowly at his pipe and anon spat expertly into the fire. 'You're a poet. In fact you're the only poet we've ever had. You write as honest men speak. You've made the thochts and aspirations o' honest working men alive – as naebody has done afore ye. Aye . . . and may never dae again. But if the world's ever to be made an honest place – which it hasna been since the Fall – then it will only be made so by honest working men takin' things into their own hands. Coorse, working men are no' a' honest. But that doesna matter. That's whaur the leaven works, Rab – and fine you ken it. I dinna ken how lang it'll tak' to work the leaven. But you've got to begin at rock-bottom – that is, on a guid solid foundation. I ken you've mixed wi' high and low. But it's your cotter, your ploughman, your blacksmith, your weaver, your soutar, your tailor – your labouring man: that's where salvation lies: wi' the salt o' the earth. Your Bible drives that truth hame time and again. The trades'll a' need to band thegither – they'll need to get haud o' a bigger idea than just banding thegither. The time maun come when there'll only be one guild – the guild o' honest labouring men; and then – and only then – will we get somewhaur. That's whaur your French mean to start – only they're letting in ower mony loopholes for men that are no' thirled to honest work. . .'

To such talk the Bard listened and said little. He felt he had everything to learn from such a man. And it was more than comforting to know that his neighbour in Dumfries was a blacksmith who read Tom Paine's *Rights of Man*.

MARIA MISCALCULATES

At the beginning of April the Bard learned that he had been made an honorary member of the Royal Company of Archers in Edinburgh. This honour had been conferred upon him mainly through the exertions of Alexander Cunningham. But, as he said to Jean:

'The Royal Archers! That's one of the maist select companies in Scotland. It seems they still think highly o' me in Auld Reckie – however little I may think o' the Big Wigs there.'

A few days later William Creech was fixing up for a second Edinburgh edition of his poems. Despite his bitter experience with the crafty and crooked Creech, he promised to give him enough new material to make up an additional fifty pages.

As always, the question of censorship obtruded. The new material – which was to include *Tam* – would have to meet with the approval of the literati and gentlemanly taste generally. The Bard knew there was no way round this if he wanted to see his work published. He finally appointed Alexander Fraser Tytler, an Edinburgh lawyer who was friendly disposed to his muse both as poet and as song-writer to Johnson's *Musical Museum*, to be the literary arbiter between himself and Creech and between Creech and Edinburgh literary taste.

Creech promised that the proposed edition would be elegant and in two volumes. There was no question of payment. Payment was beneath Creech's dignity – besides, he held the copyright for the first Edinburgh edition. All the Bard asked for was a few books and a few copies of the new edition, when it came out, to present to some of his friends. Creech was only too glad to clinch such a favourable deal.

Maria Riddell had returned from Edinburgh happy from her meetings with William Smellie. Now her book was a-printing. And kilting her skirts and displaying her cavalry legs, she executed a few reel steps. Maria was cock-a-hoop.

'What did I tell you when I returned from Edinburgh,

Robert? Now our wonderful Smellie is going to print my Voyages!'

'Well . . . Congratulations! So you got round Smellie, did you?'

'A most wonderful man. He purrs like a great tom-cat.'

'Purrs?'

'Most charmingly!'

The Bard just couldn't imagine Smellie purring. But he said nothing. It was just conceivable that Smellie had succumbed to Maria's charms.

'You met him at Craigdarroch's?'

'Our first meeting. Even Walter was charmed with him. Then I saw him in his office in the Anchor Close. He pointed to the desk where you'd sat correcting the proofs of your Edinburgh edition. Then we had a drink at your Crochallan Club place. What a pity ladies are not admitted to your Club!'

The Bard raised his eyebrows.

'You went into Dawney Douglas's did you? What the devil has old Smellie been telling you?'

'Don't be jealous of the philosopher! And he's not so old . . . in years maybe – but still the gallant! Oh, very much, very charmingly so!'

'No, Maria! Smellie may have taken to purring. But the charming gallant – no, no: never!'

'I insist both charming and gallant. Not as the gay bucks of Edinburgh are charming and gallant. But in his own old-fashioned way yes – and very touchingly so. He insists that he's publishing my Voyages solely on its merits.'

'Just so. . . . Who else did you see?'

'I can't remember all the interesting people I met. Peter Hill, your bookseller, was speiring – is that the word? – for you. Oh yes; and Mr Fraser Tytler. . . And dear old William is coming down to Woodley Park in the summer — '

'You mean Smellie?'

'Certainly! He promised Walter and me — '

'By the Holy! If Smellie comes to Dumfries — Well, there'll be one night at least that won't be a ladies' gathering.'

Maria came close to him and pretended to adjust his cravat.

'He said I was to ask you for a read of your Song Book – your Crochallan Book. You know, Robert: you mustn't treat me like a child. . . I would keep it a secret — Maybe just for one night?'

The Bard thought: 'One hand she put to my cravat —' Yet he felt the blood mounting to his cheeks.

'Smellie's been filling your head with nonsense, Maria. I ken of no Song Book. And Smellie had no right to use my name in any such connection.'

'You're such a poor fibber, Robert. You did promise there would be no secrets between us. . . And, you see, Walter told me about some of your songs — '

'Listen, Maria: Smellie may be a sinful old devil – he may be a lecherous old beggar in matters where I've nae concern; but I should have thought that your husband was indeed the gentleman — '

'You mean there are things you don't share with your Jean?'

'I mean that and more. A song that men may share in company over a bottle is one thing — '

'Robert! Don't tell me you're such a miserable Puritan — ?'

'Puritan enough, Maria. . . Of course, I know I'm only a ploughman turned gauger. But I was brought up to respect the delicacy of female — '

'Aren't you being a bit silly, Robert?'

'You are welcome to any opinion — '

'Perhaps you could tell me where I could get a few pairs of gloves – French kid? They're contraband, aren't they?'

Maria hadn't expected to be caught in the wrong so blantantly. It wasn't going to be easy to handle Robert Burns. And though she had extricated herself quickly and expertly from her untenable position, she couldn't help a wave of intense personal resentment passing over her. The Bard had made her feel over-bold and grossly indelicate. She didn't mind giving away Smellie. After all, Smellie no more than the Bard was a gentleman; but she could have bitten out her tongue for having given away her husband – and herself – in the process.

She had shown her over-anxiety to gain access to the bawdy world that she knew men shared in common. She bitterly resented her exclusion from this world. There was only one man who could really make her privy to that world, the man who, from what she could gather from Smellie and Walter, reigned supreme there. And he had repulsed her –

had made her feel a naughty and highly-indelicate importuner. She might never even get him to kiss her now... He had erected a barrier between them. It wasn't how she had expected things would turn out.

Maria had always found men easy to handle. She had never experienced the slightest difficulty in keeping them in their place. When she didn't want them to become amorous she had known no difficulty in freezing them. To get any man she wanted to kiss her had never been difficult. She had made Smellie perform like a dancing bear. She had had Robert Burns answering her beck and call – until now.

Maria sometimes regretted she had married so young and to a man so fundamentally illiterate as Walter Riddell. On the other hand, marriage was a protection. From behind the safety-wall of matrimony she could operate with a great deal of safety and security. She had no intention of remaining faithful to Walter Riddell. Marriage, like any other state, had its legitimate field of exploitation. And if she wanted to exploit Robert Burns – or any other man – sexually, there was nothing in her morality that was going to stand in her way. Maria was fundamentally selfish. She had always had her own way. She had never had reason to doubt that her own way was better than any other way. A loyalty to any other value than her own interest was foreign to her. Even in her enthusiasm for the French she was self-centred. The Fall of the Bastille meant for Maria the fall of all the social barriers that limited her freedom and her pleasure.

YOURS TO COMMAND

Summer came and the Stinking Vennel stank more unwholesomely than ever.

Jean was harassed with the children. Robbie could not always be kept indoors – he was in his seventh year. Frank, at three years, was toddling about the floor-head and getting himself into all kinds of mischief. And with the twins at the crawling stage, it was a difficult time.

Jean's good nature was unfailing; but there were times when she did feel the strain and showed it. She felt the house an intolerable prison and the worst possible place to bring up children. She could never leave the door open for the stair was steep and narrow: a death-trap to toddling and crawling infants.

The only consolation she had was that Robbie was a quiet and exemplary boy. He could look after the younger ones while she went shopping, and he could be trusted to take Frank by the hand and set off for the Sands. But Jean had a terror of the Nith. It fascinated Frank, who was vigorous, unruly and adventurous.

Jean had always to make two journeys a day to the Nith to clean the hippens. At the end of the day she often felt tired, exhausted – and at times frustrated.

True, the Bard was an ideal father. He came home regularly and took his share of the nursing. Unlike most married men he occasionally – when Jean was sore pressed – took the pail of hippens to the Nith himself. But though he saw to Robbie's education and fed one or other of the twins at the table, Jean insisted that he must have leisure to get on with his writing.

Often he did his work sitting at the table-end, with the twins crawling about his feet and Frank climbing on the back of his chair and Robbie practising his writing opposite him, while Jean baked, washed or mended.

The truth was that the Bard was both proud and fond of his children and delighted in their company.

But by eight o'clock he would set off to the Mid-Steeple as the mail-coach came in, that he might collect any correspondence and hear the latest news. There he was certain to meet many of the folks he knew. Sometimes he passed from group to group for he had friends and acquaintances in most circles. He might stand and crack with George Haugh and his cronies and then move over to the shop-keepers and men like Wattie Auld, the saddler. Some of the young clerks and apprentice lawyers would be honoured by his company for a few moments. They were extremely deferential to him. He was something of a hero and a legend: Mr Burns the poet. That he was an Exciseman was an irrelevance. Mr Burns earned his bread and butter in the Service: his fame was a poet's fame; and he was Scotland's Bard.

On a fine night he could spend a pleasant hour at the Steeple. But sometimes when his head was busy with a song and the mail brought him a letter from Johnson, or a parcel of proofs from Creech, he would do little more than nod to his friends and retire to his room at the Globe. Sometimes there were letters he didn't want Jean to know about. Sometimes he read his mail over a modest beer and retired to the vennel; but if there was nothing pressing him, and the company in the public room was inviting, he would tarry and enjoy a social hour. And when some of his boon companions called for him, men like Syme or Willie Stewart or John MacMurdo, there would be a session. . .

At other times Riddell would send his coachman with a message to the effect that he was at the King's Arms, the George or the Assembly Rooms. If it wasn't Robert Riddell, it would be Maria and some of her friends or Sir Robert Laurie or Fergusson of Craigdarroch or Maxwell of Carruchen or Captain Hamilton, his landlord, or ex-Provost Staig or Provost David Blair . . . and nearly always they had friends with them who wanted to be introduced. . .

Sometimes the Bard managed to dodge these invitations. On a pleasant evening he often went for a stroll along the banks of the Nith and, if he was in the vein, he preferred his own company. Folks didn't wonder at these solitary rambles – that was Mr Burns the poet and the eccentricity was understandable.

Sometimes he resented the intrusion on his privacy and rebelled at being shown off as one of the attractions of the town. But men like Riddell, Laurie, Craigdarroch and Staig were his local patrons as well as his gentry friends: they could get his letters franked or conveyed free of charge to their destinations. They were men of influence who could promote his welfare in many ways and in many quarters. The more influence he could win, the more likely was he to gain promotion in the Excise – and this was still his chief practical ambition. . .

But only too often he paid too dear a price for his social hours with the gentry. Summoned to the King's Arms and introduced to the company, it was impossible to tear himself away until his host gave the signal.

Inevitably there was heavy drinking and late hours. . . And sometimes in drink he forgot to bridle his tongue.

When toasts were called he was not always judicious or politically discreet. Sometimes visitors were offended. It was all very nice to be introduced to the ploughman-turned-gauger-poet – very interesting and intriguing. But when the poet did not know when to speak and when to hold his tongue; when he sometimes went to the unheard-of length of

71

addressing them: of boldly airing his views in bold and forth-right language – then difficulties arose. Often enough strangers were at once astonished and spellbound and recognised that they were in the presence of supreme genius – and were grateful. But lesser men became uncomfortably conscious of their stature and took offence.

It was all very well for Robert Riddell to roar out that if anyone wanted to meet Caledonia's Bard he had only to say so and he, Squire Riddell, would summon him forthwith. It was perfectly in order that the poet should shortly make his appearance and be introduced and shown off. But it was a very different thing when he took command of the con-versation and treated their views – as often happened – not only with scant courtesy but with blistering contempt.

Inspiring, bold John Barleycorn! For it was only too true that in drink the Bard let all caution and prudence go to the winds and spoke his true thoughts – or almost.

Never did he reveal all of himself at any one time. Drink might make him contemptuous of caution; but it never made him a fool.

Only perhaps to Jean did he reveal his deepest and his most private thoughts.

Sometimes when he returned late from a meeting with the gentry and their friends, Jean would be bitter.

'Anither of thae nichts?'

'Well . . . ye ken how it is, Jean. . .'

'Aye: I ken what you'll be like in the morning. Dae your gentry frien's never think you've to work for your living?'

'I know —'

'Weel, God Almichty, Rab! if you ken what makes you dae it?'

'You wouldna hae me offend Glenriddell, would you?'

'You could tell Glenriddell you had to get up in the morning!'

'That would be a nice thing to announce to a company. A' richt, Jean, a' richt. . . It's just that you dinna understand everything.'

'Maybe I never professed to understand everything, Rab. But I ken the drink doesna agree wi' you – and that you canna be expected to stand up to thae seasoned topers. They can lie i' their beds a' day and hae servants to attend their every whim. I've nae objection to you haeing a nicht on occasion. But it's happening too often.'

'Right as always, Jean. But I've got a splitting head – and I'm tired, Jean. God, I'm tired. . .'

Jean turned away. She hated to nag at him. And her anger wasn't really at him but at the Glenriddells and their like. He was too good for the gentry. If they thought they were being kind to him by filling him with their damned rotten drink she had another name for it.

His Dumfries friends could be divided into separate and interpenetrating groups. Syme, MacMurdo and Willie Stewart had access (under certain terms and conditions) to the Riddells, Fergussons and Lauries. Collector Mitchell, Supervisor Findlater had access to the friendship of Syme, MacMurdo and Stewart. With the exception of the gentry, all of them had various degrees of access to the friendship of the Hyslops of the Globe. The Provost and the baillies were in a class by themselves; but the Bard was on the friendliest terms with the men who watched over the town's interests. But there was a large number of friends who occupied special positions. Lawyer David Newall, Dr James Mundell, brewer Gabriel Richardson, Captain John Hamilton – these did not necessarily mix with any of his other friends. There were friends he had made in the course of his Excise duties; there were Masonic friends; there were tradesmen and shopkeepers; there were working men who often approached him for advice. . . Indeed within six months of his taking up residence, he was perhaps the best known man in Dumfries. There was certainly no other man who had friends and acquaintances in so many circles.

So many folks claimed friendship with him that the wonder was he was ever at home; and the greatest wonder perhaps lay in the fact that he was so seldom under the influence of drink.

But the man who was most accessible to the Bard and whose company – on the whole – he enjoyed most was John Syme.

And now that Syme had sold his Barncailzie estate and had almost finished with the building of a small house on the twenty-three acres he had purchased out at Ryedale, near Troqueer, on the other side of the Nith, the friendship became warmer. The Stamp Office, where Syme worked as next-in-command to Distributor Maxwell, was immediately below the Bard's rooms in the Vennel, so that their friendship had every opportunity of ripening. . .

Jean, however, was never able to warm to Syme and Syme,

73

in turn, found Jean a bit formidable – if not terrifying. Seldom was Syme in the Bard's house other than for the briefest visit.

The Bard and Syme understood each other on this matter without the exchange of words. There was nothing forbidding about Mrs Syme, however. She was pleasant enough in a dull insipid way. She was no conversationalist. Her interest in art or literature or politics or life was so limited that immediately her first son arrived she abandoned all pretence at interest. She was, however, an excellent cook – when she could be bothered; and she had found a servant of whom she could make a companion and was training her to be almost as good a cook. This Martha had a palate for strong ale laced with gin and Mrs Syme was developing a like taste. When time hung heavily on their hands, they drank and played cards in the kitchen.

The arrangement suited Syme. He wasn't a man who was capable of any large emotions or big gestures. But he was arranging to make Ryedale a snug little croft. His only regret was that he was no longer Laird of Barncailzie but, more simply, John Syme, Esquire, of Ryedale.

The Bard spent many a pleasant evening at Ryedale. Here he could relax in ease and comfort. And here too he was out of reach from the importuning of his gentry friends.

On the other hand he could not reject formal invitations to the houses of the gentry. And when Riddell wanted him to meet a celebrity like Joseph Farington, the painter, he invited him out to Friars Carse and treated him as a privileged guest.

'You must meet with Burns, Farington: Scotland's Poet and a remarkable fellow. I hae him often to dinner. . . Yes: he was a ploughman and a tenant-farmer. He is in the Excise at the moment in Dumfries at £70 per annum. No: he is totally self-educated. Has a little French but no Latin. But a genius, Farington – an able fellow. Only . . . take no offence at his manner of talk. He talks boldly – and with authority – and wi' a lot of thundering good sense. . . Of course no one, least of all Burns, pretends he's a gentleman. You need have no qualms on that account: he knows his place.'

But there it was. Riddell had a kind heart towards him and liked his company; but he had to apologise for his social inferiority.

There were times indeed when the Bard worried overmuch about his social status. In a sense the approbation of

the gentry flattered him and, though much of the flattery
found him unmoved, something of the sense of it did get
under his skin. He had yet to meet the man who could best
him in general conversation; but in social position he was at
the bottom of the ladder; and even were he to acquire the
wealth of an Indian nabob he would still remain the social
inferior of the Glenriddells of Scotland. Often he was angry
with himself, for no matter how he boasted of his manly
independence, he was always secretly pleased when invitations
came to dine at Friars Carse or Woodley Park or Maxwelton
House. He liked to meet fine ladies and be introduced to
distinguished visitors. After all: he was Scotland's Bard. It
was a proud title and one that could only be held by one
poet at a time. . . But when he sought to argue himself into
the position that he was, in a sense, flattering the gentry by
his presence, he knew he was arguing a false case.

And then he would round on himself and spit the gentry
out of his mouth and sing the unmatchable distinctions of
the rustic maid and the labouring peasant – until Maria
Riddell swooped down on him and coaxed and cajoled and
flattered him; and he flushed with pleasure at the coaxing.

And yet, however much he was flattered or commended, he
never bartered his opinions or changed them with his dress.
Politely – and even maybe with a touch of deference – he
would place his knee-booted foot on the drawing-room carpet;
but it was the boot of an independent poet and never that
of a flunkey.

GAY LANDSCAPE

Walter Riddell drained his glass greedily and then replen-
ished it. He had more or less a perpetual hang-over. His wife
put down the letter she was reading.

She caught the cold inquisitive eye of her husband.

'It's from the Bard – care to read it?'

Walter made a gesture of negation.

'Aren't you paying too much attention to Burns?'

'In what way?'

'Maybe you find him amusing?'

'Don't you?'

'Yes: on an odd occasion. I ken my brother mak's a deal

of him. But then he's got odd tastes, y'know. I mean: what's so special about Burns after all? He has a great reputation with the ladies. But – eh — '

'Yes. . . ?'

'I dislike the idea of you being in his company – alone.'

'When was I?'

'I forbid it: that's enough!'

'Isn't my lord and master a bit surly to-day?'

'Listen, Maria. We're in Scotland. Try to remember that. The family name counts for something in these parts – always has done. Burns is a case in point. But not the only one. Married gentlewomen in Scotland do observe some proprieties that you seem to take a delight in – er – scorning. I know you don't have a very high opinion of my sister-in-law at Carse; but at least nobody gossips about her.'

'So you wish me to mould my manners on Mrs Robert Riddell? Why didn't you marry someone like her?'

'You're not Elizabeth Riddell and I don't want you to be Elizabeth Riddell. But I don't want my wife to be the subject of county gossip.'

'No: you want me to be dull and docile like the others. Isn't life dull enough here – of itself? You like a gay time yourself. You like having people here: you like getting beastly drunk on every possible occasion. You like me to sit at the harp and sing – a talented wife. But you don't like me to sit in the corner and talk politics and poetry with Robert Burns!'

'You think I'm nothing but a stupid soldier. You ken damn fine, Maria, that all your talk is only the merest fiddle-faddle. It's only hot air. Of course: since it amuses you – and since it appears to amuse Burns — '

'Really, Walter! Anyone overhearing you would conclude that you were jealous — '

'Of Burns?' Walter made a sound that he hoped would be taken for derision. 'You can take him to bed – that's how jealous I am.'

Maria gathered her papers from the table. She averted her face and left the room.

Walter poured himself another drink.

The truth was that his wife was much the more popular of the two. But her unconventional vivacity was embarrassing. Maria was much too clever and much too keen at displaying her cleverness. And now that she was having her book published. . .

Yes; and she was pregnant too. Maybe plenty of babies would bring Maria to a graver sense of her social responsibilities.

Walter Riddell looked out across the grasslands of Woodley Park, golden green in the early summer sunshine. Setting up as a landed gentleman was costing him plenty – and he wasn't getting as much thrill out of the experience as he had expected. Reports from his sugar plantation in Antigua could be brighter. If he were out there he'd flay the hide off somebody. . . Maybe he'd ride over to Carse and sound his blustering big brother for a loan. Maria's dowry had been damned disappointing.

SWEET FALLS THE EVE

Jean Lorimer of Kemys Hall was in her seventeenth summer, the Bard in his thirty-third. Yet for some two years a curious relation had grown up between them.

Jean, under the name of Chloris, had become the established model for certain of his love songs for Johnson's *Museum*. Maybe he deceived himself that he really needed Chloris for his model or even that he needed any model. Certainly he drew a quantity of inspiration from her that, if indeterminate, was by no means negligible.

Chloris was young and fresh and almost unbelievably fair. She was no fool: she had lively intelligence and was possessed of all the natural instincts of a whore. Not that she whored.

At seventeen she was far from being a virgin. But she was wholly opportunist in her approach to men and indeed to the world. She kissed and cuddled as naturally as she breathed, and when she liked a lad she expected to be kissed and cuddled.

The Bard had a deep respect for her virginity: this was still, to him, inviolate. But she had successfully overcome his resistance – and it had been stubborn – to kiss and cuddle her.

But the Bard had sometimes a guilty qualm about those over-ardent embraces and he was ever reassuring both himself and Chloris that their attachment was platonic – that he did no more than worship the Eternal Youth that made her so transcendingly radiant.

And Chloris was always ready to reassure him and assist in the self-deception.

'Surely there can be nae harm in a kiss – especially when we're no' lovers?'

'And can never be.'

'But should we worry aboot that?'

'No. . . But would folks believe us?'

'It's funny to hear you worrying about what folks think.'

'But I maun worry – for your sake. What would John Lewars think if he found you in my arms like this?'

'Och, I'm sure I've tellt you often enough that Johnny Lewars doesna ken how to kiss or how a lass likes to be hugged. A lesson wad dae him a lot of good.'

'It's you will need to teach him.'

'But how can you teach a boy that doesna want to be taught? Jean and you are affa keen that I should hang my bonnet up wi' him — '

'You could dae waur. I ken Lewars as you dinna and I tell you you couldna get a better lad in the South.'

'You tellt me a while back that I was never to marry unless it was for love.'

'Aye: I suppose I did.'

'Well?'

'I'll say nae mair. You've gotten a lang memory, Chloris.'

'Onyway: you've taught me what to expect in a lover.'

'Damnit, you needed nae teaching, you flaxen-haired — '

'Go on! Say it!'

'Sit doon here and cool your dowp while I read you the second variation o' Craigieburn Wood. I'm on the point of sending it off to Johnson. I'm determined to get it right. It's got to be sung slowly – and wi' as much expression as possible. . .

'Sweet closes the evening on Craigieburn Wood, and blithely awaukens the morrow; but the pride o' the spring on the Craigieburn Wood, can yield me naught but sorrow.

'And now the chorus – and here the expression should be heightened. . .

'Beyond thee, dearie, beyond thee, dearie, and O to be lying beyond thee; O sweetly, soundly, weel may he sleep that's laid in the bed beyond thee.'

'That's one o' your best songs yet – but who's supposed to be lying beyond me?'

'Weel: there could be a few chosen candidates for that position. I had in mind Johnnie Gillespie. He was passionately fond o' you.'

Chloris gave a slightly nostalgic shrug. 'He wasna bad – but I've had better.'

'Guid kens who you'll get to satisfy your affection, Chloris. . . But as far as this song's concerned: you're the pride o' the spring o' Craigieburn Wood and it's a lover – un-requited – like Gillespie that's singin'.'

He crooned over the rest of the song to her. Chloris was delighted with it. She was highly flattered that the Bard found her such an inspiring model. Yet she was in some way afraid of him. They spoke frankly to each other – much more frankly indeed that she had ever thought possible. And yet she held back from asking him to make love to her fully and freely, without let or hindrance. Maybe he was frightened that she would make some claim on him. How could she tell him that she didn't love him in that possessive sense at all? How could she tell him – without betraying a hidden coarse-ness – that she wanted the physical experience without any emotional consequences whatsoever? Couldn't he see that she just wanted the immediate physical consummation and that it was possible for her to crave for this without any talk of love, of flaxen hair and blue eyes . . . indeed what was all this poetic dressing-up for if it didn't lead to physical consumma-tion? How could he be made to realise – without offending him – that though she might be his poetic model, the lassie wi' the lint-white locks, she was also Muirland Meg; that she wanted to fee a lad or be feed by him; that though she went east or west her physical condition would remain unaltered and ever clamorous.

Yet she was frightened to offend him: frightened that she would appear coarse in his eyes. Frank and uninhibited as was their relationship, he still had not shared one secret with her. She had a secret about him – and it was a guilty one. He had given her father his collection of bawdy songs. And when her father was away for a couple of days, and her mother was lying in a drunken stupor, she had read every song in the book. Nothing she had read had shocked her. She had known life was coarse and vulgar and bawdy – real honest life was like that. But all the time folks pretended it wasn't. There, sex

79

was honestly displayed and the real business of a man and a lass made plain for all to see – and without any polite nonsense of worshipping and loving and adoring. She might be the pride of Craigieburn Wood; but for all that Johnnie Gillespie wanted to be in bed with her – and at least there was sense in that.

But the Bard knew nothing of what Chloris was really thinking. For him, Chloris was the ideal rustic maiden, all virtue and modesty and all that was ideally becoming to her seventeen sweet summers. Fine he knew he could have seduced Chloris. Nothing easier. But her freshness and her youth protected her. And as he was not in love with her he could afford to regard her as an ideal-in-the-flesh.

And yet, if they were not lovers, they were curiously fond of each other.

'You're a wonderful man, Robert. You must get a lot o' fun makin' a sang.'

'A lot o' fun, as you say. It's no' just as easy as it looks either. I've spent a lot o' time on Craigieburn Wood – and not wholly because it was your birthplace.'

'Aye: it was bonnie at Craigieburn. . . But it's nice here too. I like Dumfries far better than I liked Moffat. There's mair life about Dumfries – and of course there's mair folks come about Kemys Ha'.'

'How's your mother behaving?'

'She's no' bad the now. It's ower a month since I've seen her really drunk.'

'If only she could keep the drink in its place. . .'

'I suppose that's asking ower much. There's plenty I'm no' supposed to ken – but – eh – but I heard my faither telling my mother how grateful he was for yon warning you sent him afore Mr Findlater cam' out.'

'For Godsake, lass, never come ower the likes o' that. If that was kent, I'd be dismissed the Service without an appeal.'

'That's what my faither said.'

'Yet you're no' supposed to ken ocht!'

'Neither I dae – really.'

'The less you ken the better. I was quizzed about you and me.'

'Mr Findlater?'

'How d'you ken?'

80

'I wadna trust yon man. He looks at you in a staring kind o' way. He'd be cruel too.'

'I dinna find him that way. He's clever and he means to get on –'

'He's gotten a cauld cruel mouth and cauld cruel een: I wadna like to be married to a man like him.'

'So that's how Findlater strikes you! Different folk see things in a different light. Aye: I believe there is a cruel streak in Findlater – a ruthless streak onyway — '

'As lang's you dinna trust him ower far.'

'Are you that much concerned for me?'

'Acht, Robert: sometimes you're no' a bit clever. Are we for wasting the wee while we've gotten thegither talking about Mr Findlater? You could at least kiss me seeing how I've inspired your Craigieburn — '

She spoke quite simply and without the slightest trace of self-consciousness. He looked into her clear blue eyes and found nothing to read there. Only the flush on her cheeks betrayed any sign of physical passion. And the Bard thought – and why his mind suddenly switched from Craigieburn Wood to the river Jed he could not explain even had he wished to; but he did think suddenly of Isabella Lindsay and then of Rachael Ainslie and remembered, almost with a physical pang, how he had never had an opportunity with them for the physical intimacy that was mutual. He had wanted them desperately and urgently – just as they had wanted him. And here he was looking at Jean Lorimer who was every inch as attractive as Isabella or Rachael and who maybe wanted him as much as they had done. And yet there was a barrier he could not explain.

Jean watched his great glowing eyes and saw them somehow soften and dim – those great smouldering eyes that did so many queer and inexplicable things to her – eyes that when you could read them spoke more eloquently and more deeply than the finest poetry.

And when their lips met, Jean Lorimer trembled with the shock of the passion that surged through her.

THE FIRST BLOW

In May, Thomas Paine, whose first instalment of the *Rights of Man* had been widely read in Great Britain and whose work had been as a flaming torch to all those who held liberal and democratic opinions, published his second instalment and was indicted for treason by the government. The government, under Pitt, and with Burke as the chief propagandist against the French, was deeply alarmed at the spread of democratic principles. They believed that Paine's work was fundamentally undermining the constitution. They had reports from their spies in every quarter that Paine's work was read with enthusiasm.

The Bard learned of Paine's indictment with surprise and indignation. But he was gratified to learn that he had managed to escape to France. There he felt he would be free from persecution and able to continue his work defending and advancing the fundamental rights of man.

He discussed the matter with Maria Riddell. Maria, of course, was furious at the government in their treatment of Paine. She considered him to be the foremost pamphleteer of the age; to be a man of intellectual audacity and courage; and the Bard could do no more than agree with her. Paine's *Commonsense* and his *Rights of Man* he had read from cover to cover many a time. But he was alarmed and Maria was alarmed that the government were now seeking through their sheriff officers, through their magistrates and through their informers and spies to bring before the government the names of all persons in the slightest way thought to be disaffected.

The Bard felt that here was the beginning of a new tyranny. The government were no longer going to sit back and take things quietly. They were going to advance ruthlessly and crush any attempt at liberty of thought and expression. They were determined, it seemed, to root out while the root appeared still young, any trace of democratic principles.

Following on the indictment of Paine came Mary Wollstonecraft's *Vindication of the Rights of Women*, and this admirable statement of women's rights in society was as widely read and acclaimed almost as Paine's pamphlet; and

Maria Riddell – since its author was a woman – was enthusiastic. . .

Throughout the country people were stirring. They thought that a new world was begun; and the fact that they had not yet taken part in it began to agitate men's minds. Even such a modest reform as the Burgh proposals had been rejected by parliament; and in Edinburgh the day after the King's birthday the people rose and stormed Dundas's house in George Square for his speech against Burgh Reform. Several of Dundas's friends had thought to disperse the mob, as they called it, with insulting and abusive language. Dragoons rode through the streets of Edinburgh with drawn swords, much to the anger of the people. And the people burned Dundas's effigy in front of his own house and stoned his windows.

This was a shattering occurrence. Here was evidence that in the capital of Scotland the people were rising; that at long last the corruption and the tyranny of Dundas was being challenged – and by the people.

Naturally those who supported the government, those whose preferments, whose jobs, whose sinecures depended upon the Dundas dictatorship, rallied to the defence of what they called the constitution – the system that granted them so many privileges.

In Dumfries the news that Dundas had been attacked in his own home caused a wave of strength to pass through all those who favoured reform and democracy.

The French had reacted generously to the arrival of Paine and proposed to honour him in some suitable manner. . .

Now everyone who was not four-square with the government and who deviated in religion or politics in the slightest way from the established order, was under suspicion. Doctor Priestley (the celebrated scientist-theologian) had been attacked in his Birmingham home by a reactionary mob led by government provocateurs. . .

In the House of Commons, Charles James Fox had risen to defend the principle of religious toleration; and in noble words Fox pointed out that to suppress men for their religious beliefs was a very dangerous principle. The very men affected might be right, and those like Fox himself (a true Trinitarian) might well be wrong. In matters of religion Fox wanted the many acts and proscriptions on the Statute Book altered, swept away, so that men could in freedom worship God as they thought best.

Edmund Burke, however, seized upon this as a pretext for launching out a fierce and vindictive diatribe not only against Priestley but against democratic doctrines and the French Revolution. In language ill-suited to any parliamentarian he linked Doctor Priestley's Unitarianism with Tom Paine's *Rights of Man* and with the Fall of the Bastille. He tried to raise the greatest prejudice against any attempt to tolerate religious freedom in Britain. He asked them in the House of Commons to notice the attack on the Bastille, 'defended alone by 96 invalids'; and he dwelt for some time on the subsequent murders.

'Such a revolution,' said Burke, 'none but wicked or mistaken men can celebrate. If they considered it an event auspicious to freedom, was there no other auspicious day to freedom that they could discover for celebration? No anniversary of the Revolution in this country – no Magna Charta to be remembered? Could they discover no other day of a Revolution fit to be celebrated than that marked by blood, by rebellion, by perfidy, by murder and by cannibalism?

'Gentlemen,' continued Burke, 'might call out "Hear, hear!" as long as they thought proper. I have asserted no more than I can prove. I will again assert cannibalism, for I have documents to prove that the French cannibals, having torn out the hearts of those they murdered, squeezed out the blood of them into the wine, and drank it. An event giving rise to such enormities is no event fit to be celebrated by Christians. . .'

In vain did Fox, in reply, point out that his motion had nothing to do with France. In vain did he point out that it was the fashion with some gentlemen to raise the French question in every debate. . .

'My opinions of the French Revolution are precisely the same now as they ever were. I consider that event as highly important and advantageous to this country and to the world; and no temporary or accidental defeat the French may suffer in their struggle for liberty will stagger my mind upon their success in the result.

'With respect to the Bastille, the destruction of which Mr Burke has so feelingly lamented, I exult at the destruction of that diabolical prison. Let me mention, in most respectful terms, a poet whom I consider one of the first of the moderns. I name Mr. Cowper, and the whole desultory poem called *The Task* I have read with the utmost delight. I quote that

84

gentleman's just description of the Bastille in the following
lines:

"Ye dungeons and ye cages of despair,
That Monarchs have supplied from age to age,
With music such as suits their sov'reign ears,
The sighs and groans of miserable men. . .!
There's not an English heart that would not leap
To hear that ye were fallen at last."

'The Bastille at that period was standing; since then it has
been destroyed. I know not why Doctor Priestley, because he
approves of the French Revolution, should be liable to
punishment from the circumstance of his being an Unitarian,
while I should be exempted from punishment though I hold
the same opinions but, in religion, am a Trinitarian. . .'

To John Syme the Bard explained himself at some length.
'Things are on the move now, John: there can be no
question about that. Before long, and maybe not so long as
we think, the British people are going to follow in the wake
of the French. . .
'The very fact that Dundas can be attacked in Auld Reekie
within the sacred precincts of George Square; the very fact
that Burke – and by the Lord, John, if ever there was a dirty,
low-down, vicious-minded votary of blood and thunder that
man is Burke! – and the very fact that Burke can lie in the
House of Commons and not be howled down for his lying,
is proof how far the government is disturbed at what's taking
place. . .
'Because, as I see it, John, man is being born anew –
everywhere. And why should we be any exception? Scotland,
in so far as I can read history, was one of the first – nay, was
the very first country, to espouse the cause of freedom. No
modern reformer has ever stated more clearly, more fundamentally the rights of man than did William Wallace. Wallace
who refused the crown of Scotland and was proud to declare
himself Governor of the Scottish Commonwealth. . . .! Aye,
it's true that down the years since the English disembowelled,
tore out the heart, quartered and beheaded Wallace, that the
principles for which he stood and which he enunciated have
been drowned many times in blood and destroyed by
persecution.

85

'Well, the French have taken up where Wallace left off; taken up maybe at a higher level. I don't know for the truth of that; but they have set to work with such strength, such resolution, that it is impossible that the principles enshrined in the French Assembly can be kept from spreading beyond the borders of France.

'The very measure of the government's panic is but proof that the ideas have in fact spread – across the Channel at least. The Tree of Liberty, John, is growing; and the government is determined that it shall not grow. But everywhere the government roots out the Tree of Liberty, a fresh tree is planted elsewhere. In their unreasoning wrath, in their terror and their agitation, I have little doubt but that the ministry of Pitt will strike terror far and wide. But what can they do if the people are determined and stand resolutely by their beliefs? You can indict an individual like Paine; you can indict a man like Doctor Priestley; but you can't indict the people – at least not for ever!

'We have got to keep calm, as I see it, John, and not allow ourselves to be provoked. Keep calm; keep resolute – and keep Paine's writings in circulation. Keep the writings of all the pamphleteers, the anonymous pamphleteers in circulation. I repeat: the people are moving; they are stirring; they are rising out of their centuries of oppression and the indifference – the deadening indifference that oppression brings when applied too long to a people.

'Never before have I felt so sanguine as to the outcome of the present tensions. You see: when I was young – before I had read much – the period when you might say my ideas were forming – they instinctively formed themselves on what Paine and the French call the rights of man. I was for the rights of man long before I read Paine. I think many people were. The virtue in Paine is that he has brought the subject clearly and sharply and brilliantly before the people.

'And I might as well confess that when I read Paine first, fired as I was, I thought it might be many years before his ideas would find general acceptance. I was wrong in that. I think the time is now. I think his ideas have been accepted. There're friends of mine in this very toon, John, who have read Paine more carefully than you or I – or at least just as carefully. They are men not of the colleges, but of the workshops and the tailors' rooms; and the mills. . . There are mechanics and young apprentices in the lawyers' offices who have firmly accepted the principles that Paine has so brilliantly enunciated. And they are determined, as I see it, not to let this generation go in default of bringing these principles into being: to compelling the government, by legislation, to act by bringing about a fundamental alteration in our constitution.

'And if I, by a poem here and a song there, can help them, then, by God, I'll help them.'

To Jean, the Bard expressed himself rather differently.

'I'll need to get a' thae pamphlets cleared out o' the house as soon as possible. . . Now, if onybody was to ask you if you saw me reading Paine's Rights of Man . . . you ken what to say?'

'What's a' this aboot, Rab?'

'It's like this, Jean. There's an outcry in parliament the new about seditious writings. The government's fully annoyed about what's been happening in France and what's happened as a consequence o' the writings o' Tom Paine and a wheen other pamphleteers. It seems they think the country's in a bad state as far as the constitution's concerned. Of course, that's rubbish. . . But then you see, Jean: it so happens that I'm an Exciseman and in government service. There's no saying what may come out of this. However, a' that you have to understand, lass, is that as far as Tom Paine's Rights of Man is concerned, and ony other pamphlets that have been lying about the house this while back and which you have heard me discussing with Geordie Haugh up the stairs: as far as a' thae things are concerned, you ken nocht.'

'Weel, I never did ken much aboot them, Rab.'

'But you've heard plenty talk o' them, Jean.'

'Aye: I've heard you talking; but I canna say it made ony great impression on me.'

'I ken, Jean, I ken. Maybe now the way things have turned out that's for the best. Mind you: I'm all on the side of France as you ken, and I'm all on the side of Tom Paine, and I'm all for democracy. In other words, Jean lass, you ken where I stand and where I've aey stood. I've aey stood for the rights of man; I've aey preached that we need more liberty, more freedom and more equality in this country – and in every country under the sun.'

'But, Rab, is there ony danger – I mean from the authorities – in having thae books aboot the house?'

'Well, there is, Jean: we micht as well face it. This government apparently has come to the conclusions that onything that goes against what Burke and Pitt and the aristocrats would like is to be banned as heresy and sedition – and stamped out accordingly. Oh, they'll have a bit o' stamping out. . .!

'Aye, lass: it's you and the bairns I'm thinking o'. I wadna want to fall foul o' the powers-that-be. I'm certain that since this rumpus in the Commons about sedition was carried that there'll be spies and informers throughout the country and that there'll be spies and informers in the toon o' Dumfries. Aye, perhaps there'll be mair spies and informers in Dumfries than onywhaur in Scotland – barring Edinburgh. . .

'By the Lord, things are moving in Edinburgh. I wish I had the ear of Willie Nicol or Willie Smellie . . . or Balloon Tytler. Aye, there's a man! I'll warrant that Balloon Tytler's in this up to the ears. He'll be writing pamphlets: or printing them. Aye, aye: Liberty's a glorious feast. . .

'You'll just need to excuse me rummaging about thae papers like this and having a word wi' you back and forward. I dinna want you to get annoyed. I dinna want you to get anxious or nervous. There's nothing to be feared o'. It's just that we're better to be on the side o' caution.'

Jean did not understand what was going on. She sat and watched Robert sift through piles of papers and documents, occasionally throwing aside some pamphlet or paper. But she sensed danger: she knew that below his careful casualness he was worried, if not agitated. In seeking instinctively to re-assure him, she tried to reassure herself.

'Weel I'm sure, Rab, I canna see what you're worried aboot. Twa or three bits o' pamphlets are no' goin' to upset the government doon in Lunnon. The twa or three folk that read them in Dumfries canna be ony threat to the constitution o' the country. . . ?'

To George Haugh the Bard was perhaps more direct.

'I was thinking, Geordie, that the best thing that could happen would be for you to tak' the pamphlets under your wing.'

'Certainly, Robert, if you'd rather hae it that way.'

'I had a bit hint from Lindlater that enquiries, in a quiet

88

way, are liable to happen in the Excise at ony time. The way the government's agitated the now he didna ken what micht happen.'

'Aye, the government's frichted, Robert: there's nae doubt aboot that. But it'll mak' nae difference to me or to my associations. We'll just need to press forward steadily with the case of reform agitation; for annual parliaments and for wider suffrage. . . I could see that the pamphlets here got wider circulation than lying in my cupboard. You ken, as far as Tom Paine is concerned, you can aey hae access to my copy here.'

'Thanks, Geordie. If you can distribute the pamphlets in a quarter where they are likely to do ony good, by all means do so. . . I hope you dinna think I'm being ower cautious?'

'No, no, Robert: no, no. A man in your position canna be ower cautious. Aye: being in the Excise is no doubt a kittle point . . . a kittle point.'

'What d'you think of the prospects yourself, Geordie?'

'Oh, weel, I canna say other than that I feel gey satisfied the way things are turning out. Mind you: there's gaun to be a lot of savagery as far as the government's concerned. I see in Edinburgh that Alexander Lockie, for throwing one stone *towards* the soldiers, or so report has it – the time Dundas's house was raided after the King's birthday – I see that Lockie has been sentenced to be banished to Botany Bay for fourteen years.'

'I saw that Geordie. The inhumanity of it, the ruthless barbarity of it makes my blood boil in a kind o' frenzy. It's when I hear o' things like that that I wish I was out of the Excise and free to play a full part in the fight for freedom. Fourteen years for throwing a stone *towards* the soldiers! Huh! What would it hae been had he hit one of the soldiers? A young lad like that banished to Botany Bay for fourteen years has his life ended before it's properly begun. . .'

'As you say, Robert: that's the end of Alexander Lockie. But then, you see, this kind of suppression works two ways. For every Lockie that's so banished and so ill-treated, a dozen men will fill his place. . . As I see it, Robert, these are but isolated examples meant to strike terror into the reform movement throughout the length and breadth of the land.'

'Well, Geordie, I have plenty on my hands at the moment. I'm busy the now on a political poem that I'll leave wi' you so that your friends can get onto the job o' making copies. I think it's a guid poem and I think you'll like it. Here's how it goes:

'Why should we idly waste our prime repeating our oppressions? Come rouse to arms! 'Tis now the time to punish past transgressions. 'Tis said that Kings can do no wrong – their murderous deeds deny it, and since from us their power is sprung, we have a right to try it. Now each true patriot's song shall be: "Welcome Death or Libertie!"'

'Proud Priests and Bishops we'll translate and canonize as Martyrs; the guillotine on Peers shall wait; and Knights shall hang in garters. Those Despots long have trode us down, and Judges are their engines: such wretched minions of a Crown demand the people's vengeance! To-day 'tis *theirs*. To-morrow we shall don the Cap of Libertie!

'The Golden Age we'll then revive: each man will be a brother; in harmony we all shall live, and share the earth together; in Virtue trained, enlightened Youth will love each fellow-creature; and future years shall prove the truth that Man is good by nature: then let us toast with three times three the reign of Peace and Libertie!'

'By God, Rab, you've got a thundering poem there! Leave me your verses and I'll copy them this verra nicht. I'll hae the lads onto it the morn – and there'll be copies a' ower Scotland afore the end o' the month. There's naebody'll ken frae me wha the author is. We canna hae you banished to Botany Bay. We need your pen working for us here —'

LIBERTY, FRATERNITY, EQUALITY

During the summer of 1792 the Bard was unusually busy. He had finished with the fourth volume of the *Scots Musical Museum* earlier in the summer. Johnson was able to publish it by the 13th of August. But his busiest time had been concerned with the correction of the proofs of the forthcoming two-volume edition for Creech. This had caused him many pains; and, indeed, so absorbed had he become in the task that he had inadvertently slipped up in certain of his Excise statements and had been reprimanded by Collector Mitchell. And although his Excise duties involved him in little physical travel, nevertheless the variety of the work and the meticulousness required in making his entries was mentally tiring –

especially since the bulk of it seemed to him a matter of soulless routine. . .

He had little time for leisure, little time for enjoying his favourite walk by the banks of the Nith, or for spending many hours with his friends in the Globe or the King's Arms. But he did take time of a fine evening to stroll up by the Meadow Walk with Jean and the children. . . And they did have visitors and he did keep in touch with many of his friends.

He rarely missed the Sunday morning service conducted by the Reverend William Inglis at the nonconformist Relief Church in the Loreburn. He preferred Inglis to any other Dumfries clergyman; and although he had visited St Michael's and Greyfriars under William Burnside, he cared little for either of them. On the other hand, the non-conformist Inglis was, both as man and as preacher, of outstanding ability. He had first come in contact with Inglis when he had lodged with the Cullies at Ellisland. For the Cullies were of Mr Inglis's faith. The talks he had had with Inglis there had convinced him of the man's forthright sincerity. When John Syme asked him why he preferred Inglis, he had replied sharply and to the point that Inglis preached what he practised and practised what he preached.

And sometimes, after the service with Inglis, he would return to the Stinking Vennel and then cross the road from his poor dwelling to the grand house af his factor, Captain John Hamilton, and partake of a generous dinner. Captain Hamilton enjoyed the Bard's company and many a cheery meal they had together. Besides, Hamilton had promised the Bard the first chance of a house that would offer better accommodation than his present home; and, truth to tell, both Jean and he were heartily sick of their mean and cramped accommodation. Though Jean had almost become inured to the many effluvia that wafted in and around the Stinking Vennel, she could not reconcile herself to the lack of an open door at ground level.

He had also struck up a friendship with Gabriel Richardson, the brewer, who lived nearby in Nith Place. Gabriel was, perhaps, the ideal type of brewer. He was burly, red-faced and jolly. He was much the same age as the Bard. They both had sons of an age and they had many other interests in common. Gabriel liked a hearty story; and a good thoroughgoing bawdy song was spiritual meat and drink to him.

Sometimes Jean would be with him at Hamilton's or

Richardson's; but the children were always claiming her attention and she could never absent herself from the vennel for long. When she did absent herself, it was only when she could get someone to look after the children. And the readiest person she could get was Mrs Haugh, though sometimes Jean Lorimer called at an opportune moment. . .

John Syme of the Stamp Office below him remained his most constant boon-companion. Now that Syme had his house finished at Ryedale and but seldom spent an evening in Dumfries, the Bard had got into the habit of calling in on him on his road home, exchanging the news of the day or submitting for his approval the latest production from his pen. Often these productions were for private circulation: an epigram on this one or that, or a political squib or even a full-length effort extolling the French or rallying the forces of freedom at home. . .

Syme invariably approved the Bard's satiric efforts. His epigrams he collected assiduously, writing them into a notebook especially kept for the purpose.

It was with Syme that he discussed his prospects in the Excise, the possibility of the success of the two-volume Edinburgh edition (which, however, would put nothing into his pocket); or went over a song with him even though Syme was no great musician. Had he had his way, Syme would have had the Bard out to Ryedale every other evening. There was no one in Dumfries, no one he had ever met before, like the Bard. Syme revelled in his company and almost totally subjected himself to his personality. Syme found life in Dumfries very dull, and his office in the Stinking Vennel little more than a prison-house from which he was always glad to escape.

Maria Riddell had taken to dropping in of an afternoon to the Stamp Office, about the time she knew the Bard would be there. Here they could talk more freely than was often possible in the George or the King's Arms. In the taverns Maria was always under the eye of the proprietor or his servants or any other visitor who happened to be around. For Maria was still very much news in and around Dumfries. Maria still attracted attention wherever she went. She was still the subject of gossip, of envy and of admiration. And Maria was still taking her revolutionary politics very seriously – for her.

Sometimes her intelligence was of a revealing kind. Maria

had innumerable correspondents: some in London, some in Paris and some in the West Indies. Maria was influentially connected, and the news she was able to give them was often of a highly diverting, though private nature.

Her descriptions of the activities of some of the leading politicians of the day were scandalous. The great Charles James Fox, it seemed, not only drank heavily as did nearly all of his parliamentary colleagues; but his endless succession of mistresses was a matter of wonder and surprise. Between drink and women and gambling, the news was that Charlie Fox had but a short course to run. And yet no one could defend the glory of the French Revolution and the aspirations of the reformers at home with such eloquence as Fox. The Bard cared little for Maria's London gossip. But it did strike him as sad that the great Charles James Fox was great only in the purpose of his oratory and that the man was so completely given over to the flesh-pots and the debauchery of his time.

It was to Lewars that the Bard explained what he knew about the French Revolution. Strangely enough, for all his intelligence and alertness, John Lewars could not understand was exactly had happened in France. And the Bard had not passed on to him the many pamphlets he had read.

'France had no parliament, John. The Court went backrupt. Louis summoned the clergy and the nobles and they couldna help him much. So he summoned what's come to be known as the Third Estate – in other words the rest o' the nation – and asked them to prepare a list o' their grievances.'

'They'd plenty o' grievances?'

'Aye – and sore ones. That was at the beginning o' things in '88. . . Weel, when the Third Estate met in May '89, they were in nae mood to be fobbed off wi' ony crafty court intriguing frae Louis. Louis tried to separate the Third Estate frae the court and the church. But the Third Estate stuck to their guns and they demanded a constitution. So they did in fact become the Constituent Assembly.

'Then came the Fall o' the Bastille – the first trial o' strength between Louis and the Assembly – for Louis and the court were for ham-stringing them. . .

'The Assembly went to work and began to consolidate themselves and provide a real constitution for France.

'First they abolished feudal rights; then they made the

historic world-shaking Declaration o' the Rights o' Man and the Citizen.

'Frae then on you ken what's happened – mair or less.

'Of course a' them that held wi' kings and courts and no democracy plotted against France. Austria and France were at war by the spring. And you ken that Brunswick's just waiting to set France on fire – if he dares! It looks as if Pitt and Dundas would like to play the same game.

'And of course Louis has been plotting and planning to this end. But they've got him tied up now where he canna do much harm. The folk o' France are giving short shrift to the enemies o' the nation. It's maybe unfortunate; but as you sow, so shall you reap. If heads hae rolled in France they were heads that had to roll – for the safety o' the nation; for the Rights o' Man – no' just one privileged class o' men. You understand?'

'I'm no' for bloodshed, Robert – that's what worries me about France.'

'Did the bloodshed never worry you afore? Folks under Louis were treated worse than mad dogs. They were treated like vermin: thrown into prison, tortured and murdered on the slightest pretext. There never was ony law in France for the folk o' France. And so, John, when criminals persist in going against the will o' a nation, they hae got to suffer accordingly. Let them desist in their criminal anti-democratic activities and not a hair o' their heads'll be touched. Let them persist – then off goes the head!'

'Is it as simple as that?'

'No . . . in practice it isn't. Innocent folk get in the road whiles – and come off worst. When men are goaded beyond endurance they seldom think on nice points o' legality. You ken weel, or should ken, that I'm the last man to favour bloodshed on ony pretext. I'm no' trying to excuse some o' the excess o' certain elements that the Revolution has brought forward. I'm only trying to understand what has happened.'

'I'm beginning to understand things a bit clearer myself. . . And what's the position now?'

'They've arrested the King. And the demand now is for a new convention to be elected by universal suffrage. They'll get it. I fancy that afore long France'll declare itself a Republic. Then the French Republic may start on the King and his associates and bring them to trial. The Bar o' the French Republic will be as the Bar o' Humanity – and Louis and his court hae a wheen crimes to answer for at the Bar o' Humanity. . . The world's bound to be a better place as a result. Everywhere tyranny, despotism and absolutism will be checked and, let us hope, overthrown – '

'And d'you think we should hae a revolution here?'

'No . . . at least no' to start wi'. We hae a parliament and we hae a constitution. Sae let's try them out. Let's hae reform – plenty o' reform. Let's hae our revolution in a constitutional way – without bloodshed and without disorder. What's to hinder us?'

'But the King — '

'Dinna worry aboot the King. The King kens brawly how Charlie lost his head and he'll no' risk losing his the same way. The King's no' the enemy – it's Pitt, Dundas, Burke – the parliamentary representatives o' the aristocracy that constitute the enemy.'

'Wad you dae awa' wi' them?'

'I would – in a constitutional manner. Gin we had a common suffrage, d'you think they would be elected? Never! Man, wi' universal suffrage the face o' Britain wad be changed overnicht – and overwhelmingly for the better.'

'I think I agree wi' you.'

'I want you to agree wi' me, John. But I want you to agree wi' me for deeper reasons. You're young. I want you to think out clearly for yoursel' what exactly France means to us and to the world. All I can say is that to reject France is to turn your back on humanity and ony belief in human progress.'

But no matter where one turned there was no escaping the effects of the French Revolution. French revolt, British reform was in the air. For the first time since the manipulated and infamous Union of 1707, the common people of Scotland and England became surprisingly united in the concept of a United Kingdom – Britain. There was enmity between English Aristocrat and English Democrat; there was enmity between Scottish Aristocrat and Scottish Democrat; there was unity between English and Scottish Aristocrat – and there was unity, deep fraternal unity, between English and Scottish (and French) Democrat. The world indeed was marshalling under two decisive banners. The banner of a revived despotic feudalism and the banner of the revolution: unity of all men of all races in democratic liberty, fraternity and equality.

It was a tremendous, world-shattering, epoch-making time. There was little wonder that the effects were felt in Dumfries. . . Little wonder too that some who should have been, by birth and upbringing, aristocrats were indeed in the democratic van; and thousands who should have been in the democratic van should have remained in sullen servility. . .

Often, in the past, the Bard had despaired of humanity – in the mass. For long enough he had been unable to see any road out for ignorant downtrodden brutalised humanity. Back in his Mossgiel days it had seemed that only the Beggars – in their freedom from morality; in their condition of being below it – were the portents of a love and a liberty yet to be.

But now a whole nation had taken to Love and Liberty – and he had been a precursor, a prophet in advance. It was he who had sung of the new principles – even before they had come to pass.

Had he not then reason for pride, for elation?

He hid this self-satisfaction from his friends; but in bed one night he spoke his inmost thoughts:

'To hell, Jean: I ken mair about Liberty, Fraternity and Equality than ony o' them! I was burned up wi' the vision of what the world should be while I was holding the plough at Mossgiel – aye, and holding you in my arms. . .

'Dinna forget that, lass. You inspired me too; you intensified my vision; increased my ardour. You see, lass, I saw you as one o' the Queens of Womankind – aye, greater, nobler, more endearing than ony queen that ever sat on ony throne.

'Aye; and you ken I speak nocht but truth here. You remain a queen, Jean – every inch and bit o' you. You did inspire me. I'd like you to understand just what I mean here. You inspired me in mony a sang – love sangs of course. For o' a' the women I've kent, lass, there's nane to haud a can'le wi' you. Noo, noo: dinna mistake me. I'm no flattering you the nicht. Let me speak o' things as I see them – looking back. In Jean Armour I saw a country lass that fired my blood; that I wanted mair than ony other lass. Aye: a' that – but something mair. I didna love you just because you were the sweetest armfu' a man could possess – though you were a' that. I saw something else in you, Jean. I saw a simple, country lass that, for essential purity and womanly dignity, stood foremaist amang womankind. Somehow you symbolised a' that was best in the Scottish peasantry – in the common folk

96

o' the land. My Beggars' doxies were puir, physically less ill-conditioned creatures. . . But you were different; and in you I saw the possibility o' the world becoming regenerated – born anew. . . And it's coming, lass – and dinna scoff or laugh at my ideas – it's coming when women like you will be reckoned first in the land. Those that toil not, nor spin not, will be despised, rejected – and cast into the outer darkness. . .

It had to come, Jean – if there's ony purpose and significance in life. I was right frae the beginning. It's in my Twa Dogs – it's in Man was made to Mourn – only now man's rejoicing! It's in my King's Birthday – damn it: what's it no' in? Even in my Dedication to Ga'in Hamilton. . . Geordie Haugh understands: maybe he's the only ane. Maybe Willie Nicol – frae a different angle. Maybe John Rankine – Rankine had a hell o' a lot o' understanding. . .'

Jean stirred and said quietly: 'There's plenty I understand, Rab; but I'm no' meikle use at puttin' my thochts into words. I weel ken that there's naebody a richt match for you. When I first got to ken you in Machlin I thocht there couldna be anither in this world wi' your brain and your gift o' words. . . I'd never ony fear o' you when you went to Edinburry – though I'd plenty for mysel'. I've met wi' a wheen o' your friends since then. John Rankine's worth them a'. I ken you think a lot o' Mr Syme – but he's a puir creature compared wi' you. Captain Grose was a man; but you'd little enough o' his company. You're richt about Geordie Haugh: he's nae fool – and he kens your worth. Willie Nicol could be a great man – only he drinks ower heavy. In the Excise there's only Johnny Lewars. Mr Mitchell and Mr Findlater – oh, they're richt enough . . . but they couldna better you in ony way. . .

'Maybe whiles you think I dinna praise you enough – I dinna mean praise either – I mean maybe you think I dinna value you highly enough. But I ken your worth, Rab, and I'm no blate at kennin' your worth compared wi' other men. I'm feared whiles to put words on what I kent in case I put my foot doon wrang. But I've read a' your verses and I think I ken what they mean – only I didna richt ken the full meaning o' Love and Liberty till the nicht; and if that's what the French are after; if that's what you and Geordie Haugh are after, then I'm wi' you. But if that Maria Riddell and Syme are after the same thing, then it'll no' work?'

'How that, lass?'

'Because oil and water will never mix.'

'But if all men and women are equal – in terms of the social contract?'

'It'll tak' a wheen generations to level things oot, Rab.'

'No' sae mony generations, Jean. Aince you tak' awa' a man's wealth and privilege and then let him find his level according to his innate worth – it doesn't tak' sae verra lang. Give Maria Riddell twa rooms i' the vennel here and ca' her oot to the Nith to wash the hippens and you'll soon find oot at the end o' a month whether the same lady has some native worth in her. . . Mind you, Jean, I'd back Mistress Maria whaur I wadna risk a groat on her man – Captain Walter Riddell wad be in the work-house at the end o' the week – and Geordie Haugh wad hae a seat in the Cabinet —'

'Aye: maybe you're richt there, Rab; and I hope you'll never forget that. . . Geordie Haugh's worth mair than a' your Dumfries frien's.'

'I ken, Jean, I ken . . . but then it's only you and me kens that. Syme would never understand that – nor Mrs Riddell . . . nor Mitchell . . . nor Findlater . . . nor MacMurdo . . . nor Willie Stewart. . . As for Glenriddell or Maxwelton or Craigdarroch: to them such a man as Geordie Haugh doesn't even exist. . . Och weel, Jean; get to sleep: it'll no' be this in the morning . . .'

KING OF THE SOUTH

On the 10th of September, Maria Riddell sent a post-chaise to Edinburgh to collect Willie Smellie and bring him to Dumfries and Woodley Park . . .

Smellie placed one knock-knee over the other and gazed with a warming look at Jean.

'Well, Mistress: so you're the Bard's Bonnie Jean. . . Noo, noo: dinna blush: you're Bonnie Jean a' richt. Robin's a lucky man, Mistress: a lucky man. . . Och, but he kens that. . . An' you've braw weans here, Mistress: braw weans . . .'

'And are you and yours in guid health and doin' weel, Mr Smellie?'

'Thank you. . . Aye: we're a daein' fine . . .'

'And how d'ye like Dumfries?'

'Oh, a grand bit o' a toon – a fine open toon – healthier than Reekie I should think. Of coorse, I can understand how you miss the green fields o' your farm at Ellisland. A pity Robin had to gie it up for the Excise. I ken, Mistress, what a steady income means to a wife and a young family; but Robin wad hae had mair independence as a farmer. True, true: there's little independence worth the name when the meal-poke's empty and the girnel's bare. . . I'm glad to learn frae your ain tongue that he's happy enough and that his prospects are good. Ho – there's naethin' to prevent Robin rising to high rank in the Excise. But – eh – he's our National Bard and should be free to employ his pen whatever way his inspiration urges him: that's what I mean.

'True enough, Mistress, the gentry could hae done much mair for him. Damnit, there's nae reason why he shouldna be on the civil pension list. When ye read o' the folk that get money that airt, it mak's you wonder . . .'

Smellie thought highly of Jean and admired the way in which she was bringing up her children. Smellie reckoned that the Bard had gotten an affectionate wife and an able and devoted mother for his children.

When Maria Riddell asked him what he thought of Jean he was surprised.

'What do you think o' her, Madam?'

'Oh . . . I suppose she's a good enough housewife – but as a poet's wife? I find it hard to think of her as the wife of our National Bard.'

'Ah, Madam, I see you ken little o' poets and less o' men and gey little about Robert Burns. The Bard couldna hae gotten a better wife — '

'Of course if Mr Smellie approves . . .'

'Noo, noo: none o' your fancy sarcasms wi' Willie Smellie. I wadna expect you to hae ocht in common wi' Mistress Burns however much common ground you could occupy alongside the Bard. . . Dinna you mak' ony mistake concerning the ties that bind the Bard and his Bonnie Jean thegither — '

'But really, Mr. Smellie! Do you find Mistress Burns beautiful?'

'Madam, you're persistent. I didna say Mistress Burns was beautiful. And I'm nae authority on the beautiful amang the ladies. Doubtless you're a' beautiful – only some mair so than others. What I said was that Mistress Burns was bonnie and weel merits the praise the Bard has bestowed on her.'

'Ah: you're an old sophist and a flatterer. I suppose you've been a terrible flirt in your day?'

'Oh, my day's no' past yet. Maybe I'm just coming to the richt age to appreciate an affair. . .'

'With a bonnie lass or a beautiful woman?'

'I told you, Madam, I was nae judge o' beauty.'

With the aid of Maria and the Provost, the Bard managed to have Smellie elected a freeman of the town. In the evening of the ceremony they were given a reception and dinner in the Assembly Rooms.

The following night the Bard and Smellie occupied a private room in the Globe.

'By God, Robin, but you've gi'en me a rare lift – you and Maria.'

'No more than you deserve, Willie. Dumfries has nae mair distinguished burghess on the roll.'

'Na, na: I'm no' a' that important – and my distinction's but sma' – but I'm sensible o' the honour — '

'And what d'you think o' Maria Riddell now?'

'God, Robin, she's a warmer. Brains, ability – and charm. We were on the ither nicht about your Jean. She was trying to draw me. . .'

'But for why?'

'There you are! Maria's a bit in love wi' you, Robin: you'll need to watch your step!'

'Bluidy nonsense!'

'As lang as you ken.'

'And what about my Jean?'

'I've already said what I think about Jean.'

'I mean Maria – what was her interest in Jean?'

'Oh – she hinted that your Jean was nae the wife for a poet.'

The Bard's eyes smouldered.

'Aye: there's twa-three o' the gentry hae hinted as much. Little dae they ken, Willie.'

'That's exactly what I told Maria. But you're no' the man I think you are if you let that worry you.'

'Worry me! 'Course maybe I hae flattered Maria back and forwards . . .'

'Naebody wad blame you for that. By God! she'd gie you a byornar thrill!'

'You think so? I'm no' sae sure, Willie. Up to a point – yes. And up to a point I'm attracted. But I'm feared the thrill wad come through the brain and no' the — '

'Aye . . . I wadna wonder at that. It wad be worth the trial – once onyway.'

'No. . . Damnit, Willie, unless there's physical passion I doubt it wad be a failure. Oh, I think Maria's gotten mair nor her share o' physical passion. What I mean is she doesna arouse physical passion in me. And yet – this is the curious bit – I am attracted by a something about her.'

'You're no' the only ane! But I ken what ye mean. I could lift a leg ower her the nicht – but what kind o' reception wad I hae the morn? You couldna be sure, could you?'

'That's correct! You're never certain o' Maria. Sometimes I feel that what she wants is to be taken without ony cere-mony. In fact she leads you up to that. But if you did, what would happen? You micht get your een clawed oot o' your head.'

'We're agreed on that side o' Maria onyway. 'Course, that's no' her only side.'

'Far from it. She's reform mad the now.'

'Aye – and vicious aboot it. By God she's a whole-hogging reformist!'

'Sincere though, Willie. And the reform movement needs a' the sincerity it can muster.'

'There's gaun to be fun, Robin my boy. And some o' it's no' goin' to be sae funny.'

'As lang as we can keep folk frae rioting. You canna riot wi' sticks and stanes against cavalry wi' drawn swords.'

'Aye . . . and there's a wheen scum amang the rioters that hae naething but destruction and pillage and looting i' their heads.'

'Exactly. And they dae nocht but harm to the true cause o' reform.'

'They gie the troops a' the excuse they need; and then it's usually the innocent that suffer. You'd need to mind your step, Robin. Situate as I am I canna come out too boldly on the reform side. A' my siller's sunk in my business and it wad be an easy thing to ruin me. Oh, there's plenty I can dae on the quiet. Fact, I'd Balloon Tytler up at me for ink and paper. I told him I couldna gie him onything but that I wad lea'e a bit parcel forgetfu'-like in Dawney Douglas's that nicht if I saw him aboot, and that if he liked to pick it up when I'd left. . . Aha: you canna be ower carefu', Robin. And talking about Balloon: you'd see that auld William Tytler o' Woodhouselea has passed beyond?'

'He has? Damned, he was a decent auld body to me, Willie. He kent a bit about music too. He encouraged me with James Johnson. Balloon Tytler and the Woodhouselea Tytlers are no' related in ony way, are they?'

'Gey far back if they are: I shouldna think sae. Mind ye: plenty folk think Balloon's mad – maybe I thocht sae my-sel' – but, by God, he's writing and printing pamphlets the now that are the talk o' the toon. Balloon's nae sheep-shank bane when it comes to turning out a reform pamphlet.'

'I'd a session wi' him once. I thocht him one o' the maist remarkable men I'd ever met wi'. Mind you: you couldna say he was normal – even allowing for a touch o' genius – but yet you couldna say he was mad either. . .'

'That's about it – a queer character wi' plenty o' brains and ideas and – poverty or no' poverty – plenty o' bluidy drive to get his road through — '

But just as they were settling down to a fruitful conversation, Bess Hyslop entered.

'Your pardon, sirs!'

'That's a' richt, Bess. You ken Mr Smellie here.'

'Mr Syme and Mr MacMurdo — '

'D'you mind, Willie, if we add to the company? They're twa guid fellows – and you've already met wi' John Syme.'

'Certainly, Robin, a bit o' Dumfries company's aey welcome.'

'Richt, Bess – show them in.'

Syme and MacMurdo were excited. Syme said:

'That's word just cam' through that the French Convention has proclaimed a Republic!'

'And King Louis?'

'Oh, he'll be for trial, I suppose.'

The excitement was immense. So that was how France was going! A Republic meant the end of the monarchy, meant an end of many things including the very concept of absolute monarchy.

MacMurdo ordered the drinks.

'No, no: allow me, Robert – and allow me, Mr Smellie.

This is an historic occasion! And we'll hae our host and hostess ben too. Damn it, the like o' this has never been afore!'

Smellie, behind the excitement, thought that the Bard wasn't so lonely in Dumfries after all. Men like Syme and MacMurdo; hosts like the Hyslops; gentry like the Park and Carse Riddells were not to be valued lightly. When he thought of all the folks, gentle and simple, that he'd met on this prolonged Dumfries holiday, he could not resist the conclusion that, outside of Edinburgh, the Bard couldn't have found a livelier town or more delightful company. It was amazing; but the Bard could draw the most gifted and the most diverse folk about him. And, damn it, the Globe was every bit as good as Dawney Douglas's. The Bard had a private room here to himself. He could sit and write in privacy; entertain a friend, male or female (Smellie knew nothing of Anna Park); or receive company like a bluidy lord. And, damn it: like a bluidy lord he received company. Proclaim a Republic in France! Huh: Robin Burns was President o' Dumfries from what he could see. By the Lord, he'd have something to report to the Crochallans when he got back. . .

They were still drinking bumpers to France and Liberty, Fraternity, Equality and Fox, Sheridan and Reform at home, and damnation to Dundas and perdition to Pitt when Maria Riddell's coachman arrived to announce that she waited with her husband for Smellie at the King's Arms.

It was decided that they would adjourn and drink a final bumper to France there.

Walter Riddell, though he drank to the French Republic, was ill-at-ease, Maria was gay and dominated the conversation. Walter wasn't so sure that he favoured a Republic in France – or anywhere else. But the county society in which he moved did: so he toed the line.

He had tried in vain to get Maria to stay at home. She was a good seven months pregnant and she was showing – not so much as Jean Burns was showing; but showing nevertheless. The Caledonian Hunt was due in October, and Maria had promised herself a round of the balls and assemblies – and the theatre which was due to open in a few days.

But Walter fumed and threatened in vain. Maria's mother was at Woodley Park in anticipation of the birth and he had to be careful.

For a moment Maria and the Bard were out of earshot in a corner.

'How's your wife, Robert? Am I showing badly?'

'Damn the fear. Mrs Burns is twice your size. When are you due?'

'The end of November.'

'Same as Mrs Burns. We've been at it thegither, Maria. No: you're no' showing onything worth. How are you feeling?'

'Glorious! The news is wonderful, Robert. I'm not going to deny myself anything. I'll have plenty to trouble about when I take to child-bed. Plenty – and I'm not looking forward to it. So let's drink, Robert – let's celebrate – and pay no attention to Walter: he thinks I should hide myself till it's all over. The flames of hell to that, Robert, and all this stuffy respectability! A new world has been born and women henceforth are going to take their place with men. But, my dear Robert! – and listen! you are my dear Robert! – I see eyes looking towards us. Let's join the company. We must have a tête à tête soon. I must have a farewell drink with wonderful erudite Willie Smellie. . .'

But Willie Smellie stood with the glass in his hand and listened to the flattery of Walter Riddell: Walter was trying to create an impression on his distinguished visitor. Smellie, as a rather overwhelmed guest, kept a check on his tongue, was polite and just a shade deferential. But there was little that missed his keenly-observant eye.

He got the Bard alone for a moment.

'Weel: I'll need to tak' this chance to say good-bye, Robin. I owe a lot to you and I want you to ken that I'm grateful.'

'Tuts, Willie — '

'Na, na, Robin. . . But if there's ocht I can do for you in the Toon yonder, just let me ken. And damnit! I ken you'll no' want to leave Dumfries – but dinna be ower lang till you pay us a' a visit at Crochallan.'

'Thanks, Willie . . . and you'll tell . . . that I was asking for their health?'

'I'll dae that. . . Man: it's a glorious town this. And you've the best o' company here. That MacMurdo's nae fool. . . Oh, and mind me to your Jean. She's the only thing I envy you, you beggar.'

Willie Smellie was driven away and then MacMurdo

mounted his beast and John Syme and he lingered over the remains of the bottle.

'I'll need to be pushing away home to Ryedale, Robert. . . What a night – a glorious, memorable night. . . I've a queer feeling that something's about to happen to me. I dinna ken what. Just something extraordinary – in keeping wi' the momentous days we're living through. . . Ever felt anything like that, Robin?'

'Many a time, John: at least I've an idea what you're feeling like . . .'

The Bard saw Syme to the bridge, where they said good-night.

Aye, aye: that was Willie Smellie away, and, truth to tell, there wasn't his equal about Dumfries. And what they would never understand was that Smellie had gone among them at half-cock. Had Smellie opened out as he was accustomed to do at Crochallan – or in his own counting-house – Dumfries would have had her eyes opened.

Aye, aye: Willie Smellie and the arrest of the French King. There were no two ways about it: it was a great and glorious time in which to be living. As John MacMurdo had said – days to be remembered with ever-glowing tribute to the end of time.

Assuming the truth of Genesis – at least the poetic truth of it. . . There was first the Creation. Then there was the Garden of Eden and the Fall. And then there was the French Revolution and the beginning of the return to the social and political Eden . . . the Eden whose rosy dawn was already glowing across the Channel from the east. . .

THE HUNT AT PLAY

But rosy dawn or grey daylight the world wagged away.

Maria Riddell's first-born went down with smallpox, much to Maria's disappointment.

On the 29th of September the theatre opened with a flourish of trumpets under the management of John B. Williamson of the Theatre Royal, Haymarket, London, assisted by George Scott Sutherland from the Aberdeen Theatre, supported by a numerous and distinguished company whose leading lady was none other than the charming and accomplished Louise Fontenelle.

For a long month, ending only with a tremendous Ball on the 30th October, the Gentlemen of the Caledonian Hunt (to whom the Bard had dedicated his Edinburgh volume) galloped through the town and the county committing every excess known to man and woman – and not a few that seemed to be new-forged from the nether regions.

The town was filled with pimps and bawds and all manner of gentlemanly and gentlewomanly flunkeys – dressmakers, wig-curlers, chamber-maids, valets, coachmen, linkboys and Lord knows what.

To say that they rioted to excess is to be guilty of understatement. It was not only that the town was sympathetic to the Reform Movement and its ideals: douce, decent folk without a thought of reform in their canny skulls and stagnant hearts were outraged and disgusted.

The shopkeepers and merchants were, of course, delighted: money flowed like water. Even the company at the playhouse – though many of their best performances were nightly ruined by the unspeakable horseplay of the young bloods – watched twenty to thirty pounds of money turned away each night for want of room. Their salaries were secured and there was every prospect of a substantial bonus.

But there was disgust for all that. The Bard watched on the fringe with mounting anger. He said to Syme:

'That's no' the Caledonian Hunt I kenned in Embro: I canna see that men like Glencairn would hae tolerated such enormities frae ony member o' the Hunt. Mind you: it's garrin' the folk think, John. Garrin' them look across the Channel; and think – and think hard. Did you ever see such druckenness in men and women supposed to be ladies and gentlemen? Did you ever see such monstrous immorality – just dirty open drucken fornication – hures wad hae mair modesty – mair respect for their bodies — '

'Aye . . . I saw a young lass, braw in her silken gown and sparkling wi' jewels, hanging onto the back wheel o' a carriage outside the Assembly. Her breasts were bare to the winds o' heaven and she was retching her pretty guts out; and her consort was in no better condition . . .'

'And that's nothing, John, to what's been goin' on in every quarter o' the toon. By God! puir folk maun be wretches . . .'

And then at long last Stephen Clarke, the organist and musical assistant-editor to Johnson's *Museum*, arrived in Dumfries on his way to give a few weeks' music lessons to the young ladies of John MacMurdo at Drumlanrig, and to the Miller girls at Dalswinton.

Clarke stretched out his long legs in the Stinking Vennel – where he paid his respects to Jean and noted down a couple of songs from her singing (he also marvelled at her rendering of *Jamie, Come Try Me*) – and then he stretched his legs in the snug of the Globe tavern.

'You're a lang, lazy beggar, Stephen! A' the same, I'm glad to see you.'

'I'm aey glad to see you, Robin. You'll die one of thae days from gross over-work. Where the hell d'you get all the energy?'

'Somebody's got to hae energy. We dinna a' earn our money as easy as you do.'

'You ken nothing about it, my dear fellow. How would you like to teach – try to teach! – those big gallumping girls music – with fingers like mealy puddings? Think that's easy? Standing over them and the sweat from their oxters would shame a skunk!'

'That would put you off making love to them!'

'Love – puff! I give it up, Robin! I never have been able to understand this passion of love. If you saw these young ladies – and not so young ladies – as I see them . . .'

'But then I dinna, Stephen. And I *choose* my women.'

'Well . . . maybe there's something I've missed.'

'I assure you MacMurdo's daughters are different.'

'Have you got your eye on one of them?'

'Well – not in that sense, Stephen – though gin I didna ken and respect their worthy father as one of my best friends. . . There's Philadelphia yonder —'

'Dinna tell me there's one named Philadelphia?'

'I admit, Stephen, it's a bit o' a mouthfu' —'

'Good God! Even that's beyond your apparently unlimited range o' rhyming —'

'Och – they ca' her Philly.'

'Thank the Lord for that! No: I couldn't get round to Miss Philadelphia — '

'You see, Stephen: between you and me and the wa', her father's a great republican – Philadelphia's in honour o' George Washington — '

'Well, God knows, Robin, I'm a bit of a republican – ye ken at least how I stand wi' him ower the water and I stand down to no man in respect of my veneration for George Washington. But had I thousand daughters and was at a loss for a name, I should never think of Philadelphia.'

'Richt then, damn you! Now listen, Stephen: I'm serious. I want to see as much o' you as I can. I've a wheen o' sangs I want you to go over wi' me. I'll meet you by arrangement at Brownhill Inn. . . I'll even come to Thornhill — '

'Yes, Robin, and I'll come to Dumfries. After Auld Reekie and the dull dogs I meet in wi' there every day, you're a different world, a different climate. . . You're an inspiration, Robin. I've told Johnson a hundred times if you could only play with your fingers a little o' the music that's inside you, you'd be the greatest instrumentalist in Scotland. And yet, God knows, in your own way you're musician for any ten of us.'

'You ken better than try your flattery on me!'

'I'm no' flatterin', Robin. Damnit, why can't you realise the full nature of your unique gifts? Where would Scottish song be without you – where would it be tomorrow or the next day but for the work you've done and are still doing? Damnit, Jamie Johnson was run dry before he met in wi' you – dry as – a — '

'Drunk man's drouth?'

'Exactly! There would never have been a second volume of the *Museum* but for you – and we're now in our *fifth*!'

'All right, all right! I can gather tunes and cobble words for them – but I need you to set them out and Johnson to print. We're in it thegither, Stephen – but let's drink to Jamie Johnson who thought out the plan in the first instance.'

'Yes, I'll drink a dozen bumpers to Jamie Johnson – but I'll drink a bumper more to you who has given his collection distinction – glorious, immortal distinction. . .'

By November the 7th, Collector John Mitchell's wife, Anne, died in her fifty-eighth year, and the Bard who thought highly of her quiet self-effacing disposition was a mourner at her grave-side in St Michael's Kirk-yard.

But by now the Bard was getting used to life's mortality: births and deaths came heads and thraws. Old familiar faces were every other day passing away – younger folks were bringing new lives into the world as had been the way of the world from immemorial time.

And despite births and deaths (and his own Jean was coming near her time), the larger affairs of men and of state pursued their steady course. It seemed almost that the larger affairs of men – in politics, religion, law, literature and the mundane arrangement of day-to-day affairs – proceeded on a rhythm independent of and regardless of the triumphs and tragedies of the domestic fireside.

And so when a certain ardent reformer, Captain William Johnson, sent out his prospectus for the *Edinburgh Gazetteer*, the Bard wrote him in the following terms:

I have just read your Prospectus of the *Edinburgh Gazetteer*. If you go on in your Paper with the same spirit, it will, beyond all comparison, be the first Composition of the kind in Europe. I beg leave to insert my name as a Subscriber; & if you have already published any papers, please send me them from the beginning. Point out your own way of settling payments in this place, or I shall settle with you through the medium of my friend, Peter Hill, Bookseller in Edinburgh.

Go on, Sir! Lay bare, with undaunted heart & steady hand, that horrid mass of corruption called Politics & State-Craft! Dare to draw in their native colours these calm, thinking villains whom no faith can fix whatever be the Shibboleth of their pretended Party.

Even Collector Mitchell and Supervisor Findlater subscribed – though they did not write incriminating letters. Many others in Dumfries did likewise.

THE MAJESTY OF WOMAN

On the 21st of November, the Bard was overjoyed when Jean was delivered of a fine baby girl. In honour of his long friendship with the Carse Riddells, she was named Elizabeth Riddell.

He did not consider it any anomaly that he was now the father of three daughters – all Elizabeths: 'Dear Bought Bess' (who was still at Mossgiel), Betty (Park) and now Elizabeth Riddell.

Jean had borne him three daughters; but they had all died. Both of them prayed fervently that Elizabeth Riddell would survive. There did not seem any reason why she shouldn't.

Two days later Maria Riddell was brought to bed and delivered of a daughter christened Sophia, in honour of whom the Bard never knew.

But the fact that the births were so close to each other somehow made the Bard feel closer to Maria.

The Royal Theatre was situated half-way down Shakespeare Street and, being built in a green field, there was ample room behind it for the parking of carriages.

A fine theatre it was with boxes and a grand circle for the gentry, and a well-raked pit for the groundlings. Even the scenery (from the brush of Nasmyth) was in every way elegant and abreast of the most daring innovations in stage decoration.

The Bard was in high spirits when on November 26th, he came to hear Miss Fontenelle in *The Country Girl*.

But he was in higher spirits still when Miss Fontenelle, at the close of *The Country Girl*, stepped forward to the footlights and, before the assembled company, read his occasional address on *The Rights of Woman*.

And Louise Fontenelle spoke his lines with rare effect:

> While Europe's eye is fix'd on mighty things,
> The fate of empires and the fall of kings;
> While quacks of State must each produce his plan,
> And even children lisp the Rights of Man;

110

Amid this mighty fuss just let me mention,
The Rights of Woman merit some attention.

First, in the sexes' intermix'd connexion
One sacred Right of Woman is Protection:
The tender flower, that lifts its head elate,
Helpless must fall before the blasts of fate,
Sunk on the earth, defac'd its lovely form,
Unless your shelter ward th' impending storm.

Our second Right – but needless here is caution –
To keep that right inviolate's the fashion:
Each man of sense has it so full before him,
He'd die before he'd wrong it – 'tis Decorum!
There was, indeed, in far less polish'd days,
A time, when rough rude Man had naughty ways:
Would swagger, swear, get drunk, kick up a riot,
Nay, even thus invade a lady's quiet!
Now, thank our stars! these Gothic times are fled;
Now, well-bred men – and you are all well-bred –
Most justly think (and we are much the gainers)
Such conduct neither spirit, wit, nor manners.

For Right the third, our last, our best, our dearest:
That right to fluttering female hearts the nearest,
Which even the Rights of Kings, in low prostration,
Most humbly own — 'tis dear, dear Admiration!
In that blest sphere alone we live and move;
There taste that life of life – Immortal Love.
Smiles, glances, sighs, tears, fits, flirtations, airs –
'Gainst such an host what flinty savage dares?
When awful Beauty joins with all her charms,
Who is so rash as rise in rebel arms?

But truce with kings, and truce with constitutions,
With bloody armaments and revolutions;
Let Majesty your first attention summon:
Ah! ça ira! the Majesty of Woman!

The Address was very well received in the boxes and the circle. The gentry thought it witty and cleverly turned.

But the elements in the pit, where the Bard sat, were more demonstrative.

111

Miss Fontenelle curtsied her respectful acknowledgements and the pit took up the Bard's name in enthusiastic acclamation.

The orchestra (such as it was) played *God Save the King*. But as had happened on several occasions lately, the pit would have none of it, and there were loud and repeated calls for the French revolutionary song *Ca Ira*. In no time the theatre was in a pandemonium of boos, cat-calls, huzzas, slogan-shouting, threats and curses.

The Bard, with his hat clamped tightly on his head, sat with folded arms and said nothing. . . But the fact that he did so didn't pass unnoticed by many of the gentry in boxes and circle. Nor were there wanting Government spies to take a note of the evening's proceedings.

Such demonstrations were becoming a feature of the theatre; and any play which contained any favourable reference to freedom or liberty was strongly in request, and favourite passages were cheered to the echo and far beyond the artistic merit of the content. William Sutherland did not dare to ignore the feeling that flowed so strongly in favour of reform and the French. His company was of the opinion that the world was being born anew and that they would benefit in the process.

FRIENDS OF THE PEOPLE

But another gloomy December was gathering about the Bard's head. Not that he felt gloomy as the month opened. Births and deaths and occasional theatrical address apart — work had to go on.

He completed his last batch of proofs for his second Edinburgh edition and despatched them to Alexander Fraser Tytler for scrutiny. This was a load off his mind — and another milestone in his literary career.

And since it was December and since he was writing to Edinburgh, he thought much of his final farewell from Clarinda a short twelvemonth ago. He was still forbidden to write to her; but he wrote to Mary Peacock instead, hungrily seeking for information. And he noted too, with a grim satisfaction, that Clarinda's cousin and guardian — the strait-laced William Craig — had been made a Lord of the Session in succession to Lord Hailes, and that he had taken the title of Lord Craig. If Nancy had waited, maybe his Lordship would have seen his way to increase her allowance.

But things were moving in Edinburgh these days. Events had moved swiftly since his last visit.

The First General Convention of the Friends of the People was being held there. Dumfries was not represented by a formal delegation. But they had secured a courier-observer and news of the Convention's activities was feverishly awaited. There was the feeling that anything could happen now and that something spectacular must happen.

Not that there was any remote possibility of revolution. Indeed few envisaged anything so drastic. True enough, there were groups of revolutionaries. There were men who believed that no reform, however drastic, could do more than patch up the constitution – men who doubted that the government of Pitt and Burke and the dictatorship of Henry Dundas would allow any measure of reform to reach the Statute Book. They laughed to bitter scorn the idea that a totally undemocratic and unrepresentative parliament could ever usher in the Golden Age by way of legislation.

As Secretary of State, Henry Dundas was the most powerful man behind Pitt. As the Dictator of Scotland he had no rival. Not only was his nephew, Robert Dundas, the Scottish Lord Advocate; but every high office was held by Dundas's favour and most of the smaller offices were held by the willing tools of the Dundas interest. He had spies everywhere. Whatever might conceivably happen to England and to the Pitt administration, Dundas had made certain that no faction could weaken his hold on Scotland.

But the reformers were optimistic – and they were bitterly opposed to the revolutionaries. The Friends of the People sought to overthrow or overturn precisely nothing. They merely urged that parliament be induced, by reasonable persuasion, to introduce some much-needed reform in order to preserve and strengthen the constitution. The Friends of the People were anxious – some thought over-anxious – to proclaim and, if necessary, to demonstrate their loyalty to King and Constitution.

The Bard, as usual, saw both sides of the argument. One part of him was all for revolution, for making a clean sweep, for ringing up the curtain on the Golden Age that was already mustering in the wings. He too doubted and had cause to doubt the good faith of those forces gathered behind Pitt and Dundas. Liberty, in the end, would have to be fought for — why not fight for it now?

But the other side of him was more cautious. The Reform Movement was led by some very respectable men: Lord Daer, Norman MacLeod the M.P. for Inverness, Thomas Muir of Huntershill. . . These were men of integrity and worth. It was inconceivable that such leading men, backed by a formidable body of honest gentlemen and citizens of worth, could be ignored and brushed aside as a rabble of treasonable elements.

No, no: something positive was bound to follow the Convention's demands. And to refuse such demands would turn the country upside down.

The First General Convention of the delegates from the Society of the Friends of the People throughout Scotland met in Lawrie's rooms at St James's Court, Edinburgh, on December 11th, 12th and 13th.

The assembled delegates numbered upwards of some 160: they represented over eighty societies who, in turn, represented some forty towns and villages situated, for the most part, in the manufacturing district bounded by Edinburgh in the east, Glasgow in the west, and on the north by Dundee.

Mr Hugh Bell was in the chair; Thomas Muir of Huntershill, an advocate, who was born and brought up near Glasgow, was Vice-President; and William Skirving was the Secretary.

Thomas Muir gave every indication of being a successful lawyer. In his late twenties, he had everything before him. But Muir was an idealist. Christianity was no cloak of hypocrisy for him. He believed his Bible. Christianity was something to be practised daily and every hour of the day. His eldership of the Kirk of Scotland was the genuine earnest of his belief.

And so inevitably, as a practising Christian, Muir was also a sincere reformer. In politics he could do no other than equate the Bible with liberty, fraternity and equality. In terms of practical politics he was prepared to compromise on the platform for universal suffrage and annual parliaments.

To Muir the French Revolution represented the greatest advance of Christ's Kingdom on earth since the birth of the Saviour. But Muir was idealistic. He was no revolutionary, though he was prepared to give his life for his reform principles. He could not envisage the possibility that the appeal to the reason and the heart of men could prove abortive.

And so, consumed with idealistic fire and fervour, Muir spoke like a man inspired. He fired the majority of his listeners. He matched the hour with his eloquence and his sincerity and, conscious of the support he got from his fellow-reformers, he was anxious to extend his appeal to the people of Scotland.

It was necessary to lay the facts before the people, to list the steps towards Reform and the people would raise their voices in unison. Against the voice of the people, what could prevail? Certainly neither Pitt nor Dundas.

Pale-faced, thin-lipped, pointed-nosed, Muir ferreted into the attack without fear for his faith was unshakable. Men listened to him with respect and with something of a sub-conscious fear. Dimly they recognised the idealist-type destined to be broken on the rough and unrelenting rock of reality and yet respecting, even revering his type as being beyond the corruptions of the eternal compromise with life and society.

Muir was brief and to the point and moved immediately that the delegates show their credentials. Skirving read these letters and it was remarkable to note that the phraseology of the French Revolution had been adopted by many of the societies giving the credentials of their delegates by opening their address as: Citizen President.

Lord Daer, eldest son of the Earl of Selkirk, whom Burns had met in the house of Dugald Stewart in Catrine in his Machlin days, rose immediately after the delegates had con-firmed their credentials and moved that there was no occa-sion for a formal election of office-bearers; that though there ought indeed to be some person in the chair whom the speakers might address, there was no occasion for a President or a Vice-President; or indeed any office-bearers. They were all met on the great principles of liberty and political equality, and therefore they ought to be jealous of all men set up in permanent positions. He therefore moved that there should be no regular office-bearers or leaders; that it was proper indeed, while the Ministry had their eye upon those whom they considered the leaders, to divide the responsibility among many, and that, at all events, every appearance of establishing an aristocracy amongst them ought to be guarded against.

Muir, of course, was quickly to the rescue and observed that no confidence ought to be placed in any man but the Convention should keep constantly in view their principles of liberty, political equality and eternal justice. He moved, and succeeded in his motion, that daily election of office-bearers should take place.

Lord Daer had paid frequent visits to France for many years. He had been in Paris when the Revolution began and he was enthusiastic for the principles of reform.

All in all, it was a most remarkable Convention; and it was clear before they had been in session many hours that the outstanding personalities dominating the scene were Thomas Muir, the Reverend Thomas Palmer from Forfar, William Skirving and Captain Johnson, the editor and owner of the *Edinburgh Gazetteer*.

Colonel Dalrymple was a forceful speaker and a man very much concerned that the Convention should in no way allow any extremism of phraseology to lead them into conflict with authority.

The sittings of the Convention were characterised by the extreme outspokenness and forthrightness of delegates from country societies. There was no attention paid to a man because of his rank or his alleged authority. Tailors and cobblers were listened to, and spoke with as much authority as the more middle-class members. But always it was Muir who came upon the scene and rose to speak with decision and authority.

By Wednesday evening the Convention had agreed on many resolutions. It was resolved, for example, that the thanks of the Convention be returned to Messrs. Gray, Erskine, the Earl of Lauderdale, Colonel MacLeod, Lord Daer and Colonel Dalrymple for their patriotic services to the cause of the people; to J. H. Tooke, Esquire, for his masterly support of freedom; to the Hon. Major Maitland, Mr Sheridan, Mr Muir, Mr Bell and Captain Johnson for their important assistance to overturn corruption; also to the Rt Hon Charles Fox for his determined speech in the last meeting of the Whig Club; and lastly to all those members of the House of Commons who had supported the cause of the people.

It was also agreed, on Captain Johnson's motion, that it be recommended to each society of the Friends of the People to expunge from the roll of its members the name or names of

116

any individual or individuals who may have acted illegally, tumultuously, or in any way to the disturbance of the public peace; and that any individual or individuals of the societies of the Friends of the People whose conduct may have been legal and orderly but who may be prosecuted by the arm of power for adhering to the cause of the people be defended by the united strength of the Friends of the People . . .

But the great decision which concerned the Convention was the form of the petition to be presented in the House of Commons and taken up there by Mr Gray. There was keen debate about this, and Palmer especially was quick to point out and keep pointing out that it was useless for the Convention not to proceed with the petition as undoubtedly the people were looking for action and would be discouraged by any delay. But, of course, Muir pointed out that it would be much better to await what the London Friends of the People decided upon so that the motion could go forward jointly, be much stronger and unite the nation in the principles of reform. He pointed out that it had not yet been decided by the London Friends of the People whether parliaments should be yearly or three-yearly.

The arguments really revolved round this vital point. The petition was to deal with two main items – annual or triennial parliaments and the right of every man to have a vote at the age of twenty-one.

The emotional peak of the Convention came at its climax. Here Robert Fowler rose and moved that: 'the Convention and all present should rise and take the French oath to live free or die.' As a man, the Convention rose and each man, holding up his right hand, repeated: 'to live free, or die.' When some of them sat down, they were on their feet immediately to a tremendous wave of applause.

But when the storm died, Colonel Dalrymple rose and said that though he was delighted with the spirit of freedom which pervaded all present, yet he must beg leave to caution them against yielding too much to enthusiasm, for they stood on perilous ground and must take care to give their enemies no ground against them. The oath, or rather vow, just made was of course harmless, yet it might be magnified by their enemies as sowing the seeds of sedition. He therefore hoped that no notice would be taken of it in their minutes or in their newspapers.

Fowler acknowledged the justice of this in the sense of the Colonel's remarks, and indicated that he meant no more by the motion than simply to impress upon the minds of all present uniformity and steadiness in the cause of freedom.

At this, there were more scenes of enthusiastic applause and, with men shaking each other by the hand and swearing eternal vigilance and fidelity to their principles, the meeting broke up, agreeing that they would meet again in May, unless some extraordinary business rendered it necessary to meet and call another Convention.

Going home, Muir said to William Skirving: 'The great work the Convention has achieved is the clearing of the air. Delegates were all agreed on general principles; but you saw what confusion there was about particular action. Above all we need clarity of aim and unity of effort. We must have pamphlets. We must have discussion and education in Reform principles. . . And out from the dedicated groups must go forth the appeal to the people. We must work hard, my friend; and we must be vigilant to guard the purity of our ideals against any contamination of violence . . .

'I look upon you, Citizen Skirving, as one of the foundation pillars of our movement – and of the new Scotland we are bringing to birth . . .'

Skirving, who was as robust as Muir was frail, held out a firm hand.

'We'll shake on that, Citizen Muir. I kenna where the road on which we hae set our feet may lead; but you can depend on me, while there's life in my body, no' to fall by the wayside. Wherever you care to lead, I'll follow aye, even to the scaffold!'

FRANCES ANNA DUNLOP

By the middle of the month the Bard paid a visit to Mossgiel and took time to spend a few days with Mrs Dunlop of Dunlop at Dunlop House which lay a little beyond Kilmarnock and near Stewarton.

Next to her God and her numerous family, there was no one Mrs Dunlop revered more than Robert Burns. Indeed some members of her family considered that Robert Burns occupied a place in her affection and admiration dangerously bordering on the morbid.

True enough, Frances Anna Dunlop was no maiden. She was in her sixty-second year and she had borne thirteen children. And although by birth and upbringing she was very much the lady of quality, fate had dealt her some hard blows, and the old Scots tradition, which was basically democratic, was strong in her.

She could be tedious and opinionated, dour and headstrong. She had written him many long rambling badly-spelled and unpunctuated and non-paragraphed letters.

But, as far as the Bard was concerned, her heart was in the right place. Of all his patrons, she had been the most consistently kind. Her interest in his welfare had been deep and genuine. She had worried about Ellisland; she had worried about his position in the Excise and had exerted herself to do what she could for him; she had worried about Jean and his children. She had sent him presents and an occasional (and welcome) five pound note.

And Mrs Dunlop had seen the best of her days and she was far from rich. True, she was often officious and nearly always somewhat tedious and prolix. But the Bard well knew her worth and his admiration (and something of affection) for her was genuine.

The evening meal over, she took him ben to her bedroom-spence, where a coal fire glowed on the hearth.

'Sit ye doon, Robert, and mak' yoursel' comfortable. Noo there's a drap o' whisky for ye – and I'm told it's the verra best. Fernitosh – ye've praised it yoursel' . . .

'And noo . . . I maun hae a' your confidential news – noo that at long last I've gotten you to mysel'.

'And your Jean's weel and gotten ower her confinement? A healthy lass, aye, and a real bonnie one. I was taken wi' her that time I saw her in Machlin. Up in three days was she? 'Course, she could owerdae that. Oh! I was gey brave mysel' – but I've aey insisted that my ain lassies tak' ten days at the verra least. Aye: I ken puir folks canna lie i' their beds a' that time unless they just canna steer. I see, I see: the wee lass is ca'd after Mistress Riddell o' Glenriddell – and they're related to the Fergussons o' Craigdarroch – oh, *and* the Lauries o' Maxwelton. A' connected through each ither! Oh then: the lass is weel named . . .

119

'No: ye havena been idle. An' you've gotten awa' your second Edinburgh edition, hae ye? And you're still writing sangs for Mr Johnson's *Museum*: just that noo ...

'And anither ane? Thomson, ye say? Fegs but your quill maun be scartin' the quires thae days!

'I'm real sorry that you're no' feeling sae weel. Thae chills and fevers that ye seem to catch back and forward maun tak' it oot o' ye ...

'You dinna think, Burns, that maybe you drink ower hard whiles? Baith you and Doctor Adair were gey fu' last nicht – though that was the wine. No: I'm no' trying to admonish you. Only I aey advise moderation.

'I'm far frae feeling weel mysel', Robert – I think I've a kind o' gout or jaundice working on me — But it's a real tonic having you here. And my cousin and your auld frien' Adair's company for you too. To listen to Rachel and Keith and you a' laughing and bantering ... it's a grand tonic.'

The pair of them conversed easily and naturally round the fireside. With the aid of a jug of hot water and a lump of sugar, the Bard had converted his whisky to a toddy and he sipped it with quiet enjoyment.

He let Mrs Dunlop do most of the talking and he allowed her to direct the conversation as she pleased. He didn't always answer her with too much truth and sometimes he turned the corner of an awkward question more adroitly than he might; but he never deceived her. After all, there were many things that did not concern her – and there were certain indelicacies that had to be avoided.

Yet he marvelled that her mind was so clear and her tongue so brisk. He watched her pale eyes and noted a yellowish tinge in the whites. He noted the scrawny neck, the fine lines round her mouth, the absent teeth, the thin much-greyed hair, the bulging marble-white forehead; the white, blue-veined knotted hands. . . She was getting on in years and the traces of physical decay were heavy on her. But her mind and her ' spirit showed little sign of diminishing power – either that or she must have been a truly remarkable woman in her prime.

And, of course, she was full of news of her family and of her two daughters who had married French refugees.

Surprisingly enough, he found her somewhat tepid about reform – and the news from France filled her more with fear than anticipation.

'Maybe I'm ower auld for reforms and the like. I greatly distrust a' thae new-fangled innovations, Robert. But I ken ine that you're fu' o' them.

'I suppose I'm a kin' o' a Jacobite. I've little time for the Hanoverians. Yet gin the Jacobites had gotten power, we'd hae had a' the trouble o' the Reformation ower again. At least he German lairdies are sworn to defend the Faith – and sae we maun be thankfu' . . .

'Ye ken that I read Thomas Paine – maist assiduously. I ken you're a' for Paine – and for reasons o' the highest principle. But I fear, Burns, that writings like Paine's will end up undermining the constitution. And I canna be expected to look on that as a guid thing . . .'

'Madam,' said the Bard, 'you will allow that we may differ on this point and on that and still be good friends. The situation that confronts us to-day is more complex than we have ever faced in our history. Yet the issue is simple. Either we are for reform and all that it means: or we are against it. . .

'That's how simple the situation is – and how complex. For, as I see it, brother may yet be divided against brother, sister against sister, father against son, and husband against wife . . . and friend against friend. Yes: just on this verra issue. Simple as the issue is, yet it is fundamental. And, as man must choose, so the nation may well be divided against itself . . .

'I hope it doesna come to this. I hope mankind in so far as Britain is concerned may resolve its differences in peace and social harmony. But in the beginning maybe – as certainly in the end – there can be no compromise. . . Not wi' the fundamental principles that stretch up and down the length and breadth o' human society . . .

'You will pardon me, Madam, that I strive to make myself plain and unambiguous. . . Therefore, though I truly sympathise with those innocent parties who have suffered in the French Revolution, nevertheless I must support the Revolution principles. . . Surely you'll agree, Madam, that the long-suffering cruelly-oppressed French people are entitled to their freedom, their liberty, their equality?'

'You wad convince me wi' the eloquence o' your tongue – gin I werena sae auld. There maun aey be a man, vested wi' the po'er o' a' guid men, to haud a nation thegither. I mean a king – or the like. . . Your French, like your Reformers, are governed by a levelling principle that's clean contrary to the law o' nature. Nature gave a few the right to govern the many, and a society that left the government of the elect few to the whim o' the many – including the rabble – wadna be worth the name o' government.'

'True, Madam, we must guard against the excesses, the blind, unthinking excesses of the rabble. But there is rabble at both ends of society. When the Caledonian Hunt and its hangers-on were lately in Dumfries, there was much rabble among them; and a disgusting and shocking rabble they were. There can be no place in decent society for either the poor rabble or the rich rabble – though the rich are more blameworthy. . .

'But I didna come to Dunlop House to threip my politics down your throat. . . You should try to understand – and I ken you do understand – what lies behind the spirit of the Edinburgh Convention o' the Friends o' the People. . . '

'My dear Burns, your eloquence could mak' murder look like a kindness. And I'm no' too auld to see the drift o things – though nae doubt I'm ower auld to agitate mysel' about things that, for me onyway, are o' sma' consequence. And twa-three bits o' reform here and there's no' gaun to mak' a deal o' difference. But we micht hae to go to war ower France – and that's nae licht thing.'

'No licht thing, Madam, as you well say. But only the evil o' politicians could put us to war wi' France – and it'll be far frae a popular war. In fact it's just the kind o' war that could verra easily turn into a civil war — '

'Burns, you'll need to put a bridle on your tongue! Politics, like drink, should be taken in strict moderation. Excess in either gangs to the head and results in irresponsibility, violence and a' the evils of unreason.'

Mrs Dunlop argued her case well. Though the Bard could easily have demolished her arguments, he did no more than state his case with reserve and in almost extreme moderation. He felt somehow that if ever the issue came to a decisive head, Frances Anna Dunlop would not be wholly on the side of the aristocrats.

Jean said: 'And how did you find a'bodies about Dunlop?
How's the mistress hersel'?'

'No' verra weel, to tell the truth. She's gotten a kind o'
gout complaint. She was bed-ridden the morning I left. And
I havena been weel myself, Jean. Oh, just one o' my toits:
kind o' fainting turns and my heart no' as steady as I wad
like it.'

'Aye: I saw you werena ower bright. You'll gang straight
to your bed after supper. I'll mak' a guid hot toddy for you.
Noo, noo: the news about the Globe can wait till the morn.
How are a' the folks at Mossgiel – did you see Adam and
Fanny . . .? No: there's nothing fresh here, and you can see
that the bairns are a' richt — But we've missed you, Rab . . .
God! you'll need to tak' care o' yoursel'; for if ocht happened
to you . . .'

It was pleasant to be back home – even to the Stinking
Vennel. Dunlop House stood in quiet caressing policies: very
calm, very dignified. The rooms very big and airy. There
were carpets on the floor and many of the chairs were up-
holstered in brocades. . . There was a great dining-room
table, much silver-ware and fine china.

But it was grand to be back with Jean and the bairns in a
small but cosy enough room and his own bits of sticks of
furniture. And Jean made the house – filled it with the
tremendous warmth of her domestic being.

He was not in any way decrying his most pleasant visit to
Dunlop House. It had been grand to be away from the
treadmill of duty; it had been strangely pleasant to walk
freely about large and spacious rooms which were still un-
crowded with a dozen people in them; it was even pleasant
to sink into a large warmed feather bed and to have hot water
and warmed towels brought to the bedroom in the morning.
Fine, too, to have company, elegance and fine conversation
round the breakfast table, with a meal that lingered on as if
eternity itself had to be wiled away; and there was no
tyranny in the great brass-faced grandfather clock. . . The
sum total of all this had constituted a glorious holiday and

added a new comfort and a new grace to the refinement of living.

And yet the Stinking Vennel, for all its mortifying and humiliating inconveniences, was superior to it. But maybe only because of Jean and the bairns – because it was his home

If he fell heir to Dunlop House and the wherewithal to support it, he would have to decline it.

Aye: he was desperate to get away from the vennel desperate to get into another house that would give him a front door and a back; bigger rooms and at least two more But if he got that he would be content for the rest of his days.

There was nothing he envied the rich, or near rich, but the measure of the wealth that conditioned their independence. . .

'Aye, aye: you've got to get awa' frae hame now and again to appreciate it. Damn it, we think we're in a queer habble here whiles – but we could be waur, lass. Oh, you ken fine I'm aey at Captain Hamilton for another house —'

'But you wadna like to bide in Dunlop House?'

'You're a witch to ken what I'm thinking – but then you aey ken what I'm thinking. . . I'm feeling better already. All right now: dinna worry. I'll gang to my bed and sip a glass o' toddy. But I'm telling you I'm better already. Gin the morn I'll be mysel'. . . If you put the pan in the bed I'll tak' Robbie here in his reading. . . And by the way, Jean, I'll hae my toddy frae this whigmaleerie cup – it's a coconut – that Mrs Dunlop presented me wi'. . .'

But, the next day, the blow fell. The Excise Board determined to conduct an enquiry into the Bard's loyalty.

Spies had been at work. There had been reports concerning his conduct at the theatre: of toasts and slogans uttered in the King's, the George and the Globe and at private dinners: of his association with undesirable elements . . .

But for Graham of Fintry, things might have been disastrous. As it was, they were disastrous enough.

Collector Mitchell and Supervisor Findlater were the first to confer in Dumfries. Mitchell was grave:

'Collector-General Willie Corbet is coming down to Dumfries to conduct an enquiry into Burns's loyalty.'

'No!'

'It'll no' do us any good if he's found to be disaffected.'

'Who the hell's been spying?'

'Who's no' a spy or informer nowadays, Alex? Has the Bard been up to anything byornar?'

'No. . . I think I wad hae heard. . . You ken where his sympathies lie?'

'We're a' in' the same boat as far as sympathy goes. But our mouths are shut: our lips sealed. I ken there's juist naebody could seal the Bard's. He's gotten nae understandin' o' his danger —'

'I wouldna say that, John – but he's sae bluidy headstrong.'

'Listen: find out what you can – discreetly. It's worth my job *and yours* to let the cat out o' the bag – but we'll need to keep ourselves richt – and warn the Bard what's coming.'

'Is that safe?'

'We canna throw him to the wolves, can we? Besides if Burns is found guilty *we'll* come under suspicion – aye, for harbouring him: for no' putting in a report.'

'I see that. To hell: this witch-hunting's goin' a bit ower far. Damnit, a' the maist intelligent folk are for reform.'

'This'll scare them. And remember we're in the Service and we'll need to go wi' the government.'

'Definitely.'

'Ye ken what this can mean to Burns?'

'Botany Bay?'

'Aye: Botany Bay – and a lang spell i' the hulks first. Now mind ye, Alex: this is no joke. I want your solemn word that you're wi' me here. We've everything to lose if we mak' a wrang move.'

'Listen, Robert: this is official and unofficial and I've nae time to lose. The Excise Board hae decided on an on-the-spot enquiry into your loyalty. Not a word! I'll dae what I can to help you. But you'll need to mak' a clean breast o' things to me. What hae you been up to?'

The Bard was shocked: he showed a trace of fear-pallor.

'What hae I been up to?'

'I want nae evasions: this is serious.'

'By God! it's serious. I've been up to nothing. I've expressed an opinion back and forwards —'

'Where?'

'Where? That's difficult to say exactly.'

'You were shouting for Ca Ira in the theatre!'

'No' me.'

'You were wi' them that did?'

'You canna choose your company in the pit o' the theatre
.. Gin it were a box — '

'Damn it, Burns, you're in a fell spot. You ken this can
mean Botany Bay for you?'

'Botany Bay – for me'?

'Aye: bluidy quick. Noo: shake yourself. I'll be cross
questioned anent your conduct, and I'll no' be able to equi
vocate. You've nae idea what an examination like this can be
This may only be a preliminary – juist the first round. Now
I'm asking you as a friend – and I am your friend as well as
your superior: hae you joined ony o' thae societies?'

'No!'

'Or written them ony letters?'

'No!'

'Weel . . . what in God's name hae you been up to? There're
spies everywhere – you ken that?'

'Well, I did and I didna. I never thocht there was onybody
spying on me.'

'Well: that was damned silly o' ye! Damnit, you're no
only an Exciseman – you're Scotland's Bard. The idlest word
fa'in' frae your lips has weight – comin' frae you. . . No
you're nae simple gauger: you're Robert Burns – worse luck
for you. A common gauger micht get away wi' a lot – you
can get away wi' nothing!'

'Well . . . I micht hae been indiscreet on an occasion –
maybe wi' a drink in me. . . You ken how it is?'

'No: I dinna ken how it is. How indiscreet hae you
been?'

'How indiscreet am I supposed to hae been?'

'That's what the Board will find out. You're hedging
Burns, and I dinna like it. You can get me into bother a
weel. . .'

'I canna get you into ony bother, Collector. Onything
ever said I said on my own authority.'

'To hell, man, you've nae authority where the Service i
concerned. You're a government servant first, last and a' the
time. The fact that you're a poet only aggravates the situation
I'm asking you to mak' a clean breast o' things and I'll see
what can be done to help you. There's a wheen o' mechanic
and working men meet about the Mid-Steeple about the hou
o' the mail. You've been heard making the damnedest wild
remarks there. Dinna deny that!'

126

'I do deny it. I may hae made a remark back and forward; but I deny that they were either wild or damned.'

'Dinna quibble, Burns: dinna quibble. This is too serious. You've even boasted republican sentiments!'

'In a general kind of way – in a theoretical manner, so to speak.'

Collector Mitchell, white and scared, thumped his desk:

'In a theoretical manner, my arse and parsley! You beggar! They'll maybe hang you for this!'

'Listen, John. I ken what you're saying's serious enough. I hae nae desire to hae my neck drawn. . . But I'm damned if I'm going to admit something I never did. I'm no' going to be coerced —'

'There's Jacobins i' the toone —'

'If there are I ken nocht about them.'

'There's Friends o' the People —'

'I ken nocht about them either.'

'Are you swearing to that: man and Mason?'

'Exactly as I've said . . .'

'See! Whatever you've done you've got to deny it. Swear to it. You've done nocht.'

'A' that I've ever said you heard me say yoursel'. You've admitted yoursel' you were for the Fr —'

'Dinna mention that word! I was never for onything but the guid o' the Service . . . and I never knew you to be otherwise. What you may hae said in an unguarded drunken moment I ken nocht about. Never even kenned ye had drunken moments – o' that sort. You understand, Robert? For God's sake, tell me you understand.'

'Yes . . . I understand. Though it's hard . . . I'm denying everything and admitting nothing.'

'Of course you've nothing to admit . . .'

'Nothing to admit.'

Mitchell wiped the beads of sweat that glistened on his corrugated forehead.

'Thank God you've gotten sae much sense. . . God, Robert, this is a bad business, a serious business. This is something that's never happened afore. By God! the government means business this time. The verra fact that I'm your superior can get me i' the wrang. I could lose my Collectorship on suspicion alone – for harbouring you. When they come doon here you've got to stand fast and prove withouten a shadow o' a doubt that you're innocent o' ony sedition or treason or disaffection... You've got to prove it!'

'You say Corbet's coming?'

'Yes.'

'Well: I stand pretty well wi' Corbet.'

'You stand well wi' naebody in a case like this. You've got to stand well by yoursel'! Have you ony men o' quality who can stand by you, who can vouch for you?'

'What about Glenriddell, Craigdarroch, Maxwelton – the Provost and the bailie — ?'

'But will they?'

'I know they will.'

'By God! I hope you're richt. I hope you dinna need their testimony. And if you dae, I hope they'll stand by you. Noo: on you go and think hard on what I've said. And mind you, Robert: much as I like ye, remember that frae noo on I'm Collector Mitchell o' the Excise and that I'm a friend to naebody but the Excise. I'll stand by you what I can – but if you mak' a mess o' things — '

The Bard fled to George Haugh, his mind in a whirl and fear in his heart. But though he knew fear such that he had to seek the relief of two privies in the space of a half mile, his convictions were unaltered and his spiritual courage undimmed.

'Listen, Geordie: they're after me – the Excise Board. They've had spies' reports. There's to be an inquiry into my loyalty. I'm told it micht mean Botany Bay.'

'Is this official?'

'I've just left the Collector.'

'Sit doon, Rab, and draw yoursel' thegither. What aboot a dram?'

'Aye: onything at a', Geordie: I've got the bluidy scour already...'

The Bard drank down a generous glass of spirit.

George Haugh was a placid, imperturbable man and yet he had the external appearance of being rough-hewn. His native intelligence was of an exceptionally high order and his spirit burned with intense reforming zeal. Folks said that he took a bit of knowing; and there were few people who really knew him.

'Gin the beggars want to pin you doon to a charge o' sedition, there's naething easier, Rab – ye ken that?'

'Aye: fine I ken that.'

'But I'm no' certain they wad want to risk that – yet.'

'Yes?'

'Things havena gone that far – yet. Noo: you're covered as far as the boys are concerned.'

'The Jacobins — '

'Dinna put words on that. Never. I'm no' sae sure o' the Frien's.'

'No: I never signed onything there.'

'No; but the Frien's are riddled with spies. But since you havena signed — '

'Nothing, Geordie.'

'Richt then. So you deny a' knowledge . . . Corbet?'

'A friend I think.'

'I hope sae. But what can they really pin on to you?'

'Hell: I've said plenty.'

'Aye; but wha kens that? Wha's prepared to stand forth and say they heard you and at the same time admit that they didna denounce you? 'Coorse, after this things'll no' be the same. This'll separate the sheep frae the goats. Plenty folk'll no' ken you noo. But they'll no' admit they kenned you in times past. I dinna want to boost ye up, Rab – but sae far I dinna see they can pin much on you – if onything. . . What frien's hae you got on the Board?'

'There's Graham o' Fintry . . .'

'Weel: get busy wi' your quill on a draft letter to Mr Graham. Tell him that you may hae expressed a mild kind o' sentiment on reform – in principle – but that that's the furthest ever you've gone . . . And mind that, if the warst comes to the warst – which in your case I doubt – we micht hae the chance o' slipping you ower to Ireland or the Americas.'

'No' that, Geordie —— No' that! I couldna leave Jean and the bairns . . .'

'You'll no' get the choice if they send ye to the Woolwich hulks. But gin you got to America you could – in time – send for Jean and the bairns. And we'd see they didna starve.'

'Could I be sure o' that, Geordie?'

'I'll gie you my hand on that. The lads'll see that neither Jean nor the bairns starve.'

'Wi' that assurance, Geordie, I think I could face onything. At least it's a great comfort to ken that. But, damn them! they're no' getting me. I'll lie my way through hell but they'll no' get me. Dirty spying vermin! I wonder who it could hae been?'

'I could think on a dozen. But dinna burn up your anger wonderin' wha it could hae been. Just concentrate on how you're goin' to get out o' this.'

'You're richt. This'll need a cool head. I'll need to think out every move. And I'll no' need to let folks see that I'm worried.'

'Especially Jean.'

'Why especially?'

'If Jean kens you're worried – and hae cause to worry – she'll show her worry. She couldna hide it. And there'll be folks watching her.'

'This is beyond tholing, Geordie — '

'It's a sair thole onyway. Listen: I'll awa' up to the Steeple and keep my ears open.'

THE PROMISE

Jean wasn't to be deceived. At first she thought he hadn't thrown off his chill. And then quite suddenly, lying beside him in bed, she knew that he was worrying.

'What are you worrying about, Rab?'

'I'm no' worrying, Jean.'

'You're no' sleeping!'

'Neither are you. What are you worrying about?'

'I just waukened kennin' you were worrying. You micht as weel tell me, Rab. If it's onything to dae wi' a lass — '

'Nothing to dae wi' ony damned lass.'

'I didna think it had.'

'But you wadna hae been surprised?'

'I'd hae been hurt.'

'But you wadna hae been surprised?'

'Dinna talk about it. You ken fine if you committed murder you wad only need to tell me — '

'What's come ower you, lass?'

'I'm asking what you're worrying about?'

'And I'm telling you I'm worrying about nothing. What hae I got to worry about?'

'You dinna need to go far to fin' something to worry aboot ...'

In the end Jean won.

'That's what Mitchell told me. But for God's sake dinna you start worryin' or that'll only mak' matters worse.'

'But Rab, Rab. . . They couldna send you to Botany Bay?'

'No . . . to be frank I don't think they could. There is . . . just the ghost o' a possibility; an' I was never much a believer in ghosts.'

'And when's Corbet coming doon?'

'The morn maybe. He micht be in Dumfries the nicht for a' I ken.'

'Weel, Rab: I'll dae onything I can – onything that you think's for the best. You ken I'll stick to you through whatever happens.'

'I ken you will, lass. . . And I canna say how sorry I am to hae brocht a' this on you. If I could only learn to shut my mouth and keep it shut.'

'No . . . I'm no' blaming you, Rab. An' you're no' to blame yoursel'. It's just no' the thing that Robert Burns should hae to go aboot wi' a padlock on his mouth – and the key lie wi' the Excise. Now . . . lie roun' and try no' to worry ony mair: ye maun get some sleep.'

The Bard suddenly found himself taking very clear, very unsentimental stock of his Dumfries friends. And particularly he began to view both Collector Mitchell and Supervisor Findlater in a new light. They had shown themselves to be men of no very great integrity or character.

The Bard wrote a long letter to Graham of Fintry defending himself against the charges that had been laid against him:

I have been surprised, confounded and distracted by Mr Mitchell, the Collector, telling me just now, that he has received an order from your Honble. Board to enquire into my political conduct, and blaming me as a person disaffected to Government. Sir, you are a Husband – and a father – you know what you would feel, to see the much-loved wife of your bosom, and your helpless, prattling little ones, turned adrift into the world, degraded and disgraced from a situation in which they had been respectable and respected, and left almost without the necessary support of a miserable existence. Alas, Sir! must I think that such, soon, will be my lot! And from the damned, dark insinuations of hellish groundless Envy too! I believe, Sir, I may aver it, and in the sight of Omnipotence, that I would not tell a deliberate Falsehood, no, not though even worse horrors, if worse can be than those I have mentioned, hung over my head; and I say that the allegation, whatever villain has made it, is a Lie! To the British Constitution, on Revolution principles, next after my God, I am most devoutly attached;

You, Sir, have been much and generously my Friend – Heaven knows how warmly I have felt the obligation, and how gratefully I have thanked you. Fortune, Sir, has made you powerful, and me impotent; has given you patronage and me dependence. I would not for my *single self* call on your Humanity; were such my insular, unconnected situation I would despise the tear that now swells in my eye – I could brave Misfortune, I could face Ruin: for at the worst 'Death's thousand doors stand open'; but, good God! the tender concerns that I have mentioned, the claims and ties that I, at this moment, see and feel around me, how they ennerve Courage, and wither Resolution! To your patronage, as a man of some genius, you have allowed me a claim; and your esteem, as an honest Man, I know is my due: to these, Sir, permit me to appeal; and by these may I adjure you to save me from that misery which threatens to overwhelm me, and which, with my latest breath I will say it, I have not deserved.

Pardon this confused scrawl. Indeed I know not well what I have written.

DANGEROUS THOUGHTS

The year 1792 passed in grim trepidation, worry and shock; and yet possibly with a new clarity the Bard realised what the world was really like and how the Excise could really operate.

When he was confronted with Corbet and the pair of them were alone, Corbet was very much the official.

'This is an unfortunate business, Burns. What hae you to say for yoursel'?'

'I've nothing to say, Mr Corbet – nothing except my regret that the Board should hae been put to ony inconvenience in the matter. I can assure you that whatever charges hae been laid against me are totally without foundation — '

'My information and the information laid before the Board — '

'And who laid the information — ?'

'I'll trouble you, Burns, not to interrupt me when I'm speaking.'

'I — '

'You'll get no information about the Board's affairs and you've no richt to ony information. You're an Excise Officer here; and it seems that you havena learned your duties in a proper manner. You must understand clearly, and without ony equivocation, that your being a one-time poet doesna concern the Board – not in the slightest. As far as the Board's concerned, you're an Exciseman twenty-four hours a day, seven days in the week and fifty-two weeks in the year. Get that quite clearly, Burns – there nae exceptions made either o' poets or pot-menders . . .

'Now, I've made exhaustive enquiries here on the spot. I'm glad to say that the charges laid against you have nae real substance. But your conduct in mixing wi' plainly-disaffected elements and certain injudicious remarks you hae let drop in public places – and public or private, it's a' the same to the Board! – hae placed you in a maist awkward position. I want your solemn word that you belong to no reforming or disaffected society.'

'I can most sincerely give you that assurance.'

'I see. But you'll admit that you have made remarks prejudicial to the Constitution?'

'No: I thought and still think that certain reforms between the legislature and — '

'Just a moment! You thought *and still think*? Well: here and now ends your thinking if you want to continue in the Service. You are not permitted to think. Your plain duty is to carry out your orders: to act on your instructions. Leave thinking out of your reckoning. You will not deem to think about the rightness or wrongness of any order: you'll carry out your duty without thinking and without questioning. You should have known this from the first day you entered the Service. In any event – you ken this now . . .

'But for the excellent report I hae got from Collector Mitchell and Supervisor Findlater, I'm afraid I should have had to take back a very different report to the Board. But –

I canna overlook what your immediate superiors have to say about you. But – and I hope you fully understand the gravity of your position – I'm giving you your last warning. On the slightest indication of any criticism of the Government or the Constitution, or the departments of the Government, not only will you be discharged: the civil authorities will be informed and advised to act accordingly. That's all I have to say officially.

'And I've only this to say unofficially. . . Watch your step, Burns – watch it verra carefully; for it's being watched for you. . . And don't be a bluidy fool. Now: I don't want you to say another word. On you go!'

'But I wish to thank —'

'I said not another word. Report back for duty.'

How he got back to Jean the Bard never knew. It seemed that he stepped out of the Excise Office and opened the door of his house.

Jean was terrified at the look on his face.

'What's the worst, Rab?'

'Admonished, Jean.'

'Oh, God be thanked for that!'

'I'm no' sae sure. Pour me some whisky or gin – a drink o' some kind. . . '

'Were they hard on you, Rab? Had you an ordeal?'

'I hardly ken what's happened, Jean. I canna believe what's happened. I've been lectured and degraded as I never believed a human being could be degraded. I'm nae longer a poet: I'm nae longer a man. I'm a bluidy creeping crawling slave to the Excise. I've no' even to be allowed to think. Not even to think, mind you! Not even in my bed at nicht: no' even when I gang to the privy. I've just to carry out orders like a weel-broke horse. That's a'. . . On the slightest evidence that I hae been guilty o' thinking I've to be thrown out o' the Excise and handed ower to the law . . .'

'Och, Rab: there's naebody can prevent you from thinking?'

'The Excise can apparently. They didna say ocht about dreams or nightmares – but I'll better no' even think if they come under the ban. No, no: I maun think. . . God Almighty, Jean! what I had to stand. . . But they've got nothing against me – no' really; or, by God, they'd hae made short work o' me. . . I doubt if I'd even hae got hame again . . .'

'Wha was doin' a' this to you?'

'Corbet – just Corbet alone: the two o' us thegither. I tried to open my mouth; but, by God, I was immediately ordered to keep quiet. I just had to stand there and tak' it a' like a weel-thrashed schoolboy. And, by God, Corbet can lash wi' his tongue!'

'The dirty brocks – bad cess to the whole lot o' them! But . . . it's a' ower . . .'

'Well, no: he's reporting back to the Board. Only it seems his report will be favourable enough. Oh, Jean lass: something's happened to me – happened inside me. . . Something's broke. . . I'm humiliated beyond even looking a human being in the face again – or ever being a human being myself again. I could greet; if greetin' wad dae ony guid.'

Jean put her arms round him.

'Greet then, Rab, if it'll dae ony guid – for I could greet wi' you. And I could slit the throats o' the beggars that hae done this to you.'

'Oh, God! An' I've to report back to duty – an' I could as soon jump into the Nith . . .'

'Weel: you're no' reportin' back to duty the noo. Them and their Excise can gae to hell and bide there! I've heard baith Mitchell and Findlater saying things in this verra hoose — '

'Dinna, Jean: dinna you start. I've thocht it a' out, Jean. It wad be bad enough in a' conscience to be thrown into the street to face beggary and destitution – but it wad be a thousand times waur if I threw mysel' out by my ain stupidity. We'll need to think hard, Jean – and no' do onything stupid or reckless or foolhardy. Oh lass, lass 'if I hadna you and the bairns to love and cherish, I think I could hae committed murder this day. You've told me often enough that if you hadna me – but, lass, if I hadna you. . . I need you mair than ever you needed me. . . And I need you mair now than ever I did. An' if I hadna you at this hour o' my travail — '

They stood there before the fire with their arms about each other and their tears mingled; and the bairns were strangely quiet. And maybe they came together then as they had never come together in physical passion; and maybe there and then their love took on a deeper significance than it had yet known; and maybe now they understood each other in a way they had never thought – nor could have thought – possible.

And so that gloomy December, or Hogmanay, drew to its

135

dark and bitter close. It seemed that Robert Burns, who considered his songs to be either above or below a money value, sold his manhood and his independence for a mess of pottage – not that he desired to sup of the pottage, but that his wife and weans might not starve.

Perhaps he should have thrown his loved wife and his loved children to destitution and poverty; perhaps his independence was more important than any wife or any children. But Robert Burns was not that kind of hero, nor that kind of martyr: he thought more of those who depended on his love and protection – and depended helplessly – than he did of his own seeming integrity. Robert Burns was that rarer individual who was to perform the unique feat of squaring more than one circle within a circle.

He was not alone in being investigated. As Secretary of State, Henry Dundas had studied his spies' reports. In consultation with his nephew, Robert, in his capacity of Lord Advocate, and his lieutenant, Braxfield, as Lord Justice Clerk, he decided to embark on a series of sedition trials that would strike terror into the Reform Movement.

Balloon Tytler was the first to be attacked, on the charge of having written or published two seditious libels. Tytler had no illusions about Dundas and his friends. He took refuge about Salisbury Crags, failed to attend the court, and was outlawed. Tytler needed no more warning. He would make for America – by way of Ireland. He could use his pen there. America was the great free land of the future . . .

And then, on the 2nd day of January, Thomas Muir was arrested and charged with circulating the works of Thomas Paine and other seditious writers. Muir refused to answer any questions concerning his conduct and was released on bail.

Balloon Tytler was an eccentric – a man of some genius but without social significance. But Thomas Muir was an advocate and an elder of the Kirk of Scotland. He was a leading member of the Friends of the People. His arrest created a sensation throughout the land.

Muir had courage as well as dignity. He almost welcomed the prospect of his coming trial. Never for a moment did the thought enter his head that his sentence – should they be able to prove him guilty – would go beyond a nominal fine. He was Thomas Muir ; and by no stretch of imagination would he be proved guilty of sedition. There was no case in law

gainst him and he had violated no law. All this, and maybe
ore, he would triumphantly vindicate at his trial.

he Bard was no lawyer. But unlike Muir he had no faith in
he law. Like Balloon Tytler, he knew there was no law for
im where Dundas was concerned.

As the shock of his interview with Corbet began to wear
ff, his anger mounted. He had been badly shaken.

Jean realised that, emotionally, he seemed to be less in
ontrol of himself than she had ever known him. This dis-
rbed her. She knew him as a man of moods – from the
epths of melancholy to the throbbing heights of exultation;
ut, unless physically ill and in fever, he always seemed to
e sure of himself. Now he seemed to be reaching out for
urety.

But never mind, Jean. The thoughts I've *got* to think; the
ords I've *got* to express will yet bear fruit – aye, even if it
ak's a thousand years. They may gag and suppress me here
nd now; but posterity will ken better. I'll get round them
et. Dinna think that I stand here defeated and humiliated
his day. Aye: one bit o' me's defeated and humiliated. But
here's mair to me than that. Ten thousand bastards i' the
xcise or Government canna tell me to stop thinking. Nor
ill they mak' me sacrifice you and the bairns to my silence.
Not only will I be Mr Facing-Both-Ways: I'll be Mr Facing-
very-bluidy-point-and-degree-o'-the-mariner's-compass.   I'll
ace every bluidy direction they ever thocht possible. But
here'll be only one direction that means onything to me or
o posterity – the true North o' the damned democratic heresy
f which they accuse me.

'Corbet thought he'd humiliated Robert Burns and brocht
im to heel like a beaten cur, did he? Beggar ten thousand
Corbets! Robert Burns'll be a match and mair than a match
or the whole damned tribe o' gutless sycophants! Corbet was
ince on my side: so were Mitchell and Findlater. To hell wi'
hem then! You'll get your bite, Jean lass: you'll get your
ite, lass and a roof to cover you and the weans frae the
lements — And I'll sleep soundly i' my bed and snap my
ingers at them . . .

'I'll be like the moudiewort – I'll burrow underground;
ut come up here and there to breathe . . . and hae my
eing. . . By God! they've done something to me the day,

137

Jean, their children or their grandchildren will live to rue. I carena how lang it may take; but I'll dae my bit and mair than my bit to usher in the day when a' sic low-life creatures are wiped frae the face o' the earth. Tell Robert Burns that he must not think . . .!'

Yet it pleased Jean to see him fighting back. He was always at his best when fighting – when his mood was in the ascendant.

When he had come in he had looked stunned – almost mortally wounded. Now, though there was a brave front on things, he had recovered sufficiently to gain something of his normal poise and his voice was now resonant and clear and his shoulders were braced. But Jean was terribly distressed and upset for all that. She would have done anything to have been able to give him real comfort and assurance. But there was no doubt that things were difficult for him – were going to be more difficult. There was no doubt now that Robert was being watched, being spied upon, and that his enemies in Dumfries or his political enemies would be waiting for him to make the first false step.

Jean feared that the Bard, despite all his caution, would sooner or later make a false step. He would say something to someone which would be overheard or repeated. Maybe he would write something that would fall into their hands. The very fact that they had told him that he must not think would be as a challenge only to think more, to think deeper and more boldly.

SAFE FRIENDSHIPS

Now that the Bard had made up his mind and recovered something of his composure and courage, he visited John Syme and George Haugh in turn and told them the circumstances of his interview with Corbet.

Syme, of course, was indignant and sympathised deeply with the Bard in the unique circumstances of his humiliation. But Syme was despairing too. He realised that if Robert Burns could be censured in such a fashion his own position was not without its danger. As Distributor of Stamps in Dumfries, even though he was known to the gentry, he was by no means invulnerable. He himself had been guilty of

138

more than one occasion of uttering sentiments as revolutionary and derogatory of the present government and of the constitution and, indeed, of the monarchy, as ever Robert Burns had been.

And, indeed, Syme wondered why he had not been spied upon too; and could he be sure that he had not been spied upon?

When the Bard left, Syme began to ponder these things carefully and to wonder and to know something of fear.

George Haugh, on the other hand, was practical. He was not surprised at the terms Corbet had used and was of the opinion that Corbet was on the Bard's side: that Corbet had given him a fright deliberately for his own good.

After all; why only Robert Burns? And why come all the way from Edinburgh to make an enquiry on the spot? And why, having done so, had he not preferred any specific charge against him?

Something must have been reported to the Excise Board of a very dangerous nature. And some friends of the Bard in the Excise Board had decided to send Corbet rather than perhaps some less-sympathetic officer. At least this was highly possible.

And Haugh, in seeking to reassure the Bard, added his own word of caution.

'I think this Corbet is on your side. The Excise Board must hae gotten a gey bad report on you. So they sent Corbet. Of course he couldna tell you he was on your side. So he tried to frighten you into keeping your mouth shut. Damn fine the Board kens that you're nae ordinary Exciseman; and had they no' been friendly disposed towards you, you'd hae been dismissed the Service without maybe ever knowing why. . . I'm no' saying the whole Excise Board is friendly towards you; but I think this Corbet and Mr Graham o' Fintry must be. If I were you I'd write to Graham and keep the richt side o' him. Tak' him into your confidence as it were. . . Tell him that you micht hae been guilty o' a wee bit verbal indiscretion but that you belong to nae Movement one way or the other: that you neither correspond wi' ony o' the societies or associate wi' ony o' them. . .

'Above all things, Rab, you maun keep the richt side o' Graham. I'm certain he's your sheet-anchor as far as the Excise is concerned . . .'

LETTER TO FINTRY

On the heels of his talk with the blacksmith came a letter from Graham of Fintry. He replied to it at once.

I am this moment honoured with your letter: with what feelings I received this other instance of your goodness, I shall not pretend to describe.

Now, to the charges which Malice and Misrepresentation have brought against me.

It has been said, it seems, that I not only belong to, but head a disaffected party in this place. I know of no party in this place, Republican or Reform, except an old party of Borough-Reform; with which I never had anything to do. Individuals, both Republican and Reform, we have, though not many of either; but if they have associated, it is more than I have the least knowledge of: and if there exists such an association, it must consist of such obscure, nameless beings, as precludes any possibility of my being known to them, or they to me.

I was in the playhouse one night, when *Ca Ira* was called for. I was in the middle of the Pit, and from the Pit the clamour arose. One or two individuals with whom I occasionally associate were of the party, but I neither knew of the Plot, nor joined in the Plot; nor even opened my lips to hiss or huzza, that, or any other Political tune whatever. I looked on myself as far too obscure a man to have any weight in quelling a Riot; at the same time as a character of higher respectability, than to yell in the howlings of a rabble. This was the conduct of all the first Characters in this place; and these Characters know, and will avow, that such was my conduct.

I never uttered any invectives against the king. His private worth, it is altogether impossible that such a man as I, can appreciate; and in his Public capacity, I always revered, and ever will, with the soundest loyalty, revere, the Monarch of Great Britain, as, to speak in Masonic, the sacred Keystone of our Royal Arch Constitution.

As to Reform Principles, I look upon the British Constitution, as settled at the Revolution, to be the most glorious

Constitution on earth, or that perhaps the wit of man can frame; at the same time, I think, and you know what High and distinguished Characters have for some time thought so, that we have a good deal deviated from the original principles of that Constitution; particularly, that an alarming System of Corruption has pervaded the connection between the Executive Power and the House of Commons. This is the Truth, the Whole Truth, of my Reform opinions; opinions which, before I was aware of the complexion of these innovating times, I too unguardedly (now I see it) sported with: but henceforth, I seal up my lips. However, I never dictated to, corresponded with, or had the least connection with, any political association whatever – except, that when the Magistrates and principal inhabitants of this town, met to declare their attachment to the Constitution, and their abhorrence of Riot, which declaration you would see in the Papers, I, as I thought my duty as a Subject at large, and a Citizen in particular, called upon me, subscribed the same declaratory Creed.

Of Johnson, the publisher of the Edinburgh Gazetteer, I know nothing. One evening in company with four or five friends, we met with his prospectus which we thought manly and independent; and I wrote to him, ordering his paper for us. If you think that I act improperly in allowing his Paper to come addressed to me, I shall immediately countermand it. I never, so judge me, God! wrote a line of prose for the Gazetteer in my life. An occasional address, spoken by Miss Fontenelle on her benefit-night here, which I called, the Rights of Woman, I sent to the Gazetteer; as also, some extempore stanzas on the Commemoration of Thomson: both of these I will subjoin for your perusal. You will see that they have nothing whatever to do with Politics. At the time when I sent Johnson one of these poems, but which one, I do not remember, I enclosed, at the request of my warm and worthy friend, Robert Riddell Esq., of Glenriddell, a prose Essay signed Catto, written by him, and addressed to the delegates for the County Reform, of which he was one for this County. With the merits, or demerits, of that Essay, I have nothing to do, farther than transmitting it in the same Frank, which Frank he had procured me.

As to France, I was her enthusiastic votary in the beginning of the business. When she came to show her old avidity for conquest, in annexing Savoy, &c. to her dominions, and invading the rights of Holland, I altered my sentiments. A tippling Ballad which I made on the Prince of Brunswick's breaking up his camp, and sung one convivial evening, I shall likewise send you, sealed up, as it not every body's reading. This last is not worth your perusal; but lest Mrs Fame should, as she has already done, use, and even abuse, her old privilege of lying, you shall be the master of every thing, le pour et le contre, of my political writings and conduct.

This, my honoured Patron, is all. To this statement I challenge disquisition. Mistaken Prejudice, or unguarded Passion, may mislead, and often have misled me; but when called on to answer for my mistakes, though, I will say it, no man can feel keener compunction for his errors, yet, I trust, no man can be more superior to evasion or disguise.

I shall do myself the honour to thank Mrs Graham for her goodness, in a separate letter . . .
Dumfries, 5th January, 1793.

Now he knew for a certainty that the Excise would not proceed against him. He knew also, however, that any possibility of a promotion was blasted. He had won sufficient victory to hold his job.

He was presently to get a very clear example of how the authorities were reacting to so-called seditious toasts. Three men from Langholm were promptly sent (two for three months and one for two months) to Dumfries gaol for this alleged offence. It was becoming clearer every day that the slightest remark thought to point towards disaffection was to be punished promptly and severely.

Feelings, however, began to run high and fierce when the news came towards the end of the month that King Louis of France had been executed by the guillotine. Everyone feared that war would result from this inevitable act. The French, having gone so far on the revolutionary road, could not turn back. But there was no saying what the end might yet be.

The Bard had no regret now that Louis had been guillotined. He himself thought no other alternative possible.

THE DEADLY BLAST

By the beginning of February the expected war broke out and there was consternation and panic throughout the land. Any sympathy expressed with the French was now clearly regarded as an offence of the first order. Not that the Friends of France and of Reform were driven underground or that they allowed their sentiments to be overturned overnight – far from it. Many felt that now the hour had struck when sides must be taken openly; when the war had either to be supported whole-heartedly or equally whole-heartedly opposed. It was felt that now indeed was the day; now indeed was the hour. And all friends of liberty and freedom and equality; all who were in favour of the forward march of humanity would have to cast their lots with the French and against the reactionary British government.

There were meetings held at every street corner: unofficial meetings where people exchanged the news and made their comments. The professional men of the societies were, of course, in a dilemma. The rank and file were pressing for action; but just what kind of action it was difficult to decide upon. Proclamations and resolutions were only the work of pieces of paper and carried very little authority. Something much more violent, more drastic was needed.

The war, of course, also provided an excuse for cowards, for the faint-hearted, and for those who could not or would not risk anything for their principles and opinions. Many of the respectable elements in the Friends of the People immediately deserted. . . But the core of the movement remained steadfast and rallied round the idea of petitioning parliament to stop the war: that the war was unjust and unjustifiable.

NEWS FROM NICOL

News concerning the Bard's trouble with the Excise had begun to penetrate most quarters of Scotland interested in such things.

Willie Nicol, who had indeed warned the Bard at their last

meeting what would happen if he interfered in politics as an Exciseman, took occasion to write him.

Dear Christless Bobbie –

What is become of thee? Has the Devil flown off with thee, as the gled does with a bird? If he should do so there is little matter, if the reports concerning thy *imprudence* are true. What concerns it thee whether the lousy Dumfriesian fiddlers play 'Ca Ira' or 'God save the King'? Suppose you *had* an aversion to the King, you could not, as a gentleman, wish God to use him worse than He has done. The infliction of idiocy is no sign of Friendship or Love; and I am sure damnation is a matter far beyond your wishes or ideas. But reports of this kind are only the insidious suggestions of ill-minded persons; for your good sense will ever point out to you, as well as to me, a bright model of political conduct who flourished in the victorious reign of Queen Anne, viz., the Vicar of Bray, who, during the convulsions of Great Britain which were without any former example, saw eight reigns, in perfect security; because he remembered that precept of the *sensible, shrewd, temporising* Apostle, 'We ought not to resist the Higher Powers.'

You will think I have gotten a pension from Government; but I assure you no such a thing has been offered me. In this respect my vanity prompts me to say they have not been so *wise* as I would have wished them to be; for I think their Honours have often employed as impotent scribblers.

Enough of Politics. What is become of Mrs Burns and the dear bairns? How is my Willie? Tell her, though I do not write often, my best wishes shall ever attend her and the family. My wife, who is in a high devotional fit this evening, wishes that she and her children may be reckoned the favourites of the Lord and numbered with the elect. She indeed leaves your honour and me to shift for ourselves; as, so far as she can judge from the criteria laid down in Guthrie's *Trial of a Saving Interest*, both you and I are stamped with the marks of Reprobation.

May all the curses from the beginning of Genesis to the end of Revelation light, materially and effectually on thy enemies; and may all the blessings of the Covenant be eminently exemplified in thy person, to the glory of a forgiving Deity!

Here or elsewhere I am always thine sincerely.

Despite the conciliatory tone of the concluding paragraphs of Nicol's letter, the Bard was stung to the quick. He had, on many occasions, writhed under his good friend's biting sarcastic vitriolic tongue. And he knew deep down that no man had more concern for his welfare than Nicol. But to be written about in what the Bard considered a cheap and sarcastic manner when his troubles were so heavy upon him, raised the devil in him; and he let stumpie scratch the paper in white heat:

O thou wisest among the Wise, Meridian blaze of Prudence; full moon of Discretion and Chief of many Councillors! How infinitely is thy puddle-headed, rattle-headed, wrong-headed, round-headed slave indebted to thy supereminent goodness, that from the luminous path of thy own right-lined rectitude, thou lookest benignly down on an erring wretch, of whom the zig-zag wanderings defy all the powers of Calculation, from the simple copulation of Units up to the hidden mystery of Fluxions! May one feeble ray of that light of wisdom which darts from thy sensorium, straight as the arrow of Heaven against the head of the Unrighteous, and bright as the meteor of inspiration descending on the holy and undefiled Priesthood – may it be my portion; so that I may be less unworthy of the face and favour of that father of Proverbs and master of Maxims, that antipode of Folly and magnet among the Sages, the wise and witty Willie Nicol! Amen! Amen! Yea, so be it!!!

For me, I am a beast, a reptile, and know nothing. From the cave of my ignorance, amid the fogs of my dullness and pestilential fumes of my Political heresies, I look up to thee, as doth a toad through the iron-barred lucarne of a pestiferous dungeon to the cloudless glory of a summer sun! Sorely sighing in bitterness of soul, I say, when shall my name be the quotation of the Wise, and my countenance be the delight of the Godly, like the illustrious lord of Laggan's many hills? As for him, his works are perfect; never did the pen of Calumny blur the fair page of his reputation, nor the bolt of Hatred fly at his dwelling. At his approach is the standing up of men, even the Chiefs and the Ruler; and before his presence the frail form of lovely Woman humbly awaiting his pleasure, is extended on the dust. Thou mirror of purity, when shall the elfine lamp of my glimmerous understanding, purged from sensual appetites and gross desires, shine like the constellation of thy intellectual powers? As for thee, thy thoughts are pure, and thy lips are holy. Never did the unhallowed breath of the powers of darkness and the pleasures of darkness, pollute the sacred flame of thy sky-descended and heavenward-bound desires: never did the vapours of impurity stain the unclouded serene of thy cerulean imagination. O, that like thine were the tenor of my life, like thine the tenor of my conversation! Then should no friend fear my strength, no enemy rejoice in my weakness! Then should I lie down, and rise up, and none to make me afraid!

    May thy pity and thy prayer be exercised for,
       O thou lamp of Wisdom and mirror of Morality!
          Thy devoted slave . . .

LIFE GOES ON

And yet, during all his troubles and trials, he managed to throw himself into George Thomson's publication and to send him song after song: to send him parcels of songs. For the Bard found that the best antidote to his troubles was to devote himself in his evenings to what was his greatest passion: the blending of words to Scottish melodies.

He learned that his two-volume Edinburgh edition had been published by Creech; but as no copies had reached him, he wrote to Creech:

I understand that my Book is published. I beg that you will, *as soon as possible*, send me twenty copies of it. As I mean to present them among a few Great Folks whom I respect, and a few Little Folks whom I love, these twenty will not interfere with your sale. If you have not twenty copies ready, send me any number you can. It will confer a particular obligation to let me have them by first Carrier.

Despite wars and rumours of wars, riots and tumults and revolutions, the everyday life of men had to go on.

Yet the Bard, becoming more and more withdrawn to his own fireside and the company of Jean, decided his eldest boy at least should have the best education Dumfries could provide. He recalled that he was a Freeman of the town; and he wrote the magistrates asking them to extend to him the privilege of having his children educated free in the High School. This the magistrates freely granted and their grant did much to restore the Bard's self-respect. It was proof that they did not regard him as a dangerously-disaffected citizen.

It was not that he was trying to climb back into favour. His political and religious views were as they had been before the enquiry into his loyalty: if anything they had hardened. But he set himself to play his own role in society and he was determined to carry out his plan. The plan was that he would establish himself as an independent citizen, independent of Royalist or Jacobite or Reformist or Revolutionary; that he would secure for himself and his family the greatest possible measure of security; that there was nothing he would not do to secure this. His help towards the principles he held would be strictly and severely underground. George Haugh alone was to be trusted to see that anything he wrote was conveyed to the proper channels in a manner which would not incriminate him in any way.

But though he made plans and stuck to them; though he worked joyfully at his songs; though he inscribed and presented copies of his new Edinburgh edition there was a cloud across the sun. Life went on and day followed day. But things could never be the same again. The world was being born anew. The capital of re-birth lay far from Dumfries. But he had become involved; he had been spied upon and informed against; he had been reprimanded and rebuked. He was a marked man. He knew he would carry the mark to his grave.

CLARINDA COMES HOME

Mrs Agnes MacLehose had made her long and tiring journey to meet her husband in Kingston, Jamaica, and had arrived there much under the weather to find a state of affairs that almost overwhelmed her.

She found MacLehose far gone in alcohol, living with at least one black woman and having a veritable squad of mulatto children running about his wooden bungalow.

MacLehose had looked at her through dull brown bloodshot eyes and sneered.

147

Yes: Nancy was welcome to return to him: welcome to share his bed again; but share it with his black woman and his brood of mulattos.

So great had been the shock that Clarinda returned to the boat, and pled with the captain to give her shelter there until the boat returned. The captain, knowing full well the state of her husband and being in fact rather taken with Nancy, granted her request at no extra cost. She was free of the ship until it returned, though she would have to find the passage money for her voyage home.

But this passage money the cautious Nancy had already reserved against just such a contingency.

Nancy wrote to her friends in Edinburgh, especially Mary Peacock, that she found the mosquitoes so trying and the climate so enervating that she was unable to stay and was returning by the boat, the *Roselle*, on which she had come out.

Clarinda had never been more humiliated, more drained of self-respect than in those weeks when she lay skulking below deck in enervating heat and foul stench . . .

She returned to Edinburgh dejected, depressed and in poor health. The fact that her cousin had been promoted to a Lord of the Justiciary was the only bright spot on her horizon. For Lord Craig, on hearing her tale, had promised to settle on her an allowance that would at least enable her to live with a degree of comfort and security she had never known.

In due course the Bard learned from Mary Peacock that Clarinda had returned. He wrote to Clarinda:

I suppose, my dear Madam, that by your neglecting to inform me of your arrival in Europe – a circumstance that could not be indifferent to me, as indeed no occurrence relating to you can – you meant to leave me to guess and gather that a correspondence I once had the honour and *felicity* to enjoy, is to be no more. Alas, what heavy laden sounds are these – 'no more!' The wretch who has never tasted pleasure has never known woe; but what drives the soul to madness, is the recollection of joys that are – 'no more!' But this is not language to the world. They do not understand it. But, come ye children of Feeling and Sentiment – ye whose trembling bosom-chords ache to unutterable anguish, as recollection gushes on the heart! Ye who are capable of an attachment, keen as the arrow of Death, and strong as the vigour of Immortal Being — Come! and your ears shall drink a tale — but hush! I must not, can not, tell it! Agony is in the recollection, and frenzy is in the recital!

But to leave these paths that lead to madness, I congratulate your friends, Madam, on your return; and I hope that the precious health, which Miss Peacock tells me is so much injured, is restored or restoring. There is a fatality attends Miss Peacock's correspondence and mine. (Two of my letters, it seems, she never received; and her last, which came when I was in Ayrshire, was unfortunately mislaid, and only found about ten days or a fortnight ago, on removing a desk of drawers.)

I present you a book: may I hope you will accept of it. I dare say you will have brought your books with you. The fourth volume of the Scots Songs is published: I will also send it you.

Shall I hear from you? But first, hear me! No cold language — no prudential documents — I despise Advice, and scorn Control. If you are not to write such language, such sentiments, as you know I shall wish, shall delight to receive; I conjure you, By wounded pride! By ruined Peace! By frantic disappointed Passion! By all the many ills that constitute that sum of human woes — a broken heart! To me be silent for ever!!! If you insult me with the unfeeling apophthegms of cold-blooded Caution, May all the — but hold — a Fiend could not breathe a malevolent wish on the head of *My* Angel!

Mind my request! If you send me a page baptised in the font of sanctimonious Prudence — By Heaven, Earth and Hell, I will tear it into atoms!

Adieu! May all good things attend you!

The truth was, of course, that hearing and guessing and reading between the lines of Clarinda's disappointment, frustration and humiliation, he was filled with a consuming desire to hear from her by her own hand, though he realised that the possibility of resuming in any way the love which had burned itself out on that gloomy December night little more than a year ago could not be expected . . .

In his loneliness and frustration, his heart did throb with a passion for Clarinda that seemed strangely at war, or in contradiction to his devotion to Jean. But then, as always,

149

Jean was there: permanent, eternal, all-loving, all-embracing, all-satisfying. Jean was like the air he breathed – necessary to his very life. In Clarinda there was a breath of different air – a holiday for the heart and the spirit.

TRIAL AND TRIBULATION

It seemed that his female friends, his loves, were undergoing a period of trial and tribulation running, in a sense, parallel to his own. For he heard from William Lorimer, with considerable agitation, that Jean had eloped with a Cumberland farmer of the name Whelpdale, and had apparently driven off to Gretna on a Gretna Green marriage. Neither Lorimer nor anyone else had any idea of where she might now be.

While the Bard wondered privately what this Whelpdale creature could be like, who had carried off his Chloris, his model, in such a fashion, the truth was easy to understand. Jean Lorimer could contain herself no longer. No longer was a flirtation – an occasional meeting with a man – of any use to her. Sex urged through her with a clamour that could no longer be denied. She had to have a man – and permanently – with her: she had to be permanently bedded. And of all the many men she had known, farmer Whelpdale was the first and only man who promised literally to take her off her father's hands and marry her.

She had met him at a ball in Moffat and Whelpdale had lost no time in making his proposal. He knew that Jean Lorimer was his for the plucking; and he did not mean to have a bite at the cherry but to have the cherry with him until it lost its flavour.

The Bard could not conceal his concern in relating this to Jean.

'Ye ken, Jean, I've had a shock the day that shouldna be a shock . . . yet is for a' that. You canna guess what has happened to Jean Lorimer?'

But Jean looked up quietly and said: 'Aye, I could guess twa things, Rab. Either she's wi' bairn or she's run awa' an' got married . . . ?'

'I don't know how you can see through brick wa's and space and time and ken what's gaun on. I don't know whether she's wi' bairn – I canna think she maun be because she's just met with this adventurer kind of a body . . . Whelpdale they ca' him: a farmer from Cumberland who has recently rented a farm here. . . But it seems she met him one nicht at a ball in Moffat and the next thing was . . . she was gone. She had flitted the nest: left a note for her father and mother that she was away to Gretna to get married there . . .'

'Weel, Rab: you shouldna be disappointed or surprised at that. I've kent for long enough – in fact I've kent frae the first day I met her – that the first man that cam' along and offered her marriage wad get her without ony bother. Oh, Jean may do weel enough for a' that . . . and I hope for her sake that she does weel: for she deserves it. And if ony woman ever needed a man to steady her blood, that woman was Jean Lorimer. I wadna hae been surprised, Rab, had she no' tempted you hersel' . . .?'

'Damn it, Jean, I canna help getting the idea whiles that you have it in your mind that I wad bairn half the women in the countryside!'

'No, na, Rab: you mauna tak' it that way. But Jean was a tidy armfu' – a nice fresh morsel for ony man. Oh, you ken yersel', Rab . . . she was desperate . . .'

'An' yet, Jean, ye kent this and never thocht onything about me being wi' her when, honest enough, I could hae bairned her a dozen times?'

'No: I didna bother, Rab. Of course I had my own quiet talks wi' Jean. Dinna think that what was goin' on between you and her escaped my notice. And I think – I may be wrong; but I think that Jean had sufficient sense no' to let ony man interfere wi' her that couldna offer her marriage. An' she canna be eighteen yet; but when I first kent her she was woman-enough for onything that life had to offer. And ony-way, now that she is married, for guid or ill, she'll be settled. She'll just need to mak' her bed as she finds it. I suppose being a farmer that they'll be weel enough provided for?'

'As to that, I canna richt say; but Lorimer himsel' has doubts about his financial worth and well-being. I tell you that man was gey sair distressed when I spoke to him.'

'Can you blame her either? You ken what her mither was like better than I dae. And her father could surely hae done mair for her than he has?'

'That's true enough. Damnit, her mother was in a gey sair state whiles. Aye, no once but dozens o' times . . . lying yonder drunk as Bacchus . . . couldna bite her finger . . . lying

151

yonder at Kemys Ha' an' the water runnin' out o' her into a puddle on the floor. Aye, my God! I ken what drink can dae and what drink canna dae. . . But it's a terrible thing when a woman, when a mother – an' no' an old mother either – tak's to drink to such an extent that she canna do better than disgust her family. . . And then, of course, Lorimer took a guid drink himsel' whiles . . .

'Oh well . . . that's the last o' Jean Lorimer . . . that's the last o' my Chloris! Though I must confess, Jean, that she served as a model for a wheen o' guid sangs. There was something about her: a freshness a peculiar kind o' virginity that made me see her – though no doubt I was just as blin' as a cuddy – as a kind o' goddess of legend. A Greek goddess: oh, as something unique in young womanhood . . .

'And let me say this, Jean, in a' sincerity: there was mony a time when Jean Lorimer despite her flaxen hair and her ringlets and her eyebrows of a darker hue – and her strange, chaste, bonnie, blue een – when she reminded me o' you when I first kent you . . .'

'Hae I lost a' my guid looks?'

'Jean lass: every day that passes adds something to you in a way that I canna describe. You maun never doubt my love for you, lass. Aye, God knows, I'm sometimes tempted; and there have been times when I hae strayed. But I really mean it, Jean, when I tell you that, of a' the women I've ever kent, there's naebody can tak' your place . . .

'There's naebody will *ever* tak' your place: there's naebody wad be allowed – though she were Cleopatra and the Queen of Sheba and the best hure that ever lived in Babylon rolled into one – to tak' your place. And I dinna think I need to assure you in ony way that my affection for Jean Lorimer and my association wi' her was in ony way improper. . . And, by God, it was affection: I liked the lassie: I would be wrong to say onything else: I liked her: she did something to me . . .'

'Aye, fine I ken that, Rab: fine I ken. I was never jealous o' puir Jean. I liked her aboot the house; I liked her way o' lookin' at things and maybe I was sorry for the lass too that she had such a sorry hame . . .

'No: I never grudged you ony association you had wi' Jean Lorimer. If you got a sang or twa out o' her that you didna get out o' me, well . . . I canna be jealous o' that either; for I have the feeling, though maybe I'm settin' mysel'

p ower far, that hadna you loved me, you wadna hae
written the sangs that you hae.'

'I'll say amen to that, Jean.'

Following on the elopement of Jean Lorimer came an invitation from Maria Riddell to say good-bye for an indefinite
period.

It seemed that Walter Riddell was going off to the West
Indies to see about the affairs of his estate there; and it
seemed that Maria's father was very ill in his Dorset house
and that she was due to visit him.

The Bard and Maria had a long talk together. Maria was
as distressed as he was about the turn things had taken with
the Reform Movement – especially the arrest of Thomas
Muir. She was able to inform him that Muir had gone off to
Paris with the intention of persuading the French to stay their
hand with regard to King Louis.

For Muir, who was essentially middle-class and essentially
constitutional, was of the opinion that any harm befalling
the king of France would have disastrous effects on the
Reform Movement in Britain.

But the French were not so naïve as to believe that their
destiny was to be thirled to British notions of respectability.
Muir himself, meeting many of the leaders of the French
Revolution, found them very different from what he had
imagined. This, together with the exhilarating climate of
Paris – which contrasted very favourably with the grim wet
west-Scotland climate – had taigled him in Paris till war had
been declared. Now he found it impossible to return and face
his trial.

As Maria pointed out, this might prove a fatal step: he
might very well, like Balloon Tytler, be declared an outlaw.

Apart from the political intelligence of the day which
Maria, with her London correspondence, was able to give him,
they talked about personal affairs too. It seemed to the Bard
that Maria, though she was concerned with her father's illness, was loth to leave Woodley Park and her two young
children in the care of a nurse.

'You know, Robert, what this means is that I'm leaving –
or I'm compelled by my lord and master to leave – my two
children behind as hostages against my return. Walter is not
at all pleased that I'm going to visit my father in Dorset; but
what can I do? A father remains a father; and mine has been

a very worthy person indeed. Should the worst befall him what would I think of myself here in Woodley Park and him lying dead in far-away Dorset?'

Maria was at a low ebb. Gone, at least for the moment were her high spirits, her bravado, her caprice. She was a woman, a mother, now reduced to facing the fundamental realities of life: of giving birth to children and of attending the death-bed of those who have given life to her. She was maturing, was Maria, and she was genuinely sorry that ever since the birth of her child in November she had seen so little of the Bard; and now she was possibly going to be absent for the summer.

The Bard expressed his genuine regret that she was leaving Despite his worries, he had missed her company . . .

Maria's leaving, following on Chloris's elopement and the sad news of Clarinda's return to Edinburgh, made him feel that his female friends were, like himself, in the depths.

As he rode away in the April dusk, a faint smirr of April rain was spreading across the green holms of Woodley Park. On the budding trees thrushes and blackbirds were pouring out their vespers to an unheeding world.

But there it was: the never-ending mystery and enchantment of spring! The grass growing green, vegetation burgeoning and birds singing their hearts out in thankfulness. Yet there was too, on that road home on his borrowed pony, the sadness that comes with the spring: the sadness that is in all bird-song however tumultuous, however rapturous may be the totality of the paean of praise that life is born anew.

As he rode home, melody after melody came to his tongue and words to fit them. Had he had paper and pen, he might have dismounted and committed to paper many a new verse, many a new lilt, many an original turn to an old phrase.

But he jogged on, the smirr of rain glistening on his coat, glistening on the mane of his pony, on into the falling night, the gathering darkness, until, when he came to the Brigend of Dumfries, he was glad to see the lights in the hostelries and to ride upwards by the Mid-Steeple and down into the Globe tavern to partake of a nightcap and in the hope of meeting with a friend . . .

No sooner had he taken his first drink than he felt the hot burning lips of Chloris on his. He recalled with a start that night, that summer's night he had sung to her his Craigieburn Wood: Sweet closes the evening on Craigieburn Wood and lithely awaukens the morrow. . . That night, when she had asked with her lips and with her body that she might be taken then and there; that night he had delicately but decisively denied her.

Now she was being taken by a man. No matter what kind of man he was, he was surely incapable of what he might have given Chloris . . .

As he felt again the burning smear of her lips, he cursed himself for being a damned sentimental idiot.

For what he had denied himself had now been taken. That he had not taken it was perhaps a tribute to his regard for Chloris – a sentimental and foolish regard.

He took a drink quickly and went through to the kitchen to meet Bess Hyslop and her husband William to order another – so that he might banish from his mind the memory of that night with Chloris, the searing of her lips . . .

THE NEW HOUSE

But the spring of 1793 was not all gloom or regret or misgiving. It had its happier moments. There was none happier than when, towards the end of April, the Bard was dining on a Sunday with Captain John Hamilton across the way and the Captain announced to him that it might be possible to give him the tenancy of a much better house in the Millbrae Vennel than that which he now occupied. The outgoing tenant had promised to leave by the middle of May. If the Bard cared to go round and have a look at it, pass an opinion, and accept, there was little fear but the house would be his.

It was a good house of red sandstone, with two good rooms on the ground floor and two good rooms upstairs (recently added) with a reasonably-sized closet between them. It had a front door as near ground level as the slope of the Millbrae permitted, and a back door opening onto a fair bit of garden. It had also reasonable attics and a chamber-end in the bedroom upstairs which could well contain a bed for a servant or a young person.

No one was more overjoyed than Jean when the Bard told her the good news.

'Oh God, Rab, that's the best news I've heard since I cam' to Dumfries. For mind you, I wasna lookin' forward to spendin' a hot summer in this stinking hole. When they ca' this place the Stinking Vennel, they didna misca' it.'

'Aye, I ken, Jean. I'll go up the morn and have a look at it I ken the house weel frae the outside... And we'll have John Lewars and his mother and sisters Jean and Jessie as neigh bours: they're just across the road. Mind you, it's a guid house – a back door and a front. I'll maybe manage to ge you up there to look at it yoursel'.'

'Ach, there's nae need for me to trouble the folk that are there the noo, Rab. For if it's what you say it is, it'll be a palace to this hole here. It's a guid warm house in the winter If it wasna for the toddlin' bairns... I'll be glad to get awa frae the trailing down there to the Nith, trailing water frae the well... That's been a sair trauchle...'

'Aye, it's been a sair trauchle, Jean. But there's a wel handy yonder on the Millbrae, though Dumfries is a damn bad place for water. Of course, the Nith's no' that far awa'... now and again I can gie you a hand down wi' the heavy things like blankets, an' we can wash them there. Bu you'll find it handy there wi' the well and the garden to do a the bits o' washing that you want.'

'That's a blessing'! No' that I'm objecting to gaun door to the Nith to do my heavy washin'. Aye, even if the Nith was ten times as far awa' as it is frae the Millbrae. But oh Rab! wi' a house o' our ain and naebody abune us and nae body ablow us, it'll be an awfu' relief.'

'Aye, Jean, it'll give us a bit more elbow-room and a bi more honest human dignity. I too hae felt ashamed while to bring a friend up that winding stair. It's no' safe ony time Aye, a dark hole...

'If Captain Hamilton keeps his word – an' I see nae reason to doubt him – we should be out o' here by the middle o' May and start a new life at the right time o' the year wi' the summer months comin' fast upon us. Aye, I'll be glad to ge stretching my legs a bit mair than I can here and, wi 'a garden at the back – just at our back door – it'll be mair than a blessing to the weans to get runnin' out and in in the sunshine and no' be a worry fa'in' down and breaking their necks on the stair.'

The Bard said good-bye to George Haugh: a good-bye tha he was leaving the Stinking Vennel, not a good-bye that he was parting.

'You see, Geordie: yon ken that what I've down below there's no' the best that could be for me or the bairns or Jean.'

'Oh, dinna worry, Rab. Mind you, I'll miss you. I'll miss being able to dodge down to hae a word wi' you; and I'll miss you dodging up to hae a word wi' me. But, damnit, you're no' leaving the town. I'll aey be pleased to see you and I hope I'll no' be a stranger to you up in the Millbrae.'

'Na, no, Geordie: I'll be mair pleased than ever to see you at the Millbrae. I confess it's been a great relief to me, especially this last twa-three months, to hae been able to confide in you when the clouds were gey dark about my head. But you and the wife'll come up to the Millbrae whenever you feel the notion; and I'll be down here seein' my friend Syme in his Stamp Office; and there's nae need for us to be strangers in ony way whatsoever. Man, Geordie, I'm grateful for a' that your friendship has meant to me since I cam' to Dumfries. Mind you: I don't know how you do it. I don't know how you've managed to go about your affairs the way you have without rousing the suspicion o' the authorities. I'm afraid, Geordie, in the matter o' politics I'm little mair than a bairn when it comes to conducting myself.'

'Noo, Rab: I'm no' goin' to allow you to say that. I've never met wi' a man what kent better what he was daein' than you do. I never met wi' a man, or heard o' a man who, wi' his pen, had such inspiration and fire in him. Never hang your head when the principles o' freedom and liberty are mentioned. My God, man, the verses you've passed on to the movement, even though they dinna ken wha wrote them, makes you stand along wi' Muir and Palmer and a wheen others as one of the leaders of these days. It's my opinion that when you and I are gone that you'll be remembered as one of the great poets; aye, the greatest poet o' democracy; of the rights of man. . . At least, Rab, that's my feeling; and wi' a cleckin' o' young bairns and sae much that you could dae wi' your pen, I've tellt you a hundred times that it wad be madness and folly to come out into the open and declare yourself.

'Now . . . away up to the Millbrae yonder and enjoy a wee bit space for yoursel' and your wife and your bairns – and they're guid bairns! – and your books. Maybe up yonder you'll get a wee bit mair peace and quiet to pursue your writings . . .'

To John Syme, below him in the Stamp Office, he also expressed his regret that he was flitting away from him.

'I canna say, John, that I'm disappointed or have any regrets at leaving the Stinking Vennel except that I'm leaving you. Not that I'm leaving you in any sense really; but it was a great privilege to come here on a late afternoon and open your door and exchange news wi' you. Oh, I'll still be about the Sands here: I'll no' be mair than a dozen steps away frae your Office most days I'm out on duty – and I'll take the liberty of calling on you as usual.'

'If you dinna, I'll think something far's wrong between you and me. Yes, I think you'll be happier in a bigger house. I know nothing about the Millbrae Vennel – I know where it is, of course, though I've never had occasion to set foot in it – but I'll be more than delighted to see you in the happier circumstances. I've often said to my wife and to our mutual friends that, knowing you as I do and having the privilege of knowing you as I did at Ellisland, seeing you cabined and confined up the stair there gave me no pleasure.'

'Maybe I could bear the inconvenience o' the vennel here more than the wife and children. The wife had a hell o' a time trying to keep thae crawlin' bairns frae getting out that door and fa'in' down that stair. The Nith's a terrible menace to young bairns . . .'

'No . . . I'm no' away out o' the town, as a friend o' mine was saying no' so long ago. No . . . I'm just stepping up the street a bit, moving up the town a wee bit. I know that my poor hospitality doesna compare wi' anything Ryedale has to offer; yet I trust, John, you'll no' be a stranger to me in the Millbrae.'

'You dinna seem to realise that it's an honour and a privilege to ken you; it's an honour and a privilege to be invited to your fireside. And I certainly winna mak' mysel' ony mair stranger to your new home than I hope you will make yourself a stranger to my office here or the freedom of Ryedale. Mind you: that's what you have – a standing, permanent invitation to come to Ryedale as and when you can; and the oftener you come the mair welcome you are.'

And so on the 19th of May the Bard moved up and out of the Stinking Vennel and took possession of the red sandstone house in the Millbrae Vennel.

He had not installed Jean and the bairns very long in the

house – he had not even set his furniture, such as it was, to rights – before Jessie Lewars was across to offer what help she could to take the youngest children off Jean's hands so as to let her get ahead with the necessary washing and scrubbing that the house demanded.

Jessie Lewars, though she was but a young lassie, was a girl that Jean took to immediately – even more warmly than she had taken to her brother, John Lewars, if that were possible; and the pitcher of hot soup that Jessie went across and procured within a few minutes was the first welcome bite they had at the end of a table in the stone-flagged kitchen with the furniture still lying unsorted and unallocated.

The sun was bright and warm, and Jean opened the back door and there was the garden, fresh in the May sunshine; and the children cried and whooped with delight as they ran about the green. She let them romp to their hearts' content where they could come to no danger and get into no trouble.

Jessie Lewars said: 'Well, Mrs Burns, you've to understand that you're our neighbours here, and that onything I can do for you I'll only be too willing to do.'

Both Robert and Jean, looking into the plain honest unassuming face of Jessie Lewars – a face that indicated kindness, tact and infinite consideration – felt they had in her a young friend who would prove invaluable. They felt too that this welcoming by Jessie was an excellent omen against their entry to the Millbrae.

Part Two

THE ROCK AND THE WEE PICKLE TOW

THE CHAIN AND THE LINK

Though the forces working for reform had been gravely depleted in their ranks, nevertheless on the last day of April, 1793, the Second Convention of the Friends of the People had met in Edinburgh. Though this Convention did not reach the high level of enthusiasm that the First Convention had, it was altogether of a higher character in relation to the attitude of the delegates and to the concrete proposals before them.

It was obvious that the Second Convention had taken on a different character since the lawyers in Edinburgh who had so largely dominated the First Convention were, to a man, absent. Muir, of course, had not returned from Paris; and the wildest rumours were circulating as to his activities there.

But if the lawyers and advocates were absent from the Second Convention, there were men like Sinclair from Glasgow who were of a harder, more elemental stuff. There were men who came from what was known as the lower orders; and they had no time for fancy phrases and less time for going into a frenzy merely on the incantation of the words liberty, fraternity and equality. These high-sounding and liberating phrases must be reduced to everyday practicalities. The Convention decided without more ado to present a petition to Parliament and to ensure that their petition was at least of some consequence so far as the numbers of the signatories were concerned.

By the 11th of May the petition was presented in parliament. There were thirteen huge petitions from Scotland alone. The petition presented by Colonel Norman MacLeod, the M.P. for Inverness, extended the whole length of the House. But, for the petitioning of parliament, it was completely ineffective. The ministry of Pitt, and the men behind him, were in no mood to tolerate the very suggestion of the possibility of reform.

But far from being dismayed, the hard core of the Reform Movement, and the harder core of the Jacobin movement, kept up an incessant propaganda against the French war, demanding the cessation of all hostilities.

163

There were many merchants, manufacturers and shop-keepers who realised that a war was not to their advantage. The spies' reports accumulated with Dundas and with Pitt; and more and more did they become alarmed that the signs of agitation in the country indicated a spreading rather than the dwindling away for which they had hoped.

The Bard noted all that was going on with considerable satisfaction, though Dumfries was far away from the centre of genuine reform agitation . . .

With very much less satisfaction he noted, as the sun grew stronger and the days longer and warmer, that he had exchanged the peculiar smell of the Stinking Vennel for an equally offensive one in the Millbrae Vennel. Almost opposite his house was a tannery and the smell from the hides and from the pits could be overpowering. But, as in the Stinking Vennel, there was the possibility that they would get used to it.

As June came round, Stephen Clarke was back in Dumfries, for he was again going out to Dalswinton and to John MacMurdo at Drumlanrig.

Clarke and he had many fruitful song-sessions. He was very interested in the fact that Thomson's publication of *Select Scotish Airs* had lately been received by the Bard. Although the volume contained only five of his songs, *Wandering Willie, Gala Water, Auld Rob Morris, O Open the Door, When Wild War's Deadly Blast was Blawn*, nevertheless these songs were of sufficient merit to arouse Clarke's enthusiasm. As they in no way interfered or detracted from what he was doing for Johnson's *Museum*, Clarke congratulated him.

It was true that it was much more handsome than Johnson's ill-printed volume with the music struck from pewter plates. Thomson's collection was in every way elegant and select, although, casting through it, the Bard was of the opinion that the more elegant it was, the less accurate it was, the less native, the less true. He considered, without any doubt, that Johnson's was the more sterling production.

But there it was: another volume of songs coming out by another editor, and himself featuring prominently in the collection! It gave him pleasure to show the volume among his friends . . .

THE REVELATIONS OF CHLORIS

The commodious quarters the Millbrae provided did not prevent the Bard from visiting the Globe tavern. There were times when he felt he could write certain letters, copy certain poems for his friends there, with a freedom, with a lack of any possible interruption not always possible at home. Although his visits to his room were less frequent than they used to be in his Ellisland days, nevertheless the Globe still remained his favourite howff.

It so happened that on one June afternoon when he was transcribing some extracts from his Crochallan Song Book (for the benefit of an Edinburgh nobleman), Bess Hyslop came up to have a word with him.

'Weel, Bess, is there ocht I can dae for you?'

Bess Hyslop looked at him rather strangely.

'Wha d'you think's speirin' for you doon the stair?'

'Oh . . . onybody could be speirin' for me, Bess: you ken that weel enough!'

'Aye; but this is a lassie. A lassie I think ye ken gey weel . . .'

'Wha is she?'

'Jean Lorimer.'

The Bard started to his feet.

'Jean Lorimer? Huh! I wonder if there's any real truth in the rumour that that scoundrel Whelpdale she eloped wi' has abandoned her?'

'Oh, I think there'll be truth enough in it, Robert. But I fancy she could tell you best herself. She cam' in here seeking her father and when she heard he wasna here she asked what the news was of Robert Burns and if he still cam' about the place; and of course I told her that there were very few places apart from the Globe you did frequent; that you were at this very moment up the stairs engaged privately with your Excise returns. She speired me if I wad ask you to hae a word wi' her?'

'Hae a word wi' Chloris? Aye, aye. . . You know, Bess – but I think I've told you this before – Jean Lorimer was the model for many o' my sangs that go under the name of Chloris. Oh, Chloris was just a foolish fancy o' mine at the

165

time because I couldna well be singin' to a Jean Lorimer when my ain Jean was at hame and – dinna mistake me now, Bess – Jean Lorimer and my ain Jean are the best o' friends and aey hae been frae the first time she came down to Ellisland. . . Aye, Jean Lorimer. . . I don't suppose you would mind if I saw her up here, Bess? I mean, if she's been deserted by that Whelpdale she may want to have a bit private word wi' me. There's twa-three folk down there already, is there no'?'

'Aye: the only place you could see her is in your room here. Will I send her up?'

'Aye, send her up, Bess, if you will . . . I mean I don't want ony scandal to be talked about my name and hers – especially in the circumstances of her late elopement.'

Presently Jean's foot was on the stair, her hand was on the door, and there she was standing and smiling. The Bard rose and shook her warmly by the hand.

'Well, well: Jean Lorimer! I'm richt pleased to see you, my dear: richt pleased to see you. Will you sit down and join me in a drink – or are you still teetotal?'

'Aye, I'm still teetotal, Robert. You micht know it'll be something very desperate that'll send me to drink; but I'll sit down here. I'm glad to see you're looking well. . . You'll have the heard the news, of course?'

'Well, I've heard rumours, Jean, but they were not of a very pleasing kind, and I didna right want to believe onything I heard. After all: you made up your mind to do what you did and it's nobody's business the one way or the other if it hasn't turned out entirely to your satisfaction.'

'Aye: I see you're no' just quite at your ease, Robert. Well, I'll put you at ease as far as my run-away marriage is concerned. I dinna think I ever was married. There was a bit o' a ceremony at Gretna; but my father has more or less convinced me that it was nae richt ceremony. There it is . . . I was much in love wi' him, Robert; and maybe I'm still in love wi' him yet in a kind o' a way. . . . But he's bankrupt: he hasna a penny; and I suspect he's fled into England. After a', you canna blame him for doin' that?'

'Maybe you werena married in accordance with the Right Reverend Gentlemen of the Kirk of Scotland; maybe you werena married in a way that would suit either an Episcopalian, a Papist or a Methodist – and maybe I'm no very much concerned whether you were or no'. But you did stay with

Whelpdale as man and wife. He did take you to be his wife and, I presume, for better or for worse. . . But if you and your father hae decided that you werena married and that the ceremony was more or less a mock ceremony, then you'll no' be the first that has been taken in wi' a Gretna Green affair. The trouble is, Jean: will the folk accept the fact that you werena married? It's hard for a woman to live down the fact that she's made a run-away match wi' a man and the match hasna turned out satisfactorily.'

'Weel, folk'll just need to think what they want to think, Robert. I'm tired and sick o' paying ony attention to what folk think. Of course, if I had been sensible and listened to respectable people I wad never hae gone awa' wi' him.'

'And was your experience an unhappy one, Jean?'

'Weel: it has turned out unpleasant enough, Robert; but I canna deny that . . . we had our moments. We're both fond o' each other. I canna regret what happened. Oh, it wad hae been nice to hae been a farmer's wife . . . to hae come back in triumph. It's no' nice to eat humble pie and beg to be taken back under your father and mother's care again. My father was gey hurt about it and my mother took to the bottle – as usual. . . There it is, Robert. Maybe I'll hae to eat humble pie for a lang, lang time.'

'Weel . . . you're in a mess, Jean: there's nae doubt about that as far as the world goes and as far as your parents go. Your parents'll come round. In time they'll get over their disappointment as countless other parents hae got over it. The time'll come when it'll never be mentioned or thocht about . . .

'Damnit, you're even bonnier looking than when you went away. You'll get another man: another love: another husband – although I suppose you'll take care this time to see that you've the ring on and the witnesses and all the oddments o' flummery that are required to make a marriage fully legal in thae enlightened days. Aye. . . Oh, you'll do well for yourself yet, my lass. But . . . since you've gone away I've thought whiles that I was a bluidy idiot – as far as you were concerned.'

'I'm glad it's you that's saying it, Robert. I wouldna hae used thae words to you before. . . But you ken that . . . maybe . . . I'm no' what I should be.'

'No' what you should be? Damnit, you're as nature meant you to be, are you no'?'

'In your words: I suppose nature made me what I am. But you ken, Robert, I'm afraid I was never intended to be . . . a guid lassie. I'm afraid that aey I looked upon men as something a lassie should hae by rights. When I met him at the Ball and he asked me to run awa' wi' him there and then and get married and lie in a warm bed, weel . . . it seemed natural to me. . . It seemed the richt thing when there he was and him in love wi' me and me in love wi' him: on the instant. . . I'll be frank. Maybe I didna need much encouragement; and maybe he needed a lot less. But I'm no goin' to blame myself; and I hope you'll no' blame me.'

'No, no, Jean: I'll no' blame you. I couldna blame you. I couldna blame you for onything you ever did; but I can blame myself for what I never did – was too frightened to do – held you in too high regard to do. Although, again, I'm quite proud that I'm looking you between the eyes and saying to myself: at least as far as Chloris is concerned I hae nothing on my conscience.'

'I ken, Robert, I ken. I did try to tell you mony a time – and mony a time you just wouldna let me tell you . . . though maybe I should hae told you . . . but . . . you ken I lost my maidenhead long before I left the school? I see you're shocked at that. I can tell *you* – and you ken I canna tell ony other body. . . If I'd had a hundred maidenheads I suppose I'd hae lost them a' the same way . . .

'I've learned a lot this last wee while; and I've promised mysel' at least I'd tell you the truth about mysel'. I ken it's goin' to hurt you; but I had something for you, Robert, and I was never in love with you . . . at least no' the way I was in love wi' him. . . But I'd like that you wad ken the truth and then you can tell me what you think o' me; tell me what you think I should dae for myself. You see: there maun be something wrong wi' me because, even yet, I'm no' in the family-way. Maybe it is that I canna be in the family-way. I've risked plenty; and though latterly I didna care because nothing ever seemed to happen – although my mother has warned me many a time never to tak' the risk. . . D'you think it's possible, Robert, that maybe I'm no' meant to hae a bairn?'

'It's rather a staggering confession, Jean, and one you didna need to make to me. But I appreciate your making it for a' that, lass. Damnit, there's nothing to hinder you having a bairn. You've met the wrong kind o' men: that's a'. My

God, lass, gin I rubbed mysel' against a lassie she was in the family-way before you could say knife. That's been my trouble. Oh yes: I know there are men that seem to be differently made. There are men hae told me something of the task it was to put their lawfully-wedded wives in the family-way; but of that I know nothing but heresay . . .

'For the Lord's sake, Jean, dinna think that because you've had a free run up to now your luck will aey hold. Not, mind you, that I'm an authority. Men and women are strange beings. There are mysteries concerning barrenness that are just beyond ony understanding. Yes, I have known of a big strong healthy woman who just refused to be bairned no matter what happened. It's possible you may be just such a lass – but I wadna like to be in your shoes and risk it. Time enough gin you were married to try for a year or twa and then you micht ken for certain. Aye, even then there's no certainty. Mony a woman's been barren till she was ower forty and had weans after that. No: don't ask me to advise you as far as that's concerned. . . Wi' the rest o' your confession, I must say I'm deeply shocked. No: I don't mean that I'm offended in ony way; but there's a different side to this business, Jean, than you think. There I was – me that's supposed to ken something about the gentler sex (mind you, I could hae taken a bit bet, aye, a certain sure bet that if ever there was a virgin you were!). . . Oh, I knew, lass, that you were keen no' to be. I ken I could hae been there long ago; but something aey held me back.

'Damnit, we've talked about this mony and mony a time; and I've told you how I felt. I suppose all the time you thought, as you said there a wee while ago, that I was just a bluidy fool.'

'Oh no, no . . . not in that sense, Robert. A fool, yes; but nobody could ever think, least of all me, that Robert Burns was a' that o' a fool. What I meant when I said that, Robert, was I was willing to give you everything and you were anxious – just as anxious as I was: I ken you! But the something that held you back needna hae held you back. Can you tell me now – now that I ken a' there is to ken – can you tell me now what held you back – what really held you back?'

'You're driving a sair bargain, lass. You ken: I really couldna tell you what held me back. Oh, I had poetic ideas about you – and maybe they were sound enough for all that. The idea that I wanted to believe that you were – oh, just –

Chloris, held my imagination. The Chloris of what we poets call pastoral poetry – the shepherdess, the goddess. . . And there you can blame me a thousand times for being the biggest bluidy fool that ever wrote a line o' poetry or turned out the measure o' a sang. . . But if we had! But if we had! Then, Jean, there wad hae been nae sangs. And I think maybe – I may be wrong – God help me; but I think the sangs were worth it . . .

'You see: you ken how we've discussed this. I remember you saying to me one night: "If a man can tak' ony lass he fancies – an' she's willing – why should a lass no' tak' ony man she fancies – an' he's willing?" But you see, Jean, there's a something about this that's no' to be reckoned on the level o' animals . . .

'Here you can blame me as you like; but I'm sticking to my point because my whole experience of life has taught me this. Jean, you worry me because, unless you watch yoursel', lass, you hae a' the makings o' a thorough-going hure. No, no, no: I dinna mean to insult you using that word; but you see that's just what a hure is. She tak's a man; and she's no' much concerned who he is or what he is as long as she gets a certain experience. And that, I suppose, is the unprofessional hure; and there's plenty o' them gaun about. Dinna mistake me: plenty o' them respectable married women who are of that category. But there's a danger, Jean: an awfu' danger. It seems to me – an' I've spoken to a wheen hures in my day – there's an awfu' danger that you'll step into the ranks o' them wha say: "Here's my body, and it's yours for whatever price you like to put on it." It's as dangerous as that, Jean.

'Oh yes: I know that there are many highly-respectable hures – and some of them are kind-hearted enough and decent enough in a' other respects. I have never looked down my nose at what are called "the unfortunates" and "our weaker sisters"; but I hae never bocht their wares either. And gin I felt that a woman was giving herself to me, either for cash or for something in kind, then I doubt I wad revolt. At least that's how I've conducted mysel' so far.

'And when you tell me what you've told me and you so young – and, damnit, when you were at the school you were bound to be innocent enough . . . when you tell me that this has been going on all the time – then I wonder what the future has in store for you. The best thing I could advise you, lass, is: put a tight rein on yoursel' and get a decent man.

He needna be a rich farmer nor a bankrupt farmer – and marry him; and, if you're blessed wi' bairns – thank the Lord! And if you're no, well . . . you'll just need to dree your weird as best you may.

'Mind you: I think you couldna be a hure – a potential hure I mean, Jean – and talk to me the way you're talking. You embarrassed me mony a night: you embarrass me more now – because I don't know that I'm the right man to answer you onything except that I think very, very deeply and very, very highly of you. And I do love you, lass . . . in my way.

'No' so very long ago in this very Globe tavern the searing o' your kisses cam' back to me when I heard o' your elopement; and they did something to me then that they didna do at the time.'

'I'm sorry if I've embarrassed you, Robert. You ken how often I've said to you – and I mean it – that you're a guid man. There's nothing bad about you, Robert Burns. . . I understand all you've said to me – at least I think I do. But the strange thing is, Robert, that I canna feel ony guilt for what I've done. My only disappointment is that I was never able to hae you when it was so easy to hae ony other body. You ken I've aey regretted that. I dinna want you to think that I cam' here to-day, or that I'm coming back again, to make up to you in ony kind o' a way – except that I can aey speak to you . . .

'And sometimes I feel I need to speak, Robert; I need to talk about things that are kept buried deep down in me. Sometimes I get worried, get . . . into a terrible state when I think I'm maybe no' as I should be. When you talked just now about hures . . . that's what I mean. I've heard about thae kind o' women that sell themselves to men; but oh! the very thocht o' it gives me the creeps. Just the same: maybe the lassie that tak's a man because she wants him is as bad as the lassie that tak's a man maybe when she doesna want but *has to want* for the sake o' the money. . . I think that's terrible. What worries me is that I shouldna want men the way I do want them. Aside from this ane here that's deserted me, I never really wanted the man for himsel' – if I can mak' mysel' clear?

'It was just a man I wanted. As lang as he wasna repulsive to me in ony way. . . That's what I mean when I say it gives me the creeps when I think of women having to do that for money.

'I used to wonder if I would never fa' in love wi' a man as others seemed to do. Oh . . . there were so many – and yet I could never think of marrying them. . . . I just never felt I was in love wi' onybody till I met him. . . . Now that that's a' by, I just wonder if I'm no' different frae a' other girls and women . . .

'D'you think, maybe, if I did marry and have a bairn or twa that I wad feel different; because if I thocht that, and a likely-like fellow did want to marry me. . . Oh, but then if I didna love him I couldna marry him. I couldna marry ony man unless I loved him the same way as I love *him*. Is that wrong too, Robert?'

'No: that's your saving grace, lass. You remember me telling you one time that your heart wad tell you when you were in love? Well, your heart has told you you were in love; and your heart, it seems, was right. But the man – the man your heart was set on – wasna right. Now that's the damnable bit: that's the uncertain bit. And by the Lord, if I ever lay my eyes on this Whelpdale I'll lay my hands on him. A man, especially at his age, knows what he's doing; knows better than to tak' a lass and damn-well ruin her the way he has tried to ruin you.

'Oh, I find mysel' whiles acting the moralist, Jean; acting as if I had some claim to being a paragon o' virtue. Maybe I'm old-fashioned; sometimes I think that. You see, sometimes I think that there's a different code o' conduct suitable to a man than to a woman. Maybe that's all wrong; maybe you should, as I've done all my life, go by the knowledge, the promptings that come from your heart. And maybe if you feel as you do about things, you're maybe right; and I'm the last man to say you're wrong, or have ony right to say you're wrong . . .

'You're given your desires, your emotions and they're yours and they're no other body's. The power that put them there put them there for reasons that are no' for you and I to understand. That, at least, is as logical as onything I can think. I never went by the book o' rules. All my life I've despised the book o' rules. But then, maybe I've flattered mysel' that what I did was right, because that was the way I wanted it.

'Now, for heaven's sake, lass, let's forget this preaching. Just try and think it out for yoursel': think out what you're doin'; what you have done; what you intend to do. . . . If it

172

ives you happiness and doesna hurt ony other body – well hen, go ahead and dinna worry. And dinna, for Godsake, hink you're peculiar or made different from other folk – at ast sufficiently to set you aside from women-kind. You're a assionate woman; you're a passionate beauty; and of course our beauty attracts men. Being attractive to men, you feel ttracted to men. Damnit, nothing more natural . . .

'No, Jean: forget what I've said. Both attitudes I suppose re right. I've tried to give you the best of both schools of dvice, and find myself contradicting myself in the process . . .

'Here you are this fine June afternoon, as nicely put-on as 've seen you – maybe no' just as radiant as I've seen you – ut, damnit, I wadna say no' as attractive as ever . . . a bit nore experienced – no' a bit more experienced but a large bit nore experienced. You've learned plenty these last months, ean: I can see that. But I'll confess to you now that, while ou were away, I was attracted to you in a way I never was when I was in your company. So now that you're back gain and sitting there. . . Mind you, it wad take gey little for ne to be tempted. . . Only the fact that I can talk this way to ou means that I have no intention of being tempted . . . eastways, no' here.

'You'll need to come round and see Mrs Burns and the airns. You'll need to resume your old visitations, Jean, and ak' up the threads again where you left off. Damnit: mind ou, I'm still singing the praises o' John Lewars. He's gey ften at the house now that he's just across the road. Oh, here're others . . . there're other young men about the town. So dinna mak' yourself a stranger, Jean – least of a' to Mrs Burns. She'll be more than pleased to see ony time you drop in. . . I think maybe it wad be best if you didna mention hat we'd have this meeting together – especially in the Globe avern. You see – no' that it concerns onybody; but we'll leave t at that, Jean . . .

'When will you come round? Will you come round to-night? I've a bit hour's work here to do and your father's naybe about the Jerusalem tavern – did you try up there? No: well he's sometimes there and sometimes he's in the King's. . . Aye, ye've tried the King's. Weel: I dinna ken onywhaur else you could try; but what about goin' round and avin' a word wi' Mrs Burns now? Or must you see your ather? If you havena to see your father you can stay till later on wi' us. You're still fit and able to walk the road home, aren't you?'

'Oh, Robert: you ken when I hear you talking like this it reminds me o' some o' thae nights we had when you were gaun ower your sangs. . . No . . . I've some bits o' things to get in the town, and now that I'm here I could come round and see Jean and you – maybe in about an hour's time would that do?'

'Nothing could be better, Jean.'

But just as they were about to part, Bess Hyslop came up the stair, knocked discreetly, came in and informed the Bard that Stephen Clarke from Dalswinton was asking for him. The Bard told her to send Stephen Clarke up and told Jean Lorimer, who wanted to depart, to wait and meet his friend.

So Clarke was introduced to Jean Lorimer. They spoke for a few minutes and then Jean took her leave.

Clarke said: 'And who, Robert, was that remarkable flaxen-haired beauty? Not your Chloris of the eyebrows of a darker hue – which I noted?'

'Yes, Stephen, that happens to be my Chloris. Maybe she won't be my Chloris again: I don't know about that; but you think . . .'

'Yes, that's exactly what I do think, Robert. Ha . . . don't tell me that your Chloris is one of your platonic affections! A man just couldna be platonic where your Chloris is concerned however much he might be platonic with regard to the sangs he made about her.'

'Well . . . there you are, Stephen! There's the girl who inspired – or, if she didn't exactly inspire, was the inspiring model for some of my best sangs. I think that: Sae flaxen were her ringlets, her eyebrows of a darker hue, bewitchingly o'crarching twa laughing een o' bonnie blue . . . was one of my better sangs. Of course I had Oonagh's Waterfall to work on.'

'I can only hope, Robert, that the young lady kens nocht of Oonagh's Waterfall!'

'In a sense, Stephen, there's nothing that lassie doesna know. She's scarce eighteen – or maybe she's just eighteen; I couldna be sure to a month. But that lassie has had more experience of the world of men than onybody you and I know.'

'Experienced in what way, Robert? I must say that where you and women are concerned, I just don't know where to

174

begin and where to end; or what to believe or what not to believe. Damn it all, you can't expect me to believe that that most virginal girl is experienced in the ways of men – the men of this world? No, no: I'm prepared to accept your statement that your affection for her is purely platonic, although. . . However, Robert: we haven't come here to discuss your platonic relation with a girl who exists – for I have lately seen her and she was in this room — Well, well: all I can say is that you're a very lucky man to have such models for your sangs. I wish to God I could find – or be interested – in such models.'

'I wanted you to meet her, Stephen, because often enough you've said to me: "Are these girls you sing about real or are they just the poet's fancy?" Mind you, I can fancy a lass richt enough along wi' the best o' them. But when you meet a girl like Chloris; when you see her as I saw her – when she was much younger – of a May morning and the blossom hoary on the thorn, the dew sparkling, the lark singing and a burn whimpling to the sea. . . Ah, if you had met her under the circumstances that I met her, even you, you long-legged lass-abjuring beggar, micht hae been tempted to mak' a sang on her!'

'Aye . . . but then *you* would meet such a girl on such a morning, when I would be getting down the Landmarket and wishing to God I were somewhere else. Aye: a poet, I see, is not only born but he must be born in certain circumstances and under a certain sign of the Zodiac. What your sign is God knows, Robert; but what about a drink?'

That night Jean said to him:

'Weel, Rab; and what d'ye think o' your Chloris now?'

'I'm worried about her, Jean . . . aye, I'm worried about her. She's no' in a very enviable position, although she's looking well and doesna appear to bear ony scars from her adventure wi' Whelpdale; but she's no' just what she should be . . .'

'No; she's no' just what she should be – the lassie's gey worried beneath the surface if you only kent it. I think she's in love wi' you.'

'To hell, Jean: let there be an end to this once and for all! I'm not in love wi' Jean Lorimer and Jean Lorimer – damnit! – is no' in love wi' me! She's just eloped wi' a man; gone through a service o' mock marriage or whatever it was she

175

went through; she's been thrown aside like a dirty rag. . .
Well: what are you tryin' to tell me?'

'I'm tryin' to tell you nothing, Rab, but what's as plain
as a pikestaff. Jean Lorimer, puir lass, has been gey disappointed. Och, I had a word or twa wi' her afore you cam'
in; and though she did her best to hide it, I could see that
she has still a notion o' you, Rab.'

'Now, once and for all, Jean: I demand that we keep
silent, you and me, about Jean Lorimer. To hell! you wad
think you were tryin' your best, doin' your best to throw me
into her arms and, for all I know, tryin' to persuade her to
throw hersel' into mine! Weel, neither you nor Jean Lorimer
nor the Lord God Almighty is going to throw me into Jean
Lorimer's arms! I'm damned if I'm goin' to be persuaded
that ony cast-off of a damned scoundrel like Whelpdale is
goin' to be thrown at me. I'm annoyed wi' you, Jean. Twa
or three times you've hinted at this and no' only hinted – but
you've spoken damned broad about me and Jean Lorimer . . .'

'Dear, dear, Rab: you get yoursel' into such a state. Oh,
I'm no' worried about Jean Lorimer . . . no' worried one wee
bit. And, since you've asked me, I'll no' say another word
about her; and maybe you'll no' say much about her yoursel'.
Because, mind you, if you're ever tempted, Rab, in the
moment o' your temptation you'll remember your words to
me – and mine to you.'

THE SWEETS OF AN EVENING

But there came a day, or an evening rather, not very long
afterwards, when the Bard did take Jean Lorimer; when the
drumming of his blood against the walls of her flesh could no
longer be denied. And he took her less tenderly, less delicately,
less affectionately than he had ever taken a woman. Chloris
felt she had won the greatest victory in her life. Now she
realised what she had always known instinctively: that, as a
lover, there was no one who could compare with Robert
Burns . . .

The Bard remembered Jean. He spat the kisses of Jean
Lorimer from his lips. He cursed himself. He cursed Jean
Lorimer. And he cursed the incessant clamouring of his
blood . . .

He had promised himself that he would not succumb to this girl; that nothing could induce him to do what she wanted. . . But now it was over he walked home in the June dusk with all nature hushed and dreaming, except an owl or two that ghosted past him and the moths that blundered about his face.

The Bard cursed himself. He felt – and he had never felt this with any woman before – that his relationship with Chloris was somehow low and despicable. The wanton, the blindly-wanton passion of Jean Lorimer disgusted him. Perhaps not disgust with Jean: perhaps the disgust was at himself for taking a woman for whom he had no real love; for destroying in the taking of her, an idol and an ideal . . .

Jean Lorimer, for her part, stretching herself down in her bed at Kemys Hall – and hearing perhaps the self-same owls hoot from the green branches of the beech trees – felt that she had won her greatest victory since she had triumphed over all the reason, all the sentiment, all the protestations of Robert Burns. It had long been to her a point of peculiar awareness that Robert Burns was inviolate. Now that she knew him, she felt there was no man that she could not know; no man in the years that lay ahead that she would not know did she so desire . . .

But beneath her triumph and her satisfaction, Chloris was aware of the bitterness of the savaging of his kisses. They were not the tender kisses he had given her in the days that were past. His lips had bruised with an intensity of passion that seemed to care nothing for the recipient of his passion. And deep, deep down, Chloris realised for the first time in her life that she had not given; she had not received; she had been made the vehicle for a passion that was as impersonal as a bolt of lightning or a roll of thunder or the shrieking of the wind in a winter's gale.

GALLOWAY TOUR

Before the summer ended the Bard and John Syme adopted a plan to escape for a few days into the Galloway countryside. This they did and the Bard returned very much refreshed to Dumfries, though resolved to have no more nights of hard drinking . . .

Syme was so taken with his jaunt with the Bard that he sat down and wrote to their mutual friend Alexander Cunningham at Edinburgh:

I had the distinguished favour and high gratification of receiving a large packet of choice pamphlets with your very acceptable letter of 24th July. They reached me on 26th, the evening before I set out with Burns on a tour through the wilds and cultivated plains of Galloway, some account of which tour I am so disposed to give you, and perhaps you are so disposed to receive, that I trust you will graciously undertake to read to the end of this (to be) very long extended epistle. I love to talk to you. I live at such a distance I can't do it frequently. You must therefore let me encroach on your ear or eye when I have a good opportunity. But first to bestow some words in answer to yours of 24th ...

Methinks I hear you saying 'confound your answering my letter; tell me where you and Burns were, what you did, what you saw, and what in short happened. Come, come, begin.' Gentle Sandy, have patience, my dear fellow. I will first tell you we did not enjoy such felicity as you and Harry experienced once on a time. We had no Tollmen to damn, and we rode equally fast and slow. We could not reap any of those exhilarations which spring from the cheerful source of contradiction. So we contented ourselves with the dull pleasure of mutual enjoyment or suffering, according as circumstances of delight or annoyance occurred.

I got Burns a grey highland Shelty to ride on. We dined the first day of our tour at Glendonwynnes of Parton, a beautiful situation on the banks of the Dee. In the evening we walked up a bonnie knowe and had as grand a view of alpine scenery as can well be found. A delightful soft evening gave it all its great graces. Immediately opposite and within a mile of us we saw Airds, a charming romantic place where dwelt Low, the author of 'Mary, weep no more for me.' This was classical ground for Burns. He viewed the 'highest hill which rises o'er the source of Dee.' He would have stayed till 'the passing spirit' had appeared had we not resolved to reach Kenmore that night. We arrived as Mr and Mrs Gordon were sitting down to supper.

Here is a genuine Baron's seat. The Castle, an old building, stands on a large natural moat. In front the River Ken winds for miles through the most fertile and beautiful holm ill it expands into a loch twelve miles long, the banks of which on the south present a fine and soft landscape of green knolls, natural wood, and here and there a grey rock. On the north the aspect is great, wild, and I may say tremendous. In short, I cannot conceive a scene more terribly romantic than the Castle of Kenmore. Burns thinks so much of it that he has long meditated on putting his thoughts in poetry descriptive of it. Indeed, I take it he has begun the work. I should be very curious to see how his mind views it. We spent three days with Mr Gordon, whose polished hospitality is of an original and endearing kind. It is not only, ask and it shall be given, seek and ye shall find, but here is what you may wish to have, take it as you incline . . .

We left Kenmore and went to Gatehouse. I took him the moor road, where savage and desolate regions extended wide around. The sky turned sympathetic with the wretchedness of the soil and treated the poor travellers to the full with a flood of misery. For three hours did the wild elements rumble their bellyful upon our defenceless heads, O, ho, twas foul.' We were utterly wet, and we got vengeance at Gatehouse by getting utterly drunk. There is not such a scene of delightful beauty in Scotland as Gatehouse. As it is a stage on the road to Ireland I will not describe it. 'Tis well known to travellers, and you likely have or will see it.

From Gatehouse we went to Kirkcudbright through a fine country, but before I bring you there I must tell you Burns has got a pair of Jimmy boots, which the wetness had rendered it an impossible task to get on. The brawny poet tried force, and tore them in shreds. A whiffling vexation like this is more trying to the temper than a serious calamity. We were going to the Isle – Lord Selkirk's – and the forlorn Burns was quite discomfited – a sick stomach, headache, &c. lent their forces, and the man of verse was quite *accablé*. Mercy on me, how he did fume and rage. Nothing could reinstate him in temper. I tried all I could think of; at length I got a lucky hit. Across the bay of Wigtown I showed him Lord Galloway's house. He expectorated his spleen against the aristocratic elf, and regained a most agreeable temper. I have about half a dozen of capital extempores which I dare not write. But I may repeat that you shall hear them sometime. I declare they possess as much point and classical terseness, if I may so express myself, as any thing I can imagine. O, he was in an epigrammatic humour indeed. I told him it was rash to crucify

Lord Galloway in the way he was doing, for though he might not receive any favour at his hands yet he might suffer an injury. He struck up immediately:

> 'Spare me thy vengeance, Galloway,
>   In quiet let me live;
> I ask no kindness at thy hand,
>   For thou hast none to give.'

. . . The interval from the first date to this has passed without my having time or mood to finish what I have still to say in continuation of our tour. I am to bring you to Kirkcudbright, along with our Poet without boots. I carried the torn ruins across my saddle despite his fulminations and in contempt of appearances – and what's more, Lord Selkirk carried them in his coach to Dumfries. I insisted they were worth the mending.

We reached Kirkcudbright about one o'clock. I had engaged us to dine with one of the first men in our country, J. Dalzell. But Burns's obstreperous independence would not dine but where he should, as he said, eat like a Turk, drink like a fish, and swear like the Devil. Since he would not dine with Dalzell in his own house, he had nothing for it but Dalzell to dine with us in the Inn. We had a very agreeable party. In the evening we went to the Isle. Robert had not absolutely regained the milkiness of good temper, and it occurred once or twice to him that the Isle was the seat of a Lord, yet that Lord was not an aristocrat. He knew the family a little. At length we got there about eight, as they were at tea and coffee. It is one of the most delightful places that can in my opinion be formed by the assemblage of every soft, but not tame, object which constitutes natural and cultivated beauty. But not to speak of its external graces, let me tell you that we found all the female beauty (as beautiful) and some strangers at the Isle, and who else but Urbani. It is impossible to pay due respect to the family by putting them forward as principal figures on this paper, when I have to tell you that Urbani sung us many Scotch songs accompanied with music. The two young ladies of Selkirk sung also. We had the song 'Lord Gregory', which I asked for to have occasion to call upon Burns to *speak* his words to that tune. He *did speak* them, and such was the effect that a dead silence ensued. Twas such a silence as a mind of feeling must necessarily preserve when it is touched, as I think sometimes has and will happen, with that sacred enthusiasm which banishes every other thought than the contemplation and indulgence of the sympathy produced.

In my opinion Burns's 'Lord Gregory' is the finest, the most natural and affecting ballad I ever met with. The fastidious critic perhaps might wish that these words 'Thou bolt of Heaven that flashes by' and 'Ye mustering thunders' had not been in such an elevated and English style. They seem to give the action of seizing fire and perdition, which is not the character of the ballad. Pass the seeming blasphemy of the criticism. It struck me by random.

We enjoyed a very happy evening – we had really a treat of mental and sensual delight – the latter consisting in abundance and variety of delicious fruits &c. – the former you may conceive from our society – a company of 15 or 16 very agreeable young people.

We got to Dumfries next day. So ends our tour. I shall not dwell longer upon it, yet I could give you many other circumstances; but recollecting how Boswell treats of his Tour with Johnson and how he tells you of his &c. &c. &c., I fear I might incur a similar contempt. I have not seen Robert since . . .

VOICE FROM THE NEW WORLD

On August 8th, Citizen Genet, the Minister Plenipotentiary from the Republic of France to the United States of America, landed at New York. At the Battery he was received by a highly-representative and respectable committee of forty gentlemen appointed for that purpose, and his arrival was signalised by the firing of a Federal salute. He was accompanied to the Tontine coffee-house, surrounded by a tremendous group of citizens who cheered every yard of his progress, and there he was addressed on behalf of the committee, on behalf of the United States of America, by Dr Pitt Smith.

Dr Smith said, among other things: 'We have the honour to address you in the name of the Republicans of this metropolis. As we had been informed of your impending arrival, we have long earnestly wished to receive you as the representative of a nation struggling in the glorious cause of freedom and humanity; of a nation animated by sentiments too congenial with our own, not to excite the warmest sympathy of friendship and exaltation.

'From the timely aid of France these United States have been brought to the full enjoyment of the blessings of civil liberty.

'The services of your countrymen in the hour of our distress were essential, were cheerfully rendered, and the despots may absurdly claim the merit of them.

'We know better to whom the sentiments of gratitude are to be directed; and we ardently wish that sentiment indelibly impressed on the hearts of our remotest posterity. We recognise in the defenders of their own, the defenders of our rights, and in the patriots of France, the defenders of America.

'We this day tender to you our hearts and through you to your nation our warm and undisguised affections. Be assured, sir, we are both ready and willing to tender you every service and assistance consistent with our reciprocal welfare, and with the duty we owe our country; nay, more exulting would we sacrifice a liberal portion of our dearest interests could we result in your behalf an adequate advantage.

'The voice of our government has, through its executive, declared the neutrality of the United States in the present war.

'We regard that sacred voice with attention; but no one is a stranger to the part all good men take in your Revolution. As the sentiment relates to question and principle, there is no neutrality. The virtuous and the wise through all ranks of society are enlisted with you! 'Tis vice, ignorance and cowardice that alone oppose the empire of truth and independence or shrink from the common cause of human nature.'

VOICE FROM THE OLD WORLD

Henry Dundas was furious that Muir had slipped through his clutches. He consulted with his nephew concerning a substitute. The Lord Advocate had several candidates for the post; but he considered that the Reverend Thomas Fische Palmer, the Unitarian minister in Dundee, was one of the most determined rebels in Scotland. He could be charged with circulating an address thought likely to arouse demonstrations against the law.

In August, Dundas decided to proceed against Palmer. But before his case could be heard, Thomas Muir – returning from Paris by way of Dublin where he had been entertained by the Society of United Irishmen – was arrested on landing at Portpatrick, loaded in chains and taken to Edinburgh . . .

Since the judges had the selection of the jurymen in their own hands, they took good care to see that the jury was well packed by members who were opposed to the principles for which Paine was indicted. To a man, the jury were all members of the Goldsmiths' Hall Association – an association which had struck Muir's name off its roll and had offered a reward for the discovery of anyone circulating Paine's works; and this, indeed, was one of the offences of which Muir was now accused.

The charges against Muir concerned the possibility of inciting disaffection by seditious speeches, circulating Paine's *Rights of Man* and other seditious works; and reading and defending the Address of the United Irishmen at the first general convention of the Friends of the People.

Addressing the jury, Lord Advocate Robert Dundas categorised Muir as not only a demon of mischief, guilty of the most diabolical conduct; but the pest of Scotland.

Muir, in a speech which made history even as he uttered it – a speech that lasted over three hours, asked: 'What is my crime? Not lending a relation a copy of Mr Paine's works; not giving away to another a few copies of an innocent and constitutional publication; but for having dared to be, according to the measure of my feeble abilities, a strenuous and active advocate for an equal representation of the people in the house of the people.'

But Muir reckoned without Robert MacQueen, Lord Braxfield, Lord Justice Clerk. Braxfield had been instructed by Henry Dundas; and he was anxious to wreak vengeance on Muir, and any like him, who had lent countenance in any way whatsoever to democratic and reform principles.

In his broadest dialect, and licking his leering lips, Braxfield said to the jury:

'I leave it for you to judge whether it was perfectly innocent or not for Mr Muir, at such a time, to go about amang ignorant country-folk; amang the lower classes o' people makin' them lay aff their wark and inducing them to believe that a reform was absolutely necessary to preserve their safety and their liberty which – had it no' been for him – they wad never hae suspected to hae been in danger . . .

'The Reformers talk of liberty and equality; this they hae in everything consistent wi' their happiness; and equality also. However low born a man may be, his abilities may raise him to the highest honours of the State. He may rise to be Lord Chancellor, head o' the law; or he may rise to be Archbishop of Canterbury, the head o' the kirk; and tak' precedence o' a' ranks but the bluid-royal. What mair equality wad they hae? If they hae ability, low birth is not against them. But that they hae a richt to representation in Parliament I deny. The landed interest alone should be represented in Parliament, for they only hae an interest in the country. In God's name, let them gang. I wish them not to stay; but I deny they hae a richt to representation in Parliament. I only maintain that the landed interest pay all the taxes. The shoon, I alloo, are dearer by almost a half than I remember them, owing to the additional taxes on leather, which the exigencies of the State require; but it is not the mechanics and labourers who pay that tax, but the proprietors o' the land; for I remember when I could pay a labourer with half the sum I do now. I am therefore of the opinion that the present constitution is the best that ever existed.'

It was a fantastic and incredible trial. The jury knew that every word that had been spoken by Thomas Muir was no less than the truth. They knew equally that every word that was spoken by Braxfield was a caricature of justice: of the bare facts of the case. The people in the court were, in so far as they were disinterested, entirely on the side of Muir.

But justice mattered nothing in this court. What mattered was the fact that Muir, in however trivial, irrelevant or obscure a way, was connected with the French Revolution. And the jury unanimously decided that any being in any way tainted with the heresies of France was automatically deserving banishment forthwith of the realm.

Many years ago, in Machlin, in the *Dedication to Gavin Hamilton*, Robert Burns had written: 'Vain is his hope, whase stay an' trust is in moral mercy, truth and justice.'

But Robert Burns was Robert Burns. There were many people in Scotland who knew there was no justice and no truth in the world for them. But for men like Thomas Muir and the middle-class elements of the Friends of the People there was a profound belief in justice and truth as eternal verities. They learned otherwise when they came up against the undisguised sentiments of the class that held dominant power.

Muir had staked everything on the verity of law: on the reality of truth and justice. He had not realised that these were but abstractions representing the innate desire of men and women for freedom in a free world. Only the few, like Robert Burns, knew there could never be anything approaching abstract freedom and that the world could never be free from the necessities of the cosmic exigencies of time and place: of the inter-relationship with man and the essential pre-requisites that made life possible . . .

So Muir was found guilty and given the sentence of transportation to Botany Bay for fourteen years.

SCOTS WHA HAE

The Bard was very deeply incensed at the savagery of Thomas Muir's sentence. He reviewed the position with regard to himself, with regard to Scotland and with regard to the general fight for liberty . . .

One fine evening at the end of August when he was taking one of his usual solitary strolls along the banks of the Nith, the tune *Hey Tutti, Taiti* dominated his mind; and he thought of Bruce standing before his army at the Battle of Bannockburn. . . . The tune *Hey Tutti, Taiti* was commonly believed to be the Scots' battle march at Bannockburn. But Bannockburn and the victory over Edward II was a long way off now, though the memory of it never failed to excite and stir the blood of all Scots patriots.

He had the vision of the Scots of the present generation lined up here and there and everywhere against the gathering forces of reaction and fighting, as the French were fighting, their Bannockburn over again. And he hadn't been enthused with this idea very long before he found himself putting the following words to the melody:

> Scots, wha hae wi' Wallace bled,
> Scots, wham Bruce has aften led,
> Welcome to your gory bed
>   Or to victorie!

Now's the day, and now's the hour:
See the front o' battle lour,
See approach proud Edward's power –
    Chains and slaverie!

Wha will be a traitor knave?
Wha can fill a coward's grave?
Wha sae base as be a slave? –
    Let him turn, and flee!

Wha for Scotland's King and Law
Freedom's sword will strongly draw,
Freeman stand or freeman fa',
    Let him follow me!

By Oppression's woes and pains,
By your sons in servile chains,
We will drain our dearest veins
    But they shall be free!

Lay the proud usurpers low!
Tyrants fall in every foe!
Liberty's in every blow!
    Let us do, or die!

He was not long in sending the tune off to Thomson, noting that though the song celebrated, or appeared to celebrate the Battle of Bannockburn, it also owed its inspiration to 'the glowing ideas of some other struggles of the same nature *not quite so ancient.*'

But he had to ensure that the song would not appear – at least for some considerable time: until the present heresy hunting had died down – as coming from his pen.

When he read the words over to Syme and later to George Haugh, both had to agree that it was nothing less than a major tragedy that his great patriotic and revolutionary song would have to circulate anonymously throughout Scotland.

Haugh said: 'Many songs you hae given the people of Scotland are anonymous; and I canna think but that a blind man could detect their authorship wi' a stick. But this glorious song, Scots Wha Hae, will, unless I'm a sadly mistaken man, take your name wi' honour and glory down the ages . . .'

No sooner had some copies of *Scots Wha Hae* been circulated than the Reverend Thomas Fische Palmer, the Unitarian minister of Dundee, was brought before the Circuit Court of Justiciary at Perth and, before Lords Eskgrove and Abercrombie, sentenced to seven years' transportation for the heinous crime of circulating an Address advocating, mildly and constitutionally, the claims for parliamentary reform and universal suffrage.

DEATH OF AN UNPRINCIPLED PROSTITUTE

On October 16th, Marie Antoinette was taken from the prison of the Conciergerie, placed in a common cart and, with her hands tied behind her back and her back turned towards the horse's tail, led to the guillotine at the Place of the Revolution.

To a storm of shouting 'Long live the Republic!' the guillotine crashed.

Her blood-streaming head was immediately given the distinction of being displayed to the citizens from the four quarters of the guillotine.

RETURN OF MARIA RIDDELL

Early in November, Maria Riddell returned from Dorset where she had buried her father, and where indifferent health had delayed her return longer than she had anticipated.

When the Bard met her at Woodley Park he found her full of her old vivacity and vitality.

The fact that Marie Antoinette had been put to the guillotine in no way dismayed her. Rather, indeed, was she elated.

'That, my dear Robert, puts an end once and for all to any possibility of a return to the throne of that dissolute monarchy. The Republic of France is firmly, irrevocably, set upon its way.'

And the Bard, who cared no more for Marie Antoinette than he did for Louis, her husband, regarded her execution as no more than historical retribution for the unspeakable

187

crimes the French royal family had inflicted upon the French people. He agreed whole-heartedly with Maria.

On the strength of this (as it seemed to the Bard on later reflection), Maria put her arms round him and kissed him with a curious frenzy. . . He found her, in the kissing, wild and insatiable. . . In the peculiar intimacy that took place; in the sudden coming together in sexual awareness, there was nothing the Bard could recognise as normal. Despite the cat-like ferocity of Maria's passion, the relationship was utterly impersonal. It was without meaning, substance or satisfaction. On the road home the Bard began to doubt what had taken place . . .

GLOOMY DECEMBER AGAIN

December, 1793, came round and proved as gloomy as any December the Bard had known in Dumfries.

The Friends of the People met in convention in Edinburgh early in the month. No sooner had they adjourned than the English delegates, Joseph Gerrald and Maurice Margarot, arrived and, together with the Edinburgh and district branches of The Friends of the People, they met as The British Convention. Their object was still universal suffrage and annual parliaments; but their language was seditious to the ears of Dundas and his henchmen. Skirving, Margarot and Gerrald were arrested. The terror against reform was about to be unleashed with the purpose and effect.

On the 9th of the month Isabella Burns was married to John Begg at Mossgiel. Though he Bard was not able to be present he sent, from Jean and himself, a gift in the way of some dress lengths.

'That's the youngest of the family – that's the pet yowe if ever there was a pet yowe in our family – married now, Jean. It leaves Nancy and Bell; but we'll just need to hope for the best as far as they're concerned.'

'Ah weel, Rab: of a' your sisters, Isabella is the maist like you. She has something o' your blood in her veins – though where that blood comes from, Guid kens: I dinna. Your father didna seem to have it; and your mother didna have it; but it's in you and Isabella – in Isabella no' to the same extent as you: Isabella's nothing compared wi' you – but I mean she's better married, Rab; an' John Begg's a guid quiet man and I've nae doubt he'll mak' her a guid husband.'

The Bard looked at Jean and thought of a pertinent reply – then thought better of it and turned away.

A week later he met Walter Auld, the saddler. Walter was very downcast. Wattie was one of his earliest friends in Dumfries and the Bard regarded him with a peculiar affection. He looked at him with sad and tired eyes.

'Oh weel, Rab: you might as well ken the news afore the whole toon kens it – or maybe the whole toon kens it gin now; but the fact is I'm bankrupt and cast out like an auld shoe. I don't know where to turn, to tell you the truth; but I was thinkin' I might haud awa' south in the footsteps o' that unfortunate brither o' yours that died in Lunnon. I might get a master saddler's job about Annan or Carlisle maybe: Carlisle might be a likelier place. But I'll need to quit Dumfries that has seen the best o' my days . . .

'It's no easy to explain either, Rab, an' yet I suppose it's simple enough. You tak' on work for men you think are men of honour; an' you mak' them graith an' you wait for payment an' you wait in vain. But a' the time that you're lying out money here an' there amang the gentry, you hae to pay for your leather, your bits an' pieces o' things. . . Weel, I owe money and there's money owing to me; and between the two o' them you suddenly find you canna mak' ends meet. And that's bankruptcy for you . . .'

The Bard looked at Wattie. There wasn't much he could say.

'Weel, Wattie: I ken something o' having a lack o' capital. I ken what it is to have bills piling up on you and nae money to pay them. Though, by God, I worked hard and aey managed to pay what I was owing. But if the dirt o' gentry havena paid ye, then bad cess to them! Bad cess to the whole tribe o' them, Wattie! For I'm beginning to doubt, in Dumfries at ony rate, if there's an honest man among them. . . And this damned useless war's goin' to ruin everybody. . . Imports are a' to hell and prices are rising . . .'

ROMP WITH THE LADIES

The drink had been flowing for a long time; and his host had been plying him assiduously with it, so that, by the end of an hour or two, the Bard had very little recollection as to where he was or what company he was in.

Certainly he remembered Maria Riddell leaving earlier in the night because, Walter still being absent, she never stayed out late . . .

As he became fuzzier and fuzzier, the men seemed to become more and more secretive and sly and furtive.

They had arranged a plot in which the Bard was to be the central figure: the central scapegoat. Of this the Bard knew absolutely nothing. They did acquaint him – the host and his second lieutenant – of the manner in which their prank was to be conducted. The ladies were all quietly sipping their tea – or were supposed to be sipping their tea – in the drawing-room. The host and his male friends planned to dash in upon them quickly and without any prior warning; and each man was to seize the lady of his choice and embrace her.

The Bard swayed uncertainly on his feet; but the talk was persuasive and insistent.

Romp with the ladies? Why, yes! He would enjoy a romp with the ladies. Since this was to be the order of the night, he would not stand back.

When they approached the door the Bard was next to the host, the second lieutenant behind him. The door opened: the host stepped aside. The Bard was unconscious of the slight push that sent him into the room.

The door was closed behind him. The hostess, with a gasp, rose quickly to her feet and came hurriedly forward. In his drunken state the Bard was conscious only of a woman's face, a woman's hair and an exposed bosom. He folded his arms around the form and impressed a kiss firmly upon the rouged lips.

There were shrieks of dismay. The hostess pummelled the Bard with her closed fists. The door opened and the men trooped through, laughing uproariously.

The hostess rubbed her lips with the back of her hand. She looked wildly accusingly at her husband.

'Take this beast out! See that he is conducted from the house! How dare you laugh at such a display! How shocking! How horrible!'

But there were women in the room who realised that the Bard had been the victim of a callous and bestial joke; and at least one of them rose in his defence.

As he stood there swaying and wondering what had happened, he slowly became conscious of the fact that he had committed an outrage: that he had been led into a trap; and that by his own host.

He stared about him in that pathetic and degrading helplessness which overtakes the drunk man who is also a sensitive man. He turned and shambled from the room . . .

He never clearly remembered how he got home; but he did get home, and Jean was both alarmed and shocked and hurt at the state he was in. He slept a drunken, physically uneasy sleep, tossing in the bed, threshing his arms and emitting wild and unintelligible words. That he was in distress, mental as well as physical, Jean realised only too clearly.

When morning came at long last to the Millbrae Vennel, he wakened to find himself alone in the bed: cold, shivering, suffering from a ghastly hang-over. He could hardly focus his eyes: eyes that were tired and red. He could hardly move his body without pain: a body that was dull and leaden.

Then he remembered suddenly, with a terrible start, something of the previous night's events. He recalled with a vividness that surprised him from the drunken mists of twelve hours his sudden embracing of his hostess, her indignation, of the consternation into which the ladies had been put; rising, starting to their feet; the defence at least one lady had put up for him . . .

He groaned, closed his eyes and lay back. But there was no peace for him, no rest. Now in addition to the torture of alcoholic poisoning came the torture of remorse, of shame, of humiliation.

Eventually he got up, washed himself in cold water, slipped into his study, closed the door, took a clean sheet of paper and wrote:

Madam,
     I daresay that this is the first epistle you ever received from

this nether world. I write you from the regions of Hell, amid the horrors of the damned. The time and manner of my leaving your earth I do not exactly know, as I took my departure in the heat of a fever of intoxication, contracted at your too hospitable mansion; but, on my arrival here, I was fairly tried, and sentenced to endure the purgatorial tortures of this infernal confine for the space of ninety-nine years, eleven months, and twenty-nine days, and all on account of the impropriety of my conduct yesternight under your roof. Here am I, laid on a bed of pitiless furze, with my aching head reclining on a pillow of ever-piercing thorn, while an infernal tormentor, wrinkled, and old, and cruel, his name I think is *Recollection*, with a whip of scorpions, forbids peace or rest to approach me, and keeps anguish eternally awake. Still, Madam, if I could in any measure be reinstated in the good opinion of the fair circle whom my conduct last night so much injured, I think it would be an alleviation to my torments. For this reason I trouble you with this letter. To the men of the company I will make no apology. Your husband, who insisted on my drinking more than I chose, has no right to blame me; and the other gentlemen were partakers of my guilt. But to you, Madam, I have much to apologise. Your good opinion I valued as one of the greatest acquisitions I had made on earth, and I was truly a beast to forfeit it. There was a Miss I — too, a woman of fine sense, gentle and unassuming manners – do make, on my part, a miserable damned wretch's best apology to her. A Mrs C —, a charming woman, did me the honour to be prejudiced in my favour; this makes me hope that I have not outraged her beyond all forgiveness. To all the other ladies please present my humblest contrition for my conduct, and my petition for their gracious pardon. O all ye powers of decency and decorum! whisper to them that my errors, though great, were involuntary – that an intoxicated man is the vilest of beasts – that it was not in my nature to be brutal to any one – that to be rude to a woman, when in my senses, was impossible with me – but —

Regrets! Remorse! Shame! ye three hellhounds that ever dog my steps and bay at my heels, spare me! spare me!

Forgive the offences, and pity the perdition of, Madam,
Your humble Slave

The letter completed, he went downstairs. He looked at Jean shamefacedly but Jean did not return his look

'There's no good o' me saying I'm sorry, Jean. I'll say I'm sorry and try to explain things when I come back. Meantime I have urgent business on hand that'll tak' me a good twa or three hours. But, lass, I'm sorry. This is something that a' the days o' our life, however long they may be, will never happen again.'

He hired a pony and rode in much physical discomfort to Woodley Park. He announced himself to Maria and was received finally – after a delay of half an hour – in the break-fast-room.

Maria had sensed there was something wrong. She was on the defensive.

'I'm sorry for troubling you at this hour of the morning – I ken you're never at home till the afternoon – but, Maria, something dreadful, something unpardonable happened last night. I was made drunk and – eh — '

He told his story. Maria became very cold.

'So for all our past friendship, Maria, I appeal to you. For my sake, for decency's sake . . . oh damn near for humanity's sake. You'll tak' this letter that I have written to Mrs Ecks and do your best to intercede on my behalf. The truth is, Maria, believe me, that I was the victim of a dastardly and rotten trick. Aye: that doesn't excuse me I know. I was filled drunk, rotten drunk, stupid drunk – by her husband. I can see it all now, alas! Last night I saw nothing and kent less. Can I ask you, Maria, to do this for me?'

Maria looked at him for a brief moment and then averted her face.

'I'll deliver your letter, Robert, later this afternoon. I shall discuss the matter first with Mrs Ecks, and try to discover the nature, the real nature of your offence. I can hardly believe it to be as grave as you indicate.

'But I did warn you last night, that you were drinking, for you, too heavily; and . . . well, if your offence has been anything like what you say it has then, of course, you do know that I cannot in any way condone it.'

'I don't ask you to condone it, Maria. I ask you to explain to our hostess that I'm not the kind of man who, either in sobriety or in drink, has ever before insulted a woman; I'm not in the habit of getting beastly drunk in the company of ladies, or, indeed, in the company of men; that I've written in the letter which you now hold in your hand a full remorseful apology; written, as I say, from the nether regions of hell.

'My God, Maria; whatever I have done I certainly am paying for it: paying for it now and will probably pay for it all my life.

'Aye; but this has taught me a much-needed lesson also. Never again . . . never again will I accept the hospitality of a man – be he ten times the gentleman he supposes he is – whom I do not know and have not proven in times past.'

Maria lowered her face as the Bard's vehemence grew.

'I will do what I can, Robert, in this matter; reluctant as I am to invade the very privacy of Mrs Ecks who, I presume, will be in no very accessible state of mind. And now if you will excuse me, for I have much to do this morning and there are domestic affairs . . .'

'Maria, forgive me for having called upon you. Put that down to my distraught state; put that down to my shame and remorse and sorrow. And my thanks to you, my eternal gratitude.'

He turned towards the door, turned again, bowed low to Maria and left the room.

OSTRACISED

In the immediate days that followed he received no word, no acknowledgment of any kind either from Mrs Ecks or from Maria Riddell.

But some nights afterwards he encountered Maria – indeed he was on the look-out for her – at the theatre. As she emerged from her carriage he approached her in the entrance of the theatre as he had often done. She saw him; but she saw him not. And, with an air of looking through and beyond him, half-turned to her companion and brushed past him as if he had never existed.

The Bard did not recover easily from Maria's brutal manner. He did write her nevertheless and told her that she had cut him; and that her cutting affected him deeply.

Here indeed the business might have ended had not Maria given tongue among her friends to certain cruel and unfeeling observations concerning the Bard: observations that came back to him directly from friends he could trust.

But perhaps, if that were possible, even more devastating

that Maria's cut, came a cut from Robert Riddell in the King's Arms not long afterwards.

The Bard was coming out of the tavern when he almost collided with Robert Riddell. He was about to hail his friend; but, like his sister-in-law, Robert Riddell stared through him and past him.

This double cut, this double annihilation, made him realise the enormity of his offence.

The cut worked both ways. The slights he had received from the Riddells and from their friends were hard to bear. He felt the injustice of them more perhaps than he had ever felt any personal injustice. But his anger rose too. After all, what was the offence he had committed? Let him examine it coolly and dispassionately now that he was removed from it . . .

Led on by a drunken host he had kissed the hostess. In a drunken party, where every man had been as drunk as Bacchus! Yes, he had committed the offence; but he had taken drunken gentlemen at their word. He, Robert Burns, had thought that even in drink they would honour their word. Yes, yes. . . The offence had been the offence of a drunk man: not a drunk gentleman. As a drunk gentleman, among gentlemen, who had the privilege of ever being drunk, he would have been forgiven. He might even have been applauded for the dashing gallantry of his exploit. But no: he was but a gauger. He was a plebeian thrust into the company of the great by virtue of his being Scotland's Bard. His manners had not been good enough for the company of drunken gentlemen and their ladies.

The more he thought of this aspect of the business, the more bitter he grew. He realised – as indeed he had realised all his life – that there was one law of social manners for those who were gentry and a very different set of laws for those who were not. And he realised too – but this time with a new clarity and a fresh bitterness – that the mere fact that he was Scotland's Bard excused him nothing; that social standing was of more importance in the ranks of the gentry than any extraneous fame or honour that might come to a man by way of worth and merit.

Sometimes he upbraided himself for having departed in any particular from the wisdom he had known between the plough-stilts on Lochlea and Mossgiel. He had travelled a very long way indeed from those days; but he should not have travelled in vain. He had been flattered, especially at Ellisland where company was scarce; he had been flattered by the attentions of the local gentry. But he had thought to repay what attention they had given him a thousandfold. And all because of one night's misdemeanour in drink he was cast aside like a drunken tinker; like a reprobate; like a raper of innocent childhood; like some foul malefactor . . .

Who were they who had turned him aside? Maria Riddell . . . Robert Riddell. . . Robert Riddell whom he had scarcely ever known to be sober. . . Huh! And Maria Riddell! Painted! Bedizened! A supporter of the French Revolution! An enthusiast for the French Revolution! An enthusiast for nothing but her own shallow vanity!

It did not help his mood any when he learned that William Skirving and Maurice Margarot had been sentenced by Braxfield to transportation to Botany Bay each for fourteen years. Joseph Gerrald still awaited trial.

He did not discuss his lapse with Syme or with George Haugh. He discussed it with nobody. He didn't even reveal to Jean the full nature, or anything like the full nature, of the circumstances that had overwhelmed him . . .

After all, the Riddells, either of Carse or of Woodley Park – though habitués of the hospitable mansion of Mr and Mrs Ecks – in no way affected his daily life in the Millbrae Vennel or in Dumfries generally. He could still carry on with his work; he could still associate with his friends despite anything that ten thousand Riddells might think or feel.

Though he was able, gradually, to dismiss the business from his mind, there did come to him – through third and fourth and fifth channels – news of the fact that Maria Riddell had so turned against him that she was making his ploughman origin the source of many jests; that she was insisting, in fact, that no man, however gifted, born in lowly station could ever be expected to conduct himself as a gentleman; that Robert Burns, though he did on many occasions give himself the air of being fit to mix with the gentry, was in fact no better than he had been born; and the coarse breeding and the coarse blood of his ancestry was telling in a way devastating to his claims to be Scotland's Bard . . .

By the beginning of January the Bard was writing to Graham of Fintry suggesting that the Excise Divisions in Dumfries be be reduced, that public money be thereby saved and recommending that, in any redistribution of the division, certain Excisemen – because of their young families – be given consideration.

Next he was writing Maria Riddell and lamenting that: 'In a face where I used to meet the kind complacency of friendly confidence, *now* to find cold neglect and contemptuous scorn – is a wrench that my heart can ill bear. It is however some kind of miserable good luck; that while De-haut-en-bas rigour may depress an offending wretch to the ground, it has a tendency to rouse a stubborn something in his bosom, which, although it cannot heal the wounds of his soul, is at least an opiate to blunt their poignancy.'

On the same day he was writing to the Earl of Buchan and Captain Miller of Dalswinton enclosing copies of *Scots Wha Hae.*

Most of the Bard's spare time was taken up with his main task of song-writing. No matter what happened to him or what befell him or how he might be feeling, he was always able to retreat to his study and forget himself in his song-writing. By February he was able to send forty-one songs to Johnson for the fifth volume of the *Scots Musical Museum* – this in addition to a good many other songs he had entrusted to Stephen Clarke's careless hands. With what he had left there was no reason why the sixth and final volume should not also be a success.

But not always did his song-writing or his odd convivial hours in the taverns banish the melancholy that lay deep at the bottom of his being. There were times when he felt that his very mind was diseased and that there was nothing could save him from the wreck of his individuality; that he was about to be swamped in the terrible waste of towering waves of grey-black melancholia that surrounded him. There were times too when he felt that there was still 'a something' which he could not adequately designate which connected man with the Divine Architect of the Universe. Though he did find a phrase to cover this relationship between the individual and the external universe – 'a something' which he called the 'senses of the mind' – yet there was always the doubt, always the uncertainty concerning an all-powerful and beneficent God and a world to come – beyond death and the grave.

But at such times he felt that there was 'a something' that had to be acknowledged, that 'something' which men at all times of doubt and difficulty (or of inspiration) call religion. He felt that when he viewed the vast miracle of nature, the miracle of the seasons, the miracle of a bursting bud and the miracle of a bird's song-note, there was some way towards an understanding of nature's God: the nature of reality . . .

This seemed to him the more necessary since so few people did he meet who had any reverence for the mystery of nature and who looked with a most casual and unseeing eye on the day-to-day miracle and mystery of life. In such moments, observing his eldest boy, young Robert, busy with his books about his desk, he felt that somehow or other he must imbue in him an awareness of the beauty, magnitude, mystery and overwhelming rapture that arose from the contemplation of nature – and somewhere, possibly, a witnessing, judging and approving God.

But when he had climbed out of the trough of his depression he regarded such essays in mysticism with a hearty realistic scepticism, and was inclined to swing in buoyancy to his other (and just as important and fundamental) belief that life was joy and laughter and friendship; that the glory of God rested in social well-being and in social harmony more than in the apparent harmony, in the external world, of birth and growth, decay and death, re-birth and growth all over again.

All his life he had swung from despair and melancholy to joy and exultation. In many of his poems and songs he had given full expression to his despair, though his finest expressions had been of the joy and acceptance of the glory and the gift of life.

BLOODY BRAXFIELD

If the year of 1793 had closed gloomily and 1794 had opened badly for the Bard, it had opened less favourably for the forces of reform. Indeed the portents indicated a reign of Dundas-directed terror.

In the middle of March, Joseph Gerrald, backed by a tremendous Edinburgh following, made a magnificent fight before Braxfield. From every angle he hurled defiance. He was the accuser, not the accused.

The brutish and besotted Braxfield roared with impotent rage. As his blood mounted to a fantastic pressure and the veins stood in livid knots on his brow, his voice rose to a throaty, apoplectic scream.

Quickly the prosecutor, Robert Dundas, would intervene to allow the Justice Clerk (of whom he was now heartily sick) to subside. Dundas regretted that his henchman did not conduct himself with a colder dignity.

'Reform!' snorted Braxfield.

'My Lord – Our Saviour Jesus Christ was also something of a reformer —'

Braxfield almost shattered the bench with his fist. Then he leaned forward as far as he could towards the unruffled Gerrald. His voice was bloodshot.

'An' meikle guid did it dae Him; He was *hangit*!'

The shudder that went through the court was like a physical impact.

But though, like Muir's defence, Gerrald's was to stir the forces of reform in Scotland, Ireland and America for many years to come, his eloquence won him no leniency from the court. Like Muir, Margarot and Skirving, he was sentenced to transportation to Botany Bay for fourteen years.

DEATH OF ROBERT RIDDELL

On the 20th of April, Jean Breckenridge presented Gilbert Burns at Mossgiel with a son. On Monday, the 21st Robert Riddell of Glenriddell died at Friars Carse. The birth of a nephew was a domestic event: the death of Robert Riddell was of public concern.

As the Bard had, on the Saturday, been discussing the illness of Robert Riddell with a mutual friend, John Clark, the laird of Locherwoods, near the Brow Well on the Solway, he immediately dashed off a sonnet and sent it to Clark as a tribute – a small heart-felt tribute – to 'the memory of the man I loved.'

As he said to Jean: 'You've nae idea, lass, what it means to me that Robert Riddell has passed away... Oh, I know that for a while past he and I havena been speaking; I ken that we quarrelled – at least it wasna Robert Riddell and me that quarrelled. . . It was that bitch Maria Riddell who cam' atween us wi' her lying rotten tongue. . . But I kent Riddell's deep-down worth, Jean, as few folk in the district kent it. Mind ye: when I first cam' to Ellisland it was Robert Riddell held out the hand o' friendship mair than ony o' the other gentry did. Aye, Riddell was a man o' worth – for a' his faults. I know he was headstrong! He was drucken: he was ill-natured whiles; and whiles he blustered and bullied. . . But as far as I was concerned, Jean, he aey had a different side o' his nature to show. Mind you: he was nae fool. Na, na. . . A lot o' the folks took him for a fool, took him for a man o' shallow parts; but I kent better. He was an antiquarian o' worth: Captain Grose wadna hae bided an hour under his roof had he no' been. . . And he was a sterling musician: a tolerable fiddler and a composer o' worth. Oh, maybe he just didna hae that fire and fight that should be in a true musician; and maybe he didna ken half that Stephen Clarke kens; but he was nae sma' musician for a' that. He had a great love for our native songs and our native worth and our history and . . . ah, damnit, it's a big loss to me, a big loss to Nithsdale that Robert Riddell is no more. Aye, and mony, mony a happy nicht I spent at his fire-side when there wasna another fire-side I could sit at in Nithsdale. You canna forget thae things, Jean – at least I canna forget them. Maybe he drank ower much. . . Who's to say? He's awa' now onyway. . . I aey had the feeling that as time went by he would get to ken the true worth o' Maria Riddell and the true worth o' mony o' the folk she associated wi'; and that our quarrel would be forgotten and that he would be friends again.'

Jean looked at him with a neutral eye.

'Weel, Rab: I'm sorry for your sake that you're feeling the death o' Glenriddell as hard as you dae. Mind you: I've nothing against the man. . . I never kent him that weel. He was often about the house yon time you were writing the ballad on the Whistle: he was gey impatient to ken how you were gettin' on wi' it. Oh, an' he was polite enough and civil enough . . . but no: there wasna the warmth to him that there was – or the worth either – in a man like Captain Grose. I'm no' forgettin', Rab – and I canna forget – how often he sent for you to the King's Arms and filled you fu' – him and his visitin' friends and – och, weel, it's a' by now and it is a pity seein' a big strong man like that cut down in his prime: it's a pity . . .'

'Yes, Jean: I know that you never saw or could see the real man that was behind the big bluff frontage o' Glenriddell. But there it was and there it is. . . The man's awa' now and I wad hae you believe that he and I – despite the difference in our stations in life, despite the difference in our education and our upbringing and a' that that could put between us – were good friends. Aye, in a peculiar sense that I canna just describe to you, Jean, we were good and true friends. We met on a plane o' friendship, shall I say, on which I hae met few people. . . Damnit, I can say nae muir. . . I'm gey sair touched at this morning's news.'

INVITATION TO LONDON

At the beginning of May, through the good offices of Captain Miller, M.P., of Dalswinton, editor Perry of *The Morning Chronicle*, London, offered the Bard a permanent job as a journalist. But the Bard was in no way taken with the idea of going to London and committing his pen to any newspaper however much he might agree with it. He had no desire to go near London at all. But he was grateful for the offer and decided that he might try his hand at some prose essays and that *The Morning Chronicle* might be the very medium to print them.

So he wrote to Captain Miller declining the offer with thanks, and sending him *Scots Wha Hae*, provided, of course, that he made certain it was not published under his name but published as something that had come into his hands by accident. He also sent him one of his new songs to the glorious old tune *The Sutor's Dochter*:

> Wilt thou be my dearie?
> When Sorrow wrings thy gentle heart . . .

He also sent four devastating lines under the pen-name of 'Nith' on Maria Riddell, headed:

> Extempore, Pinned to a Lady's coach –
> If you rattle along like your Mistress's tongue,
>   Your speed will out-rival the dart:
> But, a fly for your load, you'll break down on the road,
>   If your stuff be as rotten's her heart.

And he also promised to correspond with Perry – provided he could provide an address 'free from spies.'

REPTILE WAT

Things were going badly with Walter Riddell who had but lately returned from his estate in Antigua. He had bought Goldielea from Colonel Goldie at a price of £16,000. He had laid out (on improvements as he thought) very much more than £2,000. And now he had sold it back to Goldie for £15,000.

As he was a trustee of his brother's estate at Carse, he did his best to arrange that Mrs Elizabeth Riddell would take a given annuity and make over to him the survivancy of the paternal estate. But unfortunately for Walter, Mrs Riddell detested both himself and Maria and managed to persuade the majority of the trustees to sell the estate for what it would fetch.

This put Walter and Maria in a quandary. To save themselves from utter ruin, Walter was forced to rent from the Duke of Queensberry the dilapidated ancient mansion-house of Tinwald.

Walter, in his bitterness and humiliation, had joined with Maria in condemnation of the Bard. He was only too glad to find that his first instinct regarding Robert Burns had been correct: that he was a plebeian; that he was, for all his boosted poetry and bardship, but a common gauger.

When word came to the Bard of Walter's comments on him, he sojourned to Syme with an epigram hot on his lips.

'Well, John, I've just heard a few things concerning Wattie Riddell; and I've been turning a few things over in my mind. . . If you'll get out that book o' yours I'll give you an epigram to tak' down . . .'

Syme had the book out in a flash and the pencil in his hand, and the Bard said:

'This is for Walter Riddell of Goldielea and now of Tinwald House:

So vile was poor Wat, such a miscreant slave,
That the worms ev'n damn'd him when laid in his grave.
'In his skull there's a famine,' a starved reptile cries;
'And his heart, it is poison,' another replies.'

PARTING WITH NANCY

The previous year's tour of Galloway had been such a success that Syme and the Bard agreed to engage in another tour before the summer ended.

And so, towards the end of June, the Bard wrote to David MacCulloch of Ardwell, Gatehouse-of-Fleet, to inform him that they were due to start on their tour, that they would be pleased to see him, and that he hoped to visit Heron of Heron's house at Kerroughtree, near Newton Douglas, that he hoped he would accompany him there, because, as he added: 'I will need all the friends I can muster for I am indeed ill-at-ease when I approach your Honourables and Right Honourables.'

Eventually he reached, in Galloway, the village of Castle Douglas (lately Carlinwark); and there in an inn, while Syme was attending to other business, he read a short and unsatisfactory letter he had received from Nancy MacLehose. . . He took out his pen and ink-horn and wrote as follows:

Before you ask me why I have not written you; first let me be informed of you *how* I shall write you?' 'In friendship,' you say; and I have many a time taken up my pen to try an epistle of 'Friendship' to you; but it will not do: 'tis like Jove grasping a pop-gun after having wielded his thunder. When I take up the pen, Recollection ruins me. Ah! my ever dearest Clarinda! Clarinda? What a host of Memory's tenderest offspring crowd on my fancy at that sound! But I must not indulge that subject: you have forbid it.

I am extremely happy to learn that your precious health is re-established, and that you are once more fit to enjoy that satisfaction in existence, which health alone can give us. My old friend, Ainslie, has indeed been kind to you. Tell him, that I envy him the power of serving you. I had a letter from him a while ago, but it was so dry, so distant, so like a card to one of his clients, that I could scarce bear to read it, and have not yet answered it. He is a good, honest fellow; and *can* write a friendly letter, which would do equal honour to his head and his heart, as a whole sheaf of his letters I have by me will witness; and though Fame does not blow her trumpet at my approach *now* as she did *then*, when he first honoured me with his friendship, yet I am as proud as ever; and when I am laid in my grave, I wish to be stretched at my full length, that I may occupy every inch of ground I have a right to.

You would laugh, were you to see me, where I am just now: would to Heaven you were here to laugh with me, though I am afraid that crying would be our first employ-ment. Here am I set, a solitary hermit, in the solitary room, of a solitary inn, with a solitary bottle of wine by me – as grave and as stupid as an owl – but like that owl, still faithful to my old song; in confirmation of which, my dear Mrs Mack, here is your good health! May the hand-wal'd benisons o' Heaven bless your bonnie face; and the wretch wha skellies at your weelfare, may the auld tinkler deil get him, to clout his rotten heart! Amen!

You must know, my dearest Madam, that these now many years, wherever I am, in whatever company, when a married lady is called as a toast, I constantly give you; but as your name has never passed my lips, even to my most intimate friend, I give you by the name of Mrs Mack. This is so well known among my acquaintances, that when my married lady is called for, the toast-master will say – 'Oh, we need not ask him who it is – here's Mrs Mack!' I have also, among my convivial friends, set on foot a round of toasts, which I call, a round of Arcadian Shepherdesses; that is, a round of favourite Ladies, under female names celebrated in ancient

song; and then, you are my Clarinda: so, my lovely Clarinda,
I devote this glass of wine to a most ardent wish for your
happiness!

> In vain would Prudence, with decorous sneer,
> Point out a cens'ring world, and bid me fear:
> Above that world on wings of love I rise,
> I know its worst – and can that worst despise.

> 'Wronged, injured, shunned; unpitied, unredrest;
> The mocked quotation of the scorner's jest' –
> Let Prudence's direst bodements on me fall,
> Clarinda, rich reward! o'erpays them all!

I have been rhyming a little of late, but I do not know if
they are worth postage.
Tell me what you think of the following:

Monody —

How cold is that bosom which Folly once fired!
   How pale is that cheek where the rouge lately glistened!
How silent that tongue which the echoes oft tired!
   How dull is that ear which to flattery so listened!

If sorrow and anguish their exit await,
   From friendship and dearest affection removed,
How doubly severer, Maria, thy fate!
   Thou diedst unwept, as thou livedst unloved.

Loves, Graces and Virtues, I call not on you:
   So shy, grave and distant, ye shed not a tear.
But come, all ye offspring of Folly so true,
   And flowers let us cull for Maria's cold bier!

We'll search through the garden for each silly flower,
   We'll roam thro' the forest for each idle weed,
But chiefly the nettle, so typical, shower,
   For none e'er approached her but rued the rash deed.

We'll sculpture the marble, we'll measure the lay:
   Here Vanity strums on her idiot lyre!

There keen Indignation shall dart on his prey,
    Which spurning Contempt shall redeem from his ire!

The Epitaph

Here lies, now a prey to insulting neglect,
    What once was a butterfly, gay in life's beam:
Want only of wisdom denied her respect,
    Want only of goodness denied her esteem.

The subject of the foregoing is a woman of fashion in this country, with whom, at one period, I was well acquainted. By some scandalous conduct to me, and two or three other gentlemen here as well as me, she steered so far to the north of my good opinion, that I have made her the theme of several illnatured things . . .

He did not know that this was the last letter he would ever write to Nancy MacLehose. He did not know, though he guessed, that with the superior pension the lately-created Lord of the Court of Justiciary, William Craig, had given her and the attention which Robert Ainslie was paying her she had no longer any pressing need to resume physical contact with the Bard.

He did not know then that this was his last letter to Nancy of 'Aince mair I hail thee, thou gloomy December'; Nancy of 'Sensibility how Charming'; Nancy of 'O May, thy morn was ne'er sae sweet'; Nancy of his Edinburgh sojourn; of his Edinburgh visits; of the inspiration for one of his greatest songs: 'Ae fond Kiss and then we sever.'

And how could he know of the wrench, of the heart-ache it was to Nancy that never more were they to meet in this world?

After he had sealed his letter, in the poor room of the poor inn of the village of Castle Douglas, he said to Syme – for Syme had returned and they were enjoying a last drink before going to bed:

'John . . . I want to tell you about a loved one I once had in Edinburgh . . .'

Syme said: 'Can I guess who she was, Robin?'

'Na, na, John: you dinna ken her. But she was one o' the finest women I ever kent. A woman whose husband had

206

treated her worse nor a brute-beast. A woman, when I first knew her, I thought was one of the most delectable, one of the most desirable women in a' Edinburgh. I never met a woman in Edinburgh – aye, frae the Duchess o' Gordon down to the commonest hure in the Cowgate – who could haud a light to her. Oh, I winna gie her name because, John, she was a woman beyond and above a' the kind o' women that you and I hae ever kent: exceptin' my Jean. . . Oh, tempestuous, ardent. . . And, by the Lord, a poetess too. . . Oh, yes, a poetess. I could give you evidence enough o' that.

'However, John, she went to the West Indies to see the husband who had deserted her; but when she got there what did she find? A husband and twa or three black women and a cleckin' o' half-castes here and there. . . Ah well! she cam' back to Edinburgh. She cam' back to Edinburgh. . . I winna attempt to tell you the songs I hae wrote about that lass. But, John, believe me, there she was: a wife wi' four weans in Edinburgh. . . God Almighty! I suppose it was love. . . And we loved and loved and better loved. . . And we quarrelled and we parted and we met again. . .

'And here we are away down in Galloway, in Carlinwark, that has been re-christened Castle Douglas to suit him wi' the mills. . . Oh well, John, we're as drunk as Bartie, baith o' us, eh . . .? You ken you're as drunk as Bartie and, by God, I'm no' able to haud my head up; but, John Syme, laird of Barncailzie, here we are, the pair o' us, in this God-forsaken hole o' an inn on our way to Gatehouse and Kerroughtree where Heron o' Heron . . .

'And what hae you or I, John, to say that onybody wi' a celestial pen wad care to tak' down? Nothing at all, John: nothing at all. Only you and I are here and we micht as well be a thousand miles awa' for a' it really matters. . . A wee bit holiday; a wee bit holiday frae Dumfries; a wee bit holiday – you frae the Stinking Vennel where I bided lang enough and me frae the Millbrae Vennel where the stench and stink is just as oppressive. However, you've left a wife and weans and I've left a wife and weans; and what the hell does it matter? Here we are and we're goin' to enjoy oursel's though there's damn the haet to enjoy oursel's wi'!

'Ach weel, John: come to bed! Come on and we'll go up to our room for there's nothin' here. . . Nothin' here for ony being' wi' a wee bit glimmerin' o' intelligence.'

'Robin, my dear bonnie boy, it's a bare place we're in the

nicht: a damned poor place. . . Oh, I meant it to be better; but Carlinwark is still a bare poverty-struck village wi' just twa or three houses down the street: kin' o' weavers . . .

'Now, Robin: I ken I've had a drink; I ken I've been awa' visitin' friends that, well . . . you dinna ken about. Auld friends frae my days at Barncailzie. . . But you would stay behind and write letters, would ye? Letters to an auld Edinburgh flame o' yours, eh? Weel, weel. . . If you want to write letters to auld women that ye kent – oh, maybe no' an auld woman – an old lover, an old flame – weel, Robin, if that's the way you want it, I'm no' the man to say you nay. No, no, no. . . We're baith as fu' as bitches, you ken. . . Aye, you said that afore didn't you? Ah weel: what should come o' a' this . . . you and me sitting here wondering, waiting . . .'

The Bard thrust his empty glass in front of him.

'If we're waiting for anything, John, we're waiting for another drink. My God, we didna come down here frae Dumfries; we havena suffered the sair backsides we've suffered just to come down here and gang to our beds . . .'

'No, no: we havena done that, Robin. The landlord wadna yield to come; but the landlady was here and certes, I think she could fetch us another drink afore we gang to our beds.'

Syme went out to the landing and called to the landlady who came up. They had more drink.

'Ha, ha, Syme, you randy . . . you randy auld friend that I hae! Mind you, I ken I'm drunk . . . and I ken you're drunk. When I was speaking to you a wee while ago about a lassie I kent in Edinburgh – a widow I kent in Edinburgh – who shall be nameless. . . Oh, you'll never – neither you nor the best man in Galloway or Nithsdale will ever get the name out o' me – but I kent a lassie worth the whole bluidy lot o' the women here – acy barring Jean . . . barring my bonnie Jean that ye hae met . . . and I ken ye dinna think sae much o' her . . .'

'You never heard me say a word against your wife, Robin?'
The Bard looked at him with blood-shot eyes:
'You didna need to say onything against my wife, Syme. Na . . And maybe my wife wadna need to say onything against you. But for the love of God, John, will ye no' understand that wives and wives and husbands and husbands and friends and friends and acquaintances and acquaintances can meet and hae their converse and hae their friendships and no' the one mingle wi' the other. Ach well . . . it's a puir place

208

this, John. But the drink's no' so bad. . . And now I'm goin'
to say damn the haet mair. . . I dinna ken about you; but I'm
goin' to my bed . . .'

The Bard rose, drained his glass and went out of the room.
But Syme was too drunk to follow him. He put his arm on
the table, rested his head on his arm and, in a few minutes,
was snoring loudly.

The Bard, in his mind, had parted with Nancy MacLehose
– and yet he had not uttered a word that conveyed to Syme
what that parting meant.

NECESSITY COMPELS

At the end of July, Isa Burns presented John Begg with a
son William. It seemed that births were coming fast and thick
among the Burns family. Jean was almost due to take to bed
herself. Before she took to bed, the Bard, in the presence of
some military gentlemen, was rash enough to give a toast:
'May our success in the present war be equal to the justice
of our case!' Several people took great offence at this. One
threatened a duel.

In the morning, when the Bard recovered his sanity, he
had to dash off a letter asking a friend to intercede on his
behalf, that he might not be reported to the Excise.

He was getting rather wearied because he had always to
square his utterances and his actions with his domestic situation. He had forgotten, when he proposed the toast, that Jean
was so near child-bed. Now, viewing Jean in her helplessness,
he had no compunction in trying to make amends for his
intellectual boldness. He would crawl on his hands and knees
to apologise – if necessary.

GLENCAIRN REMEMBERED

On August 12th, Jean was brought to bed and delivered of
a fine boy who was christened James Glencairn Burns.

And the Bard thought, as the Reverend William Mac-
Morine of Carlaverock christened him, that he had indeed
remembered Glencairn and all that he had done for him.

A new arrival had come to Dumfries in the shape of Doctor William Maxwell, who set up house in Irish Street, round the corner from the Stinking Vennel.

Before long Maxwell had got in touch with Syme, Syme had got in touch with the Bard, and the Bard had got in touch with the two of them; for Doctor William Maxwell was no other than the Dr Maxwell whom Burke, in the House of Commons, had spoken against in connection with an alleged order of thousands of daggers from Birmingham to be delivered to the French. In this, of course, there was no truth whatsoever. But it was true that he had spent many years in France and, as a member of the National Guard, had been present at the execution of King Louis. As a memento of that occasion, Maxwell possessed a handkerchief he had dipped in the king's blood. That he was a Roman Catholic of the ancient Maxwell family of Kirkconnell in no way damped his extreme revolutionary ardour. He was some months younger than the Bard.

In a very short time Maxwell and Syme were the greatest of friends. Questions were flung at Maxwell concerning the French position and Maxwell replied in the most enthusiastic terms. So much so that the town of Dumfries began to recognise in Syme and Maxwell and Burns the three most daring and revolutionary figures, that is, figures that were to be observed in the open.

But, Dr William Maxwell apart, life flowed pretty much in Dumfries as it had done during the past year. Sometimes the Bard saw Chloris, and sometimes he didn't.

In October Stephen Clarke left Dumfries for Edinburgh and their farewell was a serious and not too-Bacchanalian night anent Scottish song . . .

And towards the end of October the Caledonian Hunt came once again to Dumfries, rioted through the town and folly and dissipation and profligacy and unprincipled wickedness held sway. The Bard, attending the races with Syme, noted the Hon. William Maule of Panmure riding out of the congested field on his high phaeton and immediately asked Syme to note down the epigram:

Thou Fool, in thy phaeton towering,
 Art proud when that phaeton's praised?
'Tis the pride of a Thief's exhibition
 When higher his pillory's raised.

HEAD OF A TRAITOR

On October 15th, Robert Watt, who had been apprehended
in May for the treason of pike-making and the organising of
'rebellion,' was beheaded in the presence of an enormous
crowd before the Edinburgh Tollbooth. When he had been
hanged, his body was laid out on a platform and, after three
vicious blows from an axe, the executioner managed to strike
his head from his body.

Holding aloft the bleeding head, he roared:

'This is the head of a traitor.'

The inhuman roar echoed throughout the realm.

HAZARD OF CONCEALING

His friendship with Chloris fluctuated a good deal. But he
came back to her from time to time and still found that she
could inspire a song in him.

There were times indeed when Chloris was a necessity. . .
With her he could escape from the drabness of his environ-
ment and the strain of events – when the drabness and the
strain became a burden.

He had overcome the bitterness of their first sexual en-
counter. They weren't in love with each other; but their
curious mutual attraction had grown into an equally curious
but deep affection which included all possible intimacy.

And Chloris still took an interest in his songs. He had just
written a new song on her which he thought good.

'So you like – My Chloris, mark how green the groves,
the primrose banks how fair?'

'You ken I like a' your songs, Robert. Aye: I like your
latest: it's in your best pastoral vein — '

'It preserves a good tune onyway – and all thanks to you.'

'So you say. . . I like your second set o' Craigieburn best

211

o' a' my songs. But I meant to ask you what was the news o' Fanny — ? Jean was saying — '

'Oh, Fanny presented Adam wi' a nice wee lass on the fourth o' the month. They've christened her Jean.'

'I'm glad to hear that, Robert. I got on weel wi' Fanny.'

'I ken you did. But you canna thole Jessie Lewars?'

Jean Lorimer gave her head a toss.

'I've nothing against her. She's ane o' thae sleekit sly ones. . . But dinna let's talk about her: you ken how I feel. . . I like your new song; and be sure and tell Fanny and Adam when you write that I'm pleased wi' the news. . . Or maybe you'd better no'.'

'Why?'

'I don't know, Robert. Sometimes I would like to write to Fanny. We used to hae our talks — Och, we were just bairns then. . . But then, if Fanny knew – weel, what you know . . .'

'Fanny wouldna like you? Damn it, lass, I've explained to you time and again how we've a' gotten our different personalities – our separate destinies . . .'

'Aye. . . So you say, Robert; and maybe that's what worries me. I havena got your brains – or faith.'

Jean seemed to blink away a tear from behind her eyes.

'But we canna occupy Nanny's spence a' nicht. It'll need to be the stable. . . Are you going through?'

'Aye: on you go. I'll hae a quick glass and say guidnicht to Nanny: we've got to keep the richt side o' her.'

FOR A' THAT

Towards the end of the month – on the 22nd to be precise – Findlater fell seriously ill and the Bard was gratified to find himself appointed "the acting Supervisor". No sooner had the notification come of his appointment than he was up to Sanquhar where on the following day, he was made a Free-man-Brother of the town.

There, with Edward Whigham, Robert Whigham, William Johnstone the farmer from Clackleith, Thomas Barker from Bridge-end and John Rigg of Cranwick Forge, he celebrated his Freeman's ticket by a great night of song and story-telling. He had always been friends with Whigham: he had always been friends with old Willie Johnstone of Clackleith. There were many people with whom he had always been friends in Sanquhar; and a royal night they had.

Before the closing of the year, the Bard wrote to Mrs Dunlop and expressed the view that his political sins, in so far as the Excise Board was concerned, seemed to be forgiven him. But he adverted to Mrs Dunlop's regret regarding the execution of the royal family in France and he wrote bold words to Mrs Dunlop. 'What is there in delivering over a perjured Blockhead and an unprincipled Prostitute to the hands of the hangman, that it should arrest for a moment, attention in an eventful hour, when, as my friend Roscoe in Liverpool gloriously expresses it —

'When the welfare of Millions is hung in the scale
    And the balance yet trembles with fate'?'

The Bard was not to know, though he might have known, that this paragraph in his letter to Mrs Dunlop was sufficient to outrage the old woman beyond any possibility of reply. What the Bard seemed to forget was that Mrs Dunlop had two sons-in-law who were refugees from the French Revolution, and who did not agree in principle with the objects of the Revolution: who were, indeed, in heart and soul Royalists.

But his deepest convictions regarding the French – fortified by first-hand accounts from William Maxwell – had hardened his feelings with regard to the French Revolution; had hardened his feelings with regard to the dictatorship of Pitt and Dundas and Burke. So that now, despite his censuring by the Excise Board, despite all the warnings that had been given him, he was more of the rebel than ever. So much so that presently he was dashing off a long letter to George Thomson in Edinburgh, with a Rabelaisian Ode to Spring, a song on Chloris and, most important, the song *For a' that, an' a' that.*

George Haugh, to whom he passed a copy of the song, was enthusiastic. Standing at his fire-side, Haugh read it over:

Is there for honest poverty
    That hings his head, an' a' that?
The coward slave, we pass him by –
    We dare be poor for a' that!
For a' that, an' a' that,
    Our toils obscure, an' a' that,
The rank is but the guinea's stamp,
    The man's the gowd for a' that.

What though on hamely fare we dine,
    Wear hoddin grey, an' a' that?
Gie fools their silks, and knaves their wine —
    A man's a man for a' that.
For a' that, an' a' that.
    Their tinsel show, an' a' that,
The honest man, tho' e'er sae poor,
    Is king o' men for a' that.

Ye see yon birkie ca'd 'a lord',
    Wha struts, an' stares, an' a' that?
Tho' hundreds worship at his word,
    He's but a cuif for a' that.
For a' that, an' a' that,
    His ribband, star, an' a' that,
The man o' independent mind,
    He looks an' laughs at a' that.

A prince can mak' a belted knight,
    A marquis, duke, an' a' that!
But an honest man's aboon his might —
    Guid faith, he mauna fa' that!
For a' that, an' a' that,
    Their dignities, an' a' that,
The pith o' sense an' pride o' worth
    Are higher rank than a' that.

Then let us pray that come it may
    (As come it will for a' that)
That Sense and Worth o'er a' the earth
    Shall bear the gree an' a' that!
For a' that, an' a' that,
    It's comin' yet for a' that,
That man to man the world o'er
    Shall brithers be for a' that.

Haugh was moved.
'It's beyond me how you do it, Rab.'
'It's a' in Paine.'
'Aye: it's a' in Tammy Paine — nae doubt. It's a' in the
dictionary too . . . but no' the way you put it down. And it's
amazing to me that despite a' the knocks you've gotten, your
faith in the brotherhood o' man is unshaken.'

'Man, Geordie, my fundamental faith in the brotherhood o' man is firmer the day than it has ever been. As you say: I've ta'en mony a sair knock. . . And I ken as much about man's inhumanity to man as the next. There's damn the doubt about man's inhumanity to man. France'll give you mony a brilliant and sanguinary lesson as to that. There're times, Geordie, when a guid case could be made out for rejecting man completely. For man can be the dirtiest, meanest, cruellest beast in creation. Damn the doubt: there's naething o' the brute creation that can rival man in bloody and brutal savagery. And it wad be easy to despair. Plenty hae despaired . . .

'But that's no' the whole story, Geordie, as well you ken. Man has his heroic side, his nobility. In our day we've had men like Thomas Muir and the Reverend Mr Palmer – and they dinna stand alone. There are obscure and unknown heroes in the fight for freedom. . . And as I see it, the fight is ever for freedom. The fight for freedom will never be won till a' men are brothers. There can be nae step towards brotherhood – universal brotherhood – until a' rank and title is abolished. Abolished frae society, frae men's minds and men's hearts. It's hard to believe in this day and generation that ony man, ony human being, born o' woman, however great, however worthy, can arrogate to himsel' the title "Lord". Christians forby – which mak's it damn-near blasphemy . . .

'But a' this is but cauld kail to you — '

'Go on, Rab – go on — '

'And I've said nothing about the most high and mighty princes — Damnit, when the auld Hebrews bowed down to a golden calf there was some sense about their bowing. . . But since man arrogated rank to himself the most diabolical inequalities hae entered into society – and into men's minds. . . So, as I see it, all rank and title maun be abolished afore we can get down to ony basis o' brotherhood.

'Equality we maun hae – and liberty and fraternity. But I pin my hopes on fraternity – on brotherhood. Unless we can come – by what pain and travail I kenna – to a realisation, to a fundamental sense o' brotherhood, then nothing follows. How can there be ony equality if we hate the sicht o' each other? How can there be ony liberty gin there's nae liking for ane another – and I mean black man and white man and yellow man . . . a' men. And even if we could achieve liberty

215

and equality, what would they be worth without fraternity? Damnit, I dinna mean by fraternity that we've got to hing about each other's necks. But when we realise that we're a' brothers, then we realise that we hae but one problem in common – how to achieve social peace and plenty.

'I've nae illusions that the road'll be easy. Man has travelled a lang sair road already; and the road may be langer and sairer yet. But – we're on the richt road now, Geordie; and France is there afore us blazing the trail – illuminating the darkness o' the world by the light o' her achievements.

'But the French are no' having it easy, for the ingrained habits o' thousands o' years are no' thrown off in a day.'

'But it's coming, Geordie: it's coming yet for a' that.'

'Aye: faith, it's coming, Rab – and your sang'll dae a lot to help it alang the road. Man, you've a great gift o' puttin' the maist complicated thochts into the simplest words – an' it's no' just that in the words are simple either: they're the richt words set doon in the richt order.'

'That's the greatest compliment I've ever been paid as a poet, Geordie. For poetry's largely a matter o' the richt words in the richt place. . . But: you'll be able to use the sang?'

'Dinna fear: we'll use the sang and send it on its road.'

'That's a' I want to ken. I dinna want to ken how.'

'And I wadna tell you, Rab: you've enough to worry aboot. You write the sangs and we'll see to the rest.'

'Naebody's ever suspected you?'

'Wha wad suspect an honest hammerman? Damnit, they think I can hardly write my ain name. It tak's a' talents to work for the new world that's coming, Rab. And it's just as weel that some o' us hae our lichts weel hidden aneath our bushels!'

A GUN IN THE HAND

It was all very well, of course, to be the birkie called a lord. It was all very well to sing of the day when man to man the world o'er should brithers be for a' that. But the cursed war with the French had reduced Dumfries almost to a standstill and the Bard's perquisites had almost vanished. He was in debt, in poverty; and he needed money urgently for his family demanded to be fed.

He wrote to the only friend he could think of in the circumstances. He wrote to Willie Stewart of Closeburn and begged that he give him three guineas that he might be able to pay his rent – or at least a sufficient part of his rent to secure a roof and four walls over his head, and Jean's head and the children's heads.

But 1795 came in with a great blast of trumpets and it seemed that France was about to launch an attack on Great Britain. The Bard, being a member of the Excise, had no alternative. He and Syme discussed the position, and it was agreed between them that they must come quickly before the town of Dumfries and their governmental superiors as men who were anxious and willing to take up arms in defence of their country.

And so, by the end of January, the Bard found himself in the forefront of the effort to establish a Corps of Volunteers. The alternative was to skulk in the background. The alternative was to be picked up, to be spotted immediately as a rebel and a subversive element and to be cast out of the Excise into the wilderness of poverty, run the risk of imprisonment and certainly of death by slow starvation. A moment's reflection of the position of Jean and the bairns and he did not hesitate.

George Haugh's advice to the Bard was that he should welcome the opportunity of joining the Royal Dumfries Volunteers.

'You have nae other road out. But you should ken as well as me, Rab, that there is nae possibility, nae danger of the French invading. The French hae enough on their hands without amassing a fleet to invade this country. No: the Volunteer Corps is a trick of the government to have an auxiliary army on the spot throughout the country to nip any possibility of the people taking to arms themselves. That's the main purpose of the Volunteers. Now, of course, you ken and I ken that there's plenty having to join the Volunteers for reasons o' their employment and the wee bit security they hae; but they're firm friends o' France: firm friends o' reform. Where would the French hae been had they no' had the sodgers on their side? And wi' the Volunteers, we'll be strengthened by such true friends o' democracy that could be a guid way o' neutralising the Volunteers. Indeed, men like yourself, wi' arms in your hands and the training how to

use them given to you by the government... I should think
that the chances o' reform are brighter now than they hae
been for many a year. You stick in, Rab, and learn your drill
and your musketry or whatever it is you're to get, and dinna
say too much... We'll see how things develop...'

At the end of January, under the chairmanship of Deputy
Lord-Lieutenant David Staig, those interested met in the
Court House.

There were many of the Bard's friends there: John Syme,
Thomas White, Surgeon James Mundell, Henry Clint of the
King's Arms, David Newall the Dalswinton factor, his land-
lord Captain John Hamilton, Samuel Clark the writer, James
Gracie the banker, and William Hyslop of the Globe.

At the following meeting, on the 3rd of February, more
of his friends joined: John MacMurdo (now Provost of
Dumfries in addition to being Drumlanrig's chamberlain),
Thomas Boyd the architect and general contractor, and
Findlater and John Lewars.

Findlater was not yet well enough to resume his duties as
Supervisor; but, as he said to the Bard:

'I just had to turn up and put down my name, Robert. We
canna let the Excise down – no' in thae kittle times. . . . I'll
be back on duty just as soon as I can – but you're doing
splendidly. Stick in! The experience'll stand you in good
stead for promotion – and you being in the Volunteers'll dae
you nae harm either. It'll dae nane o' us harm. But I'll need
to get back to my bed – the cauld's getting into my bones . . .'

There were enemies of the Bard there too. Men like
Francis Shortt, the Town Clerk, who was also Secretary of the
Loyal Natives Club . . .

But his friends were in the majority.

As David Newall said:

'Weel . . . Robert: a very successful evening. Glad to see
you here – how's everything wi' you and yours . . . ? Aye:
things are bad. Oh, couldna be worse. Everything's rising in
price . . . and there's scarcity. Of coorse . . . of coorse I wasna
thinking about that – wi' the imports dropped to nothing
there'll be next to nothing by way o' perquisites for you
Excisemen. Aye: a ruinous war. . . But then what wars arena
ruinous? Yet what are we to do . . .? Na, no: I dinna think
we'll hae ony trouble in Dumfries – there's nae real rabble o'
disaffected about the town. But then you see, Robert: gin
things were getting a deal worse. . . Aye: that's right – gin

218

the meal was rising much higher – or there cam' a real scarcity. . . Aye, aye . . .

'We'll look real braw in our uniforms. I took particular note o' the details – a blue coat half-lapelled wi' red cape and cuffs . . . and R.D.V. on the gilt buttons. A white cashmere vest — Ah, but easy dirtied, awfa easy dirtied – and the white trousers and the half-gaiters. . . . The hat should be nice though, real perjink. It says here: a round hat turned up on the left side wi' gilt buttons, a cockade and a black feather. . . There's a wheen o' gilt buttons. . . Aye. . . You've hit the nail on the head there, Robert! Gin we can drill and bear arms as weel as we can dress. . . Aye, that's it! Coorse, we'll be a' richt under Colonel De Peyster. . . A real old warrior, the Colonel. They tell me he did wonderful service oot yonder in America and Canada – especially wi' the Indians. And mind you, I think it wad be chancy enough wi' the Redskin craiturs – oh, no' to be trusted . . .

'This twa hours o' drilling twa nichts i' the week – mind you, it's heavy enough. By the time you travel back and forward, it fairly eats into the nicht. Oh . . . I see: just till we're proficient. Just that – and then it'll be down to once a month or thereby . . .

'You havena been in for a wee while – the lassies aey like to play the piano for you. I was forgetting, of coorse: you're Acting Supervisor – for Findlater. That's an honour too. You've gotten on weel wi' the Excise. And nae regrets at leaving Ellisland? Na, na: you were a wise man. Though damnit, Robert, you put out a lot o' hard work on Ellisland. Exactly: for John Morine to reap the benefit. Coorse, Morine has what you unfortunately lacked, Robert: the wherewithal. Aye: damn few o' us wad cut much o' a figure without the wherewithal. Maist essential in ony walk o' life; but mair sae in farming. . . A spell o' keen frost or twa-three weeks blatter o' rain at the wrang time and whaur are you gin you canna fa' back on Mr Gracie? Oh, a guid balance at the bank wi' James Gracie and you can snap your fingers at the weather . . .

'And you're still finding time to turn oot a sang or twa? I see: you're writing for *twa* publications in Edinburry! I was forgetting: the lassies had your last volume – Thomson's was it no? I think I heard them say that they preferred Johnson's *Museum*. . .

'I maun sae you're looking weel, Robert. Coorse, you can

keep drier now that you're aboot the town. Aye: you'll hae to ride out a bit too now that you're the Supervisor. A good man, Mr Findlater. . . But then we a' hae our ups and doons, our guid days and our bad days. That's life; that's how it goes. And sometimes I think when we're weel and like oursel's we're no' nearly thankfu' enough . . .

'Certainly I'll mind you to Mr Miller. Guid-nicht then, Robert – and mind and look in the first chance you hae!'

David Newall went his way and the Bard and Syme and John Lewars proceeded with Will Hyslop to the Globe.

Syme said: 'Since David Williamson, Willie Johnston and Rae have joined, I suppose we'll need to order our uniforms from one or other o' them?'

John Lewars said: 'From what I hear, Williamson's about the best tailor in the toon . . .'

Hyslop said: 'I hope they're no' for makin' a profit out o' us: we're a' in the same boat . . .'

Syme said: 'Of course they'll need to get their cost back: they canna be expected to work for nothing.'

The Bard said: 'You can be damn certain nane o' them will work for nothing. Only I hope the uniform winna be too dear: I've nae money to throw awa' – though I think it'll be a nice enough outfit. What d'you think, John – you that's been in the army?'

'It should look verra weel indeed, Robin. We'll be a handsome corps when we're drilled and turned out for inspection.'

'Braw sodgers – apprentice sodgers! Ah weel: I hope we never need to go into action. Maybe our appearance'll be enough to intimidate ony possible enemy. David Newall was saying we'd a wheen o' gilt buttons about our uniform – and a' to be stamped R.D.V.'

Hyslop said: 'I doubt but you're no' too keen, Robert, on the Royal Dumfries Volunteers?'

'Dinna mistake me, Will. I'm keen enough and I'll do my bit to mak' the corps a success. Why no'? We're in it – and it's up to us to mak' it a success. We've gotten a fairly democratic set o' rules drawn up. We hae the power to fine and censure our officers: we hae the power to expel: we can call meetings and alter the rules by a majority vote. I verra much doubt gin there's a mair democratic corps i' the nation . . .'

'True enough, Robin: we can make the Royal Dumfries Volunteers exactly what we like. And the fact that we hae the electing of our officers in the first place is proof enough o' that.'

The upshot was that John Hamilton was elected First Captain; John Finnan, Second Captain; David Newall and Wellwood Maxwell, First Lieutenants; and Thomas White and Francis Shortt, Second Lieutenants.

From the seventy-odd members the Captains, in turn, drew the names of those to serve in their respective companies. The Bard found himself in Number Two Company under Captain John Finnan, together with such friends as Syme, Lewars and James Gracie . . .

SODGER LADDIE

When the Bard donned his uniform for the first time and sallied forth to his first full-uniformed parade, Jean said:

'You're a braw sodger, Rab. I never saw you looking mair handsome!'

'So I'll pass muster?'

'You'll do that and mair. But I canna help feeling it wad be a pity to soil a brew uniform like that wi' fechting!'

'Aye: you're richt there, lass. But you can rest assured that ony fetchin' we dae will be damned sham fechin' . . .

'And how dae you like your Daddy in his military braws, Robbie? What's that you say, Frankie? Ah, you run-deil ye! Run across and tell Mr Lewars that I'm ready. So you'd like to be a sodger when you grow up, Robbie? Ah, laddie: by the time you grow up I hope and trust there'll be nae need for sodgers.'

The Bard did get some excitement from being in the Volunteers. Just as he had always been an excellent dancer, so now he found that as far as foot and musketry drill was concerned, he made an excellent soldier. His movements were smart, accurate and precise. This, added to his robust figure and stout frame, allowed him to cut quite a figure. His company was justly proud of him.

But he had not yet adjusted himself mentally to the Volunteers. His views had not changed in any particular. In his heart he still warmed to the French people.

How, indeed, could he be otherwise? He had been born a rebel, had lived all his life as a rebel, and would surely die a rebel. Certainly he was rendering unto Cæsar; but he was fully alive to the nature of his rendering.

There were those who sneered at him for joining the Volunteers. They reckoned he had joined in order to keep his Excise job. There was an odd rebel here and there who regarded him in uniform as something of a renegade, an apostate, a turn-coat, or something of an abject coward whose boasted independence was no more than the independence of a braggart.

But he was dependent on the Excise; and he was responsible for the welfare of his wife and children. He had argued out the problem with himself many times. And always he had come back to the conclusion that his first duty was to Jean and the children; his god, his king, his ideals, his poetry came a long way after that. Even his own personal comfort came a long way second. If it wasn't his sacred duty to provide food, clothing and shelter for his wife and children, then whose duty could it be?

If a man was selfish enough to sacrifice his wife and children to the conceit of his ideals – that was his responsibility. But the Bard's ego was not made of such unutterable selfishness.

A dedicated rebel might marry a dedicated rebel and they might fight for their ideals as well as they knew. All honour to them. But such dedicated rebels had no right to bring children into the world and risk their welfare and happiness.

Ah yes: a man must resist tyranny and oppression when it came upon him and his kind. Tyranny, oppression and injustice he must resist even unto death. But here was a different problem – a different set of conditions. The two must not be confused.

He had long argued the problem with himself. And though he had discussed the ins and outs of its many facets with Haugh and Lewars and Syme, he often failed to remember the dual role he had to play in society. There were occasions when he failed to dissemble – times when his tongue ran ahead of his discretion.

Such an occasion came at the end of a Volunteer dinner when the bottle was pushed around and toasts were bumpered.

When his time came for a toast, he rose and said:

222

'May we never see the French – and may the French never see us!'

There was some applause at this; but there was some dissent too.

Men like Lieutenant Shortt were incensed. What the hell did Burns mean? What the hell kind of toast was this anyway? Was there some subtle disloyalty in it? Maybe not. But there was no need for any damned subtlety or ambiguity in the Royal Dumfries Volunteers. Francis Shortt and his kind glowered and scowled.

Going home, John Lewars said:

'It's no' for me to criticise, Robert; but I dinna think you should hae made that toast. I heard Shortt saying he was going to raise it wi' the committee.'

'What was disloyal about my toast?'

'I ken you could argue about it . . .'

'The Dumfries Volunteers werena enrolled to fight the French. We're supposed to deal wi' civil disturbances.'

'Then why bring in the French? What's the good o' getting in the wrong wi' our enemies? D'you no' think you're playing richt into their hands? Of coorse: I ken I've nae richt to criticise, Robert.'

'Coorse you've a richt to criticise. . . I'll never learn sense. If Shortt likes to raise the matter wi' the committee — Aye: I suppose they could construe my toast as being somehow disloyal . . .'

'Aye: or disaffected.'

'Some day, John, when it's ower late, I'll learn to act on Corbet's orders – to act and no' to think. However . . . I've been turning ower a sang in my mind for the Volunteers – a sang wi' a sting in the tail. . . But a necessary sting, John. No, no: it's no' ready yet. The idea has been rumbling about my skull for a day or twa now. Dinna worry about the sting in the tail o' my sang. It'll be patriotic enough for Francis Shortt and the Loyal Natives: patriotic and loyal enough for onybody; and it'll wash the taste o' my toast out o' their loyal gabs. . . Mind you, John: there's aey the chance that the richt folk micht lose the day in France. There's just the chance that the big land-owners and the rich merchants may get the upper hand o' the people – for the time being. Then there micht be the possibility o' an invasion o' Britain. No: I dinna think sae mysel'; but it's a probability.'

223

'You mean that as a result of this internal quarrelling amang the Jacobins — ?'

'The Revolution could turn in upon itself and devour itself – encouraged by its enemies, of course.'

'That would be a terrible disaster after a' that's happened!'

'It would be. But remember that forces hae been liberated that can never be enslaved again. Even ideas hae been liberated and thae ideas canna be taken out o' the heads o' men... France could go through a sairer time than she's yet gone through. Forces could emerge that would embark on a policy o' conquering instead o' liberating. Maxwell fears that. Should that happen, then our duty is clear: we would oppose that; and for the time being we'd need to rally ahint Billy Pitt.'

'It's beyond me.'

'Why should it be beyond you? Damnit, things dinna come clean cut and divided into neat squares. No, no: the edges are ragged and the patches are irregular. Progress is *torn* frae the wab o' time: no' cut neatly to the measure wi' the tailor's shears. And no' always is the swatch torn clean frae the wab. Maybe just torn half-through – or hanging by threads. And sometimes the threads are picked up and an attempt made at a join. . . History, John, is a queer mixty-maxty o' ups and downs and turns and twists, advances and retreats. The one thing certain is that it's never a straight line. And you're looking for a straight line, John. Your mind's set alang a straight line – there's no' a twisted bit in you. You're young, and you're full o' ideals; and you want to go straight to your goal. You expect a' men o' guid-will to gang wi' you. Oh, I wadna hae you otherwise. . . But you'll live and you'll learn. You'll learn first to compromise – or seem to compromise. You'll hit your head against the wa' a wheen o' times – and then you'll learn to gang round it. You'll learn to side-step. You'll learn, in short, to jowk and let the jaw gae by you as I've said mony a time. But deep down you'll haud to your principles, your ideals. You'll learn to keep your hopes bright and your faith steady. And you'll learn to wait for every opportunity to advance . . .

'You can learn frae that mistake o' mine to-night. That was the wrong time to give that toast. No' the wrong place, mark you; but the wrong time. And yet the enemies o' France – the true France – in the Volunteers will have to think it ower and reflect that we're no' a' just the gullible sodgers they

224

tak' us to be. You'll mind that my toast got a gey round o' applause too. . . But yet: for me it was a mistake and a mistake I'll need to repair as soon as I can.'

THE STING IN THE TAIL

At the beginning of March he went across the Nith to Mavis Grove and saw Colonel De Peyster.

The Colonel was glad to see him. He admired the poet greatly, for he dabbled in versifying himself: and he was something of an atheist. He poured a drink and insisted that he draw in his chair to the fire.

'It's a cold night, Burns. We must look after you. You're the pride of the Volunteers, y'know. No other corps has Scotland's National Bard enrolled in its ranks. How d'you get along with Captain Finnan? Yes: a good man, Captain Finnan. He has the welfare of his men at heart. And that, with strict discipline, is the essence of a soldier. Not that we're as strict as we would be in the army. After all, we're only part-time soldiers and volunteers; and many of our privates are gentlemen. But for all that, I aim to have you a damned crack corps yet, Burns. I'll have you a credit to the King and your colours yet!'

Colonel De Peyster was tall, spare and lanthorn-jawed. His face was lined, his complexion a light coffee colour, his hair greying: his pale eyes were alert and sometimes he narrowed his eyelids mischievously. The Bard had a great regard for him.

'Now, Burns: I hear you've made a song for the Volunteers?'

'I have it here, Colonel. And if you approve of it, I intend to have a number of copies thrown off for the corps?'

'No: you read it over to me. A poet knows best how his work should go.'

'Thank you, Colonel: I appreciate that.'

He unfolded his sheet and read:

'The Royal Dumfries Volunteers – to the tune Push about the Jorum. You know the tune?'

'Give me the opening bar. . . . Yes: I have it. A good strong beat in it too: make a good march. Go on.'

'Does haughty Gaul invasion threat?
    Then let the loons beware, Sir!
There's wooden walls upon our seas
    And volunteers on shore, Sir!
The Nith shall run to Cornsincon,
    And Criffel sink in Solway,
Ere we permit a foreign foe
    On British ground to rally!

'Oh, let us not, like snarling tykes,
    In wrangling be divided,
Till, slap! come in an unco loun,
    And wi' a rung decide it!
Be Britain still to Britain true,
    Amang ourselfs united!
For never but by British hands
    Maun British wrangs be righted!

'The kettle o' the Kirk and State,
    Perhaps a clout may fail in't;
But Deil a foreign tinkler loon
    Shall ever ca' a nail in't!
Our fathers' blude the kettle bought,
    And wha wad dare to spoil it,
By Heavens! the sacrilegious dog
    Shall fuel be to boil it!

'The wretch that would a tyrant own,
    And the wretch, his true-sworn brother,
Who would set the mob above the throne,
    May they be damned together!
Who will not sing *God save the King*
    Shall hang as high's the steeple;
But while we sing *God save the King*,
    WE'LL NE'ER FORGET THE PEOPLE!'

'That's a damn fine song, Burns. Perfect. But we must have a wider audience than this for it. You must give it to the public prints. This should be a national song – taken up from one end of the country to the other. Can I have a copy right away?'

'That's your copy, sir – I've a draft at home.'

'Thank you, Burns: thank you indeed. I'll treasure this with

226

your other manuscript verses. I still think your Look Up and See a thundering good satire.'

'Then you approve of my sending to Edinburgh to have a hundred copies struck off – with the music. My friend Clarke whom you met — '

'Clarke the organist? An excellent musician. But I insist on paying the expense. Not at all, Burns – I insist: that's an order and that's an end on't. By God! this'll put our corps on the map – bring them before the British public. Another drink? Damnit, the occasion merits a bottle. Does my brother-in-law MacMurdo know about this?'

'No. . . not yet. I thought I'd give you the maidenhead o' it.'

'The maidenhead o' it? That's a damn nice way of putting it. I love that, Burns. Had there been a dinner coming off soon, you could have given the entire bluidy corps the maidenhead o' it. . . By the by, MacMurdo was telling me something of a collection of bawdy songs that you have – he tells me some of them are damn good. I'd promise to look after it carefully and keep it under lock and key. . . I was suggesting to my brother-officers that we might put you forward for a lieutenancy at the first vacancy. . . But it was pointed out that your superior in the Excise, Mr Findlater . . . glad you appreciate the delicacy of the position. Quite correct: there's absolutely no dishonour in remaining in the ranks – rather otherwise. And, of course, as our Bard you have a rank second to none . . .'

So the song went to Edinburgh and Clarke was so taken with it that instead of setting it to *Push about the Jorum*, he composed for it himself. And the broadsheets came back – words and music – and were distributed among the Volunteers and their friends.

It was published in early May in *The Edinburgh Courant, The Dumfries Journal* and *The Caledonian Mercury*.

All over the country the reformers, who were also constitutionalists, took it up with fervour – for the sting in the tail was also the leaven that worked the whole.

As Lewars said: 'I understand what you mean now, Robert. That's a master stroke – 'While we sing God save the King we'll ne'er forget the People!' Only you could hae thocht o' that and fitted it in sae neatly.'

'Thank you, John. But notice that sting in the opening

line – there's a' the difference in the world atween Haughty
Gaul and the French people. We'll ne'er forget the people –
whatever their nationality or creed or colour . . .'

THE PASSING OF FRIENDS

In February, Peggy Kennedy died at Daljarrock; but the
news didn't reach him till early in March when he received
the news of the death in Edinburgh of James Dalrymple of
Orangefield and Willie Cruikshank of the High School.

Jean knew Peggy Kennedy by sight and was sorry to hear
the news.

'You'll mind o' Peggy Kennedy frae Daljarrock? She was
Gavin Hamilton's guid-sister. My first published sang was to
her: Young Peggy blooms our bonniest lass. . . She'd a bairn
to Captain Andrew MacDoual o' Logan – Sculduddery
MacDoual – you ken what he was like. It seems they went
through a marriage ceremony which MacDoual denies.
Robert Kennedy's fighting the case of course. But how it'll
go Peggy'll never ken now. . . I'm mair upset about Willie
Cruikshank: he was one o' my best Edinburgh friends, Jean.
Dalrymple was the first Ayr man I met when I first entered
Edinburgh – I owe a lot to him too. Damnit, my friends are
dying right and left . . .'

Jean didn't like to say much about the subject of death:
she preferred not to think about it.

MARIA RIDDELL REPENTS

As spring came in in 1795, Maria Riddell could not help
thinking of the Bard and of her foolishness towards him.
This foolishness she regretted bitterly because she knew she
was in the wrong, knew that the Bard was incontestably in
the right. Yes, the Bard had made a social mistake; but had
he really . . . and what had been the nature of his mistake?

Maria Riddell, sitting in the draughty old house of Tinwald
which Walter had rented from the Earl of Queensberry and
where she was left for long periods on her own with her
children, had time to reflect on the value of social contacts.

Of the men she knew in Dumfriesshire and the adjacent ounties; of all the men she knew in England, all the men he had known in the Leeward Isles; of them all there was not ne of them who could hold a candle to Robert Burns.

She missed his conversations, she missed his personality, he missed watching his tremendously expressive face (with he eyes glowing and dimming and smouldering and the lips ursing or expanding) . . . missed the modulations of his aptivating voice as a sally of wit or profundity of truth came rom him. She missed his laughter too – his rich mellow aughter that came after a sally . . .

She missed Robert Burns.

The problem for Maria was how to win back first his espect and then possibly his friendship. Life had dealt sorely vith her since Walter had had to re-sell Woodley Park to Colonel Goldie (their debts had been fantastic); and she knew now the cheap hollow man of straw Walter really was.

Maria knew she would have to make the first overtures owards a reconciliation. These she set in motion. . . She was ratified to find the Bard, though cautious and discreet, eemed willing to reciprocate. It was now only a question, hought Maria, of an inch-by-inch re-entry into his steem . . .

The Bard was as keen to resume the relationship as was Maria. True, she was capricious, she was cruel, she was headstrong. She was a spoiled child of fortune; she could be vulgar; she was cat-like in her amorousness; she talked too much, too long, too quickly and too often; she was no beauty and yet – there she was . . . Maria Riddell! She had entered he Bard's life at Dumfries. She had brought something into his life and she had, as quickly, taken that something out of his life. The Bard was hurt and humiliated, resentful; but his regard for Maria, his desire for her company was still here.

For Maria was also witty, vivacious, intellectually daring: commanding and often enough brilliant in her talk; and still fundamentally a Republican! Still, fundamentally, Maria stood four-square with all she thought the French Revolution meant. She had not bowed the knee in any one respect to the aristocrats, as she and her friends called the men behind Pitt, Dundas and Burke.

The Bard, knowing all this from first- or second-hand, was glad when she did make her overtures. Though cautious, because of the hurt to his pride, he did come more than half way to meet her . . .

Somehow the feeling came to him these days – though it was a feeling he had known off and on all his life – that he had not long to live. Now the feeling came oftener to him and he reacted more gloomily. He did not want to die: there was no reason why he should die. There was his family of young children: there was his Jean. He was happy with his children and happy with his wife. He was not too unhappy with his work. He was supremely happy in his work for Johnson and for Thomson. No . . . there was no reason why he should die or why he should want to die . . .

Yet the feeling came to him again and again. Not maybe a a feeling . . . perhaps as a vague and dreadful kind of premonition that he had not long to live: that slowly but surely death was gathering to meet him in a final wrestling match in which he would be the loser.

Of course his spirits had got a lift up when he had been promoted to act as Supervisor in Findlater's place. And since his duties carried him hither and yont he had little time for introspection and little time for literary pursuits.

When Findlater resumed his duties in April, the Bard did not really know whether to be glad or sorry. Glad he was that he had proved his worth; that he had proved his ability to carry on the duties of a Supervisor; but he was glad too, now that spring was come again, that he would be able to devote more time to his song-writing . . .

FIRESIDE FRIENDS

Jean was supremely happy in the Millbrae Vennel. She had her children growing lustily and well and she had the companionship of Jessie Lewars. There was only one blight on the horizon, one fear, one difficulty, one heartbreak. It was that, though her boys thrived and looked like thriving, her only daughter, Elizabeth Riddell, pined and wasted. The doctors found nothing wrong with her. There was no organic weakness. Jean was deeply devoted to her. She was the Bard's pet ewe. And here she was, coming into her third year, and still she pined and lingered . . .

The Bard spent most of his time at home. He delighted in his children: he delighted to give them what education he could; and he worked hard, feverishly hard, on his song-writing. Of an evening when the children were laid by, he would encourage Jean to sing him over this lilt or that lilt. Jean, with Jessie Lewars nearly always in attendance, was glad to relax and sing for him.

They had a comfortable and spacious house. When darkness came it was grand to have a fire lit in the spence – to the left hand of the kitchen – and have a quiet meal together. . . Happy nights they had indeed; and happy nights with company when Findlater, and occasionally Syme and Jean Lorimer, and maybe her father, or Bess Hyslop came up from the Globe and joined them at the table or in a song; or Agnes Haugh, with her eldest bairn, might come up; or George Haugh saunter in himself of an evening, after the mail had arrived, and have a quiet and friendly word with them at the fire-side.

Maybe the Millbrae Vennel, for all its drawbacks, was the happiest home they had known. Certainly in the Millbrae they had room to move about, and they had at least one good room where they could entertain their friends and engage in the art and the satisfaction of social intercourse.

The plain, kind-hearted Jessie Lewars, like her brother John was devoted to the Bard. There was nothing that either of them would not have done for him. Jessie, though she was devoted to the Bard, was no less devoted to Jean. She learned much from Jean: learned from Jean's kindness and humility and from her stoical uncomplaining philosophy. They talked much of the Bard: Jessie with open-eyed rapture and Jean with the steady glow of confidence in her eye and in her talk.

'You ken, Jessie, there's just nae man like Mr Burns. You think that and I think that. You *think* that and I *ken* it in a way that you canna; but there you are. . . Sometimes you wonder at him doing this and doing that. . . Sometimes you wonder at him staying out late and coming home a wee bit fu'; but ah! Jessie lass, that's nothing. Thae are but sma' things. The wonder is, lass, that he's as happy at hame as he is; because he just needs to put his face out on the street there and this ane's hailing him and the next ane's hailing him; or the Provost's wanting him up to his hoose; or this ane or that ane o' the nobility's wanting to hae him ower to the King's Arms or the George. . . If he listened to a' their invitations he would never be hame. . . He likes company – ye ken he likes company. He's fond o' me and he's fond o' you and he's fond o' the bairns; but oh! he's awfu' fond o' the hoosefu' o' friends round the fire-side and a bit bite on the table. Him talking away . . . talking . . . talking . . . in a way that nane o' them can talk so that the whole lot o' them hae to sit and listen. Oh, I've tellt you how we've had our ups and downs, Jessie; but maistly ups. You see, being married to a man like Mr Burns: being married to a genius is, in itself, an unco responsibility. And am I the proud woman to hae that responsibility! I kent Mr Burns when he was much socht after in my ain town o' Machlin; when he was the talk o' the town and the country forby; when he was young and free and didna care – didna need to care – whaur he lichted o' what took his fancy. Aye, if you'd kent him in Machlin you'd hae kent anither side to his character . . . But whereve he's gane, Jessie, he's won hundreds o' friends: hundreds o' good steady friends that swear by him. Oh yes: baith men and women . . . baith men *and* women. Maybe some folk feel I should be jealous o' the women. But . . . I'm no jealous Jessie. I ken them and I ken Mr Burns; and I ken that nane o' them hae much chance where his wife and family are concerned. Indeed, where his wife and family are concerned, they hae nae chance at a'. That's how, Jessie, I hae nae fear o' him and nae jealousy o' him – o' his women friends I mean; for I ken him, and I ken the trueness that's in him.'

Poor Jessie Lewars! Kind, considerate and gentle in her words and looks. About the same age as Jean Lorimer. Sadder, maybe, by the recent death of her sister, also a Jean. . . Sometimes when she was about the Bard's closet and she was bringing him a drink or a bowl of brose, he would put his hand to her lithe waist, let it drop and feel the strength and plumpness of her hips. . . And Jessie would make no motion of withdrawal but smile with her eyes and murmur:

'Oh, Mr Burns, Mr Burns . . .'

And the Bard would say: 'Ah, lassie: be on your ways, my dear; you'll mak' a guid wife to a guid man some day.'

To which Jessie would reply: 'I'm in nae hurry, Mr Burns – there's nocht to hurry about.'

That was the truth in so far as Jessie Lewars was concerned. There was no hurry; no hurry about anything in this life. Everything would be fulfilled in due course – and if things verena fulfilled, well . . . that was another way of fulfilment. Though sex was a glimmer and a gleam in Jessie's life, not yet was it clamant.

Jean had experienced a different quality of passion at Jessie's age; and yet in their acknowledgment of necessity, in their quiet and unchallenging acceptance of destiny, they had everything in common. Maybe it was because of this that Jessie Lewars always drew herself away from Jean Lorimer. Instinctively, and without a word being spoken, they disliked each other. Maybe they didn't even dislike each other: they just knew instinctively that they had nothing in common. So they tolerated each other but had absolutely nothing to say in each other's presence. Both Jean and the Bard had noted this.

Jean said: 'It's no' difficult to understand either, Rab. Jean's Jean and Jessie's Jessie and that's a' that's to it.'

'And yet you like baith o' them, Jean?'

'Just as you do – though maybe for different reasons! Maybe I see a bit o' myself in Jessie and a bit o' myself in Jean. What about you?'

'Me? Ho! Jeanie kens life in a way that Jessie'll never. Jeanie'll be true to nae man though she'll be true to hersel' – or what she kens as hersel'! Jessie'll be faithful unto death: if she gets the richt man. And if she doesna? Oh, she'll still be faithful – unto death.'

'Aye, you've got them weighted in the balance, Rab. I think you're richt; but, like you, I like the baith o' them. . . But I fear for Jeanie Lorimer where I dinna fear for Jessie Lewars . . .'

Jean felt closer to the young than she did to the old – she even felt closer to young men like John Lewars and Adam Scobie than she did to John Syme or Alexander Findlater. She delighted in young folks and enjoyed the superiority that being a young mother of a young family gave her. She had little of her husband's gift of being able to be at complete ease with male or female company of whatever age.

But Jean, though her heart went out to the young folks, was no fool. She liked Mrs Haugh, Mrs Lewars and Mrs Hyslop. . . There were matronly problems she could discuss with them she couldn't discuss with the maidens . . .

And so Jean's life flowed placidly enough in the Millbrae Vennel and she was never lonely there as she had often been

233

in the Stinking Vennel – though she reckoned that her firs married years in Ellisland with Nancy and Fanny had, so far been the best years in her life.

Often she sighed for Ellisland; for the green summer field and the pleasant-singing Nith. . . And maybe her sister Nel and her brother Adam and the green acres that had seemed to be their own . . . and the kye and the horse and the chickens. In many ways Ellisland had been her golden dream.

True, there had been bleak bitter months of winter and long dark nights; and rain and wind and a terrible loneliness and isolation. . . But always the spring had come and the promise of life re-born and renewed.

Strangely enough husband and wife rarely if ever discussed their Ellisland days . . .

VISIT FROM NICOL

When Willie Nicol, in August, paid his yearly visit to Dumfries and his estate at Laggan Park, he was in an unusually depressed mood.

'I havena gotten ower Willie Cruikshank's death, Robert We were great friends as weel as colleagues. There's naebody can take Cruiky's place.'

'It's a sair time o' deaths, Willie. I thocht highly o' Cruikshank – as highly as I thocht o' onybody in Edinburgh. And now Smellie hardly a month cauld: there's just naebody to replace a man like Smellie. Smellie was a genius and a character. Without him Auld Reekie's empty.'

'Aye: you thocht highly o' Smellie.'

'Did you no'?'

'Aye . . . highly enough. But then I never had your pitch o' enthusiasm, Robert. There's never ony half-measures where you're concerned. Dinna scowl noo: I appreciated Smellie's worth – mony a rare battle o' words we had. Mony a battle ower you too. Smellie cam' back frae his visit here and told me you were happier placed in Dumfries than ever you could hae been in Edinburgh. I told him I doubted that – for I ken Dumfries and Smellie didna.'

'Dumfries! In mony a way I loathe the sicht and smell o' Dumfries. Oh, I'm lucky enough. I've got good friends in Dumfries – and I'm glad to have them. Of course there're nae

Willie Nicols or Willie Smellies in Dumfries. What the hell is there in Dumfries? Yes: Smellie was taken wi' it – but he was fêted like the lion he was. But work-a-day Dumfries – what's in it? Aye: there's the theatre that while awa' a nicht or twa in the back-end. There's twa-three guid howffs. . . But the town itself is nothing to me – though it may mean something to my laddies that are growing up in it. I could shake the dust o' Dumfries frae my shoon the morn wi' nae regret, Willie. Strange, isn't it? I ken Machlin and Tarbolton and Ayr and Kilmarnock like the back o' my hand. Aye: I ken he big feck o' Auld Reckie – for I was interested in every stane o' it. But here, Willie, I just earn my living – and dree my weird. Damn it, if I was awa' the morn the only thing I'd mind is the Globe and the Mid-Steeple – aye, and the walk down the banks o' the Nith. Though even the Nith means nothing but a pleasant stretch o' water. How different frae the river Ayr. . . I think it is, Willie, that by the time you reach thirty your mind has set. Yes: the mind's keener in some ways; but in others it doesna register visual impressions the same. Ten years ago I could tell you where I was and what I was doing. Aye: I could tell you what the weather was like. To-day! I could hardly tell you what I was doing last week. Damnit! I could tell you how mony cobble stanes were round Johnnie Dow's door in Machlin when I couldna tell you what's in front o' my ain door here in the Millbrae.'

'Yes, Robert: that's how the mind goes. I remember Latin verses I translated as a student. If I translated a verse the nicht I wadna mind in the morn. But you think deeper the aulder you get . . .'

'Dae you? I wonder? Experience wears its pattern on the mind, of course. And we learn caution and we shun folly – up to a point. But I'd give a lot to have the brain I had when I first cam' to Edinburgh – aye, or on my last year on Mossgiel. My brain was afire then and nae experience, however simple, but what was turned to account – and for me to good account.'

'But you're still turning out a guid sang?'

'And some no' sae guid. But I'm no idle, Willie. Mind you: it's far harder work making a sang to a prescribed melody than writing a verse or twa clean aff-loof as it were.'

'And you think a' this sang-writing's worth while? Jean was telling me that you'll hae her or Miss Lewars singing awa' at a time for hours on end?'

'Aye, I think it's worth it. Why else wad I dae it? I'm no' only daein' this for our generation but for the generations yet to come. And if you think this is my damned egotism at work I think you're wrang.'

'Sangs hae a way o' goin' out o' fashion.'

'And they hae a way o' comin' back into fashion. There'll aey be folk interested in sangs. I'm far frae thinking that a' my sangs are masterpieces – some o' them are damn near trash. But they'll dae till a better poet puts better words to them. My only hope is that later generations, going ower Johnson's and Thomson's work, will be thankfu' that we rescued as much for them to work on and improve and better – where they can. Scottish sang, Willie, is like Scottish history – a process wi' a remote beginning and an end naebody can see. It goes on frae generation to generation and sometimes the generations are fruitful and sometimes barren. But then that's life. Sometimes history seems to stand still and then it gives twa-three loups and jumps into another century. History has jumped a century since I was born. When I was born we were just getting ower the Rebellion – my sons are born in the first years o' the French Revolution – and the world can never be the same again.'

'So you're still thirled to your damned unlucky politics?'

'Never mind whether I am or no'. I'm no' talking as a politician – I'm talking as a mere observer of the march o' history of human destiny. And I think I understand history now as I never richt understood it afore.'

'And what good has it done you?'

'A' the good in the world, man. Once you understand history and how it moves and works, then you understand human destiny and you understand how the individual fits in wi' destiny. . . And wi' this understanding there comes deep peace, an acceptance o' the ebb and flow o' things.'

'And then you look for a tub like Diogenes?'

'Damn the fear. . . It's no' something I can argue about for, in a way, it's a serenity that's got to be experienced. . . And it's no' an experience that comes through sitting on your backside and lookin' up the lum.'

'Weel. . . You're for sitting down now and philosophising?'

'No: it doesna help the daily struggle much. But it helps reflection – contemplation. The daily struggle goes on and damn often it seems a poor shabby way for a man to earn is brose – a gauger's work. If I hadna my sangs to justify my existence, Willie, I doubt I'd give way to melancholy – ye, or suicide. A man's energies should be used for what e's maist fitted for – whether it's ploughing a rig or playing he fiddle – or teaching Latin to the generations as they come long.'

'Ah weel, Robert, as for teaching Latin, I've only this to ay. I've been at it a while noo; and I see damn few scholars hat mastered enough Latin to profit by it. Some acquired nough to scrape through Law or the Kirk or Medicine; but ew appreciated the great classical authors – aye, I could ount them a' on the one hand. And maybe that's a' there's to it. Earn a living, provide for your wife and weans and our auld age . . . and to hell wi' ocht that gets in your road. But for you things are sae different. You've gotten the Bard's Crown o' Immortality. You are one o' the immortals – while ou're still living! And you'll be a greater immortal when ou're dead – twa-three hunder years after you're dead. But, s long as you live, you hae the satisfaction of knowing you're cotland's Bard. . .'

'You've aey upheld me in that honour, Willie. But dinna hink that the responsibility o' being Scotland's Bard hasna veighed or doesna weigh wi' me now. Maybe that's one ' the reasons why I tak' my sang-writing as seriously as I lae.'

'Aye . . . but we can be ower serious, too, Robert. . . But here's one thing I canna tak' seriously – that's you being a odger in the Dumfries Volunteers!'

'How no'?'

'Scotland's Bard – wi' a gun ower his shoulder! Oh, I ken vhy you did it and I approve o' your reasons. But there's a ligh, even a ludicrous incongruity about the whole business.'

'Listen: I ken how to load a gun and I ken how to fire it. I ven ken something about hitting the target. What the hell's udicrous about a poet fechtin' – provided he's fechtin' in the ight cause?'

'There's nae poet should be fechtin'. Fechtin' is for sodgers; nd a true poet can never be a sodger. It's a bluidy farce and cruel farce. When you wrote them the Dumfries Volunteers hey micht hae excused you takin' up arms. I canna forgive hem that, Robert – makin' a sodger out o' you.'

'Maybe you think they should have given me a bluidy big astle and a pension o' a thousand a year?'

'And why not? Give me one good reason!'

'To hell wi' reasons, Willie. I'll take my chance in life as I go along. An odd favour here and there I'll ask. . . But by and large I'll take what comes to me without privilege. I was born into poverty. All my life I've struggled to keep my head above the water by virtue o' my ain efforts. This way at least I keep my feet on the earth and maintain something o' my ain self-respect. Privileges! Let me enjoy the privilege o' taking you down to the Globe and giving you a drink, for I never saw you glummer – and I want to tell you about the visit I had frae Robert Cleghorn frae Saughton Mills – you remember Cleghorn at Crochallan . . . ?'

DOUBLE AFFLICTION

Elizabeth Riddell pined and made no progress. When Jean's sister was down on a short visit, the Bard and she agreed that the bairn might be taken to Mossgiel. The country air there and the country produce – the milk and the eggs – might help her.

So Elizabeth Riddell was taken off to Mossgiel.

The Bard took very ill. The rheumatism which had troubled him all his life now became chronic. . . He struggled from his bed and he struggled to his work; and he struggled on his work and he struggled home and went to bed. . . There was no rest there except maybe in the early hours of the morning. . .

Then came word from Mossgiel that Elizabeth Riddell had died.

The Bard was too ill to go and bury his daughter in Machlin kirk-yard: too ill physically and maybe too sick at heart.

Jean and he wept much at the loss of their only surviving daughter: the daughter they had tried hard to give a chance in this life. She had died despite all their care and all their trouble.

The blow was doubly hard in that he still had two daughters christened Elizabeth: Elizabeth Park . . . and at Mossgiel, Dear-Bought Bess who thrived and had every appearance of being a lively vigorous lass. Elizabeth Park, although more delicately made and delicately formed, had every promise of womanhood.

But neither Dear-Bought Bess nor Elizabeth Park – dear though they were to him – could make up for the loss of Jean's Elizabeth. He felt the loss more than he had felt the loss of any child of his before.

For many days Jean feared for his health and his sanity . . .

NEW HOPE

The Bard's illness was short, if severe. By the beginning of November he had, as if by a miracle, regained much of his old strength. With growing strength, he became confident and even buoyant.

He had been elected to the committee of the Volunteers, and on the 5th he attended a meeting and received congratulations from his comrades on his recovery. Neither he nor the committee was to know that he would never be able to attend another meeting.

So confident was he of the future, and so confident was Jean, that they thought to have another child in the hope that it might be a girl and so compensate for the cruel loss of Elizabeth Riddell . . .

DEATH OF RESPONSE

Strange that Dumfries as a town meant nothing to the Bard. He knew its streets and wynds, closes and vennels; but they meant nothing to him. They did not register. Not even did his favourite walk by the Nith register with him. Yes: as a pleasant walk it registered: a flowering thorn, a mavis singing registered. . . But neither the mavis nor the thorn belonged, as such, to Dumfries or the Nith.

The Nith was a pleasant river; but it could not mean to him what Ayr or Doon or Stinchar had meant and still meant to him.

He knew every cobble stone in Machlin and Tarbolton. He would have been hard pressed to say which streets in Dumfries were cobbled and which were not. He would have had to *think* about such a question had it been addressed to him.

Nothing in Dumfries mattered, for nothing had character

or associations. His mind carried little of the details of the interior of the King's Arms or the George or the Assembly Rooms – or the Jerusalem Tavern.

He knew every crick and cranny in Gavin Hamilton's office. But for all the times he had dined at Captain Hamilton's there was little of the furniture he could recall. Nor had he any wish or necessity to recall.

His eyes was still as sharp as ever for a face, a gait or a gesture; his ear as keen and sensitive as ever to a phrase or an unusual intonation.

But for the stone and lime and brick of which Dumfries was built; for its shape and form he cared nothing. He was a stranger. He would always be a stranger. It was too late now to take root.

Even the theatre, as theatre, mattered nothing to him. He noted the boxes; he observed the stage. But only the actors and the audience interested him – and not always the audience.

He had many friends in Dumfries and warm enough friends in all ranks of society.

But in Dumfries there was no John Rankine, no Daddy Auld – not even a Holy Willie. There was no Smellie, Nicol, Cleghorn or Cunningham. No Black Jock Russell, no Johnnie Dow or Dawney Douglas or Nance Tinnock or John Dowie.

There were good friends; but friends of the day and the hour . . .

THE COLD BLAST

The Decembers in Dumfries had grown successively gloomy. But December in 1795 proved to be the gloomiest.

His rheumatic infection flared up and he was stricken with a violent fever.

Dr Maxwell came and prescribed; but without any seeming effect.

The Bard tossed and raved for days and nights. Many times Jessie Lewars feared he was dying. She nursed him when Jean was seeing to the children or snatching an hour's sleep. . . She nursed him quietly and efficiently.

As he came out of his fever he looked at Jessie and said:
    'Oh dear, lass: I must have been gey ill; but I mind o' you

back and forward: mind o' your angel-presence and touch. I hope I wasna too ill a patient for you.'

'Mr Burns: nae matter how ill you were – and you were gey ill – you couldna be too ill for me to help what I can. It's been a gey privilege, Mr Burns, to hae nursed you when Mrs Burns wasna here to attend to your wants and your needs.'

The Bard looked at Jessie Lewars, looked at her with a fresh eye as his fever abated. He saw a quiet comely lass. And the rhythm of a song was hot upon him ...

He asked her what her favourite tune was – gin she had a favourite. She told him; and when next she came to his bed-side he read the words to her:

> ' O, wert thou in the cauld blast
> On yonder lea, on yonder lea?
> My plaidie to the angry airt –
> I'd shelter thee, I'd shelter thee.
> Or did Misfortune's bitter storms
> Around thee blaw, around thee blaw,
> Thy bield should be my bosom,
> To share it a', to share it a'.

> 'Or were I in the wildest waste,
> Sae black and bare, sae black and bare,
> The desert were a Paradise,
> If thou wert there, if thou wert there.
> Or were I monarch of the globe,
> Wi' thee to reign, wi' thee to reign,
> The brightest jewel in my crown
> Wad be my queen, wad be my queen.'

Jessie wept a little and said: 'Oh, Mr Burns, I'm no' fit to hae a sang like that made on me ...'

'Dinna be a silly lass, Jessie. There's the song I made on you. I mean every word o' it ... and I only hope it'll be a remembrance o' the mony days that hae passed since we first cam' to the Millbrae Vennel. Now haud up your head, lass, and dinna be ashamed o' the song I've written for you.'

And Jessie stood there by his bed-side, plump and plain and straight-forward and yet somehow angelic and girlish and innocent.

The Bard stretched out his hand and his hand wandered,

feeling her person; and Jessie put her arms round him, kissed him and said:

'Mr Burns, you shouldna . . . you shouldna . . .'

'Hoots, lassie, you're young . . . and I'm a dying man . . .'

'Oh, dinna die, Mr Burns, dinna die . . . for if I could die for you I wad die . . .'

'Jessie: dinna be a fool, lass: dinna be a fool for yoursel'; but . . . aey keep near me . . . aey keep near me. There's something about your flesh, your youth and your innocence that gars me want to live . . . gars me want to get better . . .'

He patted her fine plump hips: 'Ah God, lass: there was a day. . . When I'm gone and buried, *you*'ll see the day.

And guid-luck to you, lass; and guid-luck to the man wha marries you. . . Aye: life's afore you . . . and life's behind me now . . .'

In his terrible illness; his terrible lassitude; his complete enervation; his tired hand coming in contact with her vital flesh did more to make him well than any medicine that Maxwell had prescribed for him.

Jessie knew that her body meant something to the Bard. something to his welfare and to his sanity; and she could not withdraw from him – and had no wish to withdraw from him. For his exploring hand gave her a feeling of well-being and of fulfilment such as she couldn't explain, but which ran through her veins and her nerves and soothed them and, in some way, fulfilled the longing that ran deep below her consciousness.

Jessie Lewars was one of those rare women the secret parts of whose body were inviolate and yet not invulnerable. She did not shrink from the touch of one for whom she had regard and love and sympathy. Jessie Lewars (and the Bard knew it and was thankful for it) was the kind of woman whose body and whose spirit were untrammelled with morality and "Thou shalt not" and yet was utterly free of any taint of lewdness.

Jean understood the attraction Jessie had for the Bard and she approved of it – especially in his illness. And Jean, whose awareness was uncanny, did not need to trouble her mind with reasons for her approval.

A REMNANT OF PLEASURE

By the end of January he was fit enough to crawl through to his desk and sit for an hour. He thought of the many friends who had been his correspondents. Gradually he would get round to a renewal of epistolary greetings. But the long silence of Mrs Dunlop worried him. Never before had there been such a silence. How had he offended her? There was nothing for it but to write and ask her. He drafted the note:

These many months you have been two packets in my debt. What sin of ignorance I have committed against so highly a valued friend I am utterly at a loss to guess. Your son, John, whom I had the pleasure of seeing here, told me that you had gotten an ugly accident of a fall, but told me also the comfortable news that you were gotten pretty well again. Will you be so obliging, dear Madam, as to condescend on that my offence which you seem determined to punish with a deprivation of that friendship which once was the source of my highest enjoyments? Alas! Madam, ill can I afford, at this time, to be deprived of any of the small remnant of my pleasures. I have lately drank deep of the cup of affliction. The Autumn robbed me of my only daughter & darling child, & that at a distance too & so rapidly as to put it out of my power to pay the last duties to her. I had scarcely began to recover from that shock, when I became myself the victim of a most severe Rheumatic fever, & long the die spun doubtful; until after many weeks of a sick-bed it seems to have turned up more life, & I am beginning to crawl across my room, & once indeed have been before my own door in the street.

> When pleasure fascinates the mental sight,
>   Affliction purifies the visual ray;
> Religion hails the drear, the untried night,
>   That shuts, for ever shuts! Life's doubtful day.

As to other matters of my concern, my family, views, &c. they are all as successful as I could well wish.

I know not how you are in Ayrshire, but here, we have

actual famine, & that too in the midst of plenty. Many day
my family, & hundreds of other families, are absolutel
without one grain of meal; as money cannot purchase i
How long the *Swinish Multitude* will be quiet, I cannot tel
they threaten daily.

Farewell! May all good things attend you!

ONE MORE UNFORTUNATE

What the Bard had said concerning the tendency of Jea
Lorimer to turn whore proved only too true. Maybe, con
sidering her home circumstances, the lass had much provoca
tion. Her mother went completely to drink; her father wa
seldom sober; and his business, as farmer and merchant, wa
on the verge of bankruptcy.

For Jean there was nothing but degradation and miser
at home; and she found herself more and more gravitatin
towards Dumfries and seeing what company she could fin
She found that virtue is its own reward in a very peculia
way.

If she walked down the street hurriedly – averting her eye
from any men – she was safe enough from any importuning
But she was surprised when she wanted to attract men tha
she had to make overt advances. She was more surprise
when her advances were brutally repulsed. The repulses cu
deep into her soul.

But there were others – plenty of them – who eyed thi
lovely fresh young girl and eagerly snatched at her charm
and her favours; and that for very little cash. Jean had not ye
learned to put any high price on her favours.

But she needed the money: needed the money for food an
for dress. She was now in the direst of poverty . . .

She found the Globe Tavern Close as handy a place t
skulk in as any. There were always men going up and down
and there were many convenient neuks and crannies abou
it . . .

On an early spring night the Bard was going down th
close from the Millbrae Vennel. In the dim light he though
he recognised the man and woman love-making in a corner
He halted inside the door of the Globe tavern. Presently th
man came in and he recognised him.

244

The Bard said casually: 'Wha was that you were wi',
ock?'

John Andrews said: 'That's Jean Lorimer: her that had
he run-away match at Gretna. . . God, Mr Burns . . . if
ou're wantin' a bit o' cheap, easy meat, Jean Lorimer's your
afest bet in Dumfries the now — And she's guid – I'll
uarantee you that!'

The Bard brushed him aside and walked up the close. He
ooked here and there. Then he came to where Jean Lorimer
vas skulking.

She said with a false gaiety in her voice:

'Oh, hello, Robert; it's you, is it?'

'Yes: it's me! Lord God! Jean Lorrimer! Dinna tell me
ou're whoring. . . . Dinna tell me you're whoring in *this*
lose . . . ?'

Jean kept her brazen front: 'That's no' a polite word,
Robert, to use to me.'

The Bard put his hand on her shoulder and said:

'Jean Lorimer. . . Has it come to this?'

She shook herself free: 'Come to what . . . ? And what do
ou care – what does onybody care what I've come to?'

'All right then: you'll no' deny that when I cam' down the
lose a minute or twa ago you were wi' a man – a man you
en damned little about – and a man wha bocht your favours.
. D'you deny that?'

'No: I dinna deny it. Why the hell should I deny it? What
l'you want me to do? Starve?'

'Starve? You could get a job, couldn't you?'

'Get a job at what? Tell me what kind o' job I could get
hat would keep me in food and clothes . . .?'

'All right. . . My God, Jean! You didna need to sink as
ow as this surely. . . Surely you could hae found some other
oad out . . .?'

'I'm listening to you, Robert Burns: I'm listening to you;
and I'm paying nae attention. . . I've been a bluidy fool a' my
days. . . I'm no' goin' to be a bluidy fool ony longer! If this
s the way I've got to earn my bread and butter – well, by
God! I'll earn it this way. . . And I'll no apologise to you or
ony other body!'

The Bard's gorge rose in a terrible anger. He grasped her
by the shoulder.

'God Almighty! Jean Lorimer! After all you've been to
me . . . that you should sink to this; that you should lower

yourself to ony man in Dumfries who has a copper or tw
to gie you. . . You! that was my Chloris: my inspiration: th
model for my sangs . . .'

'Aye . . . I was the model for your sangs; and what th
hell did I get out o' being the model for your sangs? Got m
head blawn up wi' ideas – ideas that you put in it — I wa
this; and I was that; and I was a lot mair . . .! Damn fine
you ken, Robert, my life doesna happen to be ony bed o
roses! Damn fine you ken! It hasna been a paradise and yo
ken it hasna been a paradise . . .!'

'No: life's no' a paradise to a damn wheen o' us, Jean. .
What's the odds about that?'

'Are you carin'?'

'Aye, I'm carin' . . . My God: you ken what you meant t
me and what I meant to you! Surely to God there's som
other road you could fend for yoursel' than this! You ke
this is goin' to lead you into stinkin' poverty and stinkin' ill
health too – and a stinkin' death at the end o' it! Listen, lass
surely you ken a better road than this: surely the sangs
wrote for you meant something more to you than this . . .?

'Well . . . you got what you wanted out o' me. . . You go
your sangs . . . and the other thing as well when it suite
you. . . There's nae mair sangs in me, I suppose; and I don'
suppose I've onything to offer *you* that's so well experience
in the ways o' the world that's of ony further interest t
you . . .'

'You're a bluidy hard woman got, Jean, that can say
things like that to me. . . How long has this been goin' on?
I suppose that's why you havena been at the house this while
back . . .?'

'Aye: that's why I havena been at the house this while
back, as you say; but no' because of you but because o
Jean!'

'All right . . . I'll no' let Jean ken anything about this. Bu
for heaven's sake, lass, can you no' keep awa' frae a place
like this — '

'It's a public place: naebody can prevent me frae coming
here . . . and there's plenty o' men goin' up and down. . . If
I want to be here I've a richt to be here; and you don't need
to recognise me if you don't want to recognise me . . .'

'Jean: how bad are things at Kemys Ha'?'

'You havena been out to see, have you?'

246

'No: I havena been out; but I can guess. . . But surely they're no' as bad as this?'

'And do you think I wad be standing here if they werena?'

The Bard put his hand in his pocket: he knew he had a half-sovereign there, treasured against emergency. He pulled it out and placed it in her hand:

'Well . . . this'll keep you for a day or twa. . . You're welcome to it, Jean. . . I'm gey sair hurt the nicht . . .'

'You dinna need to be too much hurt, Robert. I don't suppose you'll be seeing me for very long. . . I'm thinking o' goin' to Edinburgh – so I don't suppose you'll see me again. I've been a silly bitch a' my days; but I'm no goin' to be silly ony mair!'

'A' right, lass: you're no' goin' to be silly ony mair! For God's sake, pull yourself together! Pull yourself together and look life in the face. Look yourself in the face and ask yourself where this degradation's going to get you! My God! you're a woman in ten thousand yet; and could be . . .'

Jean turned her head away: 'Aye, for a poet – for a mad hour wi' a poet I'm a woman in ten thousand. But for a' day and every day and seven days in the week, what am I? And what is there for me? Me – that was married! Me – that's only the leavings o' a decent lassie in the eyes of decent men!'

She opened her hand and looked at the gold coin and said: 'But thanks, Robert; and nae hard feelings for a' that has passed atween you and me. Dinna think too badly o' me . . .'

She turned quickly and ran up the close.

The Bard stood and watched her till she vanished. He wondered if perhaps it was not his duty to take a turn out to Kemys Hall at the first opportunity and have a long and serious talk with Jean; or whether he should have a talk with her father. He knew the Lorimers were in a pretty wretched state. In fact he was disgusted with them at Kemys Hall, to think that they had gone down in drink to beggary so rapidly. Yet . . . Jean Lorimer . . .

He did not go back to the Globe; but made his way instead to the Jerusalem tavern. He did not want to run the risk of meeting Jock Andrews in the Globe: he was frightened that he might be tempted to strike him. As it was, he had barely the physical energy to pull on his boots.

But, indeed, not only were the Lorimers in a measure of distress: the whole town of Dumfries was feeling the terrible pinch of the times. On Saturday, the 12th of March, as carts were coming into the town and making for the quay, loaded with meal, the poorer elements – starved by the scarcity and high price of meal to the point of revolt – seized the carts and proceeded to sell the meal at the very much reduced price of 2/4d per stone.

Meal riots were taking place all over the country; and the situation was ugly enough in all conscience; but on the Sunday morning – and despite the Sabbath – a great crowd of people went out from Dumfries into the surrounding districts and, raiding farms, brought back into the town great stores and bags of meal which they proceeded to dispense amongst the most needy. For a moment it appeared that the sorely tried good folk of Dumfries might become completely out of hand. But the Angusshire Fencibles made a parade of the town and knots of guards from them were posted on all roads and at strategic points. Defeated and sullen the people retreated.

But most of them had laid in a fair stock of meal and, for the first time in months, were able to satisfy the hunger-pangs of themselves and their children.

The Bard looked on the revolt with every sympathy. He himself knew, and his children in the Millbrae Vennel knew, just what the scarcity and excessive cost of meal meant in the way of unsatisfied and hungry bellies.

A LAST LOOK ROUND

John Syme looked at the Bard with some anxiety.

'This spring weather's no' bringing you round the way you hoped, Robin?'

'No . . .'

'What does Maxwell say? You've been to Doctor Brown too, haven't you?'

'They keep talkin' about a flying gout.'

'But you're no' getting back your strength the way you wad ike?'

'No. . . Sometimes I fear the worst, John.'

'You mauna do that, Robin. You maun keep your spirits up!'

'What wi'?'

'What hae you aey kept them up wi'?'

'It's hard to keep the body thegither in thae bluidy times far less the spirit. And Will Hyslop's spirits are nae guid either – even if I could afford them.'

'Aye . . . the times are bad – and they'll continue bad till after harvest. Let's pray it'll no' fail.'

'Weel may they pack Dumfries wi' their damned military. But if the harvest fails the military winna avail much —'

'Damn it, Robin, I ken things are bad. But we canna hae ony bloodshed.'

'I pray there'll be nae bloodshed. I ken ower weel wha's blood'll be shed. . . But can you see the authorities acting wi' either sense or humanity? Hae they ever acted wi' sense or humanity? For myself', John, I'm past caring – but I've gotten a wife and weans. I'm on half-pay – and if ocht was to happen there would be nae pay. . . And you ask me to keep my spirits up . . .?'

'Robin, you ken —'

'I'm but joking, John. Dinna say a word. There'll be some road out for me: there aey has been.'

'Of course there has.'

John Syme knew the danger of suggesting anything in the way of charity to the Bard.

'I got the present o' a rare bottle o' port the day – you'll join me in a glass?'

'You're sure it was a— No: I'm sorry, John. I'm that damned conscious o' my poverty I feel I'm an impostor on my friends.'

'Robin, man: surely you ken I wad share my last bottle wi' you – aye, and my last shilling gin it cam' to that. This was a present: so you can drink the lot wi' a clear conscience if no' wi' a clear head.'

'I'll sip a glass wi' pleasure, John. Damnit, I never was able to drink – except like some silly woman. But my bumpering days are past. In my present state my constitution just canna tak' it.'

John Syme was worried about the state of his friend's health. But he was not alarmed. He had often been ill but had always rallied. No doubt he would rally again. It was just that he was taking longer about it.

A blatter of spring rain rattled on the window. The Bard shivered. He could get little heat about his bones these days. Syme poured out the port. His desk was a confusion of papers and documents. The Bard had difficulty in clearing enough space to set down his glass: he couldn't hold it for long for his hand shook.

Dr William Maxwell looked in. He joined them in a glass.

'How are you feeling to-day, Robert?'

'No worse, Doctor.'

'Yes. . . Avoid getting wet at all costs.'

He shook the rain from his hat into the fireplace. Doctor Maxwell was austere. His intellect was sharp but brittle. There were times when he could display emotion; but strangely enough, such were the contradictions and tensions within him that even emotionally he was brittle. The tone of his voice was thin tenor . . .

They were an oddly contrasted trio. Syme: placid, lazy, inclined to enthusiasms – but without enthusiasm. Maxwell: dry, arid, intellectual and thinly emotional. And the Bard: given to enthusiasms with enthusiasm; and yet gifted with an intellect beyond any of his friends.

Yet, isolated as they were in Dumfries society, they were bound by their common interest in discussing and hoping for a state of society broader, more humane, more cultured, more libertarian than that which prevailed . . .

The severely-circumscribed intellectual life of Dumfries dictated this. Maxwell knew little or nothing of the Bard's songs and poems; but he bowed to the strength of his personality. He knew when he was in the presence of genius, even although the quality of that genius was beyond his understanding.

Maxwell said: 'There is a suggestion going round the town, Robert, that Craigdarroch's coachman was drunk that night and the coach capsized?'

The Bard raised his eyes slowly to the pale thin face.

'Well, I don't *think* he was. . . He was a canny lad; but he may hae been for a' that. Onybody can be drunk ony time. Why the hell blame the coachman? He took the turn too quick in the dark and Craigdarroch broke his neck . . .'

'I was just wondering, Robert, if perhaps a drunken coachman was indeed responsible for Craigdarroch's death? You knew him well?'

'Yes, I knew Alexander Fergusson of Craigdarroch almost as well as I knew any of the local gentry. He was a great friend as well as a relation of Glenriddell. I celebrated a drinking bout they had in my ballad, The Whistle, which you have probably read; and well . . . what does it matter? Riddell's dead . . . Craigdarroch's dead. . . Maybe I'll by dead next!'

'Death isna a very pleasant subject for conversation, Robert?'

'No, no, death isna a very pleasant subject for conversation any time. . . I remember in one of my poems saying: But why, o' Death, begin a tale?'

'Well . . . I just thought it was damned unfortunate that a man like Fergusson should meet his death through the drunkenness of a coachman . . .'

'As I say, he broke his neck. . . I once broke my knee through the carelessness of a drunken coachman; but that was in Edinburgh. . . Oh, a very interesting experience! Of course, a man can get over a broken knee when he canna get over a broken neck . . .'

John Syme looked uncomfortable. He looked appealingly towards Maxwell for him to change the subject. He saw the Bard was in a strange dark mood.

'Aye,' the Bard continued, 'there's been a lot o' deaths recently – a lot o' friends o' mine hae died; but what think you o' the news that seems to me more important than ony death, ony recent deaths – not excepting the death o' James MacPherson, the celebrated author of Ossian – what think you o' the intelligence that Muir has been rescued by the Americans from Botany Bay?'

'Yes . . . I'd be glad to think that that were true, Robert. No doubt the Americans intend rescuing Muir from Botany Bay; but it is no more than a rumour . . .'

'Well, it's a rumour I hope is well founded, for Thomas Muir could still play a big part in the world yet. It seems to me to say everything for the great American nation that Washington would send a boat a' the way to Australia to effect his rescue.'

'Yes, Robert, I know; but we mustn't depend or build up our hopes too much on mere rumour.'

'Oh, a rumour like that could be false: we canna tell yet.

Confirmation is still lacking; but, mind you, I think that we'll still see Muir back in Scotland – or at least back in France. I pray that Muir may be spared to us; may be spared to France, to America, and to Scotland.'

'Yes, Robert: I hope that these wild rumours have some foundation in fact.'

In desperation Syme said:

'What's your latest sang, Robert – I know you always have a sang on your desk?'

'A sang? Why should I rack my puir brains trying to write a sang? My sang-writing days are finished, I'm afraid, John.'

Maxwell shifted uneasily in his seat.

'But why should you think that, Robert? You've no reason to think that you'll not write for years and years and many years yet?'

'D'you think so, Doctor?'

'Yes, I do, Robert.'

'Well, it's nice to hear you say so; but I've written damned few sangs this spring: fewer than I've done since I started writing sangs. . . The mood's no' on me to write . . .'

'But you're not well – you're recovering from a very severe attack of rheumatism and chills, Robert. Naturally you're not back yet to your normal vigorous health . . .'

Suddenly the Bard rose and put down his glass.

'You'll excuse me: I've a call to make and I've got to be in my bed early these nights . . .'

He turned and left them.

They both saw him to the door and then when he, with head bent and bowed shoulders, walked slowly up the Stinking Vennel, they returned to the room and Syme said:

'I don't like the shape or the mood o' our Bard at all. Can you give me any assurance, Doctor, that things'll turn out as you hope?'

Maxwell cleared his throat. 'I'm only a physician, John: I'm not a worker of miracles. It may be that I'm wrong; but I honestly see no reason why the Bard should not recover and be restored to his usual health.'

'Aye; but his illness has dragged on a long time, Doctor. You can see – at least I can see beneath his mood to-night an element of despair that I havena noticed so clearly before.'

'Well, of course, John, you know the Bard, as you call him,

nore intimately than I do; but as I say, I see no reason why
ie shouldna recover from his present protracted illness. He's
a stout man, naturally a strong man: he has a robust frame,
a robust constitution. He is subject to chills and to rheu-
natism; but arena' we all more or less?'

'Aye, nae doubt we are; but at the same time, Doctor,
here's a quality about the Bard; there's an underlying despair
hat troubles me greatly. Oh, I've seen the Bard depressed
many a time. I've seen him in the depths of despair. I've
had him in my house when he was – I wouldna like to say
how depressed myself – I suppose we're all subject to fits of
depression – and maybe it's just a fancy o' mine – maybe it's
ust a fancy – but I dinna like the shape o' him at all . . .'

Maxwell looked uneasy. 'Well: is there anything you suggest can be done for our friend that isna being done . . .?'

'Oh no, no, Doctor: don't think in any way that I'm at
all criticising your medical treatment. Far from it. The Bard
knows, and I know, and most intelligent people in Dumfries
know that we are privileged indeed to have in our community
here a doctor of such skill such knowledge, as you. Of that
here's no' the slightest doubt. Far be it from me to interfere
n your province and suggest that things could be done that
could possibly have escaped your notice. No, no, Maxwell . . .
t's just that I know the Bard of old – have known him for
some five years now. I've grown to love the man very very
deeply. I've seen him in most of his moods: been with him
in most of his moods; and I know that he has his ups and his
downs: his moods of exaltation and his moods of depression.
But I confess – this is all I'm trying to say – I've never sensed
before the feeling that . . . well, that he's maybe no' going
to get over this illness too easily . . .'

Maxwell looked into his glass of port for some time before
he answered.

'There's every possibility, John, that the Bard is at the
moment seized with an illness that may be fatal. You and I at
the moment may be seized with a fatal illness though we do
not know that. But I do give you my assurance that, as far
as medical knowledge goes, I see no reason to believe that,
with a continuation of the treatment – with rest and good
food – that our mutual and worthy friend may not outlive, in
years and usefulness, either of us.'

'I'll say Amen to that. I'll say Amen to that any time of
the day or night; for if anything were to happen to Robert

Burns then I just dinna think I could tolerate biding abou
Dumfries.'

At the top of the Stinking Vennel the Bard met George
Haugh and they stopped to have a chat.

'God, Rab, you're no' lookin' ony too weel yet. Are you
takin' care o' yoursel'?'

'Well, Geordie, I've just come frae my doctor and he
assures me that there's no really so much wrong wi' me! As
for takin' care o' mysel' – how are you and the bairns getting
on ony better than Jean and my bairns are getting on? I
mean: as regards a bite o' decent food?'

'We're managin', Rab, but it's a fell struggle. My God,
but times are bad – for puir folk. I mind where in your Twa
Dogs you say "But surely poor folk maun be wretches" . . .
I can stand a bit of starvation – and even our weans can stand
a bit o' starvation; but I doubt, Rab, that you'll need to tak'
care o' yoursel' . . .'

The Bard looked straight into Haugh's grimed face.

'It seems to me, Geordie, that my friends are expectin' me
to die soon.'

Haugh's arm shot out and his hand gripped the Bard's
shoulder.

'By God, Rab, you canna say that to me: you daurna say
that to me. Man, it's just that you're ill and just . . . that
under ony circumstances we canna afford to lose you. You
maunna tak' me up wrang there, Rab: you maunna. I've nae
right to tell you to tak' care o' yoursel' exceptin' the fact that
a guid bit o' you doesna belong to yoursel'. It belongs to the
folk. You're our Bard, and I'd be a damned poor friend on the
one hand and a lover o' your poems an' sangs on the other if
I didna ask you to tak' care o' yoursel'.'

But the Bard continued to look quietly, sombrely, almost
unmeaningly at George Haugh; and the smith dropped his
hand.

'Frae you, Geordie, I wad tak' almost ony advice; but I'm
really no' a great deal interested in advice ony longer. I'm
just hoping that, gin the warm days come again, I'll recover
some o' my spirits. But dinna think either, Geordie, that I'm
melancholy or creepin' about pitying my condition and my
lot. Damn the fear o' that! I'm enjoying such moments as I
have. . . I'll need to push on, Geordie, for geeting cauld is the
most damnable thing that can happen to me: my muscles and

ny bones just – damned get – into knots. I just a' stiffen up wi' this bluidy cauld. Mind you: we could hae better weather or the time o' year. . . But I'll tell you what, Geordie: I'm no' out so very much now and you ken where I bide in the Millbrae weel enough. Ony night you like I'll be pleased to see you and the wife: baith Jean and I will be glad to see he pair o' you. Ony night you like, Geordie, and there's nae need to gie us ony warning. I'm never out late and Jean's aey here.'

He turned and walked away from George Haugh. Haugh urned and walked away and then turned and looked back and watched the Bard's gait, sighed, and shook his head.

The early spring had come to Dumfries in bursts of sunshine and blatterings of rain and sleet. The Nith was swollen and drummed monotonously over the caul. The folks hurried about the ill-paved streets and vennels. The faces of the labouring folks were pinched and white . . .

Yes, it was a sore time. The Bard took a shiver. He wanted warmth and company. Yet he knew he was but poor company.

He looked towards the Mid-Steeple that stood grey and austere in the grey evening light.

He was a stranger in a strange land. No voice came to him in the warm Westland tongue of Ayrshire. He recalled his lines written in Ellisland on Jenny Geddes – And aey a Westland look she throws as tears hap ower her auld brown nose.

Yet the West was not for him any longer. He would be as big a stranger in Machlin to-night as he was in Dumfries. Folk grew up, married, died, aged. . . An odd one remained though, even in the odd one, the quality of friendship changed with the changing years.

He turned again and gazed towards the Mid-Steeple crowning the canny brae of the High Street. He felt terribly lonely and withdrawn. So little there was that mattered in the end of all things.

He asked himself why he had turned twice to look up towards the Mid-Steeple. Did he hope for a sign there? Fine he knew there were no signs anywhere – unless they were everywhere.

Automatically his slow steps took him towards the Globe. Then a young woman barred his path.

'Pardon me – yes – Mr Burns? You *are* Robert Burns?'

255

'Madam — ?'

'Hae you forgotten me? I'm Grace Aiken, daughter o' Robert Aiken in Ayr.'

'Grace Aiken! Lord God, how cam' you here?'

'I'm visitin' my auntie here — Are you well, Mr Burns?'

'Am I weel? Huh! Why shouldna I be weel, Grace? You've grown into a – grand lady.'

'I'm still Robert Aiken's daughter, Mr Burns.'

'And your father?'

'Well . . . very well indeed. He asked me to look you up. Will you no' come up to my aunt's wi' me . . .? You seem cold.'

'Aye, Grace woman. . . No: you'll need to excuse me. I'm in the Millbrae Vennel – ask onybody. I'm cold, Grace – and getting cold is perdition. . . I've been ill this while back wi' a rheumatism and a kind o' a fever . . . but I'm real glad to hae met in wi' you in Dumfries.'

'I'll tell my father — '

'Aye, tell your worthy parent how much I was speirin' for him. Aye: Bob Aiken read me into fame. . . You'll forgive me that I'm no' just what I might be . . .?'

His teeth rattled in his head: his voice faltered.

Grace Aiken held out her hand and bade him good-bye. She was profoundly distressed at his appearance. She had remembered him as a man of great strength and vitality.

Grace too turned and watched him almost totter across the street. Obviously he was very ill.

Automatically the Bard tottered up the close to the Globe and, just as instinctively, tottered ben to the kitchen fire.

Bess Hyslop looked up as he entered, swept the cat from the chair with her hand and turned the chair towards the fire.

'Come and get a heat, Robert, for God's sake.'

'Thanks, Bess, thanks. It's getting bitter outby.'

Bess changed a cleek on the swee, hooked on a pot of hen-bree that was simmering at the back and rattled the poker between the ribs.

'You should be in your bed, Robert.'

'To hell: some folk die i' their beds!'

'There's company ben the room – but you'd rather hae a bowl o' hen-bree?'

'You're an angel, Bess. You'll get your reward up above. I'm no' fit for ony company – and a bowl o' your hen-bree'll dae me mair guid than a' th drink was ever brewed.'

'Are thae doctors daein' you ony guid?'

'What the hell can a doctor dae? No' that I'm ungratefu',
Bess . . . far from it. But a doctor's just a human being wi'
some skill wi' the knife or wi' medicine. There's much they
an dae – the best o' them – to help a body in distress and
pain; but what dae they really ken or what can they really
ken about life – and death? You've an idea what happened
tween Anna Park and me up the stairs there. It wasna
planned and it wasna socht for. But it happened. And the
bonniest wee lass is up there in the Millbrae as a result.
There was our ain lass, Jean's and mine; and she died. . .
What can a doctor ken beyond his knives and his drugs? Oh,
'll dae what the doctors tell me – and I'll no complain. But
've nae trust in miracles either.'

'Robert – what's come ower you? You're no' yoursel' –
nd havena been this year.'

'Who am I, gin I'm o' no' mysel', Bess?'

'You're no' the Robert Burns I kent when you first cam'
here. Anna wadna ken you the nicht!'

'Maybe no'; but my Jean will.'

'You were blessed wi' your Jean. How you twa met on
his earth will aey be a mystery to me: you couldna hae been
better matched.'

'We couldna.'

'Then, Robert, could you tell me how Anna and you got
thegither?'

'I could tell you. But would you believe me? Could I be
sure I was tellin' you richt?'

Bess stirred the soup with the ladle and then filled the
bowl.

'I'm as bad as Anna: I'd believe onything you said.'

The Bard brought the horn spoon near his lips and then
blew.

'By God, wife: that's a guid taste a' hen-bree.'

'Gin I thocht it wad dae you guid — '

'Noo, noo, woman: keep a grip on yoursel'. Coorse it'll
dae me guid. . . Words, Bess . . . they can wing you to heaven
or plunge you in hell. I ken something about words. . . But
before the words come, something's mair important.'

'What?'

'Thocht – emotion – a prompting frae the heart – a whirl o'
the brain. The Guid Book says: In the beginning was the
Word, and the Word was wi' God. Easy enough for a skilful

seducer to deceive a country girl – or a toon girl – wi' the glamour o' his gab. But you ken fine there was naething like that atween Anna and me. A man and woman comin' thee-gither – that's been goin' on since the beginnin' o' time and it'll go on till the end o' time. Men hae made rules and regulations to prevent it – but in vain. Oh, aye, an odd man here and an odd woman there will shackle themselves wi' the chains o' morality till they canna move. But, on the whole, humankind pay nae mair nor lip-service to morality – however it may be sanctioned or blessed.'

The warmth of the first was pleasant to the Bard's bones: he supped his soup with some relish.

Bess Hyslop looked down at him from her standing position by the fire.

'But we're no' just brute-beasts, Rab. Or are we?'

'Aye: there's a gey lot o' us waur nor brute-beasts. But there is such an emotion as love – or at least affection – and that leavens the beast in maist o' us.'

'Aye. . . I suppose so . . .'

'It's a question has aey worried you, Bess?'

'It has . . . back and forward. I seem to hae missed a lot in life. Oh, I ken it was my ain fault to start wi'. . . You ken, Rab: you're one o' the few men I'm safe to be alane wi'. Men are aey puttin' oot their hands. . . Anither bowl?'

'No: that'll dae me, Bess. I never was a big eater. Sometimes I think my stomach's givin' up on me.'

'God! I wish I saw you better.'

'I wish I was weel enough to go back to the Excise. It's nae easy job wi' wife and weans and half-pay. Damnit, it took me a' my time on full pay.'

'I ken. I was talkin' to Jean aboot it. Still: better half-pay than nae pay at a'. What wi' the war, the scarcity and the price o' things, we've had to dig into our bit savings . . .'

'Aye: we're a' in a bonnie mess. Thank your stars you hae nae sodgers billeted on you.'

'Dinna say a word: I micht get them yet. That wad finish everything. There's naebody wad come aboot the place. Oh, the officers were here – but William handled them the richt way.'

'And yet it's a pity for some o' thae young laddies in the Fencibles. They'll be gey often hame-sick.'

'I suppose sae. But it's no' lang till they learn to drink – and that's where every penny goes.'

'You canna blame them: it's a damned unnatural life.'

They blethered away by the fireside – the Bard and the iendly landlady. . . Blethered for the sake of company and om friendship.

Then Will Hyslop came through and they blethered a bit ore. The Bard refused anything to drink and went home rly.

When he was gone, Will Hyslop said to his wife:

'Rab's no makin' progress: I doobt but that it'll tak' mair or a guid summer to put him back on his feet. Damnit, he as near totterin' the nicht — And naething to drink . . .'

'I'm worried aboot him, Will . . . and Jean and the bairns.'

'They say this Doctor Maxwell's no' worried aboot him.'

'Aye . . . but Doctor Maxwell never saw Robert in his rime. He was a sturdy weel-set up man when he first cam' ere.'

'And yet, Bess, he was never ower strong i' the stomach. Ie was a puir drinker.'

'Oh, but you couldna say he ever was a heavy drinker or nything like it. Maybe on an odd occasion when there was ecial company — '

'True . . . but I've kent him on an occasion – when there as nae company but when there was something on his mind drinking gey desperately.'

'Ah weel: mair often I've kent a bottle o' porter dae him r the nicht.'

'Who are we to judge the like o' the Bard? Damnit: he's ' o' genius, fu' o' thochts and ideas. . . I've heard eloquence ae his lips the like you wadna hear doon in parliament. ye: fu' o' genius – and that' something we ken nocht aboot.'

ortified by his hen-bree and the warmth and rest by the fire, ae Bard went up the close and down Shakespeare Street and own and up the Millbrae to his home.

He could not remember any other time in his life when his aind had been so detached – so neutral. He had talked with is various friends; but he had made no contact with them. Iaybe in his heart he had desired contact with them; but, if , his mind had remained a stubborn blank.

Nothing registered in his mind. Maybe a little with Bess [yslop. And what did that matter? His mind told him it idn't matter: that nothing mattered. Bess Hyslop alone had aattered – a little. Grace Aiken . . .? His mind refused to

hark back to Auld Ayr . . . that was past him forever. Geor
Haugh . . . decent upright reforming Geordie, the soul
honour and decency and a sterling representative of the sa
of the earth. Yet his mind wouldn't respond to Haugh
idealism.

When you set Truth down on the bare bones of her arse
the cold rock of Reality, what did she amount to? Nothin
Just nothing. It didn't matter. The heart struggled to gi
meaning by way of emotion. But the brain wouldn't respon
So the heart was aey the part aey . . . or was it when t
brain was dull and cold and unresponsive . . .? Maybe
wasn't his brain that was defective but his heart? Maybe t
not-caring came from the heart too tired and exhausted a
flawed to care any longer? Maybe the brain was out of tou
with the heart or the heart with the brain?

When he came in Jean looked at him suddenly – and b
trayed fear and apprehension. Immediately she assumed
casual air.

'How are you noo, Rab?'

'Just the same. The bairns i' their beds?'

'Aye. . . Robbie waited up for you. He's left some lesso
on the table he wanted to ask you aboot.'

The Bard looked at the open book and the exercise pape
He closed the book and passed his hand across his brow.

'Onybody been here?'

'No' a soul, Rab.'

'I suppose we'll better awa' to our bed?'

'I've some thin gruel — ?'

'I'd a bowl o' hen-bree at the Hyslops —'

'How's Bess?'

'Bess . . .? Oh, aye. Bess: oh, she's fine – everybody's fin
He strode the flagged floor and took the horn ladle a
filled the drinking glass with water.

Again Jean shot him a sudden apprehensive glance. S
was relieved to see that he was stone-cold sober.

'Onything worry you, Rab?'

'Me? No: nothing worrying me, Jean . . . except that
should go to bed; but I dinna want to go to bed.'

'D'you want to read or write?'

'God, no! I dinna want to read or write.'

'What d'you want to dae?'

'If I kent, Jean . . .'

'Will you no' sit doon?'

'Hell! I've been sittin' a' nicht . . . a' afternoon . . .'

'What's wrang, Rab?'

'God! If I kent, Jean . . . if I really and honestly kent. . .
othing means onything to me ony mair . . .'

'It's just that you're . . . no' richt yet.'

'I'm far frae richt, lass. . . Ach! it's just the mood I'm in:
ll pass. Everything passes. If only I was fit enough to go
ck to work . . .'

'You're no' ready for goin' back to work.'

'And yet I should be . . .'

'No. . . You've been gey ill. . . Gie yoursel' a month yet.'

'D'you think a month will put me richt, Jean?'

'I'll work a lot o' odds . . .'

'Aye: it'll dae that onyway.'

'Maybe if you took a turn up to Mossgiel — '

'Mossgiel? And Isa and Jean Breckenridge big wi' child!
ou canna get near Mossgiel for bairns and women big wi'
airns. . . Gibby took a while to get started and Isa's only
arted; but it looks gin I'll be left far ahint. No' that I'm
orrying . . .'

'Aye, you're worrying, Rab — I wish I saw you otherwise.'

''Deed, lass, I wish I could worry — could care enough to
orry. Oh, I've worried plenty; but I seem to be beyond that
ow. . . I mean for mysel' — Oh, for you and the bairns I
orry plenty.'

The Bard did a couple of paces and a turn on the kitchen
ags. Jean knitted abstractedly by the fire. Neither could bring
emselves to put words on what lay between them.

If death claimed the Bard, what would happen? He felt
at death was near to him; but he did not want to admit
s presence openly. There was always the possibility that he
ould turn the corner and jowk death yet.

Jean also knew that death was near; but she too feared to
dmit his presence. That would almost amount to admitting
m closer — accepting him.

The Bard had now only one secret fear — that he might
e before Jean was delivered of her child. It was due about
e end of July . . .

Part Three

THE POOR MAN'S DEAREST FRIEND

CONDEMNED

r William Maxwell said: 'There's nothing for you, Robert,
ut that you must get to sea-bathing quarters. . . The Solway
omewhere . . . and horse-riding for your liver . . . and
mercury, laudanum and port wine . . . that's the cure.'

'And what do you think is wrong with me, Maxwell?'

'Nothing, Robert, that medicine and exercise won't clear
p. . . A flying gout maybe . . . maybe an enervating fever;
ut you must go immediately, for you're very low, very low
deed. If you don't, I won't answer for the consequences.'

'I see . . . I see . . .'

'No . . . I don't think you do see, Robert.'

'There's the Brow Well yonder on the Solway beside John
lark of Locherwoods . . .'

'Excellent . . . sea-bathing. . . You must go in every day
t high tide, completely immerse yourself and then take
our mercury. Excellent for the liver and the laudanum for
e nerves. Oh yes, Robert: we'll have you fit and well in no
ime . . .'

The Bard said nothing about horse-riding to Maxwell. To
ean he said:

'I'm going down to the Brow Well, Jean. It seems it's my
nly hope. Sea-bathing and medicine. . . God, lass, that we
hould have come to this — '

'Tell me, Rab: just how bad are you feeling?'

'Like death, Jean: just like cauld death. But I'll gie auld
loven-clootie's haunts an unco slip yet . . . at least I'll dae
ny best. Now you're no' to worry, Jean . . .'

'God, Rab, how can I help worrying? I ken you're ill —
ou've been ill this while back. And me wi' this bairn
oming . . .'

'Aye, the bairn coming's a worry, lass. Everything's a
worry where we've nae money and we're living a gey puir
and-to-mouth existence . . .'

'Could Gilbert no' help you?'

'Aye, Gilbert's owing me plenty and he's kept a damned
accurate account of onything o' the capital sum paid back. . .
I've gone into that time and again wi' Gilbert — but you ken
here's no' a spare penny lying about Mossgiel . . .'

'No . . . and my folks hae little enough. Ye ken how little work there's been this while back.'

'Lass, I dinna like leaving you; but there's Maxwell advice to me. I'll just need to go down to the Brow Well and do my utmost to get better. There's nae other road out: maun get better – better enough to get back to the Excise and full pay. This half pay's just slow starvation.'

Jean did not like to tell him just how ill she thought he was. She felt he hadn't enough strength left to face the truth about himself. And the truth to Jean was that he was dying. Dying slowly, but dying by inches every day. Yet she was not utterly without hope. She had known him to lie at death's door before this and then make such a recovery as to be twice his old self.

Time and time again she had faced the question: If he died? But it was a question she couldn't face. If he died she would just have to die with him for there was no envisaging a future without him. But what of the children? What of the infant kicking in her womb? No, no: she could only live for the day and in dread of the morrow. She was utterly helpless in the hands of fate and, in her present womb-laden state immobile as well as helpless; and she had only Jessie Lewars to comfort her . . .

THE WELL

In the Davidsons' mean and miserable ale-house close by the Brow Well, he got lodgings. They were acceptable because they were cheap and in close proximity to the Well and the Solway shore.

The Well was a rough hole in the ground lined with boulders, and the chalybeate water looked rusty and had a wersh metallic flavour. Beside it was a rough bench of drift planks. Sometimes ill people and old people came and drank the waters, rested and went on . . .

It was a heartless July. Sometimes the sun shone and there was a measure of ease in its comfort and warmth. But for the most part the cold wind blew across the leaden waters and often it rained.

At times the incoming tide would rush across the grey brown sands with a cruel treacherous sneer. . . And at such times it took all his courage to leave his clothes behind the

266

wind-stunted thorn and venture into the water. But maybe
his was his only hope of salvation. He waded in – cold,
shivering, gasping . . . his heart pounding, his teeth rattling. . .
Almost sobbing, he went in to the arm-pits and then he felt
he sea might suck him under and, in near-panic, he would
turn for the shore.

He rubbed himself with his towel, but he hadn't the energy
to bring life to his blue and white mottled skin. He pulled
the clothes on his half-dry shivering body and then he took
his mercury and his draught of port.

And he was nauseated . . .

He did not know that Maxwell, in his blind medical ignorance, was killing him with a regimen that would have
destroyed a man with ten times his constitution. The laudanum, the mercury, the port wine played havoc with the
metabolism of his stomach. Now nothing would lie on his
stomach but a thin gruel. . . His blood became thinner and his
flesh fell away and his heart became more and more distressed. He became less and less able to endure the ghastly
shock of wading into the heartless sneering shivering Solway
tide.

He crawled about during the day seeking shelter from the
biting wind and exposing himself to any blink of sunshine
that might bring warmth to his chilled bones. At nights he
shivered in his mean bed – never really warming – for warmth
had gone from his aching body.

Everything about him was a wreck: except his mind and
his resolution. He wasn't dead yet – not just yet. He had work
to do. He must see Jean safely past child-bed. . . He had some
songs to finish.

Oh yes: the fear of death had often held him and plunged
him into melancholy. When death comes to a being prema-
turely, there is fear and terror and a terrible loneliness. But
when death comes to pay no casual visit but to claim his
own, there is often enough no fear, no terror, but almost a
feeling of relief until maybe death becomes impatient and
tightens his grip – then for a moment there may be pain and
terror and struggle . . .

Deep down the Bard knew he was dying: that he hadn't
long to go. This was the rock of his keenest awareness; and
he rested on that rock and accepted it. There was nothing now
to fear: nothing to hope for; nothing to resist; nothing to
rebel against. He was finished. It only remained for him to

walk across his brief stage with some dignity and some manhood.

But the sun sometimes shone and he sat by the Brow Well and ran his fingers across the harp of melody; and the thin tinkling ghost of a tune came across his memory and he tried words for it: tried words to blend with the notes. *Rothiemurche's Rant.* A difficult tune but one in keeping with his mood and his seat by the Well.

Aye: strathspey time. But soft and low . . . and with plenty of true pathos. 'Sweetest maid on Devon's bank.'

Aye, Peggy Chalmers and Charlotte Hamilton. . . The banks of the Devon. . . Oh Peggy, Peggy: gin you were here to see me now . . . to speak to me . . . now that I'm purged of any trace of grossness that ever was about me! And oh! to be on Devon's banks wi' you and Charlotte and the summer warm and still and vibrant wi' love . . .

COMMANDS FOR THE NEXT WORLD

Maria Riddell had come down from Lochmaben, from the seeping dampness and rawness of Halleaths . . . had come down to the Solway shore seeking sea air and freshness and a change.

Maria heard of his presence at the Brow Well and sent her carriage for him.

His heart lifted up when he read her note. Crushing it into his pocket he entered the carriage. . . But when he came to where Maria was dwelling he braced himself proudly, for he knew he would never see her again. Of all his friends, and of all the gentry, Maria alone had sent her carriage.

Maria was engaged on a frame of embroidery when he was shown into her. She was sitting in the window catching the light of a watery sun.

He closed the door behind him and, head erect, strode with utstretched hand towards her. Maria was almost turned to tone. The shock at his appearance was almost terrifying. The tamp of death was clearly upon his features. . . Maria lutched convulsively at her sewing and then threw it to the oor and rose. The outstretched hand still came towards her. The death-mask cracked in a smile.

'Well, Madam, and what are your commands for the next vorld?'

'Oh, Robert, Robert . . . how glad I am to see you. . . Come: tell me how you're feeling: you're getting well . . .?'

'Alas, Maria! my sands are nearly run. Oh, there's a grain r twa left in the glass . . . I winna die on your hands —'

'Oh, Robert, Robert: please . . . you're getting well again. You've been ill before —'

'It's no use, Maria. We have our entrances and our exits. . . 've no real regrets. I've met wi' death before: he's no' such n ill fellow as some moralists make out. And no bluidy entimentalism, Maria. . . Though sensibility, yes. I'm a dying nan and that's a' that's to it. Now let's talk sensibly and ationally – and in friendship. Friendship, Maria: you and me ave been a cuple of bluidy fools – schule-bairns! Enough o' hat. And I'll confess, Maria, that I've been human enough nd jealous enough to hae written some damned ill-natured hings about you. But – you deserved them. Damned, Maria, admired you more than ony woman in Dumfriesshire . . . nd then you. . . Ah well: we'll let that go. You've made your mends and I've made mine . . .'

'And I'm grateful, Robert, that you've done so – and so obly . . . generously. . . Life has taught me sharply how to alue men and manners. Aye – I was young and inexperinced . . . I just didn't know. . . Didn't know anything really. knew I was clever. Oh, yes; and I was proud, vain, infinitely onceited with my cleverness. What I didn't know was that knew nothing about life. . . What I did know was that you vere the one man in all my world who knew everything bout life. But life has taught me . . . taught me bitterly at Tinwald and at Halleaths. . . It's so easy to be clever, Robert: o difficult to be wise. . . Do believe me that I forgive you all he nasty things you have written and said about me, if only ecause I have greater sins to ask you to forgive me.'

'Maria lass: it's too late now for you and me to weep on ach other's bosoms . . . too late. Aye, I can see that life's

dealt hardly wi' you; but you'll get over that and it'll do yo
a' the good in the world. Life's the only true teacher – gin y
can discipline yourself to be a good pupil . . .'

The Bard put down his teacup.

'Aye, a cuppie o' tea . . . aye, aye! You ask about th
future? There's nae future. . . It's ower late now for ony ta
o' the future. There's just nae time. . . Oh! had I time there
much I would like to correct. There're poems o' mine i
circulation I would like to withdraw and destroy. There's m
Crochallan Song Book I would like to get back into my hand
– no' that I'm ashamed o' onything it holds; but just that it
sure to be misunderstood and circulated among folk that ha
only dirty evil i' their minds. And mony an ill-gotten epigra
I penned – no' that I'm retracting onything. . . But just that
dinna want to be remembered by an ill-gotten line or tw
And damnit, Maria! such is human nature that folks'
treasure a bawdy line and a satiric line when they'll cast asid
a truly inspired lyric as being commonplace and dull. Aye
had I time I'd retract a' that ever came frae my pen an
scrutinise every line afresh . . .'

Mercifully, Maria refrained from saying that there migh
still be time. . . To her everlasting regret she knew the Bar
was already beyond that. He was a visibly dying man.

But even with the hand of death on his shoulder what
man he still was! Proud, dignified – and, oh God! ho
infinitely great and noble beyond all other men she ha
known . . .! Maria struggled not to break down.

Not to break down. . . 'Oh, Robert, Robert — '

'Maria . . .! Oh, there was a day, Maria, when I would ha
wept for my fate . . . but that's a' by wi' . . . Calm yourself
woman! Oh, when I've away you can drop a silent tear fo
me . . . *but I'm no awa'* yet. And I've plenty to face afor
then. I've my Jean and my bairns . . .'

'Robert . . . I'm only woman — '

'And I'm only poet . . . bard . . . husband . . . father. .
No, no: dinna draw the curtain. I see little enough o' th
sun . . .'

They parted. He kissed Maria on the forehead and his kis
had the coldness of death . . .

'May God bless and comfort you, Robert. . . Oh, m
dear . . .'

'Steady, lass. . . If it's up-bye, I'll put in a guid word fo you and – if down below. . . But we'll no' think on that . . .'

He sank back into the sweet-smelling leather of the chaise. The July sun was behind rachled grey clouds and the Solway stretched grey and forbidding towards the English shore. . . Puir Maria – a decent lass – brought to the bones of her arse by time and circumstance.

DEBTOR'S GAOL

And the sword broke from its thread and crashed but an inch from his skull. Tailor Williamson in Dumfries had made his Volunteer uniform and the bill came to £7 6/-. Now the cunning, cautious, excellent business man, with the soul of a business man, having heard that the Bard was dying, got his lawyer, Matthew Penn, to write a letter threatening him. . . Scotland's Bard might be a-dying; but a bill was a bill and £7 6/- was £7 6/-. Tailor Williamson wasn't going to be done out of his bawbees by death. There was the alternative of the debtor's gaol. . . Tailor Williamson had no scruples in the matter of a dying poet – his country's Bard. Damnit: a debt was a debt! Unleash the hounds of the law: he was owed money by Scotland's National Bard – and what in the contra balance was Williamson, tailor in Dumfries, private in the Royal Dumfries Volunteers?

The threatening letter from Williamson's lawyer came eventually to the Bard at the Brow Well. He had braced himself to meet Maria Riddell: he had no defences against the law.

They would throw him into the debtors' gaol, would they? Even as they had threatened his father in Lochlea when he lay on his death-bed. . .

God knew he was prepared to die. But not in the debtors' gaol . . . not with Jean giving birth . . .

That day he viewed the racing sneer of the Solway's tide – and kept his clothes on. Gaol? God forgive them. . . What was he to do? Where was he to turn . . .? He couldn't let any of his Dumfries friends know that he hadn't paid for his Volunteer uniform. No, no . . . never that!

God's eternal curse on Williamson! But roast him to a cinder . . . he must be paid £7 6/-: he must be paid.

CURSED NECESSITY

In desperation he wrote to James Burness in Montrose:

My dearest Cousin,

When you offered me money-assistance little did I think I
should want it so soon. A rascal of a Haberdasher to whom
I owe considerable bill taking it into his head that I am
dying, has commenced a process against me, and will infallibly put my emaciated body into gaol. Will you be so good
as to accommodate me, and that by return of post, with ten
pound. O, James! did you know the pride of my heart, you
would feel doubly for me! Alas! I am not used to beg! The
worst of it is, my health was coming about finely; you know
and my Physician assures me that melancholy and low spirits
are half my disease, guess then my horrors since this business
began. If I had it settled, I would be I think quite well in a
manner. How shall I use the language to you . . .? O do not
disappoint me! But strong Necessity's curst command . . .

I have been thinking over and over my brother's affairs
and I fear I must cut him up; but on this I will correspond
at another time, particularly as I shall need your advice.

Forgive me for once more mentioning by return of Post.
Save me from the horrors of a gaol!

My Compliments to my friend James, and to all the rest. I
do not know what I have written. The subject is so horrible
I dare not look it over again.

Farewell . . .

And then in desperation to George Thomson in Edinburgh:

After all my boasted independence, a curst necessity com-
pels me to implore you for five pounds. A cruel scoundrel of
a Haberdasher to whom I owe an account, taking it into his
head that I am dying, has commenced a process, and will
infallibly put me into gaol. Do, for God's sake, send me that
sum, and that by return of post. Forgive me this earnestness,
but the horrors of a gaol have made me half distracted. I do
not ask all this gratuitously; for upon returning health, I
hereby promise and engage to furnish you with five pounds'

272

worth of the neatest song-genius you have seen. I tried my hand on *Rothiemurche* this morning. This measure is so difficult, that it is impossible to infuse much genius into the lines –

> Fairest maid on Devon banks,
>   Crystal Devon, winding Devon,
> Wilt thou lay that frown aside,
>   And smile as thou wert wont to do?

> Forgive me!

DEAREST LOVE

And then, on the 14th of July, he wrote to Jean:

My dearest Love,

I delayed writing until I could tell you what effect sea-bathing was likely to produce. It would be injustice to deny that it has eased my pains, and I think has strengthened me; but my appetite is still extremely bad. No flesh nor fish can I swallow: porridge and milk are the only things I can taste. I am very happy to hear by Miss Jessie Lewars that you are all well. My very best and kindest compliments to her, and to all the children. I will see you on Sunday.

Your affectionate Husband . . .

NO PLEASING NEWS

My God! that he should have to write to Thomson and Cousin James in this fashion; but he must not die in a debtors' gaol on a cold stone floor against iron bars. He must see Jean delivered – must see the child of his death-bed . . .

But calmness and reason triumphed and again he waded out into the cold sea, oxter-deep. Calmness came and calmness stayed with him. All right: all right. . . He would evade the debtors' gaol. He would pay his debts. . . Thrice-accursed Williamson would be paid. The Dumfriesshire Volunteers – God Almighty! The Price of Freedom! To be flung into gaol because he couldn't – through illness and misfortune – pay for his uniform to defend his country. Ah, Williamson! thou man of honour and probity and commercial trader's morality: thou must be paid – and by God! paid thou shalt be: £7 6/-.

But death was growing wearied. He tightened his grip. The Bard wrote to brother Gilbert:

Dear Brother,

It will be no very pleasing news to you to be told that I am dangerously ill, and not likely to get better. An inveterate rheumatism has reduced me to such a state of debility, and my appetite is totally gone, so that I can scarcely stand on my legs. I have been a week at sea-bathing, and I will continue there or in a friend's house in the country all the summer. God help my wife and children, if I am taken from their head. They will be poor indeed. I have contracted one or two serious debts, partly from my illness these many months, and partly from too much thoughtlessness as to expense when I came to town that will cut in too much on the little I leave them in your hands. Remember me to my Mother.

Yours

NOT CELESTIAL GLORY

Death's grip tightened still further. There was no more port at Davidson's. He went out and walked towards Ruthwell: maybe at the inn there . . .

His mind was a blank: he was confused. . . He must get port in order to swallow the mercury . . .

The landlord at Ruthwell handed him his bottle of port. The landlady, drying a pewter pint, eyed him from the background. The Bard felt in his pockets. He had no money: no change. He explained to the landlord. He apologised. Then he felt the seal that depended from his watch-chain.

Maybe as security . . . till he could get back? The landlord eyed the stone . . .

'Yes, certainly!'

But the landlady's heel came smack on the floor.

'No, no . . .' said the landlord: 'you can pay me another day.'

The Bard clutched his bottle and wandered out in a daze.

'Gommeril!' said the landlady to her husband. 'Did you no'
n that was Robert Burns, Scotland's Bard?'

'God Almighty! You dinna say, wife? Robert Burns!'

'Aye . . . he's taking the waters at the Brow for his
alth . . .'

'God, wife: it'll tak' mair nor the Brow Well waters to
e Mr Burns right . . .'

THE LAST LAP

ow death was at his elbow all the time – and was becoming
apatient. There was no word from the Millbrae Vennel. He
rote to John Clark of Locherwoods and got a boy to deliver
e letter.

y dear Sir,

My hours of bathing have interfered so unluckily as to have
ut it out of my power to wait on you. In the meantime, as
e tides are over I anxiously wish to return to town, as I
ave not heard any news of Mrs Burns these two days. Dare
be so bold as to borrow your Gig? I have a horse at com-
and, but it threatened to rain, and getting wet is perdition.
ny time about three in the afternoon, will suit me exactly.

Yours most gratefully and sincerely,

It rained the whole way to Dumfries along the Bankend
oad.

John Clark's man was uncommunicative: the Bard was un-
ommunicative. He tossed and swayed and now the wind and
ain were in his face – now chilling the left side of his face . . .

Below St Michael's Kirk the horse stopped at the Millbrae
ennel.

The Bard dismounted with difficulty. The impatient driver
heeled the horse.

There was nobody about. The Bard looked down the vennel.
hank God he hadn't more than a few yards to go! He
eached the door of his house, stretched out his hand to
eady himself. . . No need to alarm Jean. He placed a
solute foot on the steps, reached for the handle of the

275

door. . . It swung inwards and he staggered inwards with it. .
Jean was at the door immediately.

'Rab, Rab . . .'

'It's a' richt, lass. . . It's just me. . . How are you?'

Jessie Lewars was there too.

'Mr Burns . . . oh, Mr Burns . . .!'

How they got him upstairs to bed they never knew. Bu
they got him upstairs. And Jean and Jessie undressed him
easing off his shirt and breeches.

He was shivering and quite unable to speak.

Jessie ran and got warming-pans . . .

Downstairs for a moment, Jean said to Jessie:

'Lord God Almighty, Jessie – he's finished. I dinna ke
what he's been through; but he's finished. D'you ken what
mean, Jessie?'

'Aye, he's gey bad, Mistress; but I wadna say he'
finished. . . He's sleeping now.'

'Sleeping? Aye: it micht be his last sleep. Make a taste c
tea, Jessie, and I'll awa' up and sit by him in case he waukens

O LORD . . .

Dr Maxwell came; John Syme came; many others came
George Haugh, William Hyslop, Gabriel Richardson . .
Mitchell, Lindlater, White . . .

It was something of a nightmare.

Jean laboured up and down the stair; and she felt the pain
of child-birth on her all the time.

Jessie Lewars was an angel from heaven.

Young Robert gripped his mother's skirt and said in ope
eyed wonder:

'Mother, is my faither no' weel?'

Jean said: 'Hush ye, Robbie: your father needs rest an
quiet. Be a guid laddie and help to keep the bairns quiet.'

Dr Maxwell came and John Syme came; and Jessie Lewa
was aey at the door. . . For word had got round the tow
that the Bard lay a-dying.

George Haugh spread the news. John Syme spread th
news. And Maxwell, Dr Brown, John MacMurdo and th
Hyslops . . .

Bess Hyslop said: 'Oh God! I hear the Bard's taken to hi
death-bed?'

William Hyslop said: 'Quiet . . . for God's sake!'

They gathered at the corners of the streets and said:

'What's the word o' Mr Burns – surely he canna be dying nd him sae young . . .!'

And Jean, passing her hands across her swollen womb, said:

'Grant me a day or twa mair, O Lord! for I'm nearly emented as it is . . .'

APPEAL

)n Monday, the 18th of July, he rallied sufficiently to ask for en and paper and wrote to his father-in-law-James Armour:

My dear Sir,

Do, for Heaven's sake, send Mrs Armour here immediately. My wife is hourly expecting to be put to bed. Good God! Vhat a situation for her to be in, poor girl, without a friend! returned from sea-bathing quarters to-day, and my medical riends would almost persuade me that I am better; but I hink and feel that my strength is so gone that the disorder vill prove fatal to me.

Your son-in-law,

THE MOURNFUL CHAMBER

Ie saw Syme, and grasped his hand firmly.

'I'm getting better, John. Yesterday I thought it was all up vi' me; but to-day I feel stronger – damned, I maun just get veel!'

'Of course you will, Robin: there's nae fear o' you.'

'No . . . no . . . nae fear o' me. . . But should onything appen, John – dinna let the Awkward Squad fire over me . . .'

'No, Robin: there'll be nae Awkard Squad. But dinna you e exhausting your strength . . .'

'Exhaust my strength? Na, na . . . I've strength enough. . . Vhat's the news o' the town? Oh, that damned wretch Villiamson . . .'

And honest John Syme sat by his bed-side and watched im: watched his glowing eyes glimmer and dim: watched heir light fade behind a curious smoke-like barrier till they ecame expressionless; watched his head sink back into the

pillow; watched his breathing become uneven and laboured
watched and waited till the Bard knew him no more.

With tears blinding him, John Syme tip-toed from th
room and went home and wrote to Alexander Cunningham:

. . . I am this minute come from the mournful chamber ir
which I have seen the expiring genius of Scotland departin
with Burns. Dr Maxwell told me yesterday he had no hopes
to-day the hand of Death is visibly fixed upon him. I canno
dwell on the scene. It overpowers me – yet gracious God wer
it thy will to recover him! He had life enough to acknowledg
me, and Mrs Burns said he had been calling on you and m
continually. He made a wonderful exertion when I took hir
by the hand – with a strong voice he said: 'I am much bette
to-day – I shall be soon well again, for I command my spirit
and my mind. But yesterday I resigned myself to death.
Alas, it will not do.

My dear friend Cunningham, we must think of what ca
be done for his family. I fear they are in a pitiable condition
We will here exercise our benevolence, but that cannot b
great, considering the circumscribed place, etc. In the metro
polis of Scotland, where men of Letters and affluence, hi
acquaintances and admirers, reside, I fondly hope there wil
be bestowed on his family that attention and regard whicl
ought to flow from such a source into such a channel. It i
superfluous in me to suggest such an idea to *you* . . .

THE EPITAPH

Again he rallied and smiled wanly at Jessie Lewars and said

'Get my pen and a bit paper, Jessie lass, like the ange
you are.'

He took the pen and paper and wrote three lines to Johr
Rankine. He got Jessie to seal the sheet and then he addressec
it to Adamhill.

'If ocht should happen, Jessie, my brother Gilbert will b
here. See that he gets this, and tell him to deliver it intc
John Rankine's ain hands and nae ither hands.'

'Oh, but naething's going to happen, Mr Burns —'

'But you'll see my wishes are carried out, lass?'

Jessie nodded.

The Bard relaxed on his pillow again. He had been dream

ng of John Rankine and, in his waking, he had been thinking
of him: re-living the Lochlea days. . . And strangely enough,
John Rankine was the one man who seemed nearest to him.
His warmth and wit and his friendship reached out to him
across the years. . . John Rankine of Adamhill – a real giant
of a man in every respect. . . The spence at Adamhill and
Annie of the corn-rigs. . . The nights in the summer's gloam-
ings – John Rankine coming back half-way with him across
the dusk-gathering rigs . . . and the call of a herd-boy bringing in the cattle coming faint across the hollows . . . and
their boots wet with the heavy dew . . .

Aye, John Rankine of Adamhill and the first glorious
bloom of his bardship. . . And Adamhill there to encourage
and enthuse him and spur him on to greater glory; with a
spoken and an unspoken faith in him that was as sweet to his
being as the breath of life itself . . . John Rankine . . . of
Adamhill . . .

He dozed again and Jessie put the letter away safely and
slipped from the bed-side to go and see how Jean and the
bairns were faring. Her mind was numb: she could not yet
realise the desperate plight of the Bard. Or maybe it was
that the nursing instinct was still uppermost where he was
concerned. But her woman's heart bled for Jean Armour.

Jean had not yet recovered from the shock of his dreadful
home-coming and the weight in her womb was dragging her
to her knees. Maxwell reckoned her time could come any
hour. . . Jean, with better knowledge, knew she had a few
days to thole yet. . . Yes: she was pained and often in dire
discomfort; but the searing, down-bearing pains were not
yet. . . She wasn't yet ready. . . Maybe the shock had something to do with the delay – if there was any delay – for her
senses were becoming curiously numb.

O, OPEN THE DOOR . . .

The end came towards five o'clock on Thursday morning, the
21st of July.

Jessie Lewars had taken the younger children to her house:
Elizabeth Park and James Glencairn.

In the room next day lay Robert and Frank and William
Nicol.

The candle-light burned steady and straight: the Bard lay

279

in a state of near-coma. Occasionally he muttered words about Matthew Penn, Williamson's lawyer; occasionally he muttered something about a debtors' gaol; and occasionally his lips moved but the words that passed from them were too faint and undistinguishable for Jean to catch.

When it was wearing beyond the break of day—Jean was glad to see the dawn coming for her vigil was heavy on her soul—then the Bard suddenly stirred and opened his eyes.

Jean felt his head and felt his feet.

He looked at her and said nothing; and somehow she knew that he was dying.

She roused young Robbie who was partly dressed and told him to run for Jessie Lewars.

Jessie came quickly enough. And even she, for all her in experience, knew that the end had come for Robert Burns.

Death had had his moments of impatience; but he seemed patient enough now.

The Bard looked at Jessie and looked at Jean and his eyes seemed to know them; but no words came to his lips. And they knew that he was looking at them from across a great chasm.

Jean said in a low but strangely-steady voice to Jessie:

'Bring in the bairns, Jessie.'

The bairns were brought in: Robert, his first-born; Francis Wallace; William Nicol.

They stood there: Robert, partly clothed; Frankie and Willie in their night-shirts.

Jean held the youngest, and, with the other hand, she grasped the hand of Robbie; and Jessie Lewars sat on the chair and held Frankie to her.

And Jean said to them:

'Quiet, bairns; and dinna be feart. . . Dinna cry. . . Your father's about to say good-bye to us a' for a wee while. And, laddies, keep in mind o' this morning; for we've all got to say good-bye some day. And I want you to mind your father.'

The children were strangely quiet: awed and maybe somehow terror-stricken at the awful solemnity of the occasion. The grey dawn crept in at the window and the candle burned with a steady flame. The Bard looked at them and seemed to see them though from a great distance. His eyes, with that look that seemed even now to come from beyond the grave, held them spell-bound.

Then a tremor shook his frame and he started slightly from his pillow. His eyes left them and stared towards the foot of the bed; and in a voice that tore through Jean with a terrible rending he cried:

'Gilbert. . . Gilbert. . . Gilbert . . .'

In a voice that was to haunt Jessie Lewars to her grave, Jean uttered, in a terrible anguish, the one word:

'Rab!'

She thrust the children from her and seized the already clay-cold hand of her husband. Kneeling on the floor and resting her head on the bed she uttered the prayer:

'Almighty God. . . Eternal Father. . . In Thy mercy and infinite understanding prepare a resting place for my husband until the day Thou callest me. . . And O Lord! be merciful until him and forgive me, O Lord, my humble words; and grant me, Thy servant, this prayer which I beseech Thee in the name of our Lord Jesus Christ. Amen.'

DAY OF ETERNITY

And on that day of eternity, the 21st July, 1796, Jean sent for John Lewars. Not really that she needed to send for him: he was there, waiting her summons And she said to him:

'John, laddie: it's no' that Jessie hasna done mair for us than we've a right to expect; but I've a last request to make o' you, laddie. You were gey near my husband: he thocht highly o' you: looked upon you in some ways as a kind o' a son. . . And laddie, I'm no' fit to do ony mair. If you canna dae it for my sake, maybe you'll do it for him that lies upstairs. . . The invitations to the funeral . . . that bits o' letters that need to be written back and forward. . . Oh, John Lewars, if you could just tak' that off my mind . . .'

John Lewars was unable to restrain his tears.

Mrs Burns: there's no' much I can dae; but there's nothing that I winna try. If you like to leave things in my hands, then I'll dae the best I can: I'll see that the invitations go out; I'll see that things are arranged to the best o' my ability; and . . . it'll be a sad, sad privilege and an honour before God and Scotland to dae ocht I can for you in this terrible hour that's come on us a' but on you mair than on ony other body.'

'It's kind o' you, laddie, to say that; and I ken he would

rather hae you daeing the bits o' business that are unfortunately necessary than ony other body in Dumfries. But laddie . . . I've a confession to mak' to you. . . And let the confession be between oursel's for I wadna hae him humbled in his death. I've nae money, laddie . . . just nothing at a'. . . You ken he's been on half-pay this while . . . and that things havena been easy. . . I canna go telling his friend Syme or Maxwell or ony o' them that I just havena a copper in the house. . . But we'll need to bury him in a decent-like manner. . . Now, John; you'll ken the best man to go to . . . and get the cheapest and yet the decentest o' coffins you can get. . . Maybe Mr Boyd wad be the man. . . I don't know. . . . Maybe Mr Boyd could gie you a cheap kind o' decent coffin. . . Tell him that I canna pay him the noo but that, God willing, he'll be paid for a' that . . .'

John Lewars said: 'I understand, Mistress . . . and I haena much mysel'; but the pound or twa I hae by me is yours.'

'No, no, laddie: no, no. . . You ken fine he wadna hae liked that. I'll get my road through . . . I'll gey my road by gin I was past my ain wee bit bother. . . Oh, John . . . if you'll just see to things and ken there's nothing to pay onybody wi' in the meantime, I'll be eternally gratefu' . . .'

John Lewars got the names of those to whom invitations were to be sent; arranged for a card to be printed in the name of young Robert Burns. He saw Thomas Boyd – the man who was the architect for the New Brig: the man who had been the architect for the Ellisland house.

Boyd said: 'So you want a coffin for the Bard, do you? Well . . . since you say it's to be on the cheapest plan, there's no a great deal I can dae, Mr Lewars. But my own way o' thinking is this: it's a shame to put a guid coffin in cauld clay. I'll gie you a coffin and I'll see that it's fully dressed – guid black cloth and a' the trimmin's – and what's below the cloth folk needna ken ocht about. Aye, I'll dae the Bard a coffin on the cheapest plan . . . and I'll no press his widow for the money – at least I'll gie her plenty o' time to pay me.'

John Lewars thanked Mr Boyd and came away thinking that if God had given him the privilege of making a coffin for Robert Burns he would have made him the finest coffin that ever contained the mortal remains of any man – and that he would not have charged a penny.

He sent an express messenger to Mossgiel to tell Gilbert and the family there the sad news . . .

Dumfries stood still. In the homes of the common folk there was great sorrow, for though perhaps they had not expressed it in so many words when he was living, now that he was dead they recognised that they had lost their greatest champion: their greatest mouthpiece.

Men like George Haugh were deeply distressed.

The plan went through the town, through the common closes and common houses of the town that they would give the Bard a burial worthy of his glory. They would carry him to the grave and his coffin would be borne on the shoulders of the poor: of those of whom he had sung; those whose cause he had championed. The feeling spread and it came to the ears of John Syme and Maxwell and many others . . .

John Syme hurried to Colonel De Peyster and told him that to all intents and purposes the rabble of Dumfries were likely to make a demonstration at the burial of the Bard. Feeling that there might be unseemly displays of emotion and agitation, Syme asked his Colonel that he be given a funeral under the charge of the Dumfriesshire Volunteers.

Colonel De Peyster said: 'Well, Mr Syme, it could be vulgar business if there was any kind of public demonstration at the funeral of the Bard – our military comrade. What I suggest you do right now is to contact the Commander of His Majesty's forces here, and sound him as to the advisability of a proper military funeral between the two regiments; and with ourselves conducting the bier, the route could be lined and the burial take place in all due solemnity and propriety.'

John Syme thanked Colonel De Peyster and got in touch with the Commander.

The Commander expressed indifference to the arrangements for the burial of a local poet – more so since he was thought to be disaffected.

'Sir,' said Syme, 'Robert Burns was no local Bard. He was the Bard of all Scotland – the greatest poet, one of the greatest men Scotland has even had the honour to claim for a son. That he was disaffected, sir, I will deny. In the Dumfriesshire Volunteers there was no more loyal and devoted soldier of His Majesty and of British rights. What I fear, sir, is that the common people in their enthusiastic ignorance may make of his burial something of a rabble. There may even be elements, sir, whose presence cannot be unknown to you, who might take the occasion to make a demonstration of a kind that the good name of the town – the good name of Robert Burns – could ill afford . . .'

And the upshot was that Colonel De Peyster and the Commander got in touch, and it was arranged that the Bard be given a full-scale military funeral, so that the poor, the disaffected, the ordinary elements might be truly kept in their places in the background.

Still Dumfries stood silent and in mourning.

The great folks of the town, too, felt a chill at his death. Many had denied him: many had denounced him; but none could deny the force of his personality or the measure of his greatness.

Now the mood of the town made itself felt. Even in the most reactionary circles there was a feeling, if not of awe, at least of decent silence. For something had departed from Scotland: a glory had passed away that would never be replaced in their day: if ever it was replaced again.

The Haughs and the Hyslops felt somehow moved in a way that a more intimate, domestic death could not have moved them.

As Haugh said to some of his colleagues:

'There has passed awa' from Dumfries a voice that was the voice of the people: a heart that beat with the heart of the people; a pen that could put in words the thoughts and the memories of all suffering mankind; and, by the Lord God! we'd be poor craiturs this day if we didna recognise the terrible loss that has befallen us. . . Aye, and you'll have heard it said that he was in the Dumfriesshire Volunteers and merits little sympathy; but we a' ken how false that is. . . And maybe me more than ony other o' you ken just what his being in the Volunteers meant to him and to us . . .'

And the news reached Mossgiel; and the news spread outwards in a more widening circle from Dumfries. It reached Edinburgh; it reached down into England; it reached the north of Scotland ; it reached Ireland. And wherever it reached, men stood still and wondered at the suddenness with which the immortal singer had been silenced . . .

Gilbert and the family at Mossgiel were numb. And Adam Armour, James Armour and Fanny Burns . . .

Gilbert hurried towards Dumfries.

Dumfries stood still and gathered itself against his funeral. Crowds gathered respectfully at the Millbrae Vennel, hoping that they might be allowed to see his body and pay their respects before the coffin-lid was screwed down on him for ever.

But the ordeal was more than Jean could bear or the children could bear; and as she was, in Maxwell's opinion, still hourly expecting, it was arranged with the mechanics, with the magistrates, with the trades, that his body be taken from the Millbrae Vennel and laid out in the Trades' House: that the multitude might be accommodated in the order of paying their respects.

So his body in its coffin was taken from the Millbrae Vennel; but before it was taken Jean went into the room and shut the door, gazed for the last time on his waxen features, noted the pain in his lower jaw and noted also the serenity which crowned his brow. And she gazed at him for a long time; and she knelt down and she spoke to him. And she spoke to God for him; and she came back and spoke to him . . .

Then Jessie Lewars came and shielded her . . .

The men tramped up the stair and carried away the coffin . . .

He lay in state fornenst the Mid-Steeple. The crowds gathered and filed past his body. Many of them brought herbs and flowers, till his coffin was a mass of green and white and yellow and blue fragrance. . . And they filed past orderly and subdued; and anon many a sob vibrated in the silence. Strong men were not ashamed to brush aside their tears and blow vigorously on their napkins . . . for such a sight had never been in Scotland before. Such a demonstration to a poet was unknown in the annals of history . . .

He lay till the 25th. On the 25th they buried him . . .

On the evening of the 24th, Gilbert Burns arrived at the Millbrae Vennel.

Gilbert and Jean looked at each other; and Gilbert's face was heavy with sorrow – and yet crossed with worry. There was much on Gilbert's conscience . . .

Jean said: 'Well, you've arrived, Gilbert, in a sad hour. . .

And there's two or three bits o' things in the way of a bit meal that I need to keep the bairns alive. . . I was wonderin', Gilbert, if – in the terrible circumstances I find mysel' – there was maybe a shilling or twa you could lend me . . .?'

Gilbert said: 'Well, Jean: things are in a gey bad shape wi' us a' at Mossgiel. I hae terribly responsibilities on my shoulders . . . the same as you hae now. . . There's no' much I can do . . . no' much at a'. . . But I've a shilling if it wad help . . .'

He took a shilling from his pocket. But he didn't hand it to Jean. He placed it on the table . . .

Jean turned away her head and said nothing.

Gilbert said: 'I'd better away up and pay my respects to his body . . .'

Out on the street he took out his notebook and noted down: 'Item loaned to Jean Armour – 1 / -.'

There came the problem of who was to conduct the service at the Bard's grave-side.

Syme was consulted and could offer no help. Maxwell was consulted; but as he was of the Romish faith he could offer less help. Jean was consulted.

She said to John Lewars: 'Send an express messenger to Carlaverock and ask the Reverend Mr MacMorine that I would like to see him. That was the man wha christened our last bairns; and that was the clergyman for whom my husband had the greatest respect. . . Mind you, they werena friends as I ever saw it. . . What they was between them is between them and the grave; but I ken that Robert wad be glad if Mr MacMorine would dae the last rites at the grave-side. . .'

The Cinque Port Calvary and the Angusshire Fencibles, with reversed arms, lined the route from the Mid-Steeple to St Michael's Kirk-yard while the military band, preceding the cortège, played the *Dead March in Saul*. The coffin, borne on the shoulders of the Dumfriesshire Volunteers, containing the mortal remains of Robert Burns, proceeded through the densely-packed streets of Dumfries. For people had been travelling on foot and on horse and in carriage for one day and for two days towards Dumfries, that they might pay their respects.

Syme was there and Findlater was there and the magistrates and MacMurdo. . . And everybody who had a claim to be anybody in Dumfries was there . . .

286

But the George Haughs stood behind the soldiers and craned their necks . . .

The muffled drums and the military band drooled out the *Dead March in Saul*; and long before they reached the end of the Millbrae Vennel, Jean heard the throbbing of the drums and the blaring of the trumpets . . .

She felt the throbbing silence that vibrated in the hushed and silent town.

Maxwell paced the room below till Jessie Lewars came down and said:

'She wants you now, Doctor . . .'

Maxwell went upstairs. Jean was delivered of a fine boy.

And even as the child passed through the portals to life, so was his father's body lowered into the left-hand corner of St. Michael's Kirk-yard . . .

As Jean's last groans escaped unwillingly from her clenched teeth, a ragged volley shattered the silence. . . The Awkward Squad had fired their Awkward Salute . . .

Jessie Lewars bathed the new-born infant and wrapped it in a warm woollen shawl . . .

The cold clay was shovelled onto the coffin of Robert Burns.

HE WHO OF RANKINE SANG

John Rankine of Adamhill rode towards Mossgiel. The sun was bright in the July sky. Great clouds banked the horizon. Larks were emptying their throats in the lift . . .

John Rankine was sad at heart. . . The death of Robert Burns weighed heavy upon him. He came by Lochlea road-end and was coming up the brae towards Largieside when he met Gilbert Burns coming towards him.

They dismounted.

John Rankine shook Gilbert by the hand.

'Ah God, Gilbert . . . but it's a sad meeting this: a sad, sad meeting. What's your news frae Dumfries?'

Gilbert, with his head hanging, told him something of the funeral and of the tribute that had been paid to the Bard.

'I'd hae gi'en ten years o' my life to hae been there; but I didna ken till it was ower late. Man, Gilbert, it was here-abouts – in fact it was just ower that knowe there that I first met in wi' Robert and heard him recite his first sang . . . his first poem. . . By God, I was taken wi' him then: I was taken wi' him in the years that followed; and in our kinda broken friendship ever since I hae been the mair taken wi' him. . . Though, by God! now that he's dead and awa' I just canna – I just canna believe it. I canna believe it, Gilbert. . . God! what happened that took him awa' sae sudden and sae young and sae fu' o' genius . . .?'

Gilbert bowed his Presbyterian head.

'The Lord's ways are very strange, John.'

Blasphemy came nigh unto John Rankine's tongue. . . But he looked at Gilbert and said nothing.

'I came ower to see you. . . The last thing the Bard wrote was a letter to you. It's sealed; and his instructions were that I was to deliver it into your hand – and into nae other body's . . .' He handed John Rankine the sealed letter.

John Rankine broke the seal, unfolded the paper and read . . .

As he read, the larks trilled and the sun-haze shimmered on the green rolling hills of Lochlea. Birds chirped and flitted in and out of the thorn bushes. . . Bees went singing over the wild flowers by the way-side . . .

John Rankine coughed. He put a hand out, grasped Gilbert's shoulder and gave it a convulsive squeeze. Then he raised his head, swallowed hard, and repeated aloud the lines the Bard had sent him from his death-bed in the Millbrae Vennel in Dumfries:

> 'He who of Rankine sang, lies stiff and deid,
> And a green, grassy hillock hides his heid:
> Alas! alas! a devilish change indeed!'

The larks trilled . . . the clouds billowed . . . the wind shook the barley and there was a song in the green thorn tree . . .

John Rankine swallowed hard and, seizing the bridle, turned the mare's head. A stone lay in his path and he kicked it savagely into the hedge.

A pocket of dust rose from each hoof as it was lifted from the road . . .

Slowly, almost imperceptibly, the great white clouds billowed in the blue sky . . .

With the back of his hand Adamhill dashed the tears from his eyes.

He who of Rankine sang . . .